She went to her favourite cutler, in Haymarket.

"Not you again," he said. "What do you do with them all?"

She wasn't in the mood. "Show me what you've got in stock."

He sighed and picked a box up off the floor. He opened it and thought for a moment. "Try that."

He had a good memory, she had to give him that. It was exactly what she looked for in a knife; the right length, width, point geometry and edge profile. The grip was just the right size for her hand. The blade was charcoal-blued; resisted rust and didn't flash in the light. Could have been made for her. Given how many times she'd been in this shop over the years, it probably had been.

"How much?"

He frowned at her. "I like to tell myself you buy them as presents for your brothers in the army. I imagine they're careless and keep losing them. Eight angels."

She had the money, but only because Oida had lent it to her.

Praise for the novels of K. J. Parker

"I have reviewed books before that I thought might someday be found to have achieved greatness...K. J. Parker is writing work after work that demands to be placed in that category."
—Orson Scott Card on The Engineer Trilogy

"A richly textured and emotionally complex fantasy...Highly recommended."
—*Library Journal* on The Engineer Trilogy
(starred review)

"[*Sharps*] is a ripping good adventure yarn, laced with frequent barbed witticisms and ace sword fighting...Parker's settings and characterizations never miss a beat, and the intricate political interplay of intrigue is suspenseful almost to the last page."
—*Publishers Weekly*

"This is another splendid offering from K. J. Parker, the British fantasist who seems incapable of writing in anything but top form."
—*Locus* on *Sharps*

"Well-crafted, powerful and downright unmissable."
—*SFX* on *The Company*

THE
TWO
OF
SWORDS

VOLUME THREE

K. J. PARKER

www.orbitbooks.net

Orbit
Hachette Book Group
1290 Avenue of the Americas
New York, NY 10104
orbitbooks.net

Originally published as an ebook serial by Orbit in 2015

First Paperback Edition: December 2017

Orbit is an imprint of Hachette Book Group.
The Orbit name and logo are trademarks of Little, Brown Book Group Limited.

The publisher is not responsible for websites (or their content) that are not owned by the publisher.

The Hachette Speakers Bureau provides a wide range of authors for speaking events. To find out more, go to www.hachettespeakersbureau.com or call (866) 376-6591.

Library of Congress Control Number: 2017951010

ISBNs: 978-0-316-27090-8 (trade paperback), 978-0-316-27087-8 (ebook)

Printed in the United States of America

LSC-C

10 9 8 7 6 5 4 3 2 1

By some curious twist of fate,
nearly all of my friends are called Ian.
To Ian, therefore, with thanks and best wishes;
this one is just for you.

PART ONE

To Saevus Andrapodiza, all human life had value. This revelation came to him in a moment of transcendent clarity as he looked out from the summit of Mount Doson over the fertile arable plains of Cors Shenei in central Permia. Every man, woman and child, regardless of age, ability, nationality, religion, sexual orientation or social class was valuable and must be treated as such. His task, he realised, was finding someone to buy them all.

As a native of East Permia, he was free from the restrictive laws of the two empires, where slavery had been illegal for a hundred and fifty years, ever since excessive reliance on servile labour had threatened to wipe out the yeoman class, from whom the Imperial army was almost exclusively drawn. In Permia, with the lowest level of population per square mile in the inhabited world, there were no such considerations. When Saevus embarked on his mission, the price of a field hand in Permia was nine oxen, thirty ewes or forty pigs, making good help unaffordable to the hard-working farmers who were the backbone of the nation. He set out to change all that.

He considered the proposition from the supply end. Because

Permia had been at peace with its neighbours for generations, the supply mostly came from breeders, who naturally had to recoup the costs of fifteen years of careful nurture, together with the ongoing expense of the brood stock. But there were wars practically everywhere else; stockades crammed with surrendered prisoners, the women and children of captured cities slaughtered simply because they weren't worth anything to anybody. Prices at the pithead, so to speak, were ridiculously cheap; the real expense lay in transporting the goods to Permia, across some of the worst roads in the world.

Perhaps Saevus' greatest gift was his vision, his ability to see clearly, his sense of perspective. Before he entered the business, slave caravans limped through the high mountain passes between Rhus and Permia in gaggles of ten or twenty, moving at the pace of the slowest lame man or sickly child; and why? Because the traders were small operators, undercapitalised, inefficient. Saevus had a ship built, at that time the biggest merchant vessel ever constructed. With a full load of seven hundred, it could cover the distance between Aelia Major and Permia in ten days, as opposed to the six weeks needed by an overland caravan to cover the same distance. The cost of the ship was staggering, but, from the moment its keel bit the surf, Saevus was saving money. Marching rations of a pound and a half of barley bread per day for six weeks amounted to sixty-one pounds of bread, at a cost of an angel sixteen. Shipboard rations, a generous pound per day for ten days—ten pounds, nineteen stuivers, a saving of eighty-five per cent. Furthermore, the mortality rate overland was between forty and sixty per cent, so half the outlay was liable to be wasted, expensive bones bleaching by the roadside, dead loss. Aboard Saevus' ship, the death rate was a trivial fifteen per cent.

War is always with us; even so, it wasn't long before Saevus Andrapodiza had dried up the pool of young, able-bodied men available for purchase, or at least generated a demand that far outstripped supply. By keeping his prices to the end user as low as he possibly could, he'd stimulated the Permian economy, doubling grain yields in under a decade, with the result that more and more Permians were able to afford a slave, or two, or five. Land which since time immemorial had been dismissed as useless was now coming under the plough, as thousands of reasonably priced hands swung picks and mattocks, shifting millions of tons of stones and hacking out terraces on windswept hillsides. More and better farms called for more and better tools, which someone had to make, from materials that someone had to fell or mine; and more money in circulation meant more people could afford the better things in life, and the craftsmen who supplied them couldn't cope without help. Permia was crying out for manpower, but all the wars in the world couldn't keep pace. For a while, Saevus looked set to be the victim of his own success.

It's a true measure of the man that he made this setback into an opportunity. Obviously, perfect physical specimens were the ideal; but life, he argued, isn't like that. Take any small family-run farm or workshop; look at who actually does the work. It's not just the man and his grown-up son. Everyone is involved—women, children, the old folks, the feeble, the sick. Saevus often talked about a farm he'd visited as a boy, where the farmer's aunt, seventy years old and missing an arm, still made a precious contribution keeping an eye on the sheep, collecting the eggs, leading the plough-horses, sorting through the store apples. Everyone is valuable—not necessarily of equal value, it goes without saying, but that's just a matter of appropriate pricing, and there were smallholders and small-scale artisans who'd be glad of any help they could get, assuming the price was one they could afford to pay. What was more, these hitherto neglected categories of livestock came with hidden benefits. Children grew into adults. Old men had skills and valuable experience. Many women had significant recreational as well as practical value. A one-legged crone might look like she's not worth her feed, but she's bound, over the course of a long life, to have learned how to do something useful, and you don't need two legs to card wool or ret flax or plait straw or sort and bag up nails: all the tedious, repetitive, time-devouring little jobs that somehow have to get done if the householder's hard work in the field or at the workbench is to be turned into money.

Saevus built a fleet of new ships, each one capable of transporting twelve hundred head, with a ninety per cent survival rate. The unit cost of getting a potential worker from battlefield or burned-out city to Permia fell by a breathtaking thirty-seven per cent. As his overheads fell, so did his prices. Now, practically everybody could afford to own a functional, useful human being.

Sadly, Saevus didn't live to see the outbreak of the East–West war, but his son Saevus II, universally known as Saevolus, was ideally placed to take full advantage when the Eastern emperor Glauca repealed the anti-slavery laws throughout his dominions, shortly followed by his nephew in the West. And only just in time. War losses and economic devastation had led to attrition of manpower on such a scale that it was virtually impossible to make up the losses of the endless sequence of major battles, or keep anything like a serious army in the field. Slave labour, however, would enable the empires to take thousands of men from the plough and the forge, freeing up whole regiments for service, while ensuring uninterrupted supply of equipment and materiel for the war effort from slave-staffed State arsenals.

The simple inscription on the base of Saevus' statue reads: *He saw the worth of every man. We shall not look upon his like again.*

When Procopius (the great composer) was fourteen years old his uncle sent him to the Imperial Academy of Music at Tet Escra to study harmonic theory under the celebrated Jifrez. Aware that the journey would involve crossing the notorious Four Fingers Pass, Procopius' uncle provided him with an escort of six men-at-arms, two archers, a personal attendant and a cook; he also sent with them the full cost of his nephew's tuition and maintenance, five thousand angels in gold. A cautious man, he had made proper enquiries about the eight soldiers, and the servant had been with the family for many years. The cook was a last-minute addition to the party. He seemed like a respectable man, and he came recommended by a noble family in the south.

The party crossed the Four Fingers without incident and began the long climb down Castle Street to the river valley. On the fourth day, just before sunrise, Procopius woke up to find the cook standing over him with a filleting knife in his hand.

"What's the matter?" he asked. The cook bent down and stabbed at him with the knife.

It was probably his phobia about blades that saved him. He rolled sideways as the blow fell, so that the knife struck him on the shoulder rather than in the hollow between the collarbones, as the cook had intended. The cook yelled at him and tried to stamp on his face; he caught his attacker's foot with both hands and twisted it, toppling him; then he jumped up and ran, passing the dead bodies of the soldiers and his servant, all with their throats cut. The cook threw the knife at him, but it hit him handle first, between the shoulders. He kept running, until he was sure the cook had given up chasing him.

Although he'd escaped the immediate danger, his situation was about as bad as it could be. The cut in his shoulder was bleeding freely. He was still five days from the nearest known settlement, with nothing except his shirt. His feet were bare. The surrounding countryside was shale rock, with a few clumps of gorse. He had no idea if there were any streams running down off the mountain; he couldn't see any, and was reluctant to leave the road to go exploring. It was a reasonably safe assumption that the cook would be following the road—where else would he go?—and he would be on horseback, most likely armed with a selection of the dead soldiers' weapons. Procopius had never fought anyone in his life. He seriously considered staying where he was and waiting for the cook to find him and kill him; he was going to die anyway, and a knife would be quicker and easier than hunger, exposure or gangrene. It was only the thought that, if he let himself be killed, the cook would prevail and thereby in some vague sense prove himself the better man; the sheer unfairness of it that convinced him to keep going and do his best to survive.

Fortuitously, the road at this point was steep and made up of loose, dry stones; a horseman would have little advantage over a man on foot. He kept up the best pace he could manage, stopping only to listen for the sound of his pursuer, until nightfall. Then he left the road and hid as best he could in the gorse, waiting for sunrise. He was so tired he fell asleep for a few hours, but was wide awake long before the sun rose.

As soon as it was light enough to see by, he carefully made his way back uphill, parallel to the road, about fifty yards off on the eastern side, until he reached the place where the cook had camped for the night. He covered his advance by using the cook's horse as cover. He took an arrow from the quiver hanging from the saddle, crept in slowly and quietly and stabbed the cook through the ear without waking him.

He made an effort to cover the body with stones but soon gave up; the clouds were gathering, and he understood the merit of getting as far along the road as he could before the rain started to fall. As well as the money, the cook had brought two full waterskins and a sack of food, mostly cheese, dried sausage and apples; also two blankets and an oilskin cape. There were also various weapons, but Procopius left them behind, as he had no idea how to use them. He took a small knife and the cook's boots, which were much too big for him.

The next two days were fairly straightforward, although he led the horse rather than rode it, even though his feet were horribly sore. On the third day, however, he came to the place where the Blacklode crossed the road. Heavy rain on the Four Fingers had swollen the normally shallow river into a flood. Procopius had no experience with such matters, but he recognised at once that he had no hope of crossing the river in that state. With no map, he had no way of knowing if there were any alternative fords or crossings. He'd been careful with the food, but at best he had just enough for another four days. He couldn't get his head far enough round to see properly, but he had an idea that the wound in his shoulder had gone bad; it was warm and tender to the touch and hurt more now than it had earlier, and he felt weak and decidedly feverish. He decided that honour had been satisfied by his defeat of the cook, and there was nothing inherently shameful in this situation about death by exposure. He sat down beside the river, cleared his mind and fell asleep.

He woke up to find a man leaning over him, in more or less the same attitude as the cook. This time, though, he didn't instinctively flinch, mostly because he was too weak and sick to move. He noticed that the stranger wasn't holding a knife.

"You all right?" the stranger said.

"No."

The stranger frowned. "How'd you get yourself all cut up like that?"

Procopius took a deep breath and explained, as lucidly as he could; he'd been sent on a journey with a large sum of money, one of the servants had tried to kill him for the money but he'd managed to get away, and now here he was, lost and alone and very sick. The stranger nodded, to show he'd understood.

"Will you help me?" Procopius asked. "Please?"

The man smiled. "Wish I could," he said. "But don't worry, it'll be all right. What happened to your face? It's a real mess."

Procopius explained that, when he was eighteen months old, his father had murdered his mother and then tried to kill him too. "Is that right?" the stranger said. "You've had a pretty rough old time, one way and another. Still, it'll all come right in the end. Believe it or not, you'll look back on all this someday and understand it was all for the best."

"Look," Procopius said, "please, can you help me? At least give me a leg up so I can get on the horse. I haven't got the strength."

The stranger smiled. "In that case, that horse isn't much use to you, is it? So, really, I might as well have it, save me foot-slogging it all the way to the nearest town to fetch help. I hate walking. I get blisters."

"You can't have it."

"Sorry." The stranger's smile grew wider, if anything. "You can't use it, and you can't stop me taking it, so tough. Tell you what I'll do. I'll buy it off you."

"I don't want to sell it. I need it."

"No you don't," the stranger said gently. "But I'm going to give you a good price for it. I'm no thief."

He gathered the reins, put his foot in the stirrup and hoisted himself into the saddle. All the provisions and the other stuff were in the saddlebags. "It'll be all right," he said, "I promise you. You're going to be fine, just you wait and see."

Procopius watched him until he was out of sight; a long time, because, from where he was, he could see the road for ten miles, so at least an hour, during which time the horse and rider gradually grew smaller and further away before dwindling down into a dot, and then nothing. During that long time, he resolved not to die, because he needed to follow the thief, catch up with him and deal with him the way he'd dealt with the cook, for roughly the same reason. But this time it looked as though that wasn't going to be possible. He was getting weaker, it was harder and harder to stay awake; when he wasn't burning hot he was freezing cold, and, really, what was the point? His weakness had proved him to be inferior. If he didn't deserve to live, he didn't deserve to live. Simple as that.

He woke up lying in the bed of a cart. The driver and his wife were taking a load of cheese to market; you poor thing, they said, whatever happened to you? And they were very kind and looked after him, they took him to the inn at Loscobiel and stayed with him until he was better, and then took him on to Tet Escra, where he was able to get a letter of credit from his uncle's bank that made good his losses and enabled him to give the cheesemonger and his wife a proper reward, appropriate to his dignity and station in life, so that was all right.

On his first day at the Academy, he presented the Principal with a manuscript: a flute sonata in three movements. He didn't mention the background to the piece, how the shape of it had come to him as he lay among the rocks hoping to die, after the thief stole his horse, because that wasn't relevant, and he didn't suppose the Principal would be interested. The Principal put the manuscript on his desk and said he'd be sure to look at it some time, when he had a moment.

Two days later, he was sent for.

"Did you write this?" the Principal asked him. He looked fierce, almost angry.

"Yes," Procopius said.

"Think carefully, and I'll ask you again. Did you write this?"

"Yes."

"All on your own?"

Procopius suppressed a smile. Very much all on his own. "Yes. Sir," he added, remembering his manners. Then he couldn't resist asking, "Did you like it?"

The Principal didn't answer that. Instead, he gave a ferocious lecture on the evils of plagiarism. It had been known, he said, for students from wealthy families to hire penniless young composers to write works which the students then passed off as their own; behaviour the Principal confessed he couldn't begin to understand, because surely anybody who did such a thing would be eaten away with shame, and what possible pleasure could anyone get from being praised and rewarded for something he hadn't done? In such cases, the penalty was instant expulsion from the Academy. He wanted Procopius to understand that; and now he'd ask the question a third time, and if the answer was yes, there'd be no penalty, not this time. Did you write this piece of music?

"No," Procopius said. "Sir. I mean, like you said, why would I want to pretend if I hadn't? I've come here to learn, not to show off."

"I see," the Principal said. "In which case, that'll be all. You can go."

The Principal never liked him after that, because he'd made a serious accusation against him and it turned out to be wrong. But all the teachers loved him and said he was the most remarkable talent they'd ever come across, and it was a privilege to be part of the making of someone who would undoubtedly turn out to be the finest musician of his generation. Procopius wasn't sure about all that. The teachers had shown him all sorts of clever ways to turn the shapes in his mind into music; he'd been shocked and appalled by his own ignorance and the fact that he hadn't been able to figure out such things for himself but had had to be shown. That felt like cheating, though apparently it was quite legitimate. For the rest of it, the shapes just came to him, without any real work or effort on his part, certainly no skill or engagement with excellence. He was given them, unearned, just as he'd always been given everything, his whole life, undeserved, simply because he was the son and sole heir of a rich man who died relatively young, and the nephew of a rich, doting uncle.

So, for a while, he made sense of it the best he could. He thought about the man who'd taken his horse. You'll be all right, the man had said, just you wait and see. And he'd said he wasn't a thief, and he'd pay a good price for the horse; and that was when young Procopius began to see the shapes, and calling that a coincidence was stretching belief much further than it could possibly go. He could make no sense of it, of course—because what would a god or similar supernatural agency want with a horse, or feel the need to pay for a perfectly unremarkable thirty-thaler gelding with such a precious and valuable commodity?—but the fact that he couldn't make sense of it certainly didn't mean that it didn't make sense, only that he wasn't smart enough to figure it out. Later, he realised that he'd simply exchanged one insoluble problem for another, with a garnish of the supernatural to excuse him from having to analyse it rationally, and simply accepted; he was one of those people from whom things are taken and to whom things are given, not necessarily proportionately; a conduit for the remarkable and the excessive, himself unremarkable and lacking in any real substance, either for good or evil.

You don't bury your mother every day, so Telamon had treated herself: a new dress and shoes, two angels twenty from the best ladies' outfitters in Moil, which was also the only ladies' outfitters in Moil and the whole of the Eastern Mesoge. The dress was dark grey wool, covered her ankles and made her look like a granite outcrop. The shoes chafed at the heel, but only came in one size. Wool is far too hot to wear next to the skin in the Mesoge in midsummer, so she was going to be uncomfortable the whole time. Appropriate. Her mother would have liked that.

She'd budgeted an angel forty for the stage from Moil to Heneca; it had been an angel forty for the last thirty years to her certain knowledge, and things just don't change east of Moil, it's impossible, like water flowing uphill. So she handed the money to the driver, who looked at her.

"Where did you say you were going?"

"Heneca Cross."

"That's another ten stuivers."

She looked at him. "No it bloody isn't," she said. "Are you trying to be funny?"

Unlikely; he didn't come across as a humorous sort of man. "Angel fifty to Heneca Cross," he said. "Angel forty'll get you as far as Cordouli. You can walk from there if you like."

Between Cordouli and Heneca Cross stands the massive cloud-wreathed rampart of the Framea escarpment. In the old days before the war, painters and refined young ladies who did watercolours rode out to Heneca Top to paint the breathtaking vista of the Western plain sprawling away into the distance. On the other hand, what with the dress and the shoes she now had precisely three angels seven, out of which she had to find the cost of the funeral and her fare home. She did some mental arithmetic and found that if she didn't eat for the next three days she could just afford the fare. She fished two five-stuivers out of the hem of her glove and handed them over.

She wasn't the only passenger in the stage. There was also an old man in a long gown, who smelled, and a stout, round-faced woman with short grey hair, who read aloud from a prayer book the whole way. When it got too dark to read, she recited from memory. She got bits wrong, but Telamon didn't correct her.

She was facing forward, so she didn't get to see the amazing vista at Heneca Top. Instead, she got a fine view of the moors: a million acres of blackened heather-stubs, because they burn off the heather at midsummer, to keep the gorse in check. Beyond that was Eyren Common, a million acres of tree stumps slowly submerging into a tangle of ferns and briars, where they'd felled Eyren forest for charcoal, for the war. So, you see, some things do change in the Eastern Mesoge, though not necessarily for the better. Trees get cut down, and people die, and gradually the reasons for dragging back to this godforsaken place get fewer and less overwhelming, so that it begins to be possible to conceive of a day when one might not have to come back ever again—

("So you're from the Mesoge," a young man had said to her once. "Very flat there, isn't it?"

"Yes," she'd replied, "except for the hills and the mountains.")

One thing that never changes; it's three hours by stage from the Top to Heneca Cross, and the road goes straight through all the places she'd known when she was a little girl. A straight line, with her life on either side of it, like the things you don't like to eat left on the side of your plate. It's very much the sort of place where people don't have what they need, so they use something else. There's no slate and no clay, so they roof their houses with turf; the sheep clamber up onto the low eaves and clump about overhead all night, keeping you awake, and your big brother thinks it's amusing to tell you that the clumping noise is dead men dancing on the roof, and you lie awake quivering. There's no trees, so the fields are divided up with barriers of dry bramble and bracken wedged between rows of blackthorn stakes, for which the technical term is dead-hedging, and the only fuel is dried peat. There are no roads, no meadows, no woods, no inns, no villages, no chapels, no big houses of the rich and powerful. Instead, the people live in turf cabins in turf-walled enclosures, supposedly to protect their sheep from rustlers, though that hasn't worked worth a damn in two thousand years. They make plain but exceptionally fine weapons in the Eastern Mesoge, and they catch passenger hawks, which sell for big money. Apart from that, it's the last place God made.

There's no chapel at Heneca Cross, but the Father comes out from Segita once a month and holds services under the old thorn tree, so that's where they bury people, in the only clay seam north of the Aiser. It's convenient, because the stage stops there, and all the very many people who've left the area can come home when somebody dies, just briefly, just long enough to splash a bit of money about, and then go home. There's a stone-built barn to store the bodies in, more or less out of the damp and nicely chilled by the knife-edged wind, two stuivers a day, until the grieving kinsfolk can get there, and the farmer's wife lays on a sit-down meal for two stuivers a head or bread and cheese standing for three-farthings. It's the closest thing in those parts to a business.

"I came as soon as I could," she told the farmer, who she hadn't seen for twenty years. He hadn't forgotten her. Like a bad penny, said the look on his face. She owed him twenty stuivers, plus an angel for the plot. You could buy a small valley of indifferent grazing for an angel, but it wouldn't be under the thorn tree, so it wouldn't be right. Right and wrong are absolute and definite in the Eastern Mesoge. No grey areas whatsoever.

He showed her the plot he'd set aside. She frowned. "That's not right," she said.

"That's all there is. Take it or leave it."

"I don't want that one. I want the one next to my sister."

The farmer looked at her. One patch of scrubby heather is pretty much like another, you'd have thought, but apparently not. "That's reserved," he said.

"Is that right? How much to unreserve it?"

"Sixty stuivers."

More mental arithmetic. She could walk down the hill to Cordouli, but that would only save ten stuivers. The farmer and his son charged twenty-five stuivers for digging a grave.

"I'll give you another twenty," she said, "and you can lend me a shovel."

She'd never dug a grave before, but how hard can it be? It's just a hole in the ground. The farmer was a kind man at heart, so he lent her a pick as well. Clearly he knew his own land. Eight inches of crumbly black topsoil, all roots and small flints, and then you were into the clay. The shovel blade wouldn't bite, it turned on the fist-sized stones, and she hurt her ankle when her foot slid off with all her weight on it. So she swung the pick—how do you swing it properly without stabbing yourself in the back? She got the hang of it eventually, and each bite of the pick loosened up a palmful of clay crumbs, unless she hit a stone, in which case there were sparks and a jolt up the abused tendons of her forearms, and a burning in her lungs from the effort. Of course, the deeper down she went, the less room there was to swing the pick and manipulate the five-foot handle of the shovel. Before long she was squatting on her heels, scooping clay in her cupped hands on to the shovel blade, levering out stones with her fingernails. Her fringe was sodden with sweat, which trickled down into her eyes, salt water like tears, which she had so far neglected to shed. She wiped sweat off her forehead and smeared it on her cheeks and neck, to cool them. Hell of a way to save twenty-five stuivers, she thought; and then it occurred to her that there were probably a dozen men within walking distance who'd cheerfully have done the job for ten, because life in the Eastern Mesoge is hard (hard and treacherous and difficult and more stones than dirt) and ten stuivers is a lot of money, in context; and she'd moved away, had it easy in the soft south, never did a hand's turn, didn't know she was born. Her mother's words, and she could hear her mother's voice in her head saying them, and wouldn't she have been angry and ashamed to see her daughter digging a grave with her own hands, just to save a penny or two, because she could afford all the fine clothes and the fancy shoes, but when it came to burying her own mother—

"Telamon," said a voice somewhere in the air above her. "What the hell do you think you're doing?"

She wanted to laugh—because of the surprise, the incongruity, the very thought of him being here of all places (unimaginable, like her mother in silk underwear); and for sheer joy, because she hadn't seen him for so long. She didn't look up, and she kept her voice absolutely neutral. "Oh," she said, "it's you."

"You seem to be digging some sort of a hole."

She turned, looked up and located him; a silly, handsome face; a clever man doing an incredibly realistic impression of an idiot. Beyond any doubt the most distinguished stranger ever to visit Cordouli Hundred, though quite possibly nobody here had ever heard of him. Not very musical, the people in these parts. "Yes," she said, dropping the pick. "Oida, what are you doing here?"

"I happened to be in the neighbourhood."

Possibly the most absurd thing he'd ever said in a lifetime of spectacular inanities. "Doing what?"

"Never you mind. Then I heard some people saying there's this beautiful, rich, sophisticated city lady visiting at Heneca Cross, so I came by on the off chance it was you."

"Go to hell."

He didn't seem to have heard her. "Why are you digging a hole?"

"It's a grave."

He was silent, long enough to say half a catechism. "You're serious, aren't you?"

"Yes."

Another pause. Then: "You need to go a bit deeper than that. Six feet is generally recommended."

"It's not finished yet."

"Would you like some help?"

She laughed out loud; it came out sounding a bit forced. "What, you, digging? That I'd like to see."

"I can dig."

"Really."

"When I was in the army we dug trenches. Miles of them."

"You were never in the army."

"Actually, I was. Never saw any action, thank God, but we dug about a million miles of latrines."

She shook her head. "You've never handled a shovel in your entire life."

He lowered himself carefully and sat on the edge of the grave, with his feet dangling. Boots by the best maker in Rasch, but carefully waxed, well looked after. "I take it there's some reason why you're doing this yourself."

"Local custom. The next of kin digs the grave. It's a mark of respect."

"Ah." He sounded uncomfortable, the way men do when the subject of grief comes up. "Next of kin."

"My mother."

"I'm so sorry. I didn't know."

She looked down at the floor of the grave. Still two feet down to go, minimum. She realised she was too tired to stoop and get the pick, let alone swing it. "We weren't close."

"Even so."

"She never liked me much."

"I find that hard to—"

"She sold me."

"What?"

After ten years of trying, she'd shocked him into empty-headedness. "When I was six years old. She sold me, to pay the rent."

As soon as she'd said it, she really, really wished she hadn't. She'd never told anyone. It wasn't the sort of thing you want known about yourself. But apparently she'd just said it, and to Oida, of all people. Curious. And she felt like she'd just drawn a knife over a kitchen-table game of shove-ha'penny.

"But that's illegal."

She laughed. "Oh, they call it indentured service," she said briskly, "limited to five years and then you're free again. Only the buyer charges you for your food and your clothes and the roof over your head, plus interest, of course, and by the time you've done your five years, what you owe's going to take you another five years to work off, and so it keeps on going. No, she had the choice, sell me or my sister. She kept my sister." She looked at him. He had that blank, thoughtful look. "This is not a nice place, in case you hadn't realised. Do you know how much she sold me for?"

"No, I really couldn't say."

"Go on. Guess."

She'd offended him, or at the very least made him very uncomfortable. She wasn't sure she wanted to, but now she'd drawn blood she couldn't stop. "I can't guess," he said. "I don't know about these things."

"Guess."

He shrugged, to signify that he was playing the game against his will. "Twenty angels."

"Fifty stuivers."

"Fifty—"

Odd, she thought; it takes actual bare numbers to get right through to him, to make him truly understand. That's so like a man; facts, not feelings. To get through to a man, you have to take the cover off and show him the gearwheels. "I know," she said. "The man who bought me was robbed. Anyway, that was my mother for you."

He was choosing his words carefully. "I can see, that's not the sort of thing you can forgive easily."

"Oh, I forgave her," she said quickly. "It's all right, I told her, when they took me away, I understand. Actually, I loved her to bits. She—" She stopped. Her voice had been about to break, and that wouldn't do at all. "Like I said, it's the local custom. We're very traditionally minded round here."

"You sure I can't help?"

It was like one of those games you play in your head on long coach journeys; consequences, improbable people doing improbable things. Imagine (let's say) Oida, being a—think of something really wacky and offbeat—gravedigger. The imagination boggles. But it was very hot and she was very tired, and she had no money, and nobody else in the wide world was going to help her. And—now she came to think of it—the offer was extraordinary, incredible. "You'll blister your hands. They're too soft."

"And yours aren't."

"Yours are softer than mine. Bet you."

"Show me."

She'd wrapped the sad scraps of her last linen handkerchief round the base of her left thumb; too little, too late. "Fine," she said, with a weary sigh. "If you really want to come down here and dig a hole, be my guest."

He reached out his arm, and she realised he was offering to help her out. He caught her wrist and pulled, gently but effectively. He was stronger than he looked. Then he hopped down into the grave (like an acrobat; no, like a nimble clown) took the pick delicately, as though it was a flute or a clarinet, and swung it easily, using its own weight and balance. He worked quickly and efficiently, minimum effort and maximum effect. He'd done this before; someone had shown him how to do it well. Digging latrines in the army? For some reason she didn't think so. She noted the way he edged himself into the corners, changing from swings to pecks in the confined space. Of course he was fresh and rested, and he was wearing stout, sensible boots and a light, tailored shirt that didn't catch and snag and fight him every move he made. But he threw the earth up out on to the pile with a fluent, almost graceful sweep of the arms, and he didn't seem to be getting tired. Damn the man, she thought. If he was a shoemaker, elves would break into his workshop in the small hours and do all his work for him.

"That ought to do it," he said. He was red in the face and his hair was plastered across his forehead. "Don't you think?"

"You want to go down another six inches."

He didn't argue; well, you wouldn't, would you, digging someone's mother's grave. But she kept him at it until he looked genuinely tired, and he grinned and said he wasn't cut out for a life of manual labour. "That'll do fine," she said, and reached out her hand to pull him up. Of course, he was two feet further down than she'd been, and he was heavier than she was; and he'd expected her to be able to haul him up out of there easy as anything. A compliment, of sorts.

"Sorry," she said, as he slid back down again and landed awkwardly on the sides of his feet. "Here, try again."

"It's perfectly all right," he said. Then he laid the shovel at an angle against the corner, stood on the handle and hopped out quite easily. "Right," he said. "What do we do now?"

"You don't do anything. This is private."

"Of course."

Stupid, she thought, a little later. Her mother's body was too heavy to lift (a strong woman, years of bending to the hoe, walking three miles to the well twice a day, a weight she'd never be able to shift as long as she lived), so she had to get behind it, arms under the armpits, hands linked across the cold chest, and drag. It wasn't an issue; she'd seen battlefields, bodies longer dead, more swollen, more shrunken than this, she'd handled them, rifled them for money, trinkets, boots, it was just a thing; you can't catch death by touch, so she dragged it, heels trailing, walking backwards, careful not to bump into the wall or foul its trundling heels on the doorpost. A coffin would've been ten stuivers extra. She lugged it to the edge of the grave, stood it upright and pitched it in. You stupid, clumsy girl, you can't do anything. Well, she thought. Then she grabbed the shovel and threw dirt on her mother's face—open mouth, blank and staring eyes, I came all this way and spent all my money and look what a mess I'm making of it. Ah well. I'll try and do a better job next time.

By the time she'd spooned in the last cupful of spoil, her hands were red raw and her back was aching, and that was good, because it was only right and proper that she should feel pain at this moment, and she wouldn't have done otherwise. She stacked the tools neatly against the trunk of the thorn tree, then went inside the house.

Oida was drinking with the farmer and his two sons. She must've walked through the door a split second after he told the punchline of a joke. The three farmers were laughing, and Oida had that grin on his face.

"I'm done," she said. "I'm going now."

Oida jumped up. "Just a moment. You're not in a tearing hurry, are you?"

She really didn't want him to see her starting the long walk to Cordouli. "I don't want to miss the stage."

"Stage isn't due in till sundown," the farmer pointed out. "Plenty of time yet."

She ignored him. But Oida was too quick. Before she knew it, he was between her and the door, thanking the farmer for the drink before she could push past him.

"I can give you a lift," he said. "Quicker than the stage. Also, my coach has springs."

She sighed. "Oida, what are you doing here?"

"I heard. About your mother."

That was entirely possible. The Lodge knew everything, even now. "So you flew to my side. How sweet."

"Yes, actually. I don't think anyone should have to face something like this on their own."

The Lodge would know all about local burial customs. And

Oida would've looked them up in a book before setting off. "My bag's on the stage."

"You can have it sent on from the depot."

Now she knew him pretty well. On a trip like this, he'd ride, not bother with a chaise or a coach, unless he was sure he'd have company on the way back. Did he know about her sad lack of money? The Lodge knows everything.

"My book is in my bag. I hate not having something to read."

"I'll lend you a bloody book."

"I don't like your books. They're boring."

Which was perfectly true. For this journey, he'd packed Pleusio's *History of the Archidamian War* and Illectus's *Aspects of Comedy*. He always took two books, in case he decided he wasn't in the mood for one of them, and he never went on the road with a book he hadn't already read. The coach was a luxury model, city-built, with curtains and padded seats.

"Not mine," he said. "Hired it in Moil. I think it belongs to the mayor."

She shook her head. "You didn't hire it. The mayor turned out to be a fan. Please, take my coach, I'd be honoured. Everything's so easy for you."

He laughed. "I earned it," he said. "I had to sit still while his loathsome twelve-year-old son murdered *Undefeated* on the clarinet."

And the mayor's son would remember that for the rest of his life, and tell his grandchildren. "People give you things," she said. "And you do nothing to deserve it."

"True," he said. "But I dig a mean hole."

She looked out of the window; familiar places, but this time she was going in the right direction. "I used to pick blueberries on this moor."

"Sounds like a pleasant occupation on a sunny day."

"Not really. They use them for dye, for army uniforms. We had to pick twelve pounds a day each, or we didn't get any food."

He gave her a weak smile; it had been an obvious trap, and he'd willingly walked into it. She thought about him, digging. He'd done it like an actor, playing a man digging a hole. He'd studied the technique, thought himself into the mindset, and actors are generally fit and active, so he'd kept it up quite convincingly for half an hour. "I ought to be in floods of tears, but I'm not," she said. "Do you disapprove? Do you think I'm shallow and heartless?"

"Are you familiar with the concept of work-hardening?"

Good answer. Of course she was; a piece of steel that gets flexed time and again eventually gets hard, just before it turns brittle and snaps. Or a piece of steel sheet that gets hammered over and over gets compressed, hard and strong, just right for a helmet or a breastplate. "I do feel things, you know."

"I know you do."

"Right. What am I feeling now?"

He considered the problem as though it was algebra. "Relieved."

She looked at him. "How do you make that out?"

"Am I right?"

"Show your working."

He smiled. "All right," he said. "You hate this place, and you hate the fact that you come from here. Now your last tie with it's gone, and it's a great weight off your shoulders."

She nodded. "It's not just that," she said. "I feel like my whole life I've been carrying the guilt of a dreadful crime, only I haven't been caught yet. And now the last witness against me is dead, and there's no proof any more. I'm free."

"The last witness but one."

She shook her head. "If only I know something happened, then if I say so, it never happened."

He thought about that for a moment. "Were you close to your sister?"

"Closer than my mother. No, I wasn't, not really. I hardly knew her."

"You left her everything in your will."

He wasn't supposed to know that, but of course he did. "I haven't got anything to leave."

"You might suddenly come into money."

"Well, she's dead now, so I guess I'll have to think of someone else. The Blue Star temple, probably. Or the Pandion library."

He gave her a solemn frown. "I'm a trustee of the Blue Star," he said: "don't even consider it. Why buy lunch for a bunch of people you never even met? The Pandion's a good thing, though. They've got the complete works of Illectus."

She frowned. "Nobody's got the complete works. A third of them are lost."

He shook his head. "They don't want it widely known, but, yes, the complete works. Not to mention two books of Orderic's *Analects* that were supposed to have gone up in flames during the sack of Haut Bohec."

Her eyes widened. "You're kidding."

"Seen them myself, with these two eyes. I wasn't allowed to read them, mind you, they won't let you do that unless you've got signed testimonials from the heads of three accredited faculties. *Five aspects of the nature of Evil* are, however, self-evident. That's all I saw, and then Father Prior closed the book and put it back on the shelf. Annoying. I'd have loved to find out what happened in the end."

"They all got married and lived happily ever after, probably."

He smiled. "No witnesses," he said. "Witnesses to what?"

"None of your business."

"I'm a human being; everything human is my business."

"Fremda, *The Girl from Beloisa*."

"Act four, but which scene?"

"Two."

"Three. Close, but no apple."

She shrugged. "I read on coaches, and I travel a lot."

"Me too," he said, and opened his book.

So she opened hers: Illectus on Comedy. She hadn't read it before. It was ghastly; impenetrable, boring and wrong. But he'd chosen it for light reading; brought two books, as he always did, so she couldn't tell herself he'd brought one for her, in anticipation of her riding back with him, and deliberately chosen something dead boring. She looked up and saw him watching her. "What?"

"Swap?"

She closed the book and put it on the seat beside her. "What were you doing in Heneca? You didn't fly to be with me in my hour of trouble, because even you couldn't possibly have known. The Father wrote to me that she'd died and an hour after I read the letter I was on the stage. And the letter hadn't been opened. I know everything there is to know about fixing seals."

He shook his head. "No, you don't," he said gently. "And the Father was under orders to report anything about your family before contacting you."

She scowled at him. "Whose orders?"

"Not mine. Really. I don't have that sort of authority, believe me."

"But you're told my mother's died before I am."

"You're a Lodge soldier." His voice was suddenly hard. "Lodge security overrides delicate sensibilities. They need to know all about you."

"What were you doing at Heneca Top?"

He sighed. "You want the truth."

"Yes. I'm kinky that way."

"Fine." He broke eye contact and looked away. "You're needed, in Rasch. Someone had to go and fetch you. I volunteered."

"That's more like it." She felt a sudden surge of anger— because he hadn't dropped everything and rushed to be with her; he was just doing a job, obeying orders. It occurred to her that he was rather an important man, whose time was not without value, and he'd taken a job that any low-grade foot soldier could've done, spent days rattling through the horrible Eastern Mesoge, put up with her vile temper, dug a grave— For some reason, that didn't reduce the anger. Quite the reverse. "Why can't you give me a straight answer the first time, instead of all this garbage?"

He shrugged, said nothing. A wise man said: the purest form

of victory is not to fight. Sometimes, this was one of them, what she wanted most in the whole world was to smash his face in. "Thank you," she said. "For the lift. I'd run out of money, you see. I was going to have to walk down to Cordouli."

"In those shoes?"

How many men actually notice shoes? Was it something he'd trained himself to do, over the years? She raised her head slightly, so that she could look at him properly. Here was a man who sang commonplace songs exceptionally well but who loved and understood Procopius and Genseric, far better than she ever would; who noticed shoes and hairstyles and the ebb and flow of hemlines; who chased women like a cat chases string, but read Illectus on Comedy for pleasure and relaxation; who lied fluently and well, but who could dig a straight-sided hole in stiff clay; who bet ridiculous sums of money on cockfights and invariably won; who basked in praise and flattery like a lizard on a rock but who believed in the Craft with unshakable faith, and would die for the Lodge without a second thought; who spent more on socks each year than her mother had earned in her whole life, but who'd pulled strings and called in favours to be sent on a degradingly routine mission in the Eastern Mesoge on the off chance that he might be some help at a bad time; who spoke eight languages and was an off-relation of the two emperors; who never told her the truth unless she gouged it out of him; who, with all the world to choose from, kept following her about and finding excuses and pretexts for being in the same place as her, a plain, scar-faced woman from the Mesoge whose mother had sold her to the blueberry-pickers. Face it, she told herself; you know how this is going to end, and nobody else on earth knows you half so well, or gives a damn. But not yet. The apple falls from the tree when the time is right, and not before.

Sometimes she played a game with him, although he probably didn't realise that was what she was doing; she'd pick some thoroughly abstruse topic, which she'd carefully boned up on in advance, and start asking him questions about it, just to see if he knew what she was talking about and was able to reply intelligently. Amazingly, he hadn't failed her yet.

"But it stands to reason that if the head pressure at the top cistern is greater than the return flow" (she'd chosen hydraulic engineering, with specific reference to the rebuilding of the aqueduct at Fail Loisir), "then an abnormally low tide in the estuary is going to back up the feeder channels and the whole system will clog up with silt."

He thought for a moment. "Not necessarily," he said. "I think they've got special bleeder pipes for that, somewhere up on the moors above Ciotal. Mind you, it's a while since I've been there."

Amazing. "Well, that's not going to help much if there's heavy spring rain and the runoff comes surging down the rines. In fact, it would make it worse."

"In that case, they'd open the sluices at Mavais Shanz, surely. I'm only guessing," he added (if so, lucky guess). "If you like, I can find out for you. I know a man who knows about these things."

Over the years she'd learned an awful lot about an awful lot of unlikely things, researching for the Game. But she'd never caught him out once. "No, that's all right, don't bother. Just idle curiosity, really."

"Fascinating subject," he said, reaching for his book. "Would you mind shifting your feet? I'm getting a cramp."

She'd accepted his kind offer and traded Illectus on Comedy for Pleusio's *History of the Archidamian War*; seemed like a good idea at the time. "Still following the cockfighting?"

He peered at her over the cover of Illectus. "You don't hold with cockfighting."

"No, but I could do with a hot tip, if you've got one."

He nodded. "Bloodspur Pride of Blemya to win the Aelian summer league," he said. "You'll get a good price because nobody fancies the breed in the middleweights, but I've seen him fight and he's got the body weight and the staying power. Have you run out of money again?"

"Yes."

Puzzled frown. "Why? You always used to be as poor as a dog because you sent all your money home. But now you've got nobody to send it to, so you should be rolling in it."

She'd never told him that was what she did. "Well, maybe I will be, from now on. At the moment, though, I could do with a small injection of capital."

Credit where it was due; he'd never offered her money, or arranged for money to come her way. A couple of times, when she'd had an angel or two, he'd deliberately won it off her playing cards. Now, perhaps, would be a good time to rub his nose in it. "Could you lend me twenty angels?"

He looked at her, the way he did when they were playing chess and she did that queen's-side swoop he never saw coming. "Sure." His hand was fumbling in his pocket.

"I don't know when I'll be able to pay you back."

"Right. On second thoughts, forget about Bloodspur in the Aelian. There's a nice little Rhaesian Grey called Fireclaw in the Domestic Stakes; the odds aren't so good but it's an absolute certainty."

She smiled. "I wouldn't bet your twenty angels on a cockfight."

He held out his hand, on which rested four gold coins. "Why not? It'd be like finding money in the street."

"I don't hold with cockfighting. It's cruel."

"This from the woman who once killed a political officer for a berth on a ship."

She smiled and took the coins. "It's like the old joke," she said: "what's the difference between lawyers and rats?"

"Go on."

"Given time, and under certain circumstances, you can get attached to a rat."

He grinned, the special grin he only used for good jokes. The book was open on his knee, cover facing upwards. When he grinned like that, you could kid yourself into thinking he was a harmless idiot. She thought: Oida and me, we've fought each other like the Belot brothers, the length and breadth of two empires, and neither of us has ever lost or ever won, and I think it's possible that we fight for the same reason they do. So, if I'm Senza, what do I do now?

They only played cards once; never again. She was sure he cheated, but she had no idea how, and it was a subject she knew a great deal about. Fortunately, they weren't playing for money.

"There must be at least six aces in that pack," she said.

He shook his head. "The regulation four. No pack's got six in it. The first pack ever made had five, if that's any help."

"Five aces?"

He nodded. "Five suits, therefore five aces. But for some reason, when they made the second pack, they cut the number down to four."

"Five suits?"

"That's right. Spears, shields, stars and wheels, and swords, which they decided to do away with. Hence the trick cards we use in the Lodge. Making a total of ninety-two."

"Rather a lump to carry around."

"Quite," he said. "And expensive, too, when the packs were made of silver. And we've managed all these years with seventy-eight, so that's all right." He gathered the cards and put them back in his pocket. "I've seen it, you know."

"Seen what?"

"The original pack," he replied. "Or at least, what they believe is the original pack, though after all this time it's really just a matter of faith. It's a sort of holy relic; they only bring it out once every fifty years or so. I just happened to be in the neighbourhood at the time, so I got a look at it, over someone's shoulder."

Clearly she was meant to be impressed (which she was). "Probably a fake."

"Probably," he said. "I mean, what are the chances of something that old surviving all those years? Anyhow, there's only a handful of people alive who could tell if it's genuine. Emperor Glauca, for one. And the head of the Lodge, of course. He's the one who looks after it, so they say."

"I don't believe there is a head of the Lodge," she said. "I think he's just a convenient myth, like the Invincible Sun."

"It's pretty bad," she was telling him. "Probably where you've been the last few months, you wouldn't have noticed particularly, but everything's falling to pieces."

"We'd sort of gathered that in Blemya," he said. "So, how many of us did they catch?"

"Relatively few. Pretty well everyone who was on record as being a Craftsman either got out before the news broke or shortly afterwards. A few, couple of hundred maybe, got caught when they closed the borders." She drew a finger across her throat. "The bitch of it is, my division's been assigned to tracing and retrieval, so I'm directly responsible for about a dozen of us going to the gallows."

"No you're not," he said, quick and firm. "If anyone's to blame, it's the genius somewhere up the ladder who thought the Lodge declaring war on both empires simultaneously was a good idea." He scowled at his feet for a moment, then added, "Which it was, it goes without saying. At a stroke, all the brightest and the best on both sides of the border are either vanished or dead, so, naturally, everything grinds to a halt."

"Except the war."

"We'll see about that," Oida said crisply. "With no clerks to organise supplies and write up the payroll, it's only a matter of time. I wish someone had told me beforehand, though. When the news broke, I was scared stiff: I thought they'd come for me, sure as eggs. After all, I haven't exactly made a secret of being a Craftsman over the years."

"Ah, but everybody knows you're shallow and insincere and you only go through the motions so as to be popular."

"Just as well, or I'd be dangling on a bit of string right now. How about you? Any suspicions?"

"I don't think so, or they wouldn't have put me on retrievals." She looked away, out of the window. Far away in the distance, she could make out a grey blur, the walls of Rasch. "So, you haven't had any bother."

He shrugged. "I come and go and nobody says anything, but I've got a lot of free time on my hands. Cancelled bookings, that sort of thing. I tell myself it's because there's no clerks to organise anything. Probably true."

"It's just that nobody likes your songs any more."

"If only. No, I'd be happy with that, if that's all it is. Tell you the truth, I'm sick of it, I'd give up tomorrow if I could. No, don't pull faces, I mean it. Slowly it's dawned on me that I'll never write great music, which is what I wanted to do when I started out. So what's the point? Nobody ever got into this business because of a burning desire to write second-rate music."

"You couldn't live without it. You're like the gods in the fairy tale. If people stopped worshipping you, you'd cease to exist."

He gave her a disapproving look, which made her want to smile. "You don't know what it was like," he said, "growing up with my brother. He was always the favourite, the smart one, the good-looking one. Also he was the heir, he was going to get all the land and the money, and either I was going to have to get out there and shift for myself, or I'd spend the rest of my life hanging round the house living off his charity, of which he has none. The only thing I could do better than him was sing and play the lute, so that's what I did. Never cared much for music when I was a kid—that came later, luckily enough—but I was like a fish that didn't like swimming. Tough, you live in the water, get on with it. And what I do have, and he's never had, is application."

She looked at him carefully, as though she could see the component that was out of place, but not how to get at it to fix it. "You don't talk about him much."

"No."

"Tell me about him."

"Have I got to?"

"Yes."

Tiny sigh. "Fine. All right. My brother Axio isn't a very nice man. I see him as a pair of scales. In one pan, you've got every good quality a man could ask for—looks, charm, brains, talent. In the other pan, you've got what it takes to make the scale balance. When I was a kid, I'd have given anything to be him. These days, I'd kill myself first. Does that answer your question?"

"No, of course not. Tell me about him. I know he got into big trouble. What did he *do*?"

But Oida shook his head. "Sorry," he said. "That's between him and me."

"Tell me what he did." Or? Or what?

She was hurting him now, pulling his tail; he didn't like it, but she didn't care. "Fine," he said. "I promised him I wouldn't go around telling people, but you want to know, so I'll tell you. When my brother was twenty-five and I was eighteen, I fell in love. She was our neighbour's daughter, and I was absolutely besotted, and she loved me just as much as I loved her. Furthermore, she was an heiress on her mother's side, so a nice chunk of property came with her—no, don't look at me like that, it's important because, if we'd got married, I'd have had my own place, a comfortable living, in the country. I'd have been your typical minor gentry, which is all I ever wanted to be. And it meant we could get married: her parents were happy and so were mine. It was the problem of me solved at a stroke, everything I could possibly wish for, I could be what the Great Smith made me to be, it was perfect. So, of course, Axio had to spoil it."

Oida was quiet for a moment. She wished she'd never said anything.

"At the time he was engaged to our cousin, a lovely girl and incredibly grand, the side of the family that had the serious money; it was perfect match for him—well, for them both. I think he genuinely cared for her, and she was dotty about him. But not to worry; Axio set about taking my girl away from me, only to find that he couldn't. He did his best, he tried everything, but, no, she loved me and she had no interest in him whatsoever. It got to be sort of an obsession with him. People started talking, and our cousin couldn't understand: it made no sense to her. She knew him so well, and she could see that my girl simply wasn't his type. I think she figured out why he was doing it. Anyway, she had no choice but to break off the engagement. Her parents made her, and he was making her look utterly ridiculous. I think that might just have been what pushed him over the edge."

She wanted to say: stop there, don't go on. Too late for that, of course.

"My brother has certain standards," Oida continued. "I don't understand them, but I assume he does. He'll cheerfully steal and kill, but he disapproves of rape; I guess he sees it as an admission of failure. So he killed her. It wasn't in a fit of temper; it was a well-organised, carefully planned light infantry operation, because by that stage her parents had forbidden him the house and she didn't dare set foot outdoors because of him. So he got up a raiding party, stormed the house, killed everybody and burned the place to the ground. Say what you like about my brother, he's a talented soldier and a fine leader of men; that place was built as a fortress and well garrisoned, and he stormed it with twenty men and no heavy machinery. He could easily have been a general if he'd set his mind to it."

She stared at him.

"Perfectly true," Oida said, "in case you were wondering. I know, because he told me all about it, in great detail. It was the night he left home in a hurry. He hauled me out of bed, smacked me around a bit and tied me to a chair. It's all your fault, I remember he told me. I'm ruined; because of you I've lost everything. I really ought to kill you, only letting you live will hurt you more. I was so scared I shat myself. I was sitting there in my own shit while he told me how he cut her throat. He showed me the knife, and how he did it—like so, with sound effects. Anyway, that's my brother for you. Any questions?"

Like a general in a civil war, who surveys the slaughtered enemy and sees his brother. "He got away with it."

"You know he did, so that's not a question. Yes, it was all deftly covered up, blamed on outlaws; they rounded up a bunch of deserters living in the forest and hanged them for it. But Axio had to clear out. He still blames me. I honestly couldn't tell you how I feel about him. After all, it was a long time ago and he's my brother. And I've done some pretty bad things since then."

Said casually, as though it was all as broad as it was long. She looked up and saw that they were getting close to the walls of Rasch. The idea was that he should get out at the fifth milestone, where he was meeting someone, while she took the coach to the livery stable in Longwall. "We're here," she said.

"So we are. Look, I'd suggest we met up later, but I'm not actually mad keen on showing my face in town right now, and you've got business to attend to."

She looked at him. "No I haven't."

A guilty look. "Actually, you have. You've got an appointment first thing in the morning." From his sleeve, like a conjuror, he produced a card; the six of swords, painted in three colours on thin limewood board. There is no six of swords in a conventional pack.

"Sorry," he said; then he closed his fist on the card, crushing it to splinters, and tossed it out of the window. "That's why I was sent to get you. The coach was so we'd make it back in time. They sent me because apparently it's quite important, and I told them I was pretty sure you'd come with me, whatever the situation at home. Anything else I may have told you was lies." He made a fist and banged on the back partition of the coach, which drew to a stop. "Good luck," he said, and swung quickly and gracefully out of the door, closing it behind him. By the time she got to her feet and leaned out of the window, he was nowhere to be seen.

"Bless me, Father, for I have sinned."

"That's what we pay you for." The curtain drew back, and she saw a long, thin nose and a pair of worried brown eyes. "You got here all right."

"Yes."

"How are things at home?"

"Normal."

He frowned, as though she'd said something uncouth. "Before we start, do you want to make a confession? Might as well, since we're here."

"Yes, as it happens. I was deliberately cruel to a friend."

"Say three Ascensions and light a candle for him." His eyes were tired, as though he hadn't slept much lately. "Actually, forget the candle. Just three Ascensions."

"Is that all?"

"Thou shalt not negotiate with the Lord thy God. Now listen."

He sounded edgy, almost (but it was unthinkable) scared. "Go on."

"Things are really bad." He stopped and took a deep breath. "They're scaling the purge up a notch or two. Anyone suspected of Lodge activity or membership at any time. Naturally we've passed the word along, but getting out is going to be really difficult; they're going to close the gates and you'll need a permit to leave the city. Naturally this is going to cause enormous problems, because it'll mean thousands of hungry mouths will be trapped inside who wouldn't normally be here long term, and of course they haven't thought about extra food supplies or anything like that. Now we can get permits, for the time being at least, but don't rely on that lasting. We'll try and get as many of our people out as we can, except for those who've agreed to stay, get caught and tortured into betraying our friends. Only it goes without saying the names we'll give them won't be Craftsmen." His voice was steady; unnaturally so. "With any luck, they'll have lynched most of the few loyal, competent officers they've still got before they figure out we've been playing games with them. Listen to me." His voice dropped, and she could feel the pressure behind it, about to burst. "The empires are going to fall, both of them. It's only a matter of time. It's only the Belot boys who're keeping the armies from turning on the emperors and tearing them to pieces, and when something happens to them—I say *when*—there'll be a carve-up like you can't begin to imagine. The only thing that can stop that is if there's a new emperor; one emperor, strong, unimpeachably legitimate and on our side. And it just so happens we have the man for the job."

Something clicked into place in her mind. She held her breath.

"He's only a distant cousin, but all the rest of the Imperial family are dead, so he's quite legitimately the heir to the throne. And the thing of it is, he's a Commissioner of the Lodge. It really couldn't have worked out better. Except, of course, for all the dead people."

She was about to choke. "Oida."

He looked at her, and her heart stopped. "Close, but no apple. Oida's the younger brother. Our man is Axio."

"But that's—"

A smile, without the faintest trace of joy. "I know," he said, "he's no angel. But he's a Craftsman to the bone, he's a born leader of men and we think he'll do a grand job. The only thing is, there's a problem."

"Too right there's a problem. He's *mad*."

He laughed. "You'd think that'd be an obstacle, but read your history book and you'll find that actually, no, it isn't. No, the problem's more delicate than that. You see, if this is going to work there's got to be just one heir. Certainty, you see. Two possibles, a choice, and we risk the whole dreary business starting up all over again, East and West, until there's nobody left alive at all."

He was making a point, but she couldn't see it. "You just said. He's the heir. All the rest are dead."

"No," he said. "Not all."

She got as far as "But—" and then it hit her. Axio had a brother.

"Think about it," he went on. "What do emperors do, after a civil war, as soon as they've got the crown on their heads? They slaughter their relatives. It's a crisp, clear message; him or nobody, him or we're back where we started, and the whole thing's been for nothing."

"But that's stupid," she heard herself say. "All right, yes, I can see what you mean about only one of them, but you've chosen the wrong one. Axio's mad. He murdered a whole family, just to spite his kid brother."

He frowned. "That was a long time ago."

"People don't change."

"Actually, they do. In Axio's case, he's got worse. But maybe you weren't paying attention a moment ago. Axio is a Commissioner of the Lodge."

"He's a psychopath."

He shrugged. "The Great Smith finds a use for every piece of steel in the scrapheap. Who's to say Axio isn't exactly the man we need? His faith is beyond question. Surely that's all that matters."

She stared at him. He was serious. "So you're actually saying you're going to murder Oida so Axio can be the next emperor."

He looked straight at her. "Not me."

She was too stunned to speak, or even move. It was impossible. It was a test of some kind, a trap, a trick.

"Oida's no fool," he went on. "It's inconceivable that all of this hasn't occurred to him already—that he's next but one in line, and we want the next emperor to be one of us. In fact, I've been half expecting him to go to ground, except he's smart enough to realise that he can't hide from us, no matter where he goes. No, he's standing his ground, because he knows it's the safest thing for him to do. He's possibly the best-known man in the world after the emperors, very high-profile, not someone who just disappears without anybody noticing. He keeps on the move, close to where there's Imperial forces, where he figures we won't go, and above all he makes sure he only has people around him who he can absolutely trust. People like you."

She managed to find her voice. It sounded strange and far away. "You must be mad. I—"

"He's in love with you. Everybody knows that. You're his best friend."

He's crazy, she thought, he's giving me all the reasons why I can't—"I won't do it."

"I'm sorry."

"Are you listening to me? I said—"

"You have to. This is a direct order."

"The hell with you and your orders."

"You can't disobey a direct order and remain a member of the Lodge." He looked straight at her, and she couldn't turn away. "You know what that means."

"I don't believe in all that stuff."

"Don't you?"

"I don't believe in anything that'd order me to do something like that."

"That's not quite the same thing, is it?" he said quietly. "Listen to me. You remember that scene in the play *The Madness of Theuderic?* We've just seen the Goddess drive the hero mad—she's right there, in front of our eyes—so that he kills his wife and children. Then the madness leaves him, and he's horrified by what he's just done. His best friend comes up to him and says, it wasn't your fault, the Goddess made you do it, you're not to blame. But he can't accept that, so his friend reminds him of all the myths and legends, about all the wicked and hateful things the gods do, to us and to each other, just for spite. But the hero says, I don't believe in any of that, I don't believe the gods are capable of evil; that's just blasphemy and lies." He paused, and smiled sadly. "But we know the friend is right and the hero is wrong, because we were there; we saw it happen. I understand, trust me. You don't want to believe. But you do. You have to, because of what you've seen."

She suddenly realised she'd been crying and hadn't noticed. "I can't do it."

"You must."

She went to her favourite cutler, in Haymarket.

"Not you again," he said. "What do you do with them all?"

She wasn't in the mood. "Show me what you've got in stock."

He sighed and picked a box up off the floor. He opened it and thought for a moment. "Try that."

He had a good memory, she had to give him that. It was exactly what she looked for in a knife; the right length, width, point geometry and edge profile. The grip was just the right size for her hand. The blade was charcoal-blued; resisted rust and didn't flash in the light. Could have been made for her. Given how many times she'd been in this shop over the years, it probably had been.

"How much?"

He frowned at her. "I like to tell myself you buy them as presents for your brothers in the army. I imagine they're careless and keep losing them. Eight angels."

She had the money, but only because Oida had lent it to her.

There was a note from the Department pinned to her door— *Where are you? Report in immediately.* Call themselves spies, she thought. She screwed it up, then left the building; not by the door, but up on to the roof, then across the handy plank she'd left hidden up there on to next door's roof, down the stairs into the cellar, which had a shared charcoal chute with the next house down the block; out through their door, which opened on to a different street. This she did in the fond hope that someone from the Department was watching her, and would report back that she was acting oddly and should be brought in immediately for questioning. If she was locked up in a cell for a week or so, she couldn't be out killing people; and it could hardly be her fault if she was arrested. But of course there was nobody watching her, and she walked away unfollowed. The Department was desperately short-staffed these days, and she simply wasn't that important.

She went to a cockfight, out back of the Equity and Redemption in Lazars Row. She bet two angels on a nice little Rhaesian Grey called Fireclaw in the Domestic Stakes. Fireclaw took slightly longer than two Ascensions and a Shorter Creed to turn his opponent into a bloody mess, with a few pathetic feathers still floating in the air long after the remains had been scooped up and dropped in the trash. Two angels at seven to one is fourteen angels. Damn the man.

She reported in at the Department. "Where have you *been*?" they yelled at her, and didn't wait for a reply; he wants to see you, right now. Sorry, which he would that be? *Him*, of course; and a finger pointed discreetly upwards.

She froze. "You're kidding."

"No I'm not. You're to report to the Director immediately. And that was six days ago. Why d'you think we've been scouring the bloody city for you?"

Please, no, she said to herself as she climbed the stairs: no more, I can't cope with anything else. It occurred to her that she could simply run away (like all the other Craftsmen); if that was what they called scouring the city, she had a fair chance of being on a boat to Blemya or the Republic before they realised she'd gone. But that would be—no. Oida was due back in town for a recital in three days' time, so she had no choice.

The Department building had been many things in its time.

It was old, and nobody knew who'd originally built it. The ground floor had been a temple to some long-obsolete god; then it had housed a garrison, and then it was a grain store, in case of siege; after a hundred years or so, oil replaced grain, and there was a fire, and when Vindex IV inherited the ruins he built yet another palace, to house one of his twenty-seven mistresses. When Vindex's grandson Lodar found himself swinging from a meathook in the Arches, the palace was extended upwards and outwards to house the Ministry of Supply, until the Third Republic fell, whereupon Spolas II gave the land to the monks of the Blue Hand, who tore down half of it, extended the other half and built a soaring belltower, decorating every square inch of the interior with dazzling neo-Archaic frescoes. When Cuon dissolved the monasteries, a mercantile consortium bought the site, using the cloisters as a ropewalk and the buildings as storage. Most of the frescoes that survived the damp were defaced during the Iconoclast crisis under Copax III; the only ones to survive were the *Annunciation* and the *Judgement of the Dead* in the lower bell-chamber, which was blocked off by fallen masonry until the Department was founded by Hunderic I and moved into its present site. The first Director naturally claimed the bell-chamber for his own, and his thirty-two successors had fiercely guarded the privilege. Accordingly, only a very few people had seen what were probably the finest surviving examples of neo-Archaic devotional art, and it was a fair bet that most of them had been in no state of mind to appreciate them.

Telamon arrived at the top of the last flight of stairs weak-kneed and out of breath, and found herself face to face with the

Invincible Sun in Glory, twelve feet high and glowing in the early evening light, filtered through yellow stained glass in a strategically placed skylight. For a moment, she couldn't think; for a moment, she was prepared to believe that she was in the presence of the real thing, not a picture. Then she pulled herself together with a snap, like a dog's jaws closing, and noticed a man sitting in the far corner of the outer chamber, gazing up at the painting. She recognised him; hard not to, because of the appalling scars on his face.

He turned and looked at her. She felt herself choke up, the way she always did when she met somebody she particularly admired.

"Sorry," he said. "I was miles away."

Procopius, principal of the Imperial Academy of Music, the greatest living composer, quite possible the greatest of all time. Then a horrible thought struck her; what was he doing here, sitting forlornly in the anteroom of the Director's office?

"I'm sorry," she said, then realised she had no idea what she was apologising for. "I don't suppose you remember me. Oida—"

"Introduced you to me after a concert." He smiled. The effect was horrible. "I'm terrible with names but very good with faces. Ironic."

She realised she was staring, and felt her face heat up like a bar of iron in the forge. "I'm sorry," she mumbled, but Procopius shook his head.

"It's all right," he said. "If I were you, I'd look at the painting instead. It's a lot prettier."

She did as she was told, and for the first time noticed that on the blazing gold cheek of the Invincible Sun there was a single, unexplained tear.

"Worth the climb, don't you think?"

"Yes," she said, and then remembered where she was. She desperately wanted to ask: what are you here for? But of course she couldn't. Procopius was gazing at the painting; she glanced at him quickly, then looked away again. He didn't seem worried, but probably he never did; the sort of man who'd look the same whether he was waiting to drink the hemlock or for the rain to stop. As discreetly as she could she pressed her fingertips together. Lord, she mouthed at the painting, please don't let him be in any trouble. Let him get out of here safe and in one piece.

Then Procopius stifled a yawn, stood up and opened a door, set so cunningly into the wall that she hadn't noticed it was there. "Come on through," he said, and went in.

It was as though the roof had fallen in on her. The door clearly led to the Director's office, the inner sanctum, the lair of the Imperial spymaster-general, the most feared and hated man in the West after the emperor himself. Procopius the musician had just opened it and told her to follow him. Therefore—

Her head was pounding, and the moment she was through the door she was faced with a scene far beyond the scope or strength of her mind; the *Judgement of the Dead*, by the most brilliant, most disturbed painter who ever lived. It was the most beautiful thing she'd ever seen, and if her legs had still been working she'd have run away; probably tripped and fallen down the stairs and broken her neck.

"I know," said a voice from a long way away, "it's a hell of a thing, isn't it? Takes a bit of getting used to, which is why I usually sit with my back to it. Tell you what. You have my chair, and I'll sit here. For two pins I'd get them to whitewash it over, except that'd be a crime against humanity."

She sat down in his chair. It was huge, and her feet didn't quite reach the ground. It had been carved out of the root-ball of a huge oak tree, and made to look like a hand closing around the sitter. The other seat was an army-issue folding camp stool, on which Procopius squatted like a grown-up perched on a nursery chair. There was no desk. In this office, nothing was ever put down on paper.

"Thanks for coming," Procopius said. "Sorry to drag you all the way up here. By the way, as you've probably guessed, I run this circus." He grinned, taking care to angle the scarred side away from her. "You don't need to be told this, but not a word to anyone, all right? It's all melodrama, of course, but the fewer people know about me, the better."

"Of course."

"Good girl. Don't look so worried," he went on, "it's good news. As you probably know, the Deputy Director in charge of recoveries is no longer with us." He drew the tip of his finger lightly across his throat. "So there's a job going, and it's yours. Smile," he added. "You're supposed to be pleased."

"I am. Thank you."

"Fibber," Procopius said gravely. "Not that I blame you, the way things are at the moment. But under normal circumstances it's a real plum; you get a seat on Faculty, and you'll be an *ex officio* member of the Security Council, which ain't bad for someone who started life as a blueberry-picker on Heneca Moor. And for what it's worth, you're only the second woman in four hundred years, and one of the very few to have made it this far up the ladder starting at the very bottom. I'd like to say it's purely on merit, but the fact that everybody else is dead or on the run did have something to do with it."

"Thank you," she repeated.

His grin widened. "Don't thank me till you've sat through your first Council meeting. Also, if you feel you've got to be grateful to someone, I did get a really enthusiastic reference from a certain mutual friend of ours. He sings like a bullfrog, but I trust his judgement when it comes to women."

Damn the man. "We've worked together on a number of—"

"He's crazy about you." Procopius was smiling; bless you, my children. "Genuinely and sincerely, if that's even remotely possible. But that's none of my business. Anyway, the job's yours. I'm afraid you can't turn it down, because you now know about me, and that information is limited to the Council and the Faculty. But you don't want to, do you?"

She forced herself to rally, like the shattered remnants of the Third Guards at Scola Hill. "What does the job involve exactly?"

He nodded his approval. "Basically, it means that instead of dashing about the place catching the enemies of the People and bringing them in, you sit behind a desk and give the orders. You don't decide who the enemies are, of course, that's my job. I send you a memo; you hand out the assignments. There's also an unbelievable amount of paperwork, without which the sun will not rise, and on top of that there's Council every evening just after compline and Faculty twice a week, and as a junior member you'll be the one landed with doing the actual work. If

it's any consolation, you get a really nice suite all to yourself at
the far end of the East wing, and a ridiculous amount of money,
to make you completely immune to bribes, and which you'll
have no time to spend. Questions?"

She was staring again, but not at the scar, which she couldn't
see. He gave her a slightly annoyed look. "What?"

"Sorry. It's nothing, really."

"Go on."

Well, she thought. "How can you do it? I mean—" Too late
now; her tongue had run away from her, like a bad dog with a
bit of old twig. "You write such beautiful music. It's—" She
hesitated; too late now. "It's all about the things we ought to be
but never can be, about everything that's wonderful and good,
the things we can't get at and spoil—"

"Thank you."

"Yes, but it's true. Everybody says so. It's like you're touching
the Divine. So how can you do that and be the spymaster? It
doesn't make sense."

He shrugged. "What you mean is," he said, "which one's
the real me, and which one do I do for a hobby?" Then, quite
deliberately, he turned his head. "Here's an old joke for you.
Man bought a black carthorse, painted the whole of its left side
white, left the right side black. Why'd you do that? people asked
him. He said: it's so that if I ever have an accident in my cart
and run someone over, it'll confuse the hell out of the witnesses.
Now run along and do some work."

It didn't matter, of course. Entirely irrelevant; because she
wouldn't be around here very long, one way or another. Like

the man walking to the gallows who stoops and picks up a ten-angel piece.

To her surprise, one of the other members of Faculty was someone she knew. "I never realised," she said.

He smirked at her. "Of course you didn't. First rule of this business, never let the right hand know what the left hand is doing." He paused, then added, "Did he make you sit facing the painting?"

"No."

"Ah. In that case, he likes you. Me he doesn't like. I had nightmares for a week."

She nodded. "No wonder he sits looking the other way."

"Like hell he does." He peered at her. "Straight up, it's true. When you go in there, he's sitting on that little camp stool and you have to lower yourself into that ghastly clutching-hand thing. He says he likes looking at it; he sits there for hours just contemplating it. No wonder he's a bit—well, you know. You would be, with that lot staring at you all day long."

She went to the bookstall that sold sheet music and bought all the Procopius he had. She could read music, just about; that is, she could pick her way through a score when she knew the piece already, but not actually hear it inside her head. If she'd hoped to find any clues there, she was disappointed. And the next day, the small cedarwood chest she'd put them in was empty, though she looked all around, all the doors and windows, and saw no signs of a break-in.

Oida had cancelled the concert he'd been supposed to be giving; no explanation. It wasn't like him, he was always so reliable,

never let the public down. He must be ill, people said, or una-
voidably detained somewhere.

She moved into the lodgings reserved for the Deputy Director
of Recoveries. It occupied a whole floor—vaulted roof and polished oak floor—and was completely empty, not even a speck of
dust. She liberated a camp bed, a chair, a small folding table and
a lamp, and set them out in the middle of the biggest room, like
the last pieces left on the chessboard. The ridiculously large sum
of money would be credited to her account with the Knights
on the last day of the month; until then, she had her cockfight
winnings and four stuivers in copper. When she remembered
about food, she sneaked down to the Buttery in the early hours
of the morning and picked the lock.

It wasn't unusual, they told her, for the Director to be absent
from Council and Faculty meetings. When he wasn't there, the
head of Finance took the chair: Cardonius, a huge slug of a man
with the biggest hands she'd ever seen. She quite liked him. He
was sensible and down to earth and never raised his voice.

"Essentially," he was saying, "we have two problems. First,
we don't know who our people are. Over half of our intermedi-
ate grade officers turned out to be Craftsmen and have defected
or been arrested; needless to say, before quitting the service,
they destroyed the registers of names and contact details of
the field officers they controlled. Since, by the very nature of
the job, our field officers operate under deep cover and go to
great pains to avoid being recognised for what they are, it's now
impossible for us to trace them, contact them or give them their
instructions; they, by the same token, don't know who to apply

to, since their only contact with us was their controlling officer. Second, we don't know how much money we have or where it is. We've always made a point of obscuring how much money we have and where we keep it; those records have also been lost. In essence, we're flowers cut off from our roots, and unless we can do something about it it won't be long before the service withers and dies. If it's any consolation, nearly all the other functions of government are more or less in the same boat, though naturally not to such an alarming extent.

"So, what are we going to do about it? First, we must see to it that we recover what we can. I want all of you to get your remaining staff to tell you everything they can remember, no matter how slight or trivial. It might be enough to trace a deposit account or a field agent. Second, we're just going to have to start again from scratch. The Director has already applied to the emperor for emergency funding, and I'm pleased to say that His Majesty has agreed to give us a sum equivalent to two-thirds of our most recent annual budget, as a one-off interim provision. Your job will be to recruit new field agents, as quickly as possible. Obviously, there simply isn't time to train them to the usual standard, added to which we don't have enough qualified, experienced officers to do the training. So we'll just have to do the best we can. It'll be messy, and a lot of mistakes will be made along the way. That can't be helped. The Director has explained our present difficulties to His Majesty, and warned him what to expect. We are officially instructed to do our best. I think I speak for all of us when I say that this Faculty would never dream of doing less."

There's two of me, she thought, as the slug-man's high, slow, pleasantly reassuring voice filled the small room. One of them could do this job. She'd relish the challenge. She'd show those complacent, idle bastards. She'd do really well at a time like this. But the other one, the real one, won't be here in a few days or a few weeks—pity, that, but it can't be helped.

"Traditionally," he was saying, "we've recruited heavily among prostitutes, minor criminals, licensed victuallers, actors, impoverished young men and women of good family, travelling musicians and the less respectable class of merchants and tradesmen. This approach has always worked well for us, and I recommend it to you as a good starting point. However, we need to be careful. The enemy will know we'll be recruiting, and why. We must expect moles, plants and double agents. Anybody approaching you and volunteering will be automatically suspect. More difficult will be those who come forward claiming to be established agents seeking to re-establish contact. It may well be that their former controlling officers, now defected to the enemy, will have briefed them most convincingly; they will probably know more about our operations at ground level than we do. And, naturally, genuine, established agents will get to know about the recruiting drive and present themselves to the recruiters. I believe we have to regard them as guilty until proven innocent, and where—as will often be the case—it turns out to be impossible for them to prove their bona fide status simply because the necessary materials are lost or destroyed— we will have to assume that they're fraudulent, and arrest and dispose of them. I regret this. Inevitably, a number of good, loyal servants of this Department will be unfairly condemned. However, I believe the threat of infiltration is great enough to warrant such harshness. It will make our job a lot harder, since established agents will learn what befalls their colleagues and either lapse and be lost to us, or even defect to the enemy out of disgust. I can tell you that the Director has considered the question most carefully and reached this decision. We, therefore, do not need to think about it, and I strongly recommend that you don't. You'll sleep easier for it, I promise you."

Just for the sheer mental exercise, she compiled in her mind a list of the field agents whose names she knew; thirty, maybe forty, nearly all of them Craftsmen. But she'd be gone soon, and her duty would be to leave behind her a list of agents she knew for a fact weren't Craftsmen, making it look as though they were. She could kill hundreds that way; hundreds of key government officers, slaughtered by a scrawled list stuck between the pages of a book. Senza or Forza Belot would do it like a shot.

"To sum up," he was saying, "the service faces the greatest challenge it has ever had to deal with in its long and distinguished history. For five hundred years, we have been the gardeners of empire. We have dug out the weeds and eradicated the pests, usually before they were able to do any appreciable damage. We have averted catastrophic wars, prevented disastrous conspiracies and revolts, suppressed dangerous ideological movements; saved infinitely more lives, treasure and cities than our very finest generals and statesmen. A wise man once said that the best fight is the one not fought. Finer still are the war not waged, the revolution smothered in infancy, the coup prevented by a swift, early, decisive intervention. A venerable trope in the philosophy schools is, if you had a chance to go back in time and stand over Hegesimon sleeping in his crib with a knife in your hand, would you strike the blow? Of course we all would; and that precisely is what we have always done, whenever humanly possible. No aspect of government has done more to preserve and benefit the State; we are government at its best, a shining example of the benefits of rule and order. Now our enemies have brought us to our knees; worse still, they have snatched our best weapons from our hands and turned them against us. We will meet this challenge, we will fight the enemy, and we will prevail. Failure is inconceivable. Bear that in mind, and, I promise you, everything else will be straightforward."

"Did he really say that?" Procopius smiled. "Things must really be bad."

She frowned. "I'm sorry?"

He laughed and poured her a drink. "You don't know Cardonius," he said. "When everything's going to hell in a handcart, he gets inspired and makes these incredibly powerful speeches. If everything's trickling along nicely, the most you'll get out of him is: any other business? Fine, meeting adjourned." He'd poured a drink for himself, but hadn't touched it. "Obviously he's scared rigid. Which is fair enough. I'm scared, God knows."

He'd carefully kept his bad side away from her. His good side was nice looking, in a solid, nondescript way. He reminded her of Oida, on his better days. But he was being nice to her, which made her flesh crawl. Time to put a stop to that.

"Why weren't you at the meeting?" she said.

He shrugged. "I had work to do. Meetings aren't work; they're a waste of my time. Cardonius does them better than me, in any case. When I'm in the chair, everybody's on their best behaviour, so nothing gets done."

"Work?"

He looked at her as though she was a grey area, then picked up the ivory box from the floor, balanced it on his knees, opened the lid and took out a sheet of paper, which he handed to her. "You read music, don't you?"

She glanced at it, and caught her breath. It was just the melody; lots of space left blank above and below for the orchestration. She looked up at him and found she couldn't speak.

"It just sort of popped into my head," he said. "And I knew if I didn't sort it out and get it down on paper, it'd be gone. That or the meeting. Would you call it dereliction of duty?"

"Going to the meeting? Yes."

He laughed. "Good answer," he said; "you turned it round and made it face the other way. Tell me, is it really annoying, being held back just because you're a woman?"

"I don't know," she said. "That's like saying, do you mind breathing air; wouldn't you rather breathe something else? It's just how it is, that's all."

"I suppose it must be." He sighed. "I've always been held back by this." He touched the side of his face she couldn't see. "I'm fifty-two years old. Did you know I'm still a virgin? It's just how it is, that's all, but I resent it like hell."

"It's different," she heard herself say.

"Of course it is. Now, then. This list of loyal agents you've got for me."

Sixty-two names. He took it from her, glanced at it, nodded. "I know about him," he said, "and those two, and them. Yes, that looks very good. All right, get in touch with them and introduce yourself."

"No need," she said. "They're all people I've worked with."

He smiled. "One of the reasons I chose you," he said. "It's stupid, isn't it? We never used to promote agents straight out of the field; they had to have done seven or ten years behind a desk first. You, on the other hand, are fresh from the battle, so to speak, so obviously you know what's going on rather better than we do."

"Thank you."

He raised an eyebrow. "My pleasure." He reached out and retrieved the sheet of music, which she'd forgotten she was still holding. "Oida tells me you're a fan. Is that true?"

"Yes."

"Got a favourite?"

"Yes," she said in a rush: "the funeral march from the Seventh symphony. You take the worst despair possible, turn it on a sixpence into the most wonderful feeling of hope, and then back again, just with a single key change." And then she thought: did I just say that? How embarrassing.

But he was nodding. "I rather liked that one," he said. "But most of my stuff is garbage. Let me know how you get on with your list."

She sat perfectly still, reeling from what she'd just said, until she realised he'd told her to go away. Then she got up and left without a word.

The best way to maintain one's cover, they taught her when she joined, is actually to be what you pretend to be. Since her cover was a deaconess of the Invincible Sun, she went to services at the Silver Horn and swung a censer in the processions. She didn't mind. If you find yourself in a temple under orders to kneel and silently pray, then silently pray, by all means.

So she turned her face toward the altar (that staggering, indigestible expression of post-Reform vulgarity, of hammered gold and gold enamelling, in which His suffering, passion and triumphant resurgence are so turgidly portrayed; except that, as very few people know, the original gold was stripped off by the Canons during the Emergency under Photius IV to pay for sails for warships; what you see now is an incredibly close, faithful copy, done in paper-thin gold sheet overlaid on lead by a man whose usual job was maintaining the temple guttering) and asked for strength to do what she had to do; that, rather than grace to refuse, or that the bitter cup should pass from her. She muttered a slightly adapted formula from the liturgy, then peeked up at the rood-screen in the forlorn hope of a sign. She saw a feather, probably from one of the pigeons which had taken to nesting in the corbels since the roof shed a few tiles during the spring gales, lodged between the clasped hands of personified Endurance, kneeling on the left hand of the Invincible Sun. The bitch of it was, it was almost certainly an omen, but she hadn't a clue what it could possibly mean.

She returned to the Department, to carry on with compiling the list of potential recruits. Some point or other came up, to do with regional excise officers in Cephal. She got up to go to the archive, then remembered that she had people to do that sort of thing for her now. So she hollered for a clerk. Nobody came. She pulled a face, got up and went down the corridor to the clerks' room.

"Someone nip out to Excise and get me Memmias Clutamen. He's in Establishments and he's got the most amazing memory for names."

They looked at her and nobody spoke. Oh, she thought, it's like that, is it? And isn't it amazing how the clerks know every damn thing that goes on around here. Then she went to the archive and looked the name up for herself. It would, of course, have been much quicker and easier to do that in the first place, even if Clutamen hadn't been disappeared.

"First," the priest told her, "it wasn't an omen, it was an augury. There is a difference, you know."

"Yes, of course. Um, what—?"

That got her a disapproving look. "An omen is notice of something that is preordained and will inevitably happen. An augury is due warning of something that will happen unless you take steps to avoid it. And what you saw was an augury."

That was reassuring but mystifying. "How can you tell?"

"Auguries involve birds. Anything with a bird in it is an augury."

She blinked, but decided to press on. "So what did it mean?"

The priest frowned. "Hard to tell."

"Yes, I thought so."

Maybe he hadn't heard her. "It's in the nature of auguries to be cryptic and ambiguous. The point is, the Invincible Sun doesn't spoonfeed us the answers. It's up to us, in the exercise of our free will, to recognise the true meaning and choose the right course of action to avoid the impending disaster."

She dipped her head in acknowledgement. "I appreciate that," she said. "But you're an expert. What do you think it means?"

"How should I know? I'm not the one who saw it."

She decided on a different approach. "If it had been an omen, you could interpret it."

"Oh yes, of course. Omens use a clearly defined symbolic iconography and are capable of explicit and unambiguous interpretation."

"I see. So if it had been an omen, what would it have meant?"

"It couldn't have been an omen. It involved a feather. Therefore it was an augury."

She set up a sort of satellite office in the taproom of the Shining Countenance. It was smaller, therefore less oppressive, and the people she tended to meet there found it less intimidating.

"Changing the subject," one of them said, "your boyfriend's in Permia."

A moment for it to sink in. "Oida?"

That got her a smirk.

"Oida's in *Permia?*"

Nod. "Apparently. Some local voivode offered him his weight in gold if he'd sing a few songs at a funeral. Funerals up there are the most amazing parties. And, no offence, Oida's been putting it on round the middle lately. Obviously an offer he couldn't refuse."

She went to her control. "Well then," he said. "Obviously, you have to go to Permia."

"But I can't."

"Actually, you can. You take a ship as far as Mirvau—"

"I can't. I'm far too busy to go swanning off. We're reorganising the whole department. I've barely got time to wipe my nose. What am I going to tell the Faculty?"

He looked at her. "I think," he said, "it's about time you stopped lying to yourself."

That stopped her short. She shivered. "Look," she pleaded, "this new job, it's the most amazing opportunity for the Lodge. I'm right in there at the core of things. Just give me a little bit of time to burrow down deep and I'll be in a position to—"

"You don't understand," he said patiently. "The world's about to end. Everything you've always known is about to fall apart. People are about to die, not by the tens of thousands but by the million. You're making plans for a future that simply won't happen. Ten years ago, you'd have been a pearl beyond price for the Lodge, except that ten years ago you'd never have got that job. But this is now. And all that matters is securing the crown for Axio. Oida has to be dealt with, as quickly as possible." He lowered his voice just a little; for effect, since there was no way they could be overheard. "Both Senza and Forza Belot have been given direct orders to shelve the war and attack Mere Barton. The only reason they aren't already on the march is that they've both lost two-thirds of their general staff, and, right now, their armies simply don't work. But you know the Belot boys. Any day now, they'll have replaced the Craftsmen they've lost, and they'll be ready to move, and you know how fast they are once they get going. It'll be a race to see who gets there first. And how long do you think Mere Barton will last? Days? A whole day? A morning?"

"I'm sorry. I didn't know."

"Of course you didn't, but you do now. And, obviously, we have the situation in hand. There are things, a limited number of things, we can do to slow them down, and we're doing them. But time is running out, and you have to do your part. You have to do it now. You have to go to Permia."

The little door of the confessional slid shut. Permia, then. A godforsaken place on the edge of the map; things came from there—furs, bulk timber, tin and copper ore, wool, dried fish, salt fish; but the haulage costs were exorbitant and the risks from robbers, pirates, foul weather and disease put off even the most determined traders—but nobody went there. The Permian chieftains were rich, stupid savages, and the ordinary people ate strangers. You'd have honestly thought a man like Oida would rather have died than go to Permia, but apparently not. Instead, he'd preferred to go to Permia rather than die. And his weight in gold, of course— Damn the man.

On her way back to the Department she stopped at the Golden Hook temple and asked to see the treasurer. He led her down into the crypt, and, below that, into the vault where the temple kept its money. They also looked after things for a select number of favoured parishioners. It wasn't her parish and never had been, but there was an oak chest with her name on it. To open it, you needed six keys, of which she had two. She took out a couple of things, and put a couple of things away. In theory at least, even the emperor would hesitate to violate the privacy of a temple deposit; also, only she and the treasurer knew about it, and he wouldn't talk if he knew what was good for him. She asked to borrow an inkwell and some paper, and wrote three letters, which she entrusted to Father Prior personally. Then she went back to the Department, where a half-platoon of the Household Guard met her at the porter's lodge and arrested her for murder.

The cell was a sandstone box with a clean, bare floor and a small window eight feet off the floor. The bed was the usual stone ledge, but there was a blanket on it, newly laundered and neatly folded. On top of the blanket was a copy of Illectus's *Aspects of Comedy*. She figured there'd be light to read by for another three hours or so. She folded the blanket into a cushion, sat down and started to read. After a while, Illectus's prose worked its special magic and she fell asleep.

She woke up in pitch darkness with a crick in her neck and the book open on her knees. She badly needed a pee. There was no chamber pot, so she got up and squatted in the far corner, feeling her way along the wall with her hands, then back again to the stone shelf. It wouldn't be very long before the darkness started getting to her; she never went anywhere without a candle and a tinderbox, which she could light by feel. She settled herself on top of the blanket, lay down and closed her eyes, so that the darkness would be voluntary and intentional. She forced herself to consider an abstruse point of theological doctrine, something to concentrate her mind on. Does the Light Eternal proceed from the Invincible Sun, or are they of one substance, indivisible? Better theologians than she'd ever be had spent their lives gnawing away at that one. She knew the arguments on both sides, including the sub-hypotheses and the counter-arguments thereto. It was mental chess, moving them around in her mind in the hope of finding a disposition of the pieces that might be made to constitute an answer. It was something she tended to do when she was very frightened and completely powerless. It helped.

Any length of time under such conditions is very, very long. After a very long time, the door opened and the cell filled with blinding light from a single shuttered lantern.

"On your feet," said a voice behind the light.

She pretended to be asleep. The light came closer. A hand closed in her hair and pulled her head up. "All right," she said. "Give me a moment, will you?"

She left the book. Her escort consisted of three Household troopers, with drawn swords. The Household Guard are the finest soldiers in the Western empire, and tend to regard jailering as below their dignity. Also, nobody likes to pull the night watch. It screws up your body rhythms. "Don't worry," she said. "I'll come quietly."

She didn't have far to go. At the end of the corridor (past twelve cells identical to hers, all with their doors open, so she was the only guest) was a small, plain room, whitewashed walls, brightly lit by four lamps mounted on high brackets, two plain chairs facing each other, their feet fixed to the floor with iron straps. They pushed her down into a chair and tied her to it with good, stout hemp rope. Then they left her alone for a long time.

Her back was to the door, so she heard rather than saw it open. A man walked past her and sat down. She didn't recognise him. He was in a Guards issue gambeson, streaked with rust, regulation red breeches and red woollen cloak; about forty-five, hair cropped to three-quarters of an inch precisely. He looked tired and preoccupied. He sat down, glanced at a small wad of papers, then put them on the floor between his feet.

"You Telamon?"

"Yes."

He nodded; she'd given the correct answer, well done. He mentioned a date. "You were an intelligence officer assigned to the garrison at Beloisa."

"Yes."

He picked up the papers, leafed through, read something, looked up. "It says here you murdered Sciro Hepsionas, a political officer, shortly before the garrison was evacuated. How do you plead?"

She looked at him. "You have no proof."

That sent him back to his papers. He selected three sheets, put the rest back on the floor. "You admitted it in four separate conversations."

"That's hearsay. Inadmissible."

"Not when it constitutes an admission."

"Anyone who says I said that is a liar."

"Mphm." He looked up from the papers. "All I'm concerned with is whether there's a case to answer, I'm not interested in the facts, just whether there's admissible prima facie evidence. Naturally, you'll have an opportunity to put your case at the trial."

She shifted a little, but the ropes were tight. "Look," she said, "what's all this about?"

He gave her a disapproving look. "Murder," he answered. "It's against the law."

"I didn't murder him. I never murdered anybody."

"Quite. But my job's to report on the evidence, and I have twelve sworn depositions. Whether they're true or not is up to the judge. This is really just a formality. How do you plead?"

"Not guilty."

He nodded; an acceptable answer, and no skin off his nose either way. "Thank you," he said. "Now, a date will be set for a preliminary hearing, at which point you will be made aware of the nature of the evidence against you and given an opportunity to state your defence. Should you wish to call witnesses, you can apply to the court for them to be summoned under subpoena. Until then, I'm remanding you into the custody of the Imperial Household." He collected his papers and stood up. "Good luck," he said, and walked out.

Maybe because she was being held by the Guards, the food wasn't half bad; she suspected it was what the soldiers were getting, probably taken out of their ration. The bread was white and quite fresh, some days it was dried sausage and a mild, crumbly white cheese, other days it was bacon and beans, with tarragon; whichever, there was always a good scoop of fermented cabbage, a bit salty but no worse than you'd get in the Countenance. She got a pint and a half of weak white wine and, on the third day, a chamber pot of her very own. On the fourth day the warder, who never spoke, took away Illectus on Comedy and gave her Paiseric's *Analects* instead. On the ninth day he brought her a nearly new copy of *The Golden Donkey*, and she was allowed to keep the Paiseric as well. Every time the warder appeared she asked for paper and a pen. It was a different warder each time. Maybe they were all deaf.

On the thirteenth day, just as the light was starting to fade, she was handed a wad of papers about the thickness of her hand. She tried to read them, but the handwriting was tiny, neat, cursive law-hand; she could make out the big decorative capitals at the start of each paragraph, but that was all. She got the general impression that this was the case against her, and then it was too dark to see.

She woke up out of an unpleasant dream which she immediately forgot, opened her eyes (but it was pitch dark, so it made no difference) and listened. No sound, but she was convinced there was someone in there with her.

All her adult life she'd made it a point to know where the nearest weapon was, or the nearest object she could use as one. In the cell there was nothing at all, which made her feel uncomfortable, like an itch she couldn't reach, or a pulled muscle. She held her breath but couldn't hear anything. Her imagination, then, or leftover horrors from the nightmare. She closed her eyes and tried to go back to sleep. She was still trying when the sun rose. She jumped up and looked for the papers. They were gone.

She hadn't read *The Golden Donkey* for years, not since the Lodge had scooped her up out of the blueberry moors and packed her off to Beal; she'd been given a copy by a fellow student, and when she'd pointed out that books weren't a lot of use to her, he taught her to read. It's a profoundly silly book, ranging from knockabout comedy to vague metaphysical speculation to softcore pornography, and just the thing for when you want to forget where you are. She tried rationing herself—a chapter, then an hour's exercise, then two hours' sleep—but her self-control wasn't up to it, and when she got to the bit where the hero has to spend the night protecting a dead body from witches changed into rats, she couldn't help herself. This is the most amazing fun, she thought, and the door opened.

She looked up, and saw a man who probably wasn't a soldier in the Household Guard. For one thing, he was too old, fifty at least, a huge man (forget-it big, as a friend of hers used to put it); bald on top with long grey sides scraped back in a ponytail, and a long, thin moustache dribbling down his hamlike cheeks. His clothes were scruffy-ordinary, and he had a sword in his right hand, rather a special one, a short concave-curved backsabre, rarely seen this far south. The blade was smeared with red sticky stuff.

She froze; he scowled at her. "Don't just sit there, come *on*," he said. His voice was higher than you'd expect from such a big, fat man, and she couldn't quite place the accent.

"Who are you?"

"You're being rescued, you stupid bitch. Come *on*."

He had a stupendous double chin, with a wart the size of a bean lodged in the fold. "Go to hell," she snapped. "Get away from me."

He rolled his eyes and took a long stride towards her. She shrank back. The only possible weapon, apart from his sword, was the chamber pot, and that was in the far corner of the cell. "You coming or not?"

"No. Get away."

He sighed, then punched her on the jaw. Her head shot back and connected with the wall, and she went straight to sleep.

*

"You're a total pain in the arse, you know that?"

She opened her eyes. Her head was splitting, her jaw ached and she felt sick. She could see rafters; she recognised them. She was in the hayloft of the Sun in Splendour, on the Cotyle road out of Rasch.

She tried to get up, but a huge hand on her throat pushed her back down and held her; not throttling her, but putting her on notice that she wasn't allowed to move. The fat man's face appeared above her. Since she'd seen him last, he'd picked up a nasty cut, from the corner of his left eye down to the bottom of the jaw. The blood was just starting to cake up.

"Who are you?"

He looked at her for three heartbeats, then took his hand away. She didn't move. "I'm Porpax," he said. "You don't know me. You're heavier than you look."

Porpax; not a common name. But there was a Porpax the city guard was very interested in talking to, concerning a spate of violent armed robberies. There were posters nailed to doors all over the place.

"What's going on?" she said.

He sat down beside her in the hay. She couldn't see the sword he'd been holding, or any other weapon. "I'm a friend of Oida," he said. "He told me to look after you."

It was almost impossible to imagine that Porpax and Oida were members of the same species, let alone friends. "You what?"

He gave her a weary look. "He had to go away a bit sudden. So he told me, you look after her, see she doesn't get in any trouble. Then you get yourself arrested and slung in the Guards, for crying out loud. That's why you're a pain in the arse."

Among the crimes attributed to Porpax the armed robber was the single-handed slaughter of a half-platoon of the Watch. "Oida's a friend of yours?"

He nodded. "I say friend," he said. "More a business friend, if you see what I mean." He picked up a stalk of hay and picked his teeth with it. "Ungrateful cow, aren't you?"

"Screw you," she said. "I don't know what all this is about, but—"

"You were in for murder. They were going to pull your neck."

"I didn't want to go."

"Tough." He looked at her, and evidently didn't like what he saw. "Oida said, if she gets herself in trouble, get her out of it. You got any idea what it takes to spring someone from the Guards? No, course you haven't, because it's never been done."

She remembered the blood on his sword blade. "If I wasn't in trouble before," she said, "I am now, thanks to you. What were you thinking of? You're mad."

He shrugged. "I did as I was told. I'm reliable, me. Never let a mate down, that's my rule."

"How much did he pay you?"

"Twelve thousand. Only he hasn't paid me yet. You're my pension. It's time I packed all this in."

The Sun in Splendour: a respectable house, used by government couriers, among others. How had he smuggled her in without being seen? Then she saw a big hessian sack lying in the hay.

"Now then," said Porpax, "if you're fit we'd better be going. Won't be long before they come here looking."

"I'm not going in the sack."

"Yes you are."

A sharp twinge of pain from her jaw made up her mind for her. She stood up so he could pull the sack down over her, then felt the world swim around her as she was hoisted up and slung with alarming ease over his shoulder. A huge hand clamped down firmly on the small of her back. She tried hard to think about something else.

"I'll do anything for money," he told her cheerfully, as their cart bounced through the ruts, jarring her teeth painfully together. "Your pal Oida came round the Charity and Grace, said he wanted a man for a job, a really nasty piece of work, he said, but someone who can be trusted. So Myrrhine, she's a friend of mine from way back, straight away she said, you want Porpax. And he said, I don't want him, he's in a lot of bother, they're looking for him all over town. And Myrrhine said, you want the best, that's Porpax. He's dead reliable and he'll do anything for money."

Listening to him was making her teeth hurt. "What exactly did he hire you to do?"

Porpax smiled. "Look after you," he said, "like you were my own kid. If you got yourself in any bother, get you out of it, and take you to a place of safety. I'm relying on you, he said, his very words: I'm relying on you to see to it she's all right, and if she gets in trouble, do whatever it takes."

"Including slaughtering half a dozen soldiers."

He turned his head. "More than that, pet," he said gently, and she shivered. "That was the Guards barracks you were in, they don't muck about. I should know, I was in the Guards fifteen years. Colour sergeant, I was, till I got in a bit of bother.

That's how come I know my way around in there. Things don't change in the Guards, see, they like their traditions. And once a Guard, always a Guard, and we look after our own, even when a man's in a bit of a fix. So when they pulled me in about that other spot of business—I let 'em, of course, put myself where they couldn't help finding me—and I said who I was, and of course all the old-timers remember me, best colour sergeant they ever had, that's what they say about me. Wouldn't argue with that, I was a right bastard in my day. No, they weren't fussed about some damnfool Watch charges. Forget about it, they said, you're one of us, you come with us and you can sit it out down the barracks till your bit of bother blows over, and then you can be on your way. So then of course I was in, which is half the battle, right? And I know who'd have which keys, and the back ways round the place they don't tell just anyone about."

She nodded slowly. "How much did you say Oida paid you?"

"Hasn't paid me yet. But I trust him. Gentleman and a scholar, everybody knows that."

She looked straight at him. "If they catch you—"

"I reckon I'm like the bloody shits. People who catch me don't live long." He grinned. There are only five colour sergeants in the Guards at any one time; it's the highest rank an enlisted man can reach. "I was going to leave town anyhow. This way, I make a bob or two. It's no bother. I do this stuff for a living."

If she'd planned the route, she couldn't have done a better job, and she reckoned she knew the fifty or so square miles north of the city better than anyone in the Service. But there were times when she looked up or jerked awake and didn't know where she was; she'd ask and he'd tell her, and suddenly it would make sense—yes, there had to be a small strip of land between this road and that, but she'd always assumed you couldn't get there, because of the mountains, or the marshes. But apparently there were droves and logging roads in those impossible places, because there they were trundling along them, and making marvellously good time into the bargain. "Did we ever offer you a job?" she asked.

"Who's us?"

"Imperial Intelligence. The spooks."

"Oh, that lot." He pulled a scowly face. "Turned 'em down," he said. "And I was in the condemned cell at the time, so you can see what I think of those bastards. Slippery. Can't trust 'em further that you can spit. No, I wouldn't soil my hands."

Still, as far as she could tell, almost directly north. "Where are we going, exactly?" she asked, on the morning of the third day.

He smiled at her. "Place of safety. Safest place there is."

"Where's that?"

"You'll know when you get there."

"Did Oida say you weren't to tell me?"

He leaned towards her and put his left forefinger on her lips. "I'm telling you nicely," he said. "Don't ask."

So she spent the rest of the morning pretending to be asleep, while she thought about various practicalities of her situation. If she'd had a knife, she'd have taken the risk and stabbed him, because there wasn't much room on the box of the cart; they were sitting thigh to thigh, and nobody's that quick. But she hadn't seen a knife, he didn't seem to carry one; he ate with his fingers, and everything else he used the backsabre for. So she thought about that. It lived on his side of the box, so she'd have to lean right across him to get to it; he left it behind when he stopped to pee, but of course he'd notice if it wasn't there when he got back. As for trying to creep up on him when he was pissing or having a shit, she considered and dismissed the idea very quickly; eyes in the back of his head, for sure. Very well, then; she could wait till he was asleep, grab the sabre and run for it. She thought about that and decided she didn't like the idea at all. She would run and run until she was exhausted, and just when she was sure she was safe, there he'd be, rested and at ease and fresh as a daisy. Curious thing; never before had she met an opponent she was afraid of—plenty that were bigger and stronger and faster, many who were better fighters, but she'd always known for a certainty that there'd be a way for her to prevail, and all she had to do was figure out what it was. But Colour Sergeant Porpax of the Guards (charged with preserving her from all harm, like an angel) scared her so much that at times she could scarcely breathe; which might just have been why Oida had chosen him. Damn the man.

"Course, this Lodge thing's making it dead easy," he was saying. "Stupid bloody idea, rounding 'em all up and pulling their necks, hadn't they noticed the Lodge is into every damn thing? So, get rid of all the Lodge types, everything grinds to a halt, which is why they can't spare more than a couple of platoons to come looking for us, and that's if they're even trying. And you'd need three full companies to find us in this country, and I'm talking about Guards, not the brickheads. It's the poor sod who's on our case I feel sorry for. He's going to have to go back to his CO and say he's let us get away, and then everything'll be his fault and his feet won't touch. We don't do excuses in the Guards. Do it right and nothing's said, just *noted, carry on*, get it wrong and they kick your arse twelve ways to Ascension. Only way to do things, of course, if you want results."

She stared at him. "You're not a Craftsman."

"Me? Do me a favour. Get in with those bastards, can't call your life your own. Never saw the point in it myself. Oh, I'm not saying some of 'em don't believe in all that crap, the Great Smith and we all come back as someone else, but I'm telling you, I don't. Load of dogshit, that's all it is. And I don't like the Lodge. Wankers, most of 'em."

Oida's a Craftsman, she nearly said. "So, no great loss, then."

"Wouldn't say that. We had a lot of Lodge types in the Guards and actually they were all right. It was just something you did if you wanted to get on, make your number with the officers. Not my way, though. I never really gave a shit what the officers thought of me. Keep out of their way and get the job done. Didn't work, of course, or I wouldn't have got into trouble." He sighed, and shifted the reins into his left hand. "Broke a captain's neck, for bad-mouthing me in front of the men. That's their trouble: they don't know when to stop."

The last landmark she'd recognised was Apoina, and that had been hours ago. Silly, really, because the road couldn't be more than five miles away to the west, and she'd been up and down it more times than she could begin to calculate. But wherever this was, she'd never been there.

"Have some more of the pickled cabbage."

She smiled. "No thanks, I'm full. Couldn't eat another thing."

"Suit yourself. I like pickled cabbage. Shame it doesn't like me." He stuck his forefinger in the jar and hooked out a matted clump of the stuff. "Gives me guts ache like nobody's business, but what can you do?"

Here was a man who brooked no nonsense, not even from his own entrails. She'd managed a fist-sized chunk of stale bread and the very last of the cheese. There were still seven jars of the pickled cabbage, enough to last for ages and ages. She was ravenous.

"The best pickled cabbage in the empire—" He paused, rubbed his chest and pulled a face. "We were on campaign with the Seventh and the Forty-third, just before young Senza took over as commander-in-chief. Good mob, the Seventh, though I gather they got wiped out in that last battle, while you were inside. You heard about that one? Anyhow, the enemy Fifteenth, Sixth and Twenty-third were all around us, so we'd dug in on the slopes of this mountain, about a day's march from Erroso. Anyway, long story short, there was a poxy little village and we turned it over pretty good, because we hadn't eaten for a week, and the cellars were jammed with the stuff, great big thin tall pottery jars with pointed ends. Food of the gods." He winced and crammed his right hand down on his chest. "Turned me up pretty bad, mind, so come the battle I was stood there in the front rank, with the Twenty-third lancers coming straight at us, and all I could think about was the pain in my tummy. Our company got a commendation for that action, but buggered if I know what went on. Funny, isn't it, the things you remember and the things you don't?"

She looked at him. He'd gone white, and he was breathing in short gasps. "Are you all right?"

"It's the brine," he said. "Rock salt: it's got more spite to it than sea salt, rots your insides. Well, if you're done we'd better be making a move. Still three good hours of daylight."

He stood up, swayed backwards and forwards, and sat down again in a heap. She noticed that his right hand was clamped on his left arm. She'd seen something like that before.

"Give me a moment," he said hoarsely. "Got a bit of a stitch. It's all right, it'll go away in a minute."

White as paper. "You've had this before?"

"Now and again. Bloody pickled cabbage. Or fried food. Fried food does me no good at all."

"Porpax," she said, as calmly as she could. "Where are we?"

He frowned at her. "I told you, didn't I? Don't ask."

"Yes, but I don't know where we are, and if anything were to happen to you, I couldn't find my way out and get help. Look, I know the road's over that way somewhere, but where does this track lead to? Is there a village anywhere near?"

Maybe there was a hint of fear in his eyes. "Don't talk stupid," he said, "it's just gas. It'll pass."

Foxgloves; someone told her once that you could squeeze the juice of foxgloves, and that sometimes helped. But she couldn't see any, and couldn't remember if it was the right time of year. She was woefully ignorant about that sort of thing. "Is there a village?"

He shook his head. "That's the point," he said. "That's why we came this way."

"But if I keep on the way we're going—"

"Shut up, will you? You're getting on my nerves."

There had to be something, besides foxgloves. "Lie back," she said; "try to breathe." She unstoppered the water bottle and splashed some on her sleeve. His forehead felt cold. "You're right," she said, "it's just gas. Serves you right for guzzling half a jar of the filthy stuff."

He nodded, a tiny movement. "That's what I said, gas. Be as right as rain in a bit. I think I'll just close my eyes for a while."

She watched him until the light faded. The last she saw, he was still breathing, just about. As soon as the sun went down, it got bitter cold. She found a blanket by feel and wrapped it round herself. She listened for his breathing and could just make it out. She fell asleep.

Dawn woke her up out of a dream which ended with Oida calling out to her: don't leave me, or something like that. She'd slept at a bad angle and she had a crick in her neck. She looked at him. He was sitting where she'd left him, propped up against a tree. His head was slumped forward on his chest and his hands dangled over his knees. She got up and lifted his left hand. It was remarkably heavy. She prodded about round his wrist searching for a pulse—she never knew where to look—then gave up. He was cold, and his face was grey. When she let go of the hand, it flopped.

So much for Colour Sergeant Porpax of the Guards, who she'd been too scared of to kill. She went through his pockets and found a sailcloth bag with twenty-six gold angels in it; nothing else. Of all the inconsiderate, self-centred—he'd known where they were, but now he'd thoughtlessly died, leaving her with two enormous, vile-tempered dray horses in the middle of nowhere. And he'd said he was reliable. She had a good mind to tell Oida to ask for his money back. Then she remembered that Oida hadn't actually paid him. Twelve thousand angels saved, just like that; if he fell in a sewer, he'd come up clutching a priceless gold chalice. Damn the man.

Very briefly she considered burying Porpax, rather than leave him for the crows and foxes and the badgers. But the ground was stony, the shovel clipped to the side of the cart was basically a toy with a paper-thin blade, and just the thought of trying to move that colossal bulk made her feel very tired. She unwound the scarf from around his neck, threw the backsabre into the cart, tricked and wrestled the horrible horses into their collars and set off for wherever the hell it was she was going.

PART TWO

The horses didn't like her, which was fine, because she didn't like them either. She wondered who they belonged to—likewise the cart, a valuable capital asset. Mine now, she decided. Twenty-six gold angels, two horses and a cart; in any town in the empire that'd make you upper middle class, if not downright rich, and she'd inherited all that against her will. Made you wonder why anybody bothered going to work. And the sword, of course, she'd forgotten that. It had to be worth an angel of anybody's money, though of course everywhere was awash with surplus military hardware these days. I could go somewhere and set up as a carter, she thought: it's a good trade, people will always want stuff moved from A to B. Or I could go to Permia; in which case, getting there would burn off every last stuiver of twenty-six angels, and she'd have to trade in the horses and rig to pay for her passage, steerage, assuming she could find a ship going there.

Pointless thoughts; so she crumbled the beeswax off the lid of a jar of pickled cabbage and pinched out a couple of mouthfuls of the foul stuff, just to keep her strength up. It gave her raging indigestion, a circumstance which for some reason she found hilarious.

*

The road had kidnapped her. Four days since Porpax died, and she was having to ration the pickled cabbage. Her knowledge of the geography and her memories of relevant maps told her that she should have crossed the Timoin some time ago—it ran directly east–west and it was forty yards wide at Angersford, not something you could easily overlook—but apparently the road knew better. She was still climbing a hill that shouldn't be there, invisible from the normal roads, marked on no map, unknown to the Imperial Survey; how could you keep something that big and tall a secret? Maybe it was a Lodge road, and the Lodge had carefully suppressed all knowledge of it—a sure sign that she was coming to the frayed end of her rope, when she seriously considered a theory like that.

Besides, if it was the Lodge's road they'd have taken better care of it. There were ruts in it eighteen inches deep—she didn't like to think what sort of carts had gouged them, or in what frequency; someone had used this road to shift a large amount of very heavy stuff, and nobody knew about it. At least the terror of guiding a seven-foot-wide cart along a road with a six-foot-six span between the ruts kept her busy, and took her mind off the appalling mess she was in.

In the end, the road cheated. It filled up a wider than normal rut with black, brackish water, seeped up from the underlying peat. The first she knew about it was a sudden bone-jarring jolt that made her teeth snap together and nearly slid her off the box into the ditch, as the left side of the cart dropped away. Then the whole rig stopped dead.

She climbed down and took a look. The left back wheel had gone in a pothole, and the force had splintered the axle. The wheel was bent up at forty-five degrees, retained by a thicket of torn wooden fibres. She dropped to her knees and yelled in fury. Then she forced herself to be calm and examined the damage.

In theory—in theory she could unlimber the horses, prop the bed of the cart up on stones, lever out the massive iron staples that pinned the broken axle to the chassis, take the backsabre, cut down a sapling and rough-hew it into a new axle, pin it back in place and remount the wheels. Piece of cake. For some reason, though, she didn't fancy that, so she cut a long piece out of the reins and used it to tie the necks of the three remaining pickled-cabbage jars together, slung the water bottle round her neck, picked up the jars and the sword and walked away.

The top of the hill came as a complete surprise, probably because it was artfully hidden in a wood. She'd been steadily climbing all day, and now the sun was just about to set. She looked up, and to her amazement she noticed that the skyline wasn't shrinking away as she approached it. On the contrary, it stayed put, and every step brought her nearer to it. This was significant. From the top of the hill she could look down, possibly even recognise something and figure out where the hell she was. She was too tired to break into a run but she lengthened her stride just a little. Each time her right foot touched the ground, she could feel the blister on the sole of her foot compress and squash. They'd been very suitable shoes for walking from the inner courtyard of the Department to her ridiculously splendid lodgings, but fifteen miles uphill on mud and flint had robbed them of their youth and beauty.

The last twenty yards or so were vindictively steep; then she stumbled on to the skyline and looked down. Immediately, a black cloud of crows got up off the heather—she was out of the wood at last—and streamed into the air in an angry, closing screw-thread. There must have been hundreds of them, thousands even.

If it involves birds, it's an augury and it can't be avoided. She knew what a thousand crows in a small area means. It's one of the less inscrutably coded symbols in the divine vocabulary.

Over the years she'd met a number of men who'd have been able to read it like a book; the degree to which the crows had stripped the flesh off the bones, the absence of stench, things like the effect of damp on cloth and leather, the beginnings of mould, the colour of rust—all useful and pertinent information, things she needed to know in order to make informed decisions about what to do next. Well, you can read the text or you can just look at the pictures. She sat down on a large stone. The crows had retreated about a hundred yards up and were wheeling in open formation, like light cavalry, yelling abuse at her. It wasn't the first time she'd seen a battlefield. You get used to things.

After a while, she pulled herself together and dragged her attention away from the foreground and on to the horizon. That big pudding-shaped lump over there could only be Hopelstanz; and the sun, considerately setting smack bang on top of it, hinted that it was due west. In which case—she felt stupid, as though she'd just walked into a wall without looking. Hopelstanz due west; in that case, the long, weary hill she'd dragged up could only be the outer foothills of the Dis Hexapeton—which made sense, in a crazy sort of a way, because the moor that separates the two ranges is about forty miles wide, and Hopelstanz looked to be about forty miles away, give or take; and she was twenty miles further north and about sixty further west than she had any right to be, and in a different province, formerly a different country, not to mention perilously close to the front line—

She got up from her nice stone and picked her way through the heather clumps and couch-grass tussocks. Hell of a place to try running away from anything; every two yards or so, you'd trip up and land on your nose. She picked over a few dead bodies, and accumulated some useful information.

They'd been shot, and whoever had shot them had been round retrieving the spent arrows, but hadn't bothered to strip off tens of thousands of angels' worth of armour, clothing and other saleable kit. Nor had Ocnisant been along to work his sanitary magic; but Ocnisant went wherever the Belot boys happened to be, so if he hadn't been here—The equipment was Western standard issue, the third-grade junk they were sending new recruits out in these days. Ambush and arrow-storm; probably what she was looking at was just the hopeless end of one breakaway unit, who lost their nerve and ran for it, and picked up a squadron of horse-archers. The rest of the battle, the main event, would probably be down the slope somewhere, and maybe that was the bit the West won, with this mess just an irrelevant sideshow that didn't affect the practical outcome.

Like she cared. Three weeks was her best guess, and by now the survivors, winners and losers, could be hundreds of miles away, making the spectacle before her none of her business. Meanwhile, if that really was Hopelstanz, if she wanted to reach civilisation (assuming some dangerous lunatic hadn't burned it to the ground), she needed to hold north by north-west, so aim for that cluster of low hills over there—

Who did she know who'd retrieve every last arrow but leave a small fortune in plunder to the damp and the rust? She stood stock still and tried to think. Surely not. The Lodge was finished, at least as a strategic force. They'd picked a fight with the big boys, realised their ghastly mistake and gone scuttling back to Mere Barton to build very high walls and very deep ditches. Most certainly they weren't sending out field armies to slaughter Western regulars a few days' ride from the walls of Rasch. They didn't have field armies to send. You can't just conjure up troops of armed men by scattering dragons' teeth. It was impossible.

The sun had almost disappeared, drenching the moor with red light. True; but you can hire armed men, if you've got the money. And if until relatively recently your people were staffing the Treasuries of two empires, maybe you'd have enough money to hire all the mercenaries you could possibly want; Cosseilhatz and Cure Hardy and Rosinholet, specialist, born-in-the-saddle horse-archers who'd kill anyone you cared to point out for a stuiver and a pail of milk. The thought hit her like a slingstone. The Lodge wouldn't have started a war it had no chance of winning, and one thing there was never any shortage of was mercenary soldiers. True, when last heard of they'd been working loyally for the two empires, but a subtle redistribution of funds discreetly arranged could change a lot of things. And it's easier to massacre a column of infantry when they haven't yet realised you're the enemy. The *bastards*, she thought. The clever, clever bastards.

While there was still light to see by, she poked around and found some more money. It was all just copper, of course, but she guessed they'd been paid just before they got their marching orders and hadn't had time to spend it on anything. She filled a small canvas satchel, somewhere in the region of six angels, and decided it was compensation for the loss of her cart and horses. Then she made herself a nest out of damp, stinking greatcoats and went to sleep.

She had a dream in which she was a princess walking along the seashore. She found a dead man lying face down in the sand, wearing rich robes of brocaded silk, sodden with water and crusted with salt, and a golden crown set with rubies and pearls, of which two were missing. She turned him over and he woke up, and so did she. But the dead men all around her were still dead, and she still wasn't a princess; she cursed herself for letting the sea get into her sleep, because dreams about the sea tended to mean she was scared about something and gave her a headache for the rest of the day.

A final rootle around among the dead produced a pair of boots which, padded with bits of torn-up scarf, sort of more or less fitted, and she blessed the fact that she had large feet, something her mother had always taken as a personal affront.

Hunger, according to the approved commentary on the Lesser catechism, is a spiritual experience which should be undergone by everybody at least once in their lives. Extended experience of hunger, the anonymous commentator says, sharpens the senses, clarifies the mind and allows one to redraw one's ethical map, with Life itself as the magnetic north.

Not true, she decided. Hunger just makes you think about food, all the damn time. Furthermore it saps your energy, and you can't see what's so important about putting one foot in front of the other; after all, the road goes on for ever, there's no end to it and no destination, so why bother?

So she gave up, and sat down on a clump of couch grass, and took her boots off, because they hurt her feet and she wouldn't be needing them any more; and, mostly because it was the only thing she hadn't tried yet, she closed her eyes, clasped her hands together like she'd been taught when she was a little girl, and prayed. Great Smith, she said (she made no noise, but her lips moved), if this is because I disobeyed your orders about killing Oida, I'm very sorry, and if this is the end I know I deserve it, but if You've still got a use for me, could you please send me something to eat, because I'm so very, very hungry. And when You've quite finished punishing me, which might well take a long time, I realise that, but when I've finally paid in full, could You please send a cart or a horse or something, because I really don't want to walk any more. Or if You'd rather just finish me off, that's fine too, only please do it now, because this is miserable.

She opened her eyes. Nothing. She felt stupid. Proving nothing, she said to herself, because the Great Smith doesn't answer prayers; it's the Invincible Sun who does that, and he doesn't exist. But you can pray to the Smith till you're blue in the face, and if what you're asking for isn't part of His design, you're wasting your breath. Also, the Smith neither rewards nor punishes, He just uses the useful material and discards the useless. In fact, whatever were you thinking of? Stupid.

A horse neighed. She turned round slowly.

There were four of them; and she should have been able to tell by the design of the bridles and the way they did their hair whether they were Rosinholet or Doca Votz or Cure Hardy, but she couldn't remember which was which, and it really didn't matter. They were all young, no more than twenty; short, golden-haired, with long, braided ponytails; grey-eyed, slim-waisted, broad-shouldered, slender forearms with fine, almost invisible golden hair and long, delicate fingers; painted saddles with no stirrups; long, thin linen shirts belted at the waist; soft moccasins sewn along the seams with thick square leather laces; pale white skins that had caught the sun and burned red. Three of them held their bows in the right hand, one in the left. All four had an arrow nocked on the string, thin dogwood shafts with short, needle-pointed square-section bodkin heads. They were looking at her as if she didn't make sense in a rational universe, and they were wondering what if anything they were supposed to do about it.

Oh, she thought. "Hello, boys," she said. "Looking for me?"

Clearly they didn't understand Imperial, which was probably just as well. Nomad humour is basic and physical—cutting off a goat's feet and setting the dogs on it, or tying a prisoner to a wooden stake and pelting him with bones. There's no word for joke in any of the seventy-six dialects.

"Are you lost?" said one of them, and the syntax was Cure Hardy but the accent was no Vei. In which case, they were probably Aram Chantat—Oida would know, damn him; for some reason he knew all about bloody nomads.

"Yes," she said, trying to remember if the Aram Chantat were one of the tribes that had strict rules about helping strangers. No, that was the no Vei. Pity.

"So are we," said the horseman. "We want to get to Pithecusa. Do you know where that is?"

Where? "Sure I do."

All four looked happy. "How do we get there?"

"Ah," she said. "You can't actually get there from here. If you want to get to Pithecusa, you have to start from Cornische, or Ennepe, or Boc Afon."

"We've just come from Boc Afon," said a different horseman.

"Splendid," she said, and smiled. "Take me there, and I can show you how to get to Pithecusa."

They looked at each other. "How are you going to get there? You don't have a horse."

"That's all right." She broadened the smile. "I'll climb up behind one of you boys."

"No," the first horseman said, "you can't, you're too heavy. The horse would go lame."

Fair point, she forced herself to concede; she was taller and bigger than all of them, and the horses were little more than ponies. Her feet would nearly touch the ground. Even so. "Well," she said, "one of you could walk, and I could ride his horse."

"We don't like walking. We aren't used to it."

"Do you want to get to Pithecusa or don't you?"

She'd shouted, and that was a mistake. Very bad manners, and, among the nomads, uncouth people don't live very long. They were looking at her sternly. "I'm sorry," she said, "please forgive me, I'm tired and hungry and you know what we're like, no idea of how to behave. I shouldn't have raised my voice. It was very wrong."

There was a still silence, maybe four heartbeats, and then one of the horsemen nodded; fault forgiven, just this once. "We do want to get to Pithecusa," the first one said, "but we're late already; we can't afford the time it'd take with you walking along with us. I'm sorry. I don't see what we can do."

"You're lost, though. You don't know the way. You'll be very, very late if you just ride around at random."

The second horseman shook his head. "You said, go back to Boc Afon. So we'll do that, and when we get there, we'll ask the way to Pithecusa. Someone there's bound to know. We don't need you to tell us how to get to Boc. We've just come from there."

She tried to think, but there was a sort of thundering inside her head, like waves breaking against a rock. "You can't just leave me here."

They didn't answer. They didn't need to.

"Fine," she said. "In that case, just give me some food. I'm starving. It's the least you can do."

One of them shook his head. "Sorry," he said. "We're a bit low on supplies. We need what we've got left."

"But I'll starve."

"We're sorry," the first rider said. "I wish we could help, but we can't."

Then he pulled his horse's head around and rode away, and the others followed immediately, as though they were all limbs of one invisible body. She stooped for a stone, but by the time she'd found one big enough to be worth throwing, they were well out of range. Then she found she didn't have the strength to straighten up, so she sat down instead.

The horsemen were receding fast, losing human shape, turning into geometric points on the straight line of the infinite road.

She thought; I can follow their trail, and that'll take me to Boc Afon, and everything will be all right. So that's fine, then, she thought, and passed out.

She woke up soaking wet. There were puddles all round her, and the air smelled of rain. There was a man crouched over her. He was taking off her left boot.

Careless, or new to the profession; he had a knife in a sheath on his belt, and its handle was closer to her hand than his. She made a grab for it, but a sort of tearing pain in her back and neck made her freeze and whimper. The man looked round. He was clearly embarrassed. He drew the knife and threw it away, about three yards. "Sorry," he said. "Thought you were dead."

Behind him she saw a horse, its reins tied to a heavy stone. The man wore a Western military gambeson with rust stains down the front and sides, and Eastern cavalryman's breeches. His boots were wrapped in tattered scarves. "Well, I'm not," she said. "What the hell do you think you're doing?"

"You look like you're in a bad way," he replied, getting the boot clear of her heel with a little tug. "What's the matter?"

"I've been walking God knows how long with no food."

"It'll be all right," he said cheerfully. "I'll ride back to Boc Afon and tell someone you're here. You'll be safe and sound in no time."

"Give me my boot back."

"You're not going anywhere, the state you're in. You don't need them. But if I'm going to ride to Boc to get help for you, I need decent footwear. Mine are a mess and the stirrups don't half chafe your feet."

The satchel of money wasn't where she'd left it, and she was prepared to bet the gold angels had evaporated from her pocket. "You realise what you're doing is murder."

He laughed. "Don't be silly," he said. "I'm going to see to it that you get rescued. Trust me."

"At least give me some food. I've paid enough for it, God knows."

"Sorry." He did look genuinely sad. "But I've hardly got anything left, just enough to get me to Boc. Wouldn't be any good if I fainted from hunger, fell off and bust my head open. Then we'd both be screwed."

The knife was only four yards away. It would get her the horse, not to mention her boots and her money back, and her life. Surely, she thought, I've got the strength to crawl four stupid yards. But apparently not.

"You just lie there and get some rest." He was fishing out the padding she'd stuffed in the boots. "Boc's only a day's fast ride away, so you'll be just fine, I promise you. I give you my word. Everything's going to be just fine." He lifted his foot, hopped around comically while he pulled the boot on. It was a bit too small. "You're lucky I happened to come along."

He got the other boot on, scrambled on to the horse. "Just take it easy," he called back to her: "save your strength." Then he splashed away through the puddles, and in due course the straight line swallowed him up, as though he'd never existed.

Two peat-diggers, an old man and his sister, found her. They were on their way to Eubine, a small village ten miles off the road, but when they saw the state she was in they reckoned it'd be better to take her to the doctor in Boc Afon. They wrapped her up in blankets and the old woman made some vegetable soup.

"She's waking up," the old man said. "Now then, just lie still. You're going to be fine."

He was small and thin, with a dark brown face and bushy white hair. He spoke Imperial with an accent you could've plastered a wall with.

"Who are you?" she replied in Tembe.

The old man smiled. "I'm Thunderbolt and this is my sister, She-Stamps-Them-Flat. Fancy you knowing Tembe. There's not many as does in these parts."

She smiled as best she could; her face didn't seem to be working. "You're a long way from Blemya."

"Too right. We came out here, what, forty years ago, for the seasonal work, got stuck, been here ever since. It's all right, apart from the cold and the damp."

"Thank you," she said.

"That's all right. We're about sixteen miles from Boc. We'll take you there first thing in the morning. There's a doctor there."

"I haven't got any—"

"Our treat," the old woman said. "Look at the state of you, out on the moor on your own like that. What happened to your boots?"

She shrugged. "A man stole them."

The old woman scowled. "Some people," she said. "Anyhow, you're all right now. You're going to be just fine."

*

The doctor said there was nothing wrong with her, and charged the old man sixty stuivers. She grabbed her finger, to pull off the ring that Oida had given her in Lonazep, and found it wasn't there any more. So she thanked them instead. They laughed. Anyone would've done the same, they said.

There was a white stripe where the ring had been. It would fade, in time.

There was a remote chance that she might be able to kid the Knights into writing her a letter of credit on her account in Rasch, so she went to the tavern where they did business in Boc, but the local agent wasn't there; he'd left three days before, they said, on business in the city, and nobody knew when he'd be back. The man who told her that was very careless with his purse. He left it lying around in his coat pocket. Inside it was an angel twenty. Back in the money again.

She hurried out and tried to find the peat-diggers, but they weren't in the market square, and they'd paid their bill at the inn and moved on. Damn them, she thought; so she went down to the taproom. No, they didn't have any tea, no call for it, so she asked for a small red wine. The man gave her a funny look, and said he'd see what he could do.

The mail coach was in, and the driver was sitting by the fire telling everyone the latest news. There had been one hell of a battle, he said, at some village called Pithecusa. Four regiments of Imperial regulars and a squadron of auxiliary cavalry had been wiped out by the horse-archers—

"Hang on," someone said. "They're on our side, aren't they?"

Not any more, apparently. The driver had got it from a couple of survivors, who'd flagged him down beside the road; one of them was in a hell of a mess, he'd taken them to the Brother's house at Imea. On the way they told him all about it, how the horse-boys suddenly fell out of the column, rode away at top speed, then looped and came back in shooting. Until the arrows started to hit, everyone thought it was some sort of showing-off display, and by then it was too late. The cavalry were shot down where they stood; the regulars formed a square, but the horse-boys rode into point-blank range, and their arrows went through regulation coats-of-plates like they weren't there. Of course, the regulars had no archery support—at least, they did, that's what the horse-boys had been for—so there was nothing they could do except stand there and get shot. Right at the end they tried a charge, which just made it easier for the horse-boys to finish them off. The two stragglers got out alive by shamming dead under a pile of bodies. No, they had no idea what made the horse-boys turn on them like that. Something someone said, maybe. That's savages for you: you never know what they'll do next.

"Four regiments," someone said, after a very long silence. "I didn't know we still had four regiments."

"Where the hell is Forza Belot?" someone else wanted to know. An apparently well-informed man replied that he was consolidating his forces for the big push, which was going to drive the Easterners into the sea and end the war by midsummer. There was an awkward pause, and then someone bought the driver a drink and changed the subject.

She moved to the back of the taproom, where three men were playing cards for money. She asked if she could join in. They laughed, and someone pulled out a chair. She asked what they were playing. I'm not sure I know that game, she told them. That's all right, they said, you'll pick it up as you go along.

Which she did, to a remarkable degree. Not all that much later, there was just one man, and his tall piles of copper had melted down to one little stub, like a cheap candle. On the table between them sprawled a brown sea of small, worn coins.

"Remind me," she said. "What do I do if I want to see what you've got?"

Pay double the bet, he told her, so she did that. He laid down five cards, one of which was the four of swords. There is no four of swords in an orthodox pack.

He leaned across the table to scoop up all the money. "Where the hell have you been?" he said. "We've been looking for you all over."

"I got lost."

"Really." He scowled at her as though everything that had ever gone wrong since the Creation was her fault. "You do realise you're putting the whole operation in jeopardy. You were given one simple thing to do—"

"I was *arrested.*" She'd raised her voice; not, perhaps, the best way to change his obviously poor opinion of her. "They grabbed me and put me in jail. What was I supposed to do?"

Maybe he hadn't heard about that. Maybe he wasn't interested. "If it was up to me," he said, "this assignment would be taken away from you and given to somebody else. But it's not, so you're just going to have to pull yourself together and get on with it. Do you understand?"

"Look." She tried her pleading face, but it had been a while and she hadn't been practising it. "Can't we go somewhere a bit less public and talk about this? People are staring."

"There's nothing to talk about."

"Let's talk about it anyway. Please?"

He thought for a moment, then sighed. "If you insist. All right, stand up and slap my face."

Ah, she thought, right. She did as she was told. He belted her right back, making her head spin, then grabbed her wrist and pulled her across the room to the stairs. Behind them, people were cheering. Savages, she thought. And they're wrong; the thing about savages is, they're so predictable.

The stranger had one of the better rooms, with a view over the stable yard. "Let's bypass the dancing around," he said, sitting on the bed and pulling his boot off. "My name is Corason and I'm a Commissioner of the Lodge, so if you're going to plead superior orders, forget it, because I outrank practically everybody on Earth."

She stared at him. "You're dead."

"No I'm not."

"Yes you *are*. You wandered off just before the big battle between Senza and Forza, the one that led to the relief of Rasch. You got shot by a horse-archer. Someone saw your body."

He nodded. "Perfectly true. Only I wasn't dead. I had a perfectly miserable ten days, and then Ocnisant's people found me and fixed me up, and now here I am, live, kicking and giving you a direct order. Here," he added, pulling up his shirt to reveal a shiny purple blotch the size of a dog's paw. "Will that do?"

"Yes. I'm sorry."

"And I didn't wander off. I was doing a job of work. And

Commissioner Axio and I saved Rasch by doing a deal, as you well know. The battle was just something personal between the Belot boys."

He said it so casually: I saved the city, the battle and all its dead were neither here nor there. "And you're here to find me."

He nodded. "You've got a job to do, and the decision is, you're the only one who can do it. Which means I have to spend days on end in this rat-hole, when I've got a mountain of work I ought to be doing, waiting for you to condescend to show up. And then I've got to take you to Blemya."

Wax in her ears? "Blemya. You mean Permia."

He looked at her as though she was stupid. "Oida's not in Permia," he said, "he's in Blemya. So that's where you're going. And me, too, to make sure you don't wander off again."

"What's he doing in Blemya?"

She'd said something amusing; he was grinning. "Buying the Blemyan army. No, seriously. We're hiring forty thousand heavy infantry for the Lodge."

She'd heard him loud and clear, but what she'd heard made no sense. "That's impossible," she said. "We haven't got—"

He shook his head. "That kind of money, no, of course not."

"So—"

He hesitated; not supposed to talk about it, but the story was too good not to share. "The East is bankrupt," he said. "So's the West, of course, but the East has actually run out of cash money: you walk into the Treasury vault and all you can see is marble floor. So, a few months back, the chief financial officer of the Eastern department of the Exchequer arranged a loan from the Knights; twenty million angels. Biggest loan ever in the history of international finance. Of course, the Knights couldn't carry that much on their own, so they laid off about half of it on the Scholars, the Poor Brethren, the Sword-blade, the Crown of Gold, all the major banks this side of Mezentia. The cunning of it was, quite apart from the East getting enough liquidity to run the war for nine months, it'd dry up all the spare money in the world, so when the West goes looking for a loan, there won't be anything left for anyone to lend them. Smart move, don't you think? Of course, it was a Craftsman who thought of it."

She had a feeling she knew what was coming. "Before—"

"Oh yes, naturally. And then, just before the trouble started and he had to make himself scarce, our man in the Eastern Treasury wrote the whole lot in strict-form letters of credit and sent it to our account with the Merchant Venturers in Blemya. So, when we send our newly hired army to obliterate the Eastern empire, we'll be paying for it with their own money. Smart."

She felt as though she'd been kicked in the face. "That's—"

"Yes. Of course, there's a downside. It'll be the end of the Knights, and eight or nine other major banks. It'll be a long time before there's any money circulating anywhere, it'll be barter and sea shells anywhere outside the main cities for the next fifty years, and that'll be very bad for pretty much everybody. But, as the saying goes, omelettes and eggs. And we did more or less the same thing with the West and the horse-soldiers, except they didn't have to borrow. We managed that with the very last of their cash reserves."

She breathed in slow and deep, and out again. "So what's Oida got to do with it?"

"What? Oh, didn't I mention that? His idea. I told you, didn't I, it was a Craftsman who thought of it."

She needed her mind to clear, quickly. "So he's single-handedly won us this stupid, suicidal war. We're actually going to beat both empires."

Corason frowned. "Don't count your chickens," he said. "Both the Belot brothers are still very much alive, and we found out the hard way just recently we can't touch either of them, not directly at least. And either of those two lunatics could crunch up our pretty new army, and then where would we be? But, yes, Oida did well there, and that's why it had to be him in Blemya negotiating the deal. Like I said, he's a smart boy. Like his brother."

"He did all that for us," she said, "and you still want me to kill him."

"Yes. You know why. It's necessary. The fact that he did us a good turn doesn't change a thing."

"Mere Barton? Oh, that's all finished," Corason said, as they clattered over the rickety bridge over the Finamor. "The Western army got there, found it deserted, burned it to the ground. Just like they were supposed to. It was only ever meant as a decoy. You know, make them think that was our home, base of operations, whatever, give them something to attack when they came after us. Of course, we had to make it look convincing, which is why we spent all that money and effort making it look nice. But you know as well as I do, the Lodge can't be confined in any one place. It's everywhere."

He was, she felt, being disturbingly informative; whatever

happened to need-to-know? Except that nothing he'd told her would be any use to an enemy, once they'd tortured it out of her. And it didn't matter that she knew all this stuff, because before very long she'd be dead. Which explained why he was being so informative.

"Corason," she said. "Am I going to get out of this alive?"

He shrugged, as though the point was trivial. "That's up to you," he said: "depends on how cleverly you go about it. You have our permission to survive, provided your survival doesn't prejudice getting the job done. Everybody reckons you're pretty smart. The secret, I've always found, is having several independent escape routes planned before you start. Lots of eggs in lots of baskets. Always worked for me."

The ship waiting for them at Languil was Blemyan, but the crew were all Lodge, from both empires. It was small, low in the water and very fast. They rounded Cuir Point with a perfect following wind, which obligingly turned southerly exactly when it was supposed to and blew them across the straits to Glous; it was obviously a tame wind, it would probably feed from your hand and lick your face if you told it to. "There's a problem," she told Corason, as the red sandstone cliffs appeared on the skyline. "About me in Blemya."

"I know all about that."

"And?"

"You'll think of something."

She clawed hair out of her mouth. The wind was playing with it, like a naughty kitten, but this wasn't a good time. "Are you coming with me to the city?"

"You bet. I don't let you out of my sight until we find Oida."

It was time for the awkward question. "You know Axio pretty well, don't you? You were telling me last night, you've worked with him a lot."

He pulled a face. "Feels like half my life."

"What's he like? I've never met him."

Corason took a moment to get his words into formation. "They say he's off his head, but that's not true at all. Or, at least, it's a gross simplification. He's no loon, that's for sure. I guess you could say he follows different rules. What I mean is, there are things he would never do, even if doing them was to his advantage. Just, not the same things you or I would have trouble with. And by the same token, lots of things we'd have problems with wouldn't bother him for an instant. His tragedy is, every bit of him was designed and bred for one purpose, being a mid-rank nobleman, but the Great Smith had other uses for him. It's as though a carpenter set out to make the best flagpole he possibly could, and inadvertently designed the perfect spear."

She thought about that for a moment. "What does he want?"

"Nobody knows. Him least of all. But one thing's absolutely sure and not susceptible to doubt in any shape or form. He's Lodge to the core, and he'll do exactly what he's told, without a moment's hesitation. That's why he's got to be the emperor."

"Does he want to be?"

"Ah." Corason grinned. "We haven't told him about that bit yet."

The first thing she did when she reached the city was borrow three angels from Corason to buy a knife with—

("That's a lot of money for an everyday utensil."

"I'm an artist. I need exactly the right gear, or I can't realise my full potential."

"Yes, but three angels. This is my money we're talking about, not Lodge funds."

"You'll get it back."

"I'd better.")

It was for her brother, she explained to the man on the cutlery stall. It was his eighteenth birthday, and the family wanted him to have something special. The man gave her a cold stare, then pulled out a box from under the table. She took her time and chose carefully.

"You know a lot about knives," the man said. It wasn't meant as a compliment.

"My father told me what to look for. Have you got anything else?"

"No."

"Oh. In that case, I'll take this one."

"Fifty stuivers."

"My father said, don't pay more than thirty-five."

The man wanted to get rid of her. "All right. What does your brother do, then?"

"He's assistant huntsman to the Duke of Aurec."

Leaving her with two angels sixty-five; to which, add ten stuivers if she sold the boots Corason had bought for her on the ship and replaced them with a cheap pair from the dead-men's-shoes stall—not enough to get far enough away in the very short space of time available to her once Corason realised she'd run out on him. But the trouble with Blemya is, there are only three directions: downtown, the sea or the desert. And she couldn't walk on water, and sand wasn't much better. Killing Corason was an option, but there was an annoyingly high level of law and order in Blemya, which meant homicide wasn't something to rush into. Also he was a Commissioner of the Lodge, whereas Oida was just another Craftsman—

So she crossed the square from the cutlers' market, followed the main street up as far as the Painted Column, then the left fork—the heat was stifling—then a short cut through the alleys that brought her out in Horsefair. The Western Embassy was the single-storey sandstone building with the iron gates.

The sentry sent for the duty officer, who recognised the five-word code that meant Imperial Security. He went white as a sheet and took her to see the deputy proconsul.

"The ambassador's not here," the proconsul explained. "He got called back home for a briefing."

She ought to have known that. "You'll have to do, then," she said. "Do you know who I am?"

The proconsul shook his head, but she could see his mind slowly grinding away: a woman, who knew the top-level code. If he knew anything at all about Intelligence, he'd realise there was only one woman of such exalted rank in the Service, and she was a wanted fugitive. But why should he? The ambassador would've known—probably—but he wasn't there, was he? She decided to make it easy for him.

"My name's Telamon," she said, and watched for a reaction, which didn't happen. "A while back, I was arrested on a murder charge. I broke out of the Guards' barracks. People died in the process."

The proconsul stared at her. "I'm not making this up," she said. "If you want, you can go away and look it up in despatches. I don't mind waiting."

"I believe you," he said.

"Splendid. Well, I'm here to give myself up."

He didn't move or say anything. She wasn't sure he was even still breathing. "I said, I'm giving myself up. Arrest me. Now."

"I can't do that."

"What?"

She couldn't help feeling sorry for him. "I can't," he protested. "For a start, I haven't got the authority, I'm only diplomatic grade six, I don't have that sort of authorisation. Also, we haven't got the facilities, or the staff. This is basically a trade delegation. We've got six rooms, three sentries, a clerk and a local woman who dusts and cleans. I'm sorry, but we just don't have the capacity here."

Calm, she told herself, calm and peaceful. "You can hand me over to the Blemyan authorities," she said, as gently as she could. "As a matter of fact, they probably want to talk to me about a couple of murders."

"I can't do that." He was genuinely horrified. "I can't go surrendering custody of an Eastern citizen without a formal warrant."

"Then get one."

"A warrant from home. Do you have any idea how long that would take? And I'm not allowed to request one, I'm only grade six, I told you. You'd need the ambassador for that."

She breathed out slowly through her nose. "Maybe I forgot to mention," she said, "I'm also a double agent for the Lodge.

And there's a three-line directive about Lodge traitors, which gives you authority."

"No it doesn't."

"Yes it does."

"No it *doesn't*." The poor man was sweating. "Besides, if that's true, there's no way I can hand you over to the Blemyans: that'd be unlawful rendition, that's a criminal offence. Please," he said, gazing at her desperately, "can't you just go away until the ambassador gets back?"

"When?"

"Not more than three weeks. Six at most."

She stood up. "I'm sorry," she said, "clearly I'm wasting your time. By the way, none of it was true. I'm not Intelligence, and I'm most definitely not Lodge. I was just playing games with you."

That left the Blemyans. She went to the Watch headquarters in Belltower Yard.

"I'm a criminal," she said. "Arrest me."

The duty sergeant looked at her and sent for the captain. "Fine," he said. "What did you do?"

"I murdered a government minister. And several soldiers."

The captain smiled. "Sure you did. What were their names?"

She realised she couldn't remember. Nor could she call to mind the dead minister's portfolio. "It was about a year ago," she said. "When Oida came here to give Her Majesty a copy of Procopius' symphony."

The captain frowned; a bell tinkling in the back of his mind. "No," he said, "that wasn't you."

"Yes it *was*."

But he shook his head. "No," he said firmly, "because they caught the man who did that."

"They couldn't have."

The captain sighed. "They did," he said. "It was my old CO who made the arrest. Look, I don't know what your problem is, but I don't think I can help you. Maybe you'd be better off with a priest, or a doctor."

"All right," she said. "Arrest me for wasting Watch time."

"Please go away," the captain said.

"Assaulting an officer?"

He grinned at her. "Maybe if I wasn't so busy."

She drew the knife and lunged at him. He sighed, smacked it out of her hand, tucked her arm behind her back, marched her to the street door and shoved her out. He shouldn't have been able to do that, but he had. She picked herself up, put her tongue out at the people who were staring at her and went back to the cutlers' market, where she bought another knife at a different stall.

"Good choice," said a voice directly behind her. She turned and saw Corason grinning at her. "Better than the first one. Shorter, and better edge geometry."

She scowled at him. "You were following me."

"Me personally? God, no, I haven't got the energy." He laid a gentle hand on her arm and led her across the street to a teahouse. "Out of interest," he said, "was that just for my benefit? Because if not, you weren't trying very hard, were you?"

"Wasn't I?"

He shook his head. "If it was me," he said, "I'd have stabbed a perfect stranger. Two, probably, to be on the safe side."

She slumped back in her seat. "Yes, and then they'd have put me in the Watch lockup, which would've been a real pain to get out of. Also, it'd have been murder."

"That doesn't seem to have bothered you in the past."

"That was *orders*."

He smiled gently. "So's this. But you could've done something a bit less dramatic. Robbed a market stall, or got in a fight without actually killing or maiming anyone. Face it," he said, "your heart's just not in it."

She didn't answer that; not straight away. "If I'd succeeded," she said, "what would've happened?"

"If you'd got yourself locked up, you mean? I'd have had to get you out again, at God knows what level of aggravation and expense. I'm really glad it didn't come to that." He poured the tea. "It says in your file that you're a real pain in the bum."

That shocked her. "Does it?"

"Oh yes. Fifteen operatives who've worked with you say, never again. You've got forty-seven discommendations and twelve provisional demerits. Also, they say you're not to be trusted with money."

"Thank you for telling me that."

"That's perfectly all right."

"Does it say anything nice about me?"

He grinned. "Now, then," he said. "This is what you need to know. Oida is at the palace, right now. His room is on the seventh floor of the West wing, with a window facing out over the main quadrangle. The windows are shuttered, and he bolts them every night before he goes to bed. The good news is, there's a hypocaust directly under the floor—of course, I forgot, you know all about the heating system, so that's probably your best way in, except he's put his travelling chest on the grill, and it's oak with heavy iron fittings, weighs about four hundred-weight. Otherwise the only way in is through the door, and the only way through the door is if it's opened from the inside. Three-ply oak, cross-grained, it'd take half an hour to cut your way in with an axe."

She'd never known Oida to travel with cumbersome, inelegant luggage. A thought struck her. "Does he know?"

"That someone's after him? Good question. We have no reason to believe he does, but he's been acting like he's scared of something. Clever precautions, though nothing explicit enough to give offence to his hosts. Like pretending he'd gone to Permia. We didn't tell him to do that."

She frowned. "I've known him a long time," she said, "and he never seems to bother about anybody wanting to hurt him. I mean, why should he? Everybody loves him; he's the most popular man in the whole world."

Corason sipped his tea, then put his bowl down gently in the middle of the table. "It's odd, isn't it? All right, yes, I personally believe that he's scared of something or somebody. I don't think it's you. If that had been the case, he'd have arranged for you to be put in the Guards, not broken out of it."

"You know about—?"

He confirmed that with a slight frown. "But," he went on, "he's skittish about something, that's reasonably certain. Not the East or the West, because they've had plenty of opportunities to nail him since the trouble started, and they've shown no interest in doing so. And apart from about a thousand outraged husbands and fathers and maybe a few of the more perceptive music critics, he has no other enemies I'm aware of, so if someone's on his case, it has to be the Lodge."

"Which is true."

"Yes," Corason said irritably, "but we know he doesn't know about that. About you, I mean, and you're the only officially sanctioned move against him, and you're on the narrowest possible need-to-know basis, and we know that's rock-solid. Also, this furtive dodging about started before the decision about him was taken, so it can't be that."

The tea was strong and a bit too spiced for her liking; also hot enough to take all the skin off the roof of her mouth. She put the bowl down again. "All right, then," she said. "In that case, it can't be anybody."

But Corason just frowned, as if a nagging tooth had started playing him up again. "Actually, it could be."

"What? You just said—"

"Be quiet and listen." He closed his eyes and opened them again. "There's something odd going on, actually inside the Lodge. Yes, I know, that's impossible, it could never happen, and I'm imagining the whole thing. But I have a horrible feeling I'm not."

She opened her mouth, but no words came.

"Cast your mind back," he said, "to that time I wandered off, as you so sweetly put it. I had an errand to run, and this dreadful woman attached herself to me. I had no idea who she was, basically she was just a nuisance, until she kicked me in the head and stole my horse. And then I found out—I won't bother you with how, just take my word for it—I found out she was Lodge. One of us. A Craftsman."

She stared at him for a long time. "That's—"

"Impossible, yes. So everybody keeps telling me: my fellow Commissioners, my superiors, everybody. I've made a point of asking everybody who had the authority to send her to spy on me, and they all said, no, that wasn't me, and I believe them."

"That doesn't make sense."

"No, of course it bloody well doesn't. In order for it to make sense, you'd have to posit the possibility of factions inside the Lodge, differences of opinion, a division, schism, something less than an absolute unity of mind and purpose. God's right hand not knowing what His left is doing." He sighed and shook his head. "Accordingly, I must have imagined it, or else misinterpreted the slender piece of evidence on which I based my conclusion that that bloody woman was Lodge. Except that now here we have Oida, acting like he knows something about Lodge business that we don't. Which is why I've condescended to tell you about it."

She looked at him. "I was wondering about that."

"Yes, well. Orders are, you're to be given all possible necessary facilities to do the job, and in my judgement, knowing about this business is a necessary facility, just in case it's relevant. Not that I think it is, but since I don't *know* what all this is about, I can't form an informed judgement as to whether it's relevant or not—" He made a despairing gesture. "I asked Axio," he said. "I asked him, would Oida take to lugging around a bloody great iron-bound chest unless he had a damned good reason. Axio just looked at me. No, of course not, he said, Oida travels light." He shrugged. "You know what this feels like? It's like I've just happened to stumble on a dirty great crack in the back wall of the Universe, and if nothing's done about it the sky's going to fall into the sea and the sun will go out and that'll be that, finished. Only, who can I tell about it? Nobody, because it isn't bloody well possible."

The waiter was hovering. She beckoned him over and paid for the tea, and he went away. "Have you asked——?"

"Who?"

"You know." She realised she had no idea how to put the concept into words. "Him. The boss."

She'd lost him. "You mean prayer?"

"No, I mean whoever's the top man. The very top. The head of the Lodge."

He gazed at her as though she was stupid. "Have you been listening to a single word I've said?"

"Yes. But——"

"In that case, no. No, of course I haven't, because I haven't got the faintest clue who he is. You know that."

"Yes, but you're a Commissioner."

"So bloody what? I don't know who the head of the Lodge is. Neither do my superiors, or their superiors. I *think*, but most definitely don't know, that the next layer up knows who he is, but for all I know there's another two, three, four levels after that." He glared at her. "You sit there and tell me you honestly believed that I know who's running everything? Dear God. You think, if I knew something like that, they'd have me running about loose? You're an idiot."

"I'm sorry."

He sighed. "Forget it," he said. "Doesn't matter. My fault, for talking to you under the misapprehension that you're a grown-up. Anyway, you now have all the information you need in order to do the job that's been assigned to you." He gave her a big, unfriendly smile. "And so," he said, "I suggest you get on with it."

The Tembe women traditionally wore voluminous gowns, head to foot, like the men's but with a scarf wrapped round the face. The idea was to protect them from sandstorms and the blistering heat. Upper-class Blemya city women had recently adopted the fashion, although in silk rather than cotton and not in desert white: flame red or saffron yellow, even actual sky-blue for the prodigiously wealthy. For an angel, she bought a yellow one second hand. It didn't quite reach her ankles, so she had to lash out forty stuivers on smart embroidered-silk flat pumps, with the moon and seven stars picked out in sequins. Possibly the ghastliest footwear she'd ever seen in her life, but they were a good fit and remarkably comfortable. The scarf tickled her nose and made her want to sneeze all the damn time, but only her eyes were visible. She inspected herself in the tinned bottom of a copper preserving pan, then spent her last remaining money on a tiny jar of kohl. She was no good at makeup and hated anything anywhere near her eyes, and it took her several goes before she got it looking right, but she reckoned she was unrecognisable.

The knife was a problem. Its unmistakable profile showed up under the thin cloth. In the end, she strapped it to the inside of her calf with strips torn from a silk handkerchief that Corason had carelessly left drooping out of his pocket. It moved when she walked and chafed annoyingly, and would almost certainly slide down her leg and trip her up if she had to run.

"Why are you walking like that?" Corason asked. "Have you hurt yourself or something?"

She lifted her hem. "If you've got a better idea."

"God, that's hopeless." He scowled, then grinned. "What you need," he said, "is a copy of Mardonius' *Analects*."

Inspired suggestion. It took an hour of hard work to cut out the middles of the pages, but the knife fitted snugly in the hollow and fell out as soon as she opened the book. And he'd been quite right. Only the *Analects* were bulky enough. "Though what a fine society lady would be doing with any book of any description is beyond me."

"I'm giving it to someone as a present, of course," she replied. "My brother. In the army. Something to read in his tent after a hard day."

Corason pursed his lips, then opened his travelling bag and took out a book. She didn't get a look at the title. It was held shut with a little brass clasp, which Corason carefully levered off with the point of her knife; then he hammered it delicately on to the cover of the *Analects* with the heel of his boot. After he'd bent it a bit, it closed just fine and stayed shut even if you shook it quite hard, but she could open it with a brush of her finger. Corason was grinning like a dog, absurdly pleased with his small triumph of craftsmanship. "My father always said I was good with my hands; he wanted to apprentice me to a jeweller but my mother wouldn't have it." He flipped the catch open and shut a couple of times, just to hear the faint click.

Corason liked the present-for-my-brother idea, though she was rapidly going off it. Don't be silly, he told her, and set about procuring her a brother in the Royal Guard.

"His name's Emmon," he said; "he's a junior captain in the

third day watch. Go to the south gate of the palace and ask for him, he'll get you inside. After that you'll be on your own, but I know you prefer it that way."

"Actually—" she said, but he wasn't listening.

She spent an hour memorising a detailed floor plan of the palace—you could buy one, quite openly, for a stuiver in the booksellers' yard—until she could close her eyes and see it perfectly clearly. The original architect had designed it so that, to the Invincible Sun looking down from the bar of Heaven, it looked like a five-petalled rose, each of the petals being represented by a gilded dome, the stigma or central boss being the porticoed circular cloister. Subsequent rulers had been more interested in convenience, efficiency and being able to get from one room to another without walking all round the circumferences of internal circles, so the flower was now worm-eaten with transverse corridors and passages; also, two of the five domes had collapsed under their own weight and been replaced by slab-sided blocks of guest rooms, reception halls, kitchens and barracks for the Guard. Her freshly minted brother would get her into the barracks area on the south side. Oida's room was on the west side, directly overlooking the central cloister. To get there, she could take the main thoroughfare, a heavily used enclosed corridor paved with the legendary Blemyan blue and white geometric tiles; or she could follow the original peripheral route, as the first architect had intended, most of which was deserted now and visited only by the servants who swept it; or she could follow the Clerks' Road, a composite agglomeration of passages that threaded in and out like cross-stitch between the offices that occupied the third and fourth floors of the South,

East and West wings. There was, of course, no map of the Clerks' Road; it was one of the mysteries of the craft, something you had to learn for yourself as a rite of passage, or be shown, just the once, as a special mark of favour by a kindly superior. As an option, everything was against it except that the Blemyans did employ female clerks, and she wouldn't look out of place there carrying a book.

Black clerical subfusc just about fitted under the shining yellow gown, though it made her sweat like a pig. Her brother greeted her with great joy at the gatehouse, hustled her into the barracks, led her up four flights of vertiginous spiral stairs and abandoned her without a word. She peeled off the yellow gown and dumped it down a garderobe. The shoes were now a problem; far too dressy for a woman clerk. She rubbed them with dust and grime mixed with spit and cut off the sequins. Just as well she wasn't on a schedule.

Getting onto the Clerks' Road was no trouble at all. She wandered around until she saw a clerk—rather, she heard him before she saw him, the clip-clop of his hard soles on the tiled floor giving her plenty of time to stoop and mime tightening a loose shoelace. He swept past without noticing her, and she followed discreetly. He led her to what was clearly some sort of hub, corridors branching off in all directions. She picked up another clerk heading west and followed him for a very long time, until she caught sight of the cloister roof through a broken pane in a stained-glass window. She waited till she had the corridor to herself, then crouched on the floor and peered up, trying to catch a glimpse of the sun. No dice; but the length and angles of the shadows on the cloister roof were just as helpful. She now knew that she was south-west, on the inside, three floors below where she needed to be. A group of four clerks surged past her, talking loudly about the insufferable cruelty of their supervisor. She tagged along behind them unnoticed until they went left and she needed to keep on bearing right, and then she came to a staircase.

She looked at it. Well, why not, she thought. It was one of those horrible screw-thread staircases with triangular treads, and there was no guide-rope or handrail. Up three flights, and she found herself confronted by a massive oak door, which was locked.

Ah well. But the thought of retracing her steps down the loathsome staircase made her feel ill, so she picked the three inches of stiff wire out of the hem of her sleeve and had a go at the lock. To her great surprise it was a piece of cake: a very old lock, therefore a very simple one, dating back to more innocent times. She opened the door carefully and found herself in a long, high gallery, with tall yellow-glazed windows, overlooking the cloister. Simple as that.

The room numbers were painted on the doors in gold leaf. She'd come out at number 46. Oida was in 238. Of course, he wouldn't be there at this time of day, but sooner or later he'd come back, and—She realised she couldn't lift her foot. Sudden cramp, pins and needles, possibly a trapped nerve, or it might just be that she didn't want to. She'd been relying so much on getting caught, but the skill and the instincts and—be honest— the simple thrill of the chase had swept her along, and now she was actually here, and of course there was no way on earth she was going to go through with it—

"Are you lost?"

He had to be a guest, not a local; the voice was wrong, also the manner. A local would be suspicious, not pleasantly amused. She turned round, and recognised the face.

"Telamon? What are you doing here?"

She couldn't actually remember his name. He was some official in the Western diplomatic service, and they'd shared a long coach ride three or four years ago; she'd been assigned to keep an eye on him, so she'd turned on the charm. No surprise that he'd recognised her immediately.

"Keep your voice down, for crying out loud," she hissed, and he looked guilty and sad, like a naughty boy. Then she flicked Corason's beautiful catch, caught the knife as it dropped out of the book and stuck it under his ribs.

She caught him before he fell—three cheers for black, which doesn't show bloodstains—and dragged him, heels trailing, as far as the garderobe, thirty-two staggering yards in the wrong direction. He looked like a small man, but she nearly broke her back heaving him up and posting him through the slot. The splash he made gave her the shivers. My trouble is, she told herself, I know far too many people for my own good.

She walked quickly up the corridor, wiping her hands on the front of her clerical smock, the book wedged securely under her arm. Maybe, she thought, that should be the other way around; too many people know me, knew me, for their own good—is there anyone I've ever known, had anything to do with, who's ever come out of it well? Not many; offhand, couldn't name one. That stopped her dead in her tracks, even though she was in a hurry to get out of sight. Everybody I've ever known long and well enough to have an effect on has suffered as a direct consequence. Everybody I meet, I injure. And I've only just realised that.

Yes, she thought (200, 201, 202) but I work for the cause, the greatest and most wonderful, the only true, the sublime, the supreme cause, I'm a tool in the hands of the Great Smith, and some of us are cutting tools, some of us are hammers, some of us are weapons. She stopped again, opposite Door 213. Do I really believe that? In Him, the Father of all Purposes? As a living being, an entity, a big, broad-shouldered man with a beard? She pressed on, Door 219. There is no big man with a beard, but there is a pattern, a shape, a force, a process, and I'm part of it and necessary to it, and I do what I have to, I do as I'm told. I'm a soldier in an invisible army, led by an invisible general; I can't see the soldiers on either side of me in the line, but I know my shield is locked in with theirs to form an invisible wall against the assault of our enemies; I know that everyone I can see is the enemy, and this is war. Room 225. I do as I'm told. The arrow doesn't second-guess the bowstring. Orders come down. I do as I'm told.

Room 238. She couldn't breathe. She picked the wire out of her sleeve. Her hands were shaking, but as soon as the wire entered the keyhole they became docile, obedient. Another old lock, with naïve, obliging wards. She felt the last one click back and gently pushed the door.

And saw Oida, who shouldn't have been there. But he was. He was squatting on a chamber pot in the middle of the floor, his kingfisher-blue robe tucked up around his waist, a strained expression on his face. He looked up and saw her.

There never was a man like Oida for comical expressions. His face went from stunned surprise to horror to deep, ineradicable shame. He hopped up, dragging his robe down his legs, tripped, stumbled, staggered back three paces, collided with the bed, lost his legs, sat down hard, overbalanced and ended up flat on his back; scrabbled upright and stared at her. She could feel her face burning red as coals on the bed of the Smith's forge. He'd knocked over the jerry; a nasty looking pool was spreading on the floor. "Shut the door, for God's sake, shut the *door*," he howled. She did as she was told. She was good at that.

He was deep-breathing, his eyes closed, getting a grip. Whatever he'd been eating lately, it hadn't agreed with him, not one bit. Probably all those cream and clarified butter sauces for which Blemya is so famous. She wanted to laugh, which was stupid.

Three long strides took her well within distance. "What's the matter?" he asked, as she flipped the catch on the book. The knife fell perfectly into her hand, no fumble. "Are you all right?" he said. "You look awful." She stabbed him.

But the knife wouldn't go in. The point stopped dead, then skidded sideways, ripping the silk of his robe. The knuckle of her thumb ran over a small, hard lump, with enough force to gouge out a small flap of skin. The head of a rivet, she realised; he was wearing a brigandine under his clothes. Then a fist appeared, and quickly grew so big it blotted out the world, and hit her eye socket. She felt her brain move in her skull, then a horrible bump as her head hit the floor, and then everything was a bit vague for a while.

She opened her eyes and saw Oida's face, alarmingly close;

he looked scared to death. He was shouting her name. "Are you all right?" he bawled at her. "Look at me. How many fingers am I holding up?"

Her left eye closed, all on its own. "One," she mumbled.

"Does this hurt?" His hand reached past her, and she felt his fingers gently probing the back of her head. "You stupid bloody cow, I could've killed you. I'm so sorry."

She looked past him, for the knife. It was almost close enough for her to stretch out and reach, but Oida was in the way. He must've seen her, because he looked round, jumped up, grabbed the knife, quickly scanned the room; he went to the door and stabbed it hard into the oak doorframe about eighteen inches off the ground. Then he lifted his foot and stamped on the handle. The blade twanged. He stamped again, harder, and it snapped off. She felt every muscle in her body relax, as though he'd just killed a scorpion or a poisonous spider. There, now; it was all the knife's fault, after all, and we'll say no more about it—

He came back and knelt beside her. "Are you feeling dizzy? Nauseous?"

"I'm fine," she croaked. "For God's sake stop fussing." She could see the small steel plates of the brigandine quite clearly through the hole in the gown; very small plates, such as you only get on the very finest, top-of-the-range bespoke jobs. Nothing but the best, naturally.

The look of terror in his eyes had faded into deep concern. "Telamon," he said, in that damned annoying serious voice, "listen to me, this is important. Did you have orders to kill me?"

"Yes."

He nodded. "Listen. Those orders were false: they didn't

come down through the chain of command." He was having trouble finding the right words, which he found infuriating. "The order to kill me could only come from the very top, and it didn't, I promise you, trust me."

She managed a valiant attempt at a grin, though it hurt. "You would say that, wouldn't you?"

"It's true. I asked him. He told me, quite categorically. He never gave any such order."

He? Who was he talking about? "Oh come on," she said, "don't be silly. You don't know the head of the Lodge. Nobody—"

"Actually I do."

It hit her harder than the punch had done. But she knew him so well. He was telling the truth.

"Long story," he said quickly. "But the important thing is, you don't have to do it."

"You know who the—" Oh, it was so typical, she wanted to hit him. "Prove it. Tell me. No, don't shake your head at me, tell me, I want to know."

He sighed and did the hand-spreading appeasing thing. "If you must know, it was purely by accident. The fact is, I've known him for years, before I found out, I mean. And he said something without thinking, which he never ever does, and suddenly it all made sense. So I asked him. And he admitted it."

"Just like that?"

"Like I told you, I've known him for years and years." He looked at her helplessly. "You know I can't tell you."

Her head was splitting. "No, I suppose not."

"I knew you'd understand." He breathed out slowly and

rocked back on his heels. "Anyway, that's it, now you know. And you don't have to do it, do you understand? It's a false order." He stood up, went away, came back with a dear little porcelain tea bowl half filled with water. "Drink this," he said. In his other hand was a damp piece of cloth. He started dabbing at the corner of her eye, and she slapped his hand away.

"I tried to kill you," she said. It came out like whining; like they were married or something.

"Yes," he said, "I know. And I hit you. Let's call it quits."

That was another thing; utterly trivial, but she had to ask. Why did she find the details of his life so irresistibly interesting? "Good left," she said. "But you can't punch your way out of a cobweb."

He grinned. "Catalauno's," he said, "just off the Goosefair in Choris. Twenty angels for a crash course of ten lessons. All the best people go there, naturally. He reckons I show great promise."

She couldn't help laughing, and it made her yelp, and he ordered her to hold still while he dabbed at her eye, and she said, oh go on, then, and let him. The cloth came away rose-coloured, so he'd broken the skin.

"I'm sorry," she said. "I'll never be able to get my head round you as a bare-knuckle fighter. Or armour next to the skin, come to that."

He pulled an unhappy grin. "I was expecting you," he said. "And believe me, I take you very seriously."

"Thank you. Actually, that's the nicest thing anyone's ever said to me, in context."

"In context." He put down the cloth and made her sip some

water from the exquisite bowl. "I know you had to obey a direct order," he said. "It's like the time I got ordered to kill Senza Belot. Did I tell you about that? Well, anyway, luckily I didn't have to go through with it, obviously. But I knew if I did, that'd be it, the end of me." He shrugged. "It's like putting a hood over a candle, you just blot out what's in your mind and press on anyway; you know you don't want to do it, but somehow it's not up to you any more. Tools in the hands of the Smith, and all that. Except it does actually feel that way, at the time." He grinned. "I still wake up sweating in the middle of the night about it, but I'd have done it."

She smiled at him. "You weaselled your way out of it, didn't you? You always do."

"No. Well, sort of. Actually, no, I was let off. Otherwise—" He drew his finger across his throat. "Something like that, it really pulls you up short."

So that was it, then, was it? Forgive and forget and promise not to do it again? Was it possible that he truly understood her, right down deep, past all the thousands of tiny interlocking steel plates? She deliberately called to mind what she'd been told about him, the first time they were going to work together. Don't trust him further than you can spit.

"It was the truffles in hazelnut and fig sauce," he said with his mouth full. "I love them, but they don't like me. They go straight through me like an arrow."

She looked up at him and pulled a stern face. "Don't eat them, then."

"It's not that easy. The queen, bless her, knows I like them, so we get them at every meal. And you can't refuse, it'd give offence."

Oida had sent down for a light snack: six kinds of fancy cured meat, baby cucumbers sliced lengthways in yogurt, little fried onion cakes with some sort of utterly delicious herbs and spices that you could only get in Blemya, and soft white wheat bread, still warm from the oven. She'd had to hide under the bed when the servant brought in the tray. Her head was aching, but she could see straight again. "You shouldn't be eating with an upset stomach," she said.

He gobbled the last of the cucumber. "Just being sociable," he said.

No further than she could spit, remember? "Sometimes I play this game," she said. "What would I do if there wasn't a war?"

He frowned. "Tricky one," he said. "Well, actually, no, it's not. If it hadn't been for the war, you'd be married to some farmer. Right now you'd probably be chopping up two hundred cabbages for pickling, or washing out guts ready for the sausage-making."

She laughed. "No farmer would've married me, with no dowry. I wonder, would the Lodge have come for me if it hadn't been for the war, or would I still be picking berries on the moor?"

He frowned slightly. "I know it's your game," he said, "but I think you said the rule was, what would I be doing now if there wasn't a war? Which I take to mean, if the war suddenly ended and we had peace."

"Ah well," she said. "In that case, I'd probably look round for the one big score that'd set me up for life, and then, I don't know. Probably I'd buy a small estate or a big farm, a long way out in the sticks."

"One big score."

She nodded. "Rob someone, or a swindle, or maybe just a really good game of cards. You know, I've been so close to it, four or five times over the years, but it's like someone's playing with me like a puppy with a bit of string. Just when my jaws are about to close, it twitches away."

"It doesn't have to be criminal. You could marry money."

She scowled at him. "Don't be silly. Also, if I did that I'd be saddled with a husband."

"Would that be so bad?"

She shrugged. "Depends. Probably."

He ate the rest of the cold meat. "I see you in a big old house, sitting in a library. West-facing, naturally. For some reason, it's raining outside and there's a big log fire. You're sitting at a desk, reading one book and with two others open in front of you, and every now and then you stop and write something in the margin."

She laughed out loud. "It's a stupid game," she said. "And the war will go on and on for ever, so what's the point?"

But Oida shook his head. "Glauca has six years to live," he said. "He dies, the war's over. But it won't come to that, because long before then the Lodge will have taken over both empires, and someone—I have a horrible feeling it'll be my brother—will be emperor over the whole lot. At which point, no doubt, new and different wars will break out. But they won't be this one." He dabbed his mouth with the hem of his sleeve; his one vulgar habit. "Which reminds me."

She looked at him. Just the slightest change in tone of voice, but it was like a tiny creak in a house that ought to be empty. "What?"

"All this is very pleasant," he said, "but you've got work to do."

"I thought we'd agreed I haven't."

"You need to do a job for me."

Her eyes widened. "Is that right?"

He nodded. "For a smart woman you can be a bit stupid sometimes. Two things. One, you don't seem to have grasped the significance of what I told you. You got a direct order, but it didn't come from On High. Do you know what that means?"

She nodded. "Commissioner Corason told me," she said. "Schism inside the Lodge. I didn't believe him."

"Do you now?"

She paused before answering. "If I don't," she said, "then I don't believe you either, in which case my orders were valid and I've got to murder you. So, yes, I choose to believe."

"Belief isn't about choice. See Monomachus' *Ethics*, books one to three."

"Screw Monomachus. What was the other thing?"

He gazed at her for a moment, then went on; "You were ordered to get rid of me. I think it would be best all round if you succeeded."

"Got you. Won't that be a problem with the negotiations?"

He shook his head. "Fortuitously, you killed me just after I'd wrapped up all the salient terms of the deal. Now, the queen really likes me at the moment, probably because of all that money and the fact I rescued her boyfriend for her—"

"*We* rescued."

"I left you out of it," he said, "safer for you, in the long run. Anyhow, she'll play along if I ask her nicely. I expect she'll give me a state funeral, quite possibly a mausoleum. I always fancied a mausoleum, on a hilltop somewhere, with lots of white marble and a free-standing alabaster sarcophagus and a shiny copper roof, only I thought, the hell with it, I wouldn't be around to see it." He grinned. "Anyway," he said, "that'll convince everybody except everybody who actually matters. What they're going to need is positive, unassailable proof."

"What?"

"My head preserved in a jar of honey would be optimum, but I don't think that's practical. This, though, would do almost as well."

"What?"

She noticed he'd raised his right hand and was pointing to his index finger. "You'll notice," he said, "this scar here. It's quite distinctive, like a clover leaf. Had it since I was nine, and Axio trapped it in a door. Packed in salt, it'd keep quite nicely."

She didn't follow. "Where are you going to get a finger just like that from?"

"Think about it. And the beauty of it is, Axio would know I'd rather die than lose this finger."

His plectrum finger. Without it, he couldn't play. "But—"

He shook his head. "Axio's a fool," he said. "He overestimates my vanity. The truth is, of course, that I'd far rather lose this finger than die, but he couldn't see that. So." He shrugged. "We'll need some salt. And a little box."

She stared at him. "Are you serious?"

"About the box? Absolutely. A bag wouldn't do nearly as well."

"Well?"

Corason's eyes were shining, or glittering; she could see the candle reflected in them. She sat down heavily. "I need a drink."

He reached for the teapot, but she shook her head. "Something stronger."

Corason raised both eyebrows. "You don't drink. It's in your file."

She looked past him, caught the barmaid's eye. "Peach brandy," she said. "Bring the bottle."

"We haven't got any."

"What've you got that's like it?"

The barmaid thought for a long time. "Applejack?"

"Is that stuff fit for human consumption?"

"Well, we drink it."

"Fetch me a bottle anyway."

The barmaid didn't move. Corason produced money. She went away.

"Well?"

She nodded.

"What's that supposed to mean?"

She didn't speak or move until the barmaid came back with the bottle. "Job done," she said, filled a tea bowl with applejack and swallowed it.

"Meaning?"

From her sleeve she produced a small rosewood box, the sort

high-ranking clerks use to keep pen-nibs and sealing wax in. She opened the lid.

"For God's sake," Corason said. "Put it away."

"Not till you've had a closer look. Here, see this scar? Seen it before?"

He reached over her hand and closed the lid. "Yes."

"That's what I meant by job done." She refilled the bowl and gulped it down. "But you don't have to take my word for it. The news'll be all over town by this evening, I expect. He was a well-known public figure, and all that."

Corason had gone as white as a corpse. "Well, then," he said. "That's that."

She looked straight at him. "No thanks? Praise? Well done, thou good and faithful servant?"

He shook his head. "If you want. Well done."

"Go fuck yourself."

He leaned back, and the chair creaked. "You got out all right, obviously."

"Obviously."

"What happened to your eye?"

"There were a few minor mishaps. Want to hear about them?"

He shook his head. "Not really."

"Then don't pretend you care."

He looked as though he'd just come home to find his mother in bed with the stable boy. "Seriously," he said, "well done. It was a job that needed doing. I know you hate me and the Lodge and everybody in the whole world because of it, but—"

"I did as I was told."

"Exactly. It's what we all have to do. The hammer strikes, the saw cuts, otherwise there's no point to their existence." He massaged his forehead, as though he had a bad headache. "Pour me a drop of that stuff, will you?"

"Buy your own."

"I might just do that." He gestured to the barmaid, but she hadn't seen him. "Well, then," he said. "Time for your next assignment. They want you to go to a place called Malla Polla—"

But she shook her head. "I'm excused duty," she said.

"Oh." She'd shocked him. "Why?"

"When Oida was dying," she said quietly, "he made me promise him something. I have to find his brother and give him a message."

"What?"

"Family stuff. I'm not allowed to tell anyone except Axio." She poured another bowl. "Don't even think about telling me I can't do this, unless you want your throat cut right now."

He shrugged. "Not up to me," he said, "I'm not your control. I'll tell them you asked for a leave of absence, on compassionate grounds."

"Compassionate. Now there's a word. Yes, you do that. Oh, and I'll need money."

"What? Oh, all right. How much?"

"How much will it cost to get me to where Axio is?"

"I don't know."

"Find out." She stood up, wobbled, caught the edge of the table. The box slipped out of her sleeve and fell on the table. Fortunately, the catch held and it didn't spill open. She retrieved it and shoved it down the front of her dress. "Be here same time tomorrow."

"I'm not sure I can get you that information."

"Here. This time tomorrow."

On her way out of the city, she stopped at the booksellers' yard and found the man who had the best selection of maps in the whole of the West. "I want a map," she said.

The man smiled. "I have many fine maps. What sort would you like?"

"I want one that's got a place called Engoi on it. It's not for me, it's for my brother."

The man's smile only wavered for a second. "We'd better look in the gazetteer," he said.

Engoi turned out to be a small village in Eysi Celeuthi, three miles east of the border between East and West. "I can sell you a map of Eysi," the man said, "but it'll be a bit out of date. Half the cities in Eysi aren't there any more, and I seem to remember Forza Belot diverted the course of the Haimon river during the Field of Crocuses campaign."

She gave him a weary look. "Noted," she said. "How much?"

The map came in a dear little brass tube embossed with flowers and vine leaves. She found a teahouse, spread the map out on the tabletop and studied it carefully. Maybe there's more than one Engoi, she thought. She rolled it back up again, and had a lot of trouble getting it back in the tube.

A shadow fell over her, making her shiver. Then a man appeared at the edge of her vision, and sat down opposite. "Hello," he said. "I don't suppose you remember me."

He was young and ridiculously tall. "Of course I do," she

replied. "You're the thief. No, don't tell me. I never forget a talent, but names take a little longer."

"I'm Musen," he said. "Corason told me you'd be shopping for maps."

She smiled at him. He'd changed since she'd last seen him. There were scars on his face and arms. His nose had been broken. It improved him. "You know Corason."

"Yes. I worked for him. He says you're going to see Commissioner Axio."

"If he says it, I guess it must be true."

"Can I go with you?"

There was one particular scar, in the middle of the palm of his left hand. She'd seen several like it over the years. It came from having your hand nailed to a plank or beam. It's a job that calls for skill and judgement, to avoid skewering the big veins on the other side. "Why?"

He grinned. "Everyone says you're the best in the business."

"Liar."

"They say you're good at getting to places and finding people. I don't like doing long journeys on my own."

"You get into trouble."

"Yes."

"That's because you steal things and get caught."

"I used to."

"Get caught?"

"Steal things. I don't do that any more. Not unless I'm told to."

She put the map in her sleeve. "Corason sent you to keep an eye on me."

"Yes. And because I want to see Axio. He's my friend."

He'd put his hands on the table. It didn't look a particularly comfortable way to sit. "When did you work for Corason?"

"I stole the pack of cards they used to buy off the siege of Rasch. Then, when he got shot after the big battle, I found him and brought him back. I've been with him on and off ever since, running errands. He knows I want to see Axio again, so he sent me to go with you."

She frowned. "Axio's your friend."

"That's right."

"Did Corason tell you why I'm going to see him?"

"No. Just that it's important Lodge business. I don't need to know."

"No, you don't, but what the hell. Listen. I have to take something for him to see, and give him a message. It's very important. If there's two of us, it doubles the chance of one of us making it. We'd be going to a very bad place. There's no people there any more, it's right on the front line, so if soldiers don't get us, we'll probably starve. What Axio's doing in a place like that, I have absolutely no idea."

He shrugged. "I don't mind. I'm used to roughing it."

"Good, because I'm not. I don't like getting wet, I hate sleeping in ditches, I'm pathetic at setting snares and spit-roast squirrel gives me the shits. I'm a *girl*, for crying out loud, I shouldn't have to do all that."

He grinned. "I might be able to help," he said.

"How could you possibly—?"

"There's this man I know."

*

It was essentially a fairy story—the lion with a thorn in its paw, or the poor fisherman's son who throws back a fish that turns out to be the Dragon King in disguise. But this time it was true.

The slave dealer Saevolus Andrapodiza, the second richest private individual in the world, had a penchant for dressing as a carter, drinking in low dives and losing large sums of money in card games. Originally he'd done it to annoy his father, and now that the old man was dead he found he couldn't break the habit. Just occasionally, though, he won large sums of money in card games, whereupon he would celebrate by getting drunk, which made him aggressive. He'd just threatened to fight any man in the bar, and an ex-soldier had advised him, in the friendliest manner possible, that he shouldn't really say things like that if he didn't mean them. But I do mean them, Saevolus replied, whereupon the ex-soldier picked him up and threw him across the room.

Sitting in a corner was Musen. He'd noticed that the little thin man had just won forty angels, and, despite having bought drinks all round three times, it stood to reason that he had most of it left. So Musen got up quietly and, as the ex-soldier lifted his boot to stamp on Saevolus' ribs, gently barred his way. Musen was a head taller than the soldier and a handspan broader across the shoulders, and he was smiling in a context where nobody would normally smile. The ex-soldier hesitated.

"You won," Musen said. "You made your point. Why spoil it?"

The ex-soldier had four friends with him, but they hadn't moved. Serving under Forza Belot, he'd learned a bit about tactics. He took a deep breath and let it out again.

Musen smiled. "Let me buy you a drink," he said.

That done, he helped the little man up off the floor, bustled him out into the street, picked his pocket and asked if he was all right. The little man groaned. Musen noticed a gold signet ring, and recognised the emblem. Far too recognisable to sell; but it occurred to him nevertheless that his new friend might prove profitable in other ways. "I'll take you home," he said. "Where do you live?"

The next morning, Saevolus woke up feeling ill. He'd forgotten about his winnings, a sum so trivial that it slipped through the meshes of his mind, but he distinctly recalled the brave stranger who'd saved him from certain death and then vanished, leaving behind no trace of his identity. It was rather miraculous, therefore, that the first person he met as he staggered out into the daylight some time later should be the mysterious hero in person.

"I wanted to know if you were all right," Musen said shyly. "Only, I couldn't very well call at the front door. Your people would throw me out looking like this, and quite right, too."

So, he went on, he'd been hanging about outside on the off chance; he was greatly relieved to see that no serious harm had been done, and now he'd be on his way.

No chance of that. I owe you my life, said Saevolus. Oh, that's all right, it's what anyone would have done. Saevolus offered money. Musen looked shocked and offended. Well, anyhow, Saevolus insisted, if ever there's anything I can do for you, anything at all—Musen thanked him, said that so long as he was all right, that was the main thing, and walked away. And if Saevolus even noticed that he'd lost his gold cloak pin and come out without any money, he certainly didn't make the connection.

"You said you were done with all that."

Musen shrugged. "I saved his life. He owed me."

"He offered you a reward and you didn't take it."

"He'd paid already." He scowled. "So I keep my hand in now and again, that's not the same as regular thieving, like going out and looking for stuff. And I really am finished with all that, I promise."

She rolled her eyes at him. "Anyhow," she said, "that's all very well, but how's that supposed to help us get to Engoi?"

"Simple. We hitch a ride with the caravan."

Which put her in her place good and proper. Brilliant. Both emperors had made it known that Saevolus' caravans, performing as they did a vital economic function, had unequivocal safe passage. Saevolus never sent his stock anywhere without a substantial escort, and it was cheaper in the long run to ship them in carts, thereby cutting transit times and preventing them from losing condition. Two civilians on foot wouldn't last ten minutes on the Great East Road, which ran straight through the heart of Eysi province, but a well-armed and supplied caravan with diplomatic credentials would have nothing to worry about at all.

"But what makes you think he's sending a caravan in that direction?"

"That would be the favour." Musen grinned. "Like I said, he owes me."

*

She assumed it wouldn't actually work. Either Saevolus would have forgotten Musen, or would pretend he had, or the favour would be too much to ask, bearing in mind the substantial cost of fitting out a caravan; or maybe he simply wouldn't be at home when Musen called, and wasn't expected back again for nine weeks.

She assumed wrong. Musen went to call, and Saevolus was at home. He was delighted to see Musen again. His debt, he said, had been weighing heavily on his mind ever since the night in question. Permians believe that if you die while under a serious obligation of honour, the person to whom you die obliged gets control of your immortal soul, and can conjure you to appear and perform magical tasks. Actually, very few Permians still believe that, and Saevolus definitely wasn't one of them, but it rankles, like a grape pip between the teeth.

Sure, Saevolus said, I can do that. In fact, it just so happens that I have an order to fill at Ana Straton, on the western edge of Eysi, so Engoi would be less than a day's ride out of my way. Then a depressing thought struck him: you wouldn't mind desperately if I didn't come with you myself? Only I've got so much to do here, and—

Musen assured him that that wouldn't be necessary. Saevolus, looking mightily relieved, promised to send his best man to lead the caravan; Bidens, splendid fellow, tough as old boots, he'll see you get there and no messing about. Then he sat down at his desk and wrote a letter of recommendation in his own handwriting, which Musen presumed Bidens could read, through dint of long practice; to him, it looked as though a mouse had fallen in an inkwell, then chased its own tail across a sheet of paper. "The plan was to leave the day after tomorrow," Saevolus said, "if that suits you. If not, I can easily reschedule."

"That'll do fine," Musen said, thanked him and left without stealing anything.

A small, high-value consignment: all skilled men, twenty to a wagon, ten wagons plus two supply carts, escorted by thirty Mi Chanso horse-archers and fourteen men-at-arms. To which was added Saevolus' personal carriage—not his best or his second-best, but his third-best was still a degree of luxury and sophistication which she hadn't encountered before, even when travelling with Oida. In the back of the coach was a tent—no, you had to call it a pavilion—with enough rugs and cushions and tapestry draught-excluders to furnish a house, not to mention the portable stove, with its incredibly ingenious telescopic flue. It was the sort of rig the emperor would've had, if only he could've afforded it. On the box there was room for a driver and two guards, who doubled as butler and lord high chamberlain; an aristocratic Blemyan by the name of Phrixus, and a gigantic Permian with decorative scars criss-crossing his cheeks and a real knack for folding napkins in the shape of roses.

"This is stupid," she said, as they rumbled along the Great East Road in gorgeous sunshine. "We're supposed to be slipping out unobtrusively, and we look like an embassy from the Great King of the Sashan. We couldn't be more conspicuous if we were on fire."

Musen shrugged. Sitting in the coach made him bored and restless. "If anyone's watching out for us," he said, "this is the last place they'd look, because of what you just said. So really, it's a good way of not being seen."

Idiot's logic, to which she had no answer. "What did you manage to find out about the cargo?"

"Not much," he replied. "Tried asking the guards, but they don't know a lot either. They're Easterners of some kind, but that's all I know."

She'd caught a few glimpses of them, nothing more; rows of men, middle-aged or older, sitting on benches in the wagons, their feet shackled to a steel bar running the length of the wagon bed. Her impression was that they were too pale for farmhands, so presumably artisans of some description. "There used to be a foundry at Straton before the war," she said, "though I'm pretty sure it got burned down. I don't know, maybe there's enough of it left to be worth rebuilding. Still, it's a bloody funny place to build a factory, right in the middle of a war zone."

"I wouldn't know," Musen said, "I've never been there."

Helpful as ever. "I can't believe you actually arranged all this. First-class travel door to door, all expenses paid." A thought struck her. "Is this Andrapodiza a Craftsman?"

Shrug. "Don't know."

No, and why should he? She should, though; a prominent public figure, rich and well-connected. It would make sense if he was. After all, Saevolus and the Great Smith were in more or less the same line of business, making even the most improbable people useful, and not giving them much say in the matter. Oida would know if Saevolus was Lodge, of course. She turned her head and looked out of the window. This close to Rasch, the landscape should be a well-ordered grid of carefully tended fields (good growing country; had to be, to feed the biggest city in the world) but it was a long time since they'd seen a human being, and the fields were waist-high grass, nettles and briars.

It wasn't like travelling with Oida, who always carried spare books and foldaway chess sets and backgammon boards that just seemed to materialise when needed out of his minimal luggage. Musen seemed content (no, wrong word; resigned) to sit staring at the floor for hours on end; occasionally he'd pull out a cheap pack of cards and stare at them instead, but he never suggested a game of anything. She had no great interest in talking to him, but on the third day of their improbable journey the silence started to get to her.

"What do you do with all the money?" she asked.

He looked up from the cards. "What money?"

She smiled grimly. "You're always stealing things," she said. "Usually small and valuable. You don't drink or gamble; you hardly spend anything. So, what do you do with it all?"

There was a short battle inside him. Then he smiled. "I put it in the bank. Where it's safe."

She blinked. "The bank."

He nodded. "I got an account with the Knights. And another one with the Sword-blade. Sort of like hedging my bets."

The Knights and the Sword-blade; oh dear. Just before she left Rasch she'd removed her trivial savings from the Knights and lodged them with the Trani Brothers, too small to be invited to join the syndicate to cover the Imperial loan. Pointless, though, because when the Knights went down— "That's very sensible of you," she said.

"Well," he grunted. "I worked hard for that money. When all this is over, I want something to show for it."

It had been Oida's bright idea, of course, to bring about the end of the world. Looking out of the window at the derelict fields, the end of the world was something she could actually bring herself to believe in. A comforting thought, in a way. If everything comes to a sudden and violent end, we won't have to clear up all the messes we've made.

Everything went fine until they reached the Mafaes, which they should have been able to cross by way of the magnificent stone bridge built by Gauda IV three hundred years earlier.

"It must have taken them weeks," she said. "Probably longer than building it."

A remarkable feat of engineering, certainly. To break the bridge, someone had had to undermine the central span, which had meant digging a shaft deep underneath the river, a hundred yards through the living rock, in order to collapse the mighty granite columns. "It was fine when we came through this way last month," Bidens assured her. "This is all new. Beats me why they bothered. I hadn't heard there was any serious fighting in these parts."

At its narrowest point, where the bridge used to be, the Mafaes is two hundred and ten yards wide and fifteen feet deep. The nearest crossing point is twenty-six miles upstream; and if you go that way, in order to get back on the Great East, you have to scramble up the Pig's Head and down the other side, which isn't possible in a wheeled vehicle. "Isn't it lucky," Bidens said, "that we happen to have with us a hundred and five professional carpenters."

She looked at him. "You're kidding."

"No shit." He turned and nodded towards a stand of tall, spindly birch. "Of course, we don't have any woodworking tools. But we do have twenty-five blacksmiths, and twelve sledgehammers."

The smiths used the sledgehammers to forge links from the spare sets of shackles into hand-hammers and tongs, using salvaged granite blocks from the bridge as anvils. Then they used the hand-hammers to forge the sledgehammers into axes, with which the carpenters cut down and rough-shaped trees into beams wide enough to span the gap, while the smiths forged iron scraps and offcuts into nails. They worked quickly and efficiently, never saying a word to the guards or each other, except when necessary for the furtherance of the job in hand. When their shifts were over, they went and sat in the wagons, with their shackles on. The work took two full days and half a morning. Musen had offered to help, but was politely told he was a passenger and mustn't exert himself.

Bidens the overseer had taken to riding with them in the coach. He hoped they didn't mind; it made such a pleasant change to have someone cultured and intelligent to talk to—apparently Musen was officially included in this category, though Bidens ignored him most of the time. He wanted to talk about the plays he'd seen in Rasch, most of which she'd missed because she'd been out of town. Bidens' idea of discussing a play was to give a detailed blow-by-blow account of the plot; and when he ran out of plays he started discussing books, most of which she'd never heard of. He was clearly a voracious reader and playgoer, though she suspected that nearly everything he read and saw went over his head like a flock of migrating geese; still, he evidently managed to get pleasure from it, in the same way as the gold miners pulverise a whole mountain to get a cupful of gold. His voice filled up the silence, which had been starting to get to her, and his regurgitated narratives of hate, lust, greed, cruelty and revenge, all wildly melodramatic and unreal, had a curiously soothing effect as they passed through the briar-smothered ruins of town and villages, or camped for the night beside thickets of the tall, red-flowered weed that grows on the site of burned-down buildings. Listening to Bidens, you could kid yourself into believing that violence was like dragons or gryphons, an imaginary monster invented to account for phenomena for which there was, in fact, a perfectly normal and natural explanation; we pretend there's this monster called war, but really it's just the houses and people dying off in winter so they can come back to life in the spring.

You can't tell someone the plot of the entire Maricas Cycle and not warm to them just a little bit. So, when she felt the time was right, she started delicately fishing for facts, and eventually she got them. The slaves were on their way to join up with the Third Army, the last, best hope of the West; their job was to build siege engines for an assault on a major Eastern city, whose fall would end the war at a stroke. The idea was, it was far easier to take the engineers to the job than lug the finished product halfway across the empire under constant harassment from the enemy. By the same token, the sight of a fully-equipped siege train would put the enemy on notice and give him time to prepare. Which city? Bidens frowned and confessed that he didn't know, although these days there weren't that many left to choose from. But she shouldn't read too much into their destination; this caravan was one of twenty, all heading east by circuitous routes, twisting and turning about and eventually meeting up where they were supposed to be. Senza Belot—this was Bidens' theory—always got his results by dashing along terribly fast in a straight line. Like a dog, he couldn't really see something unless it was moving. The best way to hide something from him, therefore, was to shift it slowly and meandering along in loops and circles; anything like that wouldn't register as a threat, and he'd ignore it.

"But Forza's just like his brother, isn't he? He thinks in lightning flashes."

Bidens shrugged. "Maybe this isn't his idea. Maybe they've got a new general. After all, Forza's done nothing at all to win the war; he just keeps it going on and on for ever. About time the West tried a new approach, if you ask me."

"I thought Saevolus was supposed to be neutral. That's why he's got safe passage."

Bidens shrugged. "Yes, I wondered about that. Wouldn't look good if he got found out. But it wouldn't come to that. I've got perfectly legitimate bills of sale that say this lot's consigned to a sawmill in Eysi. It's not there any more, of course, it got burned down five years ago, but I don't know that officially." He ate an olive, offered her the jar. "My guess is, by the time it all comes out, the plan will have worked and the war'll be over and Saevolus will be well in with the winning side." He grinned. "More likely, he's doing something equally devious for the East at the same time, so they sort of cancel each other out. Fact is, everywhere's so desperate for manpower these days, nobody's going to pick a quarrel with Saevolus, no matter what he does, so long as he's not too blatant about it."

"Now that's not something you see every day," Bidens said.

She looked up from the book he'd lent her—she already knew the story, in great detail, but something to read is something to read—and glanced out of the window. At first, nothing registered; just open fields, with men cutting down briars and loading the brash on to carts. Then, "My God," she said. "People."

They hadn't been at it long, to judge by the area that had been cleared. "Probably some of ours," Bidens said, with a hint of pride. "Though we haven't sold many farmhands in the empires, you just can't get the stock. Still, it's nice to see waste being put back into productive use."

One of the field hands stooped and picked something up. He was maybe thirty yards away. Without thinking, she threw herself on the floor. "Get down," she yelled.

Musen followed her, dragging Bidens down with him. "What's going on?" he asked, as the coach stopped suddenly. "What the hell are you playing at?"

Tough as old boots, Saevolus had said; well. "Shut up," she said, and Musen put his hand over Bidens' mouth.

The carriage door swung open. "Out," someone said. He sounded confident, and in a hurry.

They were piling the bodies of the horse-archers on to the piles of cut briar. The men-at-arms had made a show of throwing away their weapons as soon as they realised what was going on, and had been spared, but the aristocratic looking Blemyan had been shot in the stomach and wasn't expected to live. They'd laid him out on the grass, and stepped over him as they went about their business.

Someone was cutting iron with a hammer and cold chisel. The man who'd ordered them out of the carriage looked them over and obviously reached the conclusion that they were no bother to anyone. "Stay there," he said and walked away. There seemed to be no reason not to do as he said. Like a dog, or Senza Belot, they only seemed disposed to attack moving targets.

"It wouldn't be the first time," Bidens muttered under his breath. "That's why we have the armed escorts: we're carrying a valuable commodity." He pulled a sad face. "I always wondered what it'd be like, to be one of them." He nodded towards the nearest wagon. "There's irony for you."

They hadn't bothered to tie up the surrendered men-at-arms, who were standing around looking forlorn and keeping out of the way. Bidens could be right, she told herself, but somehow she didn't think so; if they were just stealing the slaves, why bother to cut off the shackles?

A short, bearded man was fiddling about with a tinderbox, trying to light one of the impromptu briar pyres. He gave up and handed the box to the huge, red-headed young man who'd been watching him struggle; a moment later there was a curl of smoke, then crackles and a spurt of flame. She noticed that Musen was looking very hard at the giant fire-raiser. "Know him?" she said.

"I think so."

"That figures. They're Lodge, aren't they?"

Musen shrugged. "Well, he is if he's who I think he is. Don't know about the rest of them."

The short man was heading towards them. At twenty-five yards she recognised him, though the name temporarily escaped her. But she'd seen him once, at a mission briefing.

"Sorry about this," the man said, and his voice was familiar. "Now you're Musen, and I'm guessing you must be Telamon. Sorry, I don't know your friend."

Musen did the little head shake that meant Not-Lodge. The short man turned to Bidens and gave him a pleasant smile. "Perhaps you'd like to go over there and join the others."

By which he meant the men-at-arms. He didn't like the sound of that; but the tall, red-headed man was now standing behind the short man; she couldn't see his face, but Bidens could. He slumped and walked away.

"I think we've met," the short man said.

Her memory stirred. "Myrtus."

"Commissioner Myrtus," he said. "I remember now, you did that job for us at Beloisa." Then he turned to Musen. "You I've heard a lot about."

Musen looked past him. "Hello, Teucer."

The red-headed man didn't answer. "Axio's looking forward to seeing you again," Myrtus said, and she realised he was talking to Musen. "I don't know, is that a good thing or a bad thing?"

"He's my friend," Musen replied, and she thought, that's not an answer to his question. But that was none of her business. "Is Commissioner Axio near here?" she interrupted, raising her voice a little. "I need to see him."

She'd reminded Myrtus of her existence. "Official business?"

"Very much so."

"In that case, yes. Tell you what," he went on, "we'll use that fancy carriage of yours. Mind driving?"

That was apparently addressed to Teucer, the red-headed man. He nodded, his eyes still on Musen. Tact, she thought; if he's driving, he doesn't have to share space with Musen. Still none of her business. "Excuse me," she said, "but weren't you—?"

Myrtus grinned bleakly. "No need to rush," he said, "but we might as well get on."

Myrtus: appointed commander-in-chief of the armed forces of the Lodge, when they made their unilateral declaration of war against the two empires. Not heard of since; hardly surprising, since the Lodge's army had melted away and Mere Barton had been evacuated without an arrow being loosed, because, of course, the war had turned out to be a very different kind of war. She wondered if they'd told him in advance and decided, probably not.

"The Lodge doesn't hold with slavery in any shape or form," he said, as the coach started to move. "Therefore, we intercept slave caravans wherever we can and set the slaves free."

"In the middle of an uninhabited moor."

Wry smile. "No, of course not, that'd be next best thing to murder. No, they're coming back with us to Engoi, as soon as we've got the shackles off. We need them to do a little job for us, and then they'll be free to go. Home, or wherever they like."

"A little job."

"You'll see when we get there."

He found talking to her boring and mildly irritating; he wanted to talk to Musen, but Musen didn't seem to want to talk. Not that it mattered. The object of the exercise was to find Axio and give him the little box. After that—well, presumably there would be a return journey, but she hadn't given it much thought. She'd be going back to Blemya—would she? No reason why she should, as far as anyone else was concerned, and quite possibly the Lodge, as represented by two Commissioners in one obscure moorland village, had some other use for her. Under normal circumstances she'd be resigned to that. She wondered what the bad blood was between Musen and the other Rhus—Teucer, though she'd have forgotten his name by this time tomorrow. If she knew Musen, she wouldn't want to be the other man; except that he seemed to be in high favour with Commissioner Myrtus, loyal sergeant and right-hand-man, and Musen, whatever his faults, seemed to have a healthy respect for the Lodge's chain of command. But if Teucer owned any small, portable items of value, he'd probably do well to keep them well hidden. And undoubtedly he knew that already, if he knew Musen. Still none of her business, but you can't help being just a tiny bit curious.

You can't tell from maps, but the picture of Engoi she'd formed in her mind was a single street, maybe a couple of dozen buildings, a single-storey thatched Brother's house, possibly a village tower, for the villagers to huddle in during cattle raids. She hadn't expected—

"That's why we need carpenters," Myrtus said. "And stonemasons—you had ten of them with you, didn't you know that?

And you can never have too many smiths on a major construction project."

A fortress; or at least it would be one very soon, once they'd dug the spur from the river to flood the moat and capped off the walls with crenellated battlements. "People look down on mud brick for defensive architecture," Myrtus said, "but actually it's got a lot going for it, provided you think massive. We're using stone for the gatehouse and the guard towers, naturally, but brick makes a damn good wall, soaks up a hell of a pounding. More give in it, you see, it crumbles rather than shatters."

No shortage of raw material; they'd dug a huge ditch, made bricks out of the spoil and a moat out of the trench. "It's a lousy position compared to Mere Barton, but so what? Who needs Nature when you've got manpower?"

And they had that all right. Slaves, naturally; but freed slaves, from both empires, doing one little job for the Lodge and then they were free to go. Myrtus wasn't entirely sure how they were being fed (Axio was looking after supply) but he had an idea they were bringing stuff in down the river on barges, from stockpiles the empires had built up (without knowing it) shortly before all the supply clerks defected ... "No," Myrtus said irritably, when she plucked up the courage to ask him straight. "No, I didn't. It was need-to-know, and they felt that if they told me, it'd cloud my judgement. So what? It's all working out fine, isn't it? And you've got no idea how relieved I was when they finally let me in on the secret. I was fully resigned to getting slaughtered."

"You're a Commissioner."

Exasperated sigh. "Meaning nothing, as you well know.

Commissioner means you get given five times as much work, that's all."

She'd been watching. Musen and the red-headed man, Teucer, hadn't exchanged a single word since they'd got here. Teucer, apparently, was the best shot in the Lodge and both empires, but instead of training recruits at Beal he was here, running errands for the Commissioner. Apparently, if the Great Smith wanted to use a pair of tongs to drive in a nail, nobody was prepared to argue.

"Axio's probably on site somewhere, shouting at the foremen," Myrtus said. "He's good at that. They're all scared stiff of him, for some reason."

The one thing she had left to do, and then the rest of the day was her own—would the end of the world be marked by a big, showy red sunset? Hard to say. Of course, someone might still have work for her. I want to go back to Blemya, she realised, and the sudden insight left her feeling giddy and stupid, like a blow to the head.

You'll know him when you see him, Corason had told her: just look for the most handsome man in the world. Yeah, right, she'd thought; but, yes, actually, he was. She first saw him standing on a low stone wall, haranguing—no other word for it—a bunch of timid looking men in stonemasons' aprons. She was too far away to hear what he was saying, but she didn't need to. He finished his remarks and the masons walked away quickly. He stayed on the wall, peering at a plan or diagram; he held it at arm's length. Long-sighted, she diagnosed. He could do with one of those magic glasses the Mezentines used to make; you screw them into your eye and suddenly you've got close vision like a twelve-year-old.

She cleared her throat. He looked up and saw her. "You're Telamon," he said.

"Is there somewhere we can talk?"

Exactly why he was so good-looking she couldn't say. She'd read a book about that once. Apparently, someone had studied the subject in detail and with proper scientific rigour, and had concluded that the difference between butt-ugly and drop-dead gorgeous was a hair's breadth short of a quarter of an inch. Well, then; move his nose up a bit and widen his mouth just a touch and round his chin off just a smidgeon and you'd have Oida.

"Sure," he said, jumping down off the wall. "This way."

He led her to a lean-to shack full of barrels. "Well?"

Her fingertips found the lid of the box. She took it out, put it on top of a barrel and opened the lid. He frowned. "A box of salt," he said. "What about it?"

Her skin crawled as she brushed away the surface layer, but as soon as he saw the finger his eyes lit up. Then he looked at her. She said nothing. He emptied the box out, picked the finger up delicately, as if he was afraid it might break if he dropped it, and held it up to the light. Then he smiled the most beautiful smile. "You did this?"

"Yes."

"Good girl." He put it down, fished about in his coat pocket and produced—guess what, a Mezentine glass; rather a good one, in a plain gold setting. "That's him all right," he said. "How did you know about it?"

Good question. "The scar? Oh, he told me."

Big grin. "Of course, you knew him quite well, didn't you?"

"Yes."

"The one that kept getting away. I can see how that would've driven him wild. Did he tell you how he got it?"

"He said you had something to do with it."

He laughed, then tucked the finger behind his ear, like a carpenter's stick of chalk. "You know what," he said, "this is probably the happiest day of my life. Allow me to buy you a drink. And a big house in town and a country estate. Unless you'd prefer a gold mine. Or both."

Remember who you are, she told herself. Remember who your file says you are. "I'd rather have cash," she said.

"Sure. How much?"

"How much have you got?"

The smile became a beam. The sun was never that bright. "Not nearly enough," he said. "I can give you a hundred angels in your hand, but that could only be a token down-payment."

"That's fine," she said. "Can I have it now, please?"

"Of course. Stay there. No, come with me, I don't want you wandering off. This way."

He walked quickly, with a bounce in his step. People got out of his way, but he didn't seem to notice. "I gather you brought my friend Musen with you," he said. "Was he any trouble?"

"No."

"Splendid. He can be a bit of a nuisance if you don't know how to handle him."

A plain oilskin tent. He dived in and came out again with a cloth bag the size of a spring cabbage, but significantly heavier. "Thanks," she said. "Do you want the box?"

He thought for a moment. "Might as well," he said, "to be going on with. When I've got five minutes, I'll have them make me one of those, what's the word, what you keep saints' bones in."

"Reliquary?"

"That's it, reliquary. I saw just the sort of thing once, it was a fair-sized box carved out of a lump of coal. Working hinges and everything. Of course, traditionally it ought to be a drinking cup made from his skull. Or I read in a book somewhere about someone who made a bow out of the bones and sinews of his enemy, which I'm not sure is actually possible, but it'd be great to hang on the wall."

She gave him a bleak smile. "Wasn't it a chair?"

"Different book." Suddenly he liked her; shared taste in literature, presumably. "A chair would do fine, actually, though you couldn't rely on it. A footstool would be better. You could always rely on my brother to fold up in a heap whenever the pressure was on."

She held out her hand. He'd forgotten about the money. "Sorry," he said, and gave her the bag. She needed both hands. "Don't wave it about," he said, "properly speaking, it's six weeks' wages for the masons, but let's not worry too much about that. Shame you didn't come a week earlier, before I paid the brickmakers."

"Give me the reading glass," she said suddenly, without knowing quite why.

His hand went straight to his pocket. "There you go," he said, and held it out to her. She put the bag down on the ground, took the glass, slipped it into her sleeve and picked the bag up again. "Don't you need it?" she asked.

"Yes, actually, but what the hell. I can get another one. There were more of them made than people think." He closed his eyes, breathed out, opened them again. "And now let's have that drink."

"No thanks."

"Sure? Sorry, forgot, you don't, do you? Very sensible. If there were more people like you, the world would be a better place. You know, this is wonderful. I feel like an enormous weight's been lifted off my shoulders. Thank you so much. You have no idea how much this means to me."

The weight of the bag was making her arms ache. "I didn't do it for you. I don't even know you."

"Of course not. Sorry, I'm just happy, that's all." He sighed. "Look, you must be worn out after your journey and everything, why don't you cut along to the mess tent and get something to eat?"

She looked at him, and just for a moment she had a vision of his body on a butcher's oak cutting table as she carefully jointed the carcass. It wasn't the sort of image that haunted her as a rule, and she wondered if she'd caught something from him. Oddly enough, though, she realised she was hungry. "Mess tent?"

He pointed. "Down the midway, third on the left. It's horrible, but you can eat as much as you like."

Actually it wasn't bad at all; there was a big all-day tureen of soup, all-sorts-of-things soup, with dry army bread that expanded to double its size when immersed in liquid, and rock-hard salt pork, and cartwheels of white crumbly cheese with a thick plaster rind. She ate till her jaws ached.

"There you are." Myrtus; she'd been busy with food and hadn't seen him coming. He looked round, then sat down beside her. "Something rather unpleasant has happened."

She swallowed her last mouthful with an effort. "What?"

Myrtus hesitated, then said, "Commissioner Corason's been murdered. They sent the news by special courier. Stabbed to death in his bed in Rasch."

It wasn't me, she very nearly said, because he was looking at her carefully. "That's terrible," she said. "Who did it?"

"That's the thing: we don't know. It doesn't make any sense. It wasn't robbery or a street brawl, he had no personal enemies."

"He was a Commissioner," she said, without thinking.

"Nobody knew that outside the Lodge."

"Then it must've been Imperial Security."

Myrtus shook his head. "You know better than that."

True; we'd have arrested him, not stabbed him in his sleep.

"You were the last Lodge officer to do business with him," Myrtus went on. "Did he say anything to you? Tell you anything?"

She went cold all over. The man asking the question was a Commissioner of the Lodge, and she was just about to lie to him.

"We discussed the job I'd just done," she said. "And he gave me my orders for this job."

"That was all?"

She couldn't bring herself to say yes, but she found she could nod.

Myrtus was tugging at his beard. "Makes no sense," he said. "People don't just get stabbed for no reason."

"Maybe there was something we don't know about."

That wasn't worthy of an answer. "Presumably he helped you, with the job you did in Blemya."

"Yes, of course. But that all went very smoothly."

"He'd have had friends, though. Dangerous people."

It took her a split second to figure out who *he* was. "No, actually, I don't think so. Plenty of friends while he was alive, but nobody who cared enough about him to do anything about it after he was dead."

(Except me, of course; and I have the perfect alibi.)

Myrtus sighed. "You're probably right," he said. "I never met the man, but I gather he didn't have any really close friends, and no family. It's a strange thing to say about the most popular man in the world, but I guess we can't really look there for a motive. Anyway." Myrtus took a deep breath, as if nerving himself to do something distasteful. "His death obviously leaves a vacancy, and you're it."

"What? Sorry, I don't—"

"They've decided to make you a Commissioner," Myrtus said. "Report to headquarters immediately for further orders. Oh, and congratulations, if you want them. Actually, it's a bloody awful job. I wouldn't wish it on my worst enemy."

He stood up; he was just a blur, because her head was swimming. "Me?"

"Yes, you. It goes without saying, your fellow Commissioners had no say in the matter. I imagine it's a reward for the Blemya thing, absolute loyalty and so on and so forth." He gazed at her as though she was an ugly new building spoiling a famous beauty spot. "You'd better be on your way," she said. "They don't like to be kept waiting."

She felt as though someone invisible was hitting her. "Headquarters?"

"Yes."

"Where's that?"

That got her a scowl of pure contempt. "Rasch," he replied. "You do know where that is, don't you?"

More news, delivered by a courier who died shortly afterwards from his wounds; Forza and Senza Belot had met in battle, sixteen miles south of Choris. They fought each other to a standstill; no reliable casualty figures yet, but the courier (who'd seen at least some of the action before running into a stray platoon of Eastern lancers, who left him for dead) reckoned that at least half, probably more, of both armies had been cut to pieces; later, on the road, he'd heard that Forza's Iron Brigade had broken and run on the left wing, while Senza's Immortals had done more or less the same on the right—impossible, because these were the great generals' crack troops, the best soldiers in the world, who'd rather die a thousand deaths than run ... In any event, there were uncorroborated rumours that Senza had withdrawn to the city, while Forza had been left with no alternative but to follow what was left of his retreating army, even though (strictly speaking, according to all the best scoring systems) he'd probably won the battle.

Myrtus and Axio immediately got out the maps; apparently she was included in the meeting, though she couldn't see she had anything to contribute. "Let's say they've each lost fifty per cent of their effectives," Myrtus said. "That's, what, twenty thousand each, give or take?"

Axio was grinning broadly. "More to the point, it sounds like they've reached the point where their best men just can't take it any more. I told you it'd come to that."

"If it's true," Myrtus conceded irritably. "But, yes, it looks like it, otherwise they wouldn't have pulled back." He'd been doing arithmetic on a scrap of paper. "They must be out of their tiny minds." He handed the paper to Axio, who whistled and gave it to her.

"What does this mean?" she said.

"It's our rough tally of how many men each side has left," Axio replied. "These columns on the right are what they've got in the field, and these are reserves they haven't called on yet. We've been keeping score for the last eighteen months."

She stared at the paper. Obviously she wasn't reading it right, because on the right-hand side, after scores of crossings-out, there were bottom-line totals of less than ten thousand under each heading, and nothing at all on the left. "I'm being stupid," she said. "Please explain it to me."

Myrtus snatched the paper back and glared at her. "It's obvious," he said. "Forza's got about nine thousand, Senza's down to about seven and a half, and there's no more reserves."

"No more—"

Axio shook his head. "Nobody left to enlist," he said. "Dead, deserted, made themselves scarce before the recruiting sergeants got to them. Both empires, by our calculations, have finally run out of men."

"No, but—" She broke off. Whatever she'd been about to say would have made no sense. "You mean, everybody's—"

Axio nodded. "Dead, or hopped it. Which means the military capability of both empires combined is sixteen and a half thousand men. We've just hired forty thousand from Blemya, and we've got thirty thousand horse-archers—"

"More like forty-five," Myrtus interrupted.

"All right, say forty thousand horse-boys. All paid for, all more or less in position." He smiled. "Which doesn't mean a damn thing," he added, "because Forza with nine or Senza with seven and a half could chew us up and spit us out, no bother at all, so we're not home yet, not by a mile. Still," he added cheerfully, "that's all right, because we aren't looking to pick a fight with either of them."

She looked at him. "I don't understand."

"We do nothing," Myrtus said sadly. "We hold our forces in reserve and avoid contact with either side. That's been the plan all along."

Axio laughed. "The plan they didn't tell him about when they made him commander-in-chief. That's why he's looking so miserable."

Nobody left; all dead, or run away. But that didn't seem to interest her fellow Commissioners. "So what's the plan?"

Axio shrugged. "Your guess is as good as mine," he said. "Now if I was running the show, I'd be looking to take out the Belot boys. Only, since that hasn't already happened, I'm guessing it's not possible, or, at least, not possible yet. Of course, we have the ace up our sleeves."

They looked at her; presumably she was supposed to be able to figure that one out for herself, if she was worthy to be a Commissioner of the Lodge. "Lycao," she said.

Axio clapped his hands. "Good girl," he said. "Yes, she's got to be the key, it stands to reason. Senza will do anything to get hold of her, that's one thing we can be sure of, and Forza knows that as well as we do. Therefore, Lycao's got to be it. How they plan on going about it, however, is anyone's guess. I don't know, maybe they'll tell you all about it in Rasch."

"I'm still going there, then."

"Of course you are," Myrtus said. "You've got orders. This doesn't change anything. Talking of which, it's time you were on your way. You can have that fancy coach you came in."

She was about to object when Axio said, "Tell you what, I'll come with you. Me and the boy. See to it that you don't come to any harm."

"You'd be a bloody fool if you did," Myrtus said quickly. "Rasch isn't safe for you and you know it."

"Safer than you think, actually," Axio said. "Everyone there who could make trouble for me is dead."

"There's a warrant out—"

"Six, actually, but that's old news. I don't suppose anybody remembers that far back. Besides, I've got friends there who'll see me right."

"You can't just go wandering off—"

Axio looked at him, and he fell abruptly silent. "Just had a thought," Axio said. "I'm my brother's next of kin. He must've been worth an angel or two. I wonder, did he make a will?"

She thought about it long and hard, when she should have been sleeping. Basically a matter of time and geometry. Three times out of five, when she imagined the scene in her head, she was able to kill Axio before Musen killed her. She considered various options for improving the odds—kill Musen first, surreptitiously half open the coach door and then kick him out, then stab Axio as he tried to catch him, find some excuse for leaving Musen behind at a way station, poison him the night before; poison Axio the night before. Try as she might, she couldn't get the odds to come out better than three in five. Also, Oida hadn't asked her to do it. Would he? She had to admit, she didn't know.

While they were loading the coach with supplies and Axio's luggage, she asked if she could have a word with him. "Sure," Axio said, and she followed him into a stable. "By the way," he went on, "I should be able to raise money in Rasch. I still owe you."

"I've got a message for you."

"What?"

"From your brother."

Axio frowned. "Before or during?"

"He asked me to deliver it just before he died."

"Ah. Right, let's hear it."

"He says, he forgives you."

"Does he indeed?"

"And he said to tell you," she went on, "the fifth card was a four."

Axio went bright red in the face. "Bastard," he snapped. "God damn it. I should've known. I really should have known."

She backed away a step. "You don't have to explain if you don't want to."

"He screwed me, is what it is. He took me for a bloody fool, and I let him." Axio sighed, and sat down on a rail. "I guess I was about sixteen, so he'd have been, what, thirteen and a bit? We were playing cards. He was a lousy card player. At least, I always beat the shit out of him. But there was this one time. We were playing Fives. You know the game?"

She shook her head.

"It's the same as ordinary Dragons' Teeth, but with five cards. And he had jack, ten, nine and some piece of rubbish, a two or a three, and I had three queens and a pair. Mine were all showing, of course, he had one card hidden, and he bet me his whole pile—sixty stuivers, I think it was, anyhow, a lot of money for us in those days. I couldn't match the bet, so I had to fold. Go on, then, I said, show me what you've got, and he refused. Said he didn't have to. I told him, he'd won, even if he'd been bluffing, and I wanted to see what he'd got. He said no, I wasn't entitled to. So I made a grab at him, and he jumped up and danced round the table a bit, I got a hold on his shirt front, and you know what he did? He ate the bloody card. Stuffed it in his mouth and chewed it up, just so I couldn't see. So I told him, tell me what it was or I'll smash your face in. He wouldn't tell me. And I kept on and on at him for years after, and he was just plain stupid-stubborn. I stole his best shirt and his new shoes, told him I'd put them on the fire if he didn't tell me what the card was. Fine, he said, go ahead, and he just stood there and watched them burn. Cracked two of his ribs once, and he wouldn't tell me." Axio sighed. "He had this nasty streak, you know, he liked to torment people, and it was the only way he knew he could get back at me. And all along it was a bloody four."

She drew a deep breath and let it out again. "You believe him, then."

"What, on his deathbed?"

She shrugged. "In his place, I'd have lied. If I'd had a queen or an eight, I mean. I'd rather leave you thinking I'd been screwing you all these years."

He gave her a look that genuinely scared her. "Four of what, did he say?"

"No. Just a four."

"Bastard. But that was always his problem. He never would admit it when he was beaten." His face stopped being scary and turned very sad. "You think he was lying?"

"I don't know. I just told you what I'd have done."

Axio shook his head and turned away. "You know what," he said. "I never realised he hated me so much." And then he burst into tears.

PART THREE

The repair to the bridge hadn't fallen to bits yet, so they had no trouble crossing the river, and the Great East was empty, so they flew along. Just as well. All her life, she'd dreaded boredom; stuck in a coach again, with nothing to read and no one to talk to. Axio slept most of the time; like a lizard, she thought, when there's nothing to do he conserves energy. Musen stared out of the window or went over and over his pack of cards, sometimes muttering under his breath, sometimes staring at them as though there was one blindingly obvious fact he knew he was missing, but he couldn't figure out what it was. The Lodge had packed them all sorts of nice things to eat and drink. Musen was the cook, and every bite and sup she took terrified her, because of what she'd nebulously planned to do to him, except that she didn't happen to have any poison with her, and noxious substances don't grow on trees, or at least they do, but you need to be able to identify them and know how to render them down. The only naturally occurring poison she knew enough about to be able to pick and use was a certain kind of green-capped mushroom, and that only grew in forests in the far South.

"Stewed chicken with mushrooms," Musen announced sadly,

pushing a bowl under her nose. Musen was a good cook, though he hated doing it. She tried picking out the bits of chicken, and wiping the sauce off when nobody was looking.

Axio snored; at night, not during the day. How he could sleep at all was a mystery to her, since he'd spent the whole day away with the fairies. It was one of those irregular snores that you simply can't ignore. You just have to lie there listening to it in horrified fascination. At least it gave her a chance to keep an eye on Musen, though he slept like a log from the moment he closed his eyes until Axio kicked him awake at daybreak.

More news at the last way station before Rasch. As a result of the big battle (not the one they'd heard about; another one), Forza Belot had been relieved of his command, and was now under house arrest at his wife's villa in the Cleir mountains. The emperor had sent an embassy to his uncle in the East, with a view to establishing a framework and timescale for preliminary negotiations; meanwhile, all the men in Rasch over fourteen and under sixty-five, including foreign nationals and resident aliens, had been called up to guard the walls in the event of a siege. The city gates were closed to everything except supply convoys; "so if you were planning on going there, you're out of luck, because they won't let you in."

Axio didn't seem particularly worried about that. He had a brief talk with Musen, which she wasn't allowed to join in; then Musen stole a horse and rode away, while they carried on in the coach as far as Beuda, the last village on the Great East that wasn't a suburb. Musen was waiting for them in the inn.

"Any luck?" Axio asked. Musen nodded, and led them to a

derelict barn on the western edge. Inside it they found a large cart loaded with barrels. "Apples," Musen said. "It was all I could get."

"Apples are fine," Axio replied. "Splendid. We're now a supply convoy."

Just to be on the safe side they painted the cart white, with some distemper Musen had managed to steal from somewhere. Attention to detail, Axio explained; the last thing we need is to get arrested for stealing a cart. Also, he added, in a whisper that Musen could've heard if he was stone deaf, it gives the boy something to do, keeps him out of mischief.

"If this is Rasch stocking up for a siege," Axio said, "they're being damned casual about it."

She was forced to agree. She'd anticipated a long, crawling line of carts and wagons, shuffling along at walking pace all the way from the Tenth Milestone to the Gate. Instead, they shared the road with three farm wagons and a big army cart, which was empty. But she didn't think it was any lack of urgency on the city prefects part. More likely, there simply wasn't any food left to buy, because there were no farmers left to grow it, and no money to pay for it.

Florian's Wall, which surrounds Rasch on three sides, is thirty feet high and ten feet thick, with guard towers every hundred yards and enfilading bastions every quarter-mile. The story goes that there was once a mountain overshadowing the city, where now there's a flat plain; Florian quarried the whole mountain to build the city wall, and still had to send out for more stone when the mountain had been used up. The story isn't true, because the walls are granite and basalt and Rasch is built on sandstone; that doesn't mean there isn't a flat plain somewhere else that was once a mountain, or a mountain range.

In the uncomfortable inner ring, between Florian's Wall and the outer ring, property has always been cheap, because that's where catapult shot and fire-arrows land during a siege; and Rasch has seen a lot of sieges. So the outer ring has traditionally been a ramshackle huddle of wattle-and-daub or wooden houses, shacks, warehouses, workshops, crammed with expendable enterprises and expendable people, a place where money is made but not spent. From time to time there's a fire, which serves the useful function of cleaning up the godawful mess, and then they rebuild and pretty soon it's all back to normal—

There had been a fire, but they weren't rebuilding. They were *ploughing*.

"Quite right," someone told them at the Poverty and Patience in Goosefair. "Prefect's orders. They torched the whole lot, and they're ploughing it up, going to grow barley and cabbages and stuff. Three days' notice they gave, and they shut the inner ring gates so the poor sods couldn't get into the city. No idea where they went: the soldiers pushed them out through the gate and told them not to come back. Makes sense, of course. They'd just be more hungry mouths to feed when Senza comes."

Quite. You could grow a good crop in the outer ring: all that ash, on top of generations of haphazard sanitation soaking away into the ground. "If Senza comes," Axio asked him, "are you going to stick around?"

The stranger shrugged. "Might as well," he said. "Nobody's going to buy my business with that hanging over us, and it's all

I've got. Anyway, a siege isn't so bad, if you're prepared for it. And they can't get past Florian's Wall, not even Senza, so it'll just be a sitting-down match. And old Glauca can't last for ever, can he?"

"This is worrying," Axio said, when they'd found a private table in the corner. "I have a nasty feeling someone in the government's got a brain, and isn't afraid to use it."

She forced a smile. "Surely not."

"It had to happen, sooner or later. Besides, they've tried everything else. Like the old saying, when all else fails, think."

"All right," she said. "So what's the new plan?"

"I should say it's quite obvious when you look at the facts. Forza's out; they're getting ready for a really long siege. So, someone has finally figured out that the war can't be won on the battlefield. Sure, they've got Forza, but the East's got Senza, and so long as those two are alive, they cancel each other out—which would be fine, except that while they've been at it, most of the male population of the empires have been turned into fertiliser. So, Plan B. Get rid of Forza, recall what's left of the army to garrison Rasch. What happens? Five minutes later, Senza arrives and sits down outside the gate. But he can't storm Florian's Wall, nobody can. So there he sits, thinking up more and more desperately ingenious ways of feeding his army. Inside the city, we sow and reap and winnow corn where the common people used to live, your basic agrarian idyll, and in ten or fifteen years' time, Emperor Glauca dies and the war's over. And the West wins, by default. The rest of the Western empire doesn't matter, it's mostly a wilderness now, and what little is left of it won't come to any harm, because the East can't spare any men from the siege of Rasch to do any real damage. Then, when the day comes when Glauca finally breathes his last and we're all just one big happy family once again—" He shrugged. "It'd be easy to say, so why did nobody think of it earlier? But to be fair, it can only work once both sides have withered away down to the bone."

She didn't ask why that would be worrying. She was sure Axio could answer that, but she didn't want to hear it.

Being in Rasch again made her skin crawl. She'd lost track of how long it had been since she'd broken out of the most secure prison in the city, leaving a trail of dead bodies behind her. It felt like a hundred years; but there must still be plenty of people here who knew her by sight. Don't worry about it, Axio said airily; you're with me, you'll be just fine. But that in itself was a contradiction in terms, so she didn't put much faith in it. "I've lost count of how many warrants there are out on me," he went on, "but I don't let it get to me. Besides, they've got other things on their minds right now. Trust me; nobody gives a damn."

They turned a corner, and suddenly they were in Golden Cross Yard. "Just a minute," she said. "Where are we going?"

"Headquarters. Weren't you listening?"

The south entrance to Intelligence was in the north-east corner of Golden Cross Yard. "I can't go there," she said. "I'll be seen. People I used to work for."

"You worry too much."

She drew back, but he grabbed her scientifically round the neck, his thumb jammed in her windpipe. Her head started to swim. She staggered. He was laughing; his other arm was holding her up; a handsome man and his drunk girl, and of course they wouldn't be looking at her, because everyone always looked at Axio. She tried to speak but couldn't. He hustled her along so fast she could barely keep her feet. He was going to turn her in to the authorities rather than kill her himself, and if she tried to shake herself free she'd fall flat on her face. Then thinking through the fog got too difficult; her strength ebbed away, and Axio swept her up in his arms, like the handsome prince in a fairytale.

"Here we are." His voice came from far away. "Steady now," and she felt the ground under her feet. Her knees buckled, but his strong, reliable arm was there to support her. "Deep breaths, there's a good girl."

It hurt so much to breathe; he'd nearly crushed her throat, and her lungs burned. "Told you it'd be fine," he said, looping her hair round his hand so that he could control her head as surely as a horseman with a tight rein."Now, take a moment to get your breath: we've got stairs to climb."

She contemplated kicking his kneecap with her heel, but she simply didn't have the strength. Across her mind flashed an image of her mother, scowling at her; be good, or the monster will get you. Well, she thought, she'd been right about that. She felt her scalp lift off her skull, and knew he'd pull it off if he felt he had to. There was a stone step under her foot, and then another one. A knee in the back of her knee straightened her leg for her.

"Come on," Axio said brightly. "We haven't got all day."

She let go, neither resisting nor cooperating; forty-seven steps. She'd been in and out and round about this building for years, but she had no idea where she was, and the heavy oak door they stopped in front of was completely new to her. Axio leaned past her and banged on it with his head. A moment later, it opened. She saw a long, narrow room like a gallery, with one small window. Three chairs facing her, one with its back to her. In two of the chairs sat a man and a woman. The man she recognised: Thratta, senior assistant archivist, nominally a big man in Security but he ran his own show off on the sidelines somewhere, and what he did and where he did it nobody else knew or cared. The other one she felt she ought to know: a striking looking woman with a thin, taut face, maybe a year or so younger than her, hair scraped back and firmly secured, as though if it got loose it might be dangerous.

"Sorry we're late," Axio sang out. He deposited her in the single chair by tripping her feet out from under her; she landed square on the seat, very neatly done. Then he sat down with the other two. "Sorry," he went on, "introductions. Well, Thratta you know, obviously. And this is 'Na Lycao."

In spite of everything, she couldn't help being fascinated; Senza's Lycao, for whom the world would be well lost. She realised she was staring. Lycao gazed back at her. Obviously, she's used to it. Everybody wants to see the most beautiful, enchanting woman in the world. Nobody can possibly imagine what he sees in her. Fine. Telamon blushed and looked away.

"Congratulations," Lycao said.

Which made absolutely no sense at all. Congratulations on what? On escaping from the Guards? Getting as far as she had before Axio brought her back? "Excuse me?"

"On your appointment as Commissioner," Thratta said. He

was a round-faced old man with a beard and no moustache; that fashion had lasted a couple of years, thirty years ago. "Excuse me, but are you all right?"

"I'm sorry, I didn't realise—" She tried to take a deep breath, but her throat still hurt terribly where Axio had creased it. "Sorry, but who are you?"

Axio laughed. "We're the Triumvirs, of course. No, hang on, you won't have heard of us. Basically, we run the Lodge, under the supreme boss. Among other things, we choose the Commission. You're here to be sworn in, remember?"

Headquarters. In a room in the Intelligence building. And Thratta—just because he was old and fat and so very, very boring, they'd all assumed he was simply marking time until he retired and drew his pension. She remembered the proverb Oida had told her once: what's the deadliest creature in Blemya? The elephant? The lion? The buffalo? The black mamba? No, the mosquito.

"Of course," she said with a smile. "What have I got to do?"

Thratta yawned. "There isn't actually a prescribed ritual, and, if there was, we haven't got time for it right now. Do you accept the job? Say yes."

"Yes."

"Splendid. In accepting the job, of course, you're automatically deemed to have bound yourself to obey all the rules and carry out the orders of your superiors without question. Do you understand?"

"Yes. What are the rules?"

Thratta smiled bleakly. "We don't know. If we need to know them, they tell us. Of course, if we inadvertently break them, ignorance of the rules is no excuse."

She nodded. "I understand," she said.

Axio burst out laughing. "Don't take any notice of him," he said, "he just likes to tease, that's all. Just raise your right hand swear you'll do as you're told. That's what I did," he added, when Thratta scowled at him.

"I promise to do as I'm told," she said. "Was that all right?"

Lycao was looking at her, and she felt all the fight drain out of her, like milk out of a cracked bucket. She managed not to apologise.

"All right," Axio said. "Now let's move on." He steepled his fingers and rested his hands on his knees. "We have a job for you."

"Yes."

"We want you to kill Forza Belot."

Dead silence, for about as long as it takes to pour a glass of wine. "You mean Senza."

Lycao shook her head. "Forza," she said.

"Very well."

Thratta raised his eyebrows. "Either she's as cool as snow or she's not going to do it," he said.

"She'll do it, don't you worry." Axio was looking straight at her. "Won't you?"

"Yes."

"There." Axio was grinning. "Done and dusted."

"But I'd like to know," she went on, "why Forza? He's irrelevant now, surely. He's been dismissed and disgraced."

"For the time being," Lycao said. "But when I kill his brother, Forza will be the best soldier in the world."

"I see." She tried to breathe. The difficulty she experienced had something to do with the imprint of Axio's thumb, but not all that much. "Can you help me out at all, or am I on my own?"

Axio laughed and clapped his hands. "See what I mean?" he said. "She's a tiger."

Thratta ignored him. "We can get you in close," he said, "and give you all the background you need. What we can't do is undertake to get you out again afterwards. If you can manage that on your own, naturally we'll be delighted to see you again."

A bell rang, somewhere not far away. She recognised it at once: the solo treble at the Golden Horn, marking the quarter-watch. "Hellfire," Axio said, jumping out of his seat, "is that the time? We'd better be making a move. They'll be wanting the room," he explained with a grin. "Thratta, can we use the back stairs?"

"If you're quick."

Axio grabbed her wrist and pulled her out of the room; as she left, she caught a brief glance of Lycao, stopping to make sure her hair wasn't coming loose. Then more stairs; up, across a landing, and suddenly she knew where she was—the far end of the archive block, directly above the stables. Now she came to think of it, the geometry of that part of the building had never made sense—

You're taking a big risk, she was about to say, then realised: no, not really. At quarter-watch, the grooms and stable boys would be having their customary unofficial break, sitting round in the tack room drinking cider. A sally port in the far corner of the main stable led directly onto the street, though only four officers of the Department had a key.

Four plus Axio; from a feed bin he produced two hooded gowns, covered in dust and chaff. He thrust one at her, slipped into the other one-handed. The key was in the pocket of his gown. He pulled her hood down over her face, grabbed the lapel and pulled her through the door into the narrow alley, then pulled the door to and locked it.

"Shame you don't drink," he said. "I'd buy you one at the Charity and Grace."

"I can't go in there."

"Can't you?"

"Barred for life," she said. "Rowdy behaviour."

He gave her a look of deep respect. "Obviously you're my kind of girl," he said. "All right, how about the Temperance?"

"The where?"

"The Temperance Vindicated. You know, in North Parade."

"I've never been there."

"Dear God. And they made you a Commissioner."

She reminded herself that in his pocket was a small rosewood box. He led the way. He knew all the short cuts. When they got there, he ordered Blemyan attar. It didn't look like that sort of bar. The man went away and came back with a dusty bottle and two tiny horn cups.

"This doesn't count as drinking," he said, and poured. She'd never had attar. It was nauseatingly sweet and tasted of roses.

"There's one question I've got to ask you," he said. "My brother could've had any woman he wanted, but he chased after you for years and you never gave him a tumble. That's right, isn't it?"

"Yes."

"Why, for crying out loud? He had all that money. He'd have married you, you know."

"Quite possibly, yes."

"You could've been a fine lady. Packed in the business, spent your time doing whatever you wanted to—reading books, isn't it? Quite the bluestocking."

She didn't answer. It didn't seem to matter.

"So why the hell not? You were quite fond of him, weren't you?"

She smiled at him. "Are you deliberately trying to annoy me?"

He looked offended. "God, no, I'm just curious. Very, very curious. I mean, it's no secret you've had a hard life, constant struggle, never had any money because you always sent every last stuiver home. You could've put all that behind you. And he was an attractive man, very charming, he could be very thoughtful and considerate when he wanted to. Smart, too. Read the same sort of books you like. And yet you never showed the slightest inclination—"

"Forza Belot," she said. "It's a suicide mission, isn't it?"

He scowled at her. "Doesn't have to be," he said, after a while.

"Really?"

"It all depends," he said, refilling her cup. "Now, I wouldn't claim to be a tactician in the Belot class, but I know there's a smart way and a stupid way of going about everything. The stupid way will get you killed. The smart way—" He turned his scowl into a smile. He really was very good-looking. "I'd need to think about it," he said. "And of course we'd need all the inside information we could get."

"We."

"Sure. Right now, the Lodge has no orders for me, which makes a pleasant change. So, what do I do with all this unaccustomed free time? I could wander off somewhere, enjoy myself, maybe make a bit of money. Or I could help you out with this job of yours. Two heads are better than one, especially when one of them's mine."

"Is that right."

"Yes, actually. This job would've been right up my street, as it happens. I look at it this way. When you want someone killed, either you send a soldier or a criminal. The soldier's got one way of thinking about things and going about things, the criminal's got another. Now I happen to be both, and very good at both, though I do say so myself. You, I would imagine, would set about this job by getting inside either passing yourself off as a servant or climbing up a drainpipe. You'll have a map and a floorplan; if you're lucky you'll have paid or blackmailed someone to leave doors and windows unbolted for you. Basically, though, you're on your own. Am I right?"

"Go on."

"A soldier, on the other hand, would think in terms of a strike force of fifty or so picked men, light cavalry; surround the place just before daybreak, wedge all the doors shut except one, set fire to the thatch, kill everyone as they come running out. Two perfectly valid approaches."

"Could I have fifty light cavalry?"

"Don't see why not. All the resources of the Lodge are at your disposal."

"Oh. I hadn't realised."

"That's because you're still thinking like a field-grade. Sure, you could have two hundred and fifty if you wanted them, or five hundred. But fifty would be about the optimum number, for speed and efficiency. You've got to get them there, remember, and five hundred horsemen can be a bit conspicuous in open country." He smiled. "I was right, you're a criminal. Nothing wrong with that," he hastened to reassure her, "but you see? Already you've deprived yourself of a great many perfectly viable options, and you haven't even started yet."

"Could I have siege engines?"

He frowned. "In theory, yes. Of course, we'd have to build them on site, or ship them prefabricated for assembly when we got there. More trouble than it's worth, in my opinion."

She beamed at him. "And if I've got an army and an artillery battery, I'd have to have a uniform to match. One of those muscle cuirasses, silver-plated, and a Mezentine helmet with a big red plume."

He sighed. "If you don't want my help, just say so. But I've read your file, I know how you go about things, and if you do this job in your usual way, you'll probably succeed and you'll probably get killed. Or I could help you. Please note, I've done loads of this kind of thing, and *I'm* still alive."

She looked at him. "What will all this cost me?"

He looked right back at her. "Guess."

"You want what Oida never managed to get."

"Correct."

She stood up. "I'll think about it," she said. "Now, will you go away or shall I?"

"I'll stay and finish the bottle," he said with a yawn. "Mind how you go. You're top of the most wanted list, remember."

She hadn't forgotten. Nor had it escaped her that she no longer had a job, therefore no income, therefore no money when she'd spent what she had on her, unless she was prepared to risk stealing. All the safe places she used to go were almost certainly known to the Department. She had no idea where she was going to sleep tonight, or where she was going to hide until bedtime, or how to contact her fellow Triumvirs. She hadn't eaten since breakfast, and the horrible sweet alcohol had made her hungry. Axio, she was quite certain, could deal with all these problems for her, and probably knew a quiet little Aelian place somewhere that did the most amazing smoked lamb casserole. "I'm still thinking," she said, and sat down again.

"Of course. I wouldn't want you to rush into anything. Have another drink. Something else."

"I don't suppose you know a good teahouse."

"As a matter of fact, I do. You'll love it."

For what? Safety? Security? Better the devil you know? It would be, she told herself, no big deal. She'd undergone more painful experiences, more degrading ordeals. Anything you can limp away from, anything that eventually heals up and leaves no obvious scar; her long-standing definition of no big deal, in context. Senza Belot had broken her arm, a guard in a corridor in Lox Dardaen had cracked two of her ribs; she'd starved, fallen from a moving coach into a thorn bush, gone two days with a dislocated shoulder; she'd been sold by her mother to the bilberry-pickers and lived for five years in a cage. She encouraged her mind to dwell on what the Department would do to her if they caught her—true, they were seriously under-staffed these days, but the brutal men in the lower pay grades hadn't been Craftsmen; they'd still be there, just doing their job and doing it very well. If not that, then, what? She supposed it was something to do with not wanting Axio to win. But Oida was alive, so his brother's victory was a deception; it wouldn't matter, it was no big deal. I should have killed him when I had the chance, she told herself; and it occurred to her that she had the chance right now. The alley they were walking down was secluded and deserted, he was off guard, or as off his guard as he was ever likely to be. She'd been successful under far more unpromising conditions (doing her job, doing it very well). Yes, she argued, but he's a Triumvir, he *is* the Lodge, a third of its heart and brain—which was impossible, surely, a monster holding high office in the institution she was sworn to obey without question, which she believed in absolutely and without reservation. The Great Smith finds use for us all, and turns our defects into talents. How many times had she been the monster, to perfect strangers, inoffensive men and women whose exist- ence had become inconvenient, soldiers and domestic servants who simply happened to be in the way? The forge doesn't call the anvil black. The hammer has no right to withhold its hard- ened face from the blow. The function of all utensils, living or otherwise, is to do as they're told.

Yes, but he's off duty, he said so himself. She didn't deign to respond to that one.

The teahouse was quiet, private and really rather charming; I must remember this place, she told herself, and come here again—and then she remembered that in all probability she wouldn't be going anywhere again, and definitely not in Rasch; but so long as she was with Axio, apparently she was safe. That safety came at a price, but it was one which, by any objective accountancy, she could afford. No big deal. Grit your teeth and get it over with, and then we can toddle along and murder Forza Belot.

They did those wonderful sweet, sticky rice cakes, and the white foam buns with sweet and savoury fillings, which she'd been convinced you couldn't get anywhere in Rasch. And for a companion she had a man who was urbane, witty, cultivated, intelligent, well-informed about a surprisingly wide range of topics. Charm came more naturally to him than to his brother. Presumably it ran in the family, like white-blond hair or a strong chin, though such traits suit some family members more than others. You knew that when Oida was being charming he was after something, even if it was only your temporary happiness. With Axio, it was more natural, more fluent, something he could do without thinking; there was no need for him to turn on the charm, the terms of the deal would inform her decision, not pretty table manners. No; he was being charming because he could, because it came effortlessly, so why not? So she tried to put herself into his mind; what's he really thinking right now, what's his mind and his will gnawing away at, what's he up to? She realised she had no idea, but whatever it was, she was at most only peripheral to it. Which didn't fit the monster hypothesis. When the monster is stalking you, you don't expect its mind to be on something else. You have a right to be the centre of attention; and if you're not, it's probably not a monster. But that wasn't true, as witness the guards and maidservants and clerks and political officers she'd stabbed to death almost absently, while thinking three moves ahead about the job in hand. Of course, that would only apply if she was the monster, too. And the only thing that kept her from being the monster was the Lodge, of which Axio was a third—

Years ago she'd owned a ring: quite old, genuine Mezentine, and the blue-tinged solitaire diamond hinged sideways, to allow you to tip a lethal dose of poison into your companion's tea bowl. But she'd lost it long since, and that was probably just as well; saved her from solving her problem the easy way, which might not necessarily be the right way. Besides, it's generally safer to suffer harm rather than to inflict it. Then at least the aggrieved party is someone you know, and who you can generally count on to be reasonable.

After two bowls of tea and a second plate of cakes, he asked, "Have you decided yet?"

In the event, it was pretty much what she'd expected; he was skilful, confident, accomplished, almost as though he was giving an exhibition or an illustrated lecture—this is how we go about this particular manoeuvre, this is something a lot of people have trouble with, but actually if you do it this way it's not difficult at all, this one is surprisingly effective, and this is my speciality, not many people can do this but I can. It occurred to her to wonder who he was giving the lesson to—and then she realised, it was obvious, who do you think?

Afterwards he slept; he snored, and hogged the bedclothes. If he had bad dreams, he gave no sign of it. As for her, the snoring made sleep impossible, so she lay staring at the ceiling until the oil in the lamp was all used up, trying to figure out how she was going to kill Forza Belot.

Axio had told her everything he knew about Forza's villa

in the Cleir foothills. Actually, it had been his wife's father's country house, a painstaking forgery of a *fin de siècle* gentleman's residence but done to a budget; the walls were brick faced with marble, the central dome was lath and plaster, the mosaics were paint, and so on. When Forza got his hands on it, he immediately saw that it was about as defensible as an eggshell, which wouldn't do at all; his wife would be left there while he was away on campaign, and Senza knew that he could end the war at a stroke if he got possession of her. So he'd misappropriated the services of half the corps of engineers and had the place done out in ashlar. There were three concentric half-moon walls, backing on to the mountain, twelve feet high and three feet thick, topped with razor-sharp flints set in mortar. The gates had been intended for the state arsenal at Laten but they got lost in the book-keeping and somehow made their way out here: three-ply oak with the grain crossed, swinging on hardened steel hinges and pintles. If the arrangements had a weakness, it was the number of men needed to garrison them. You'd need fifty for the outer wall, forty for the middle and twenty-five for the inner. Entirely practicable and in accordance with the standard loss ratios for a frontal assault—five to one for the outer wall, so by the time you'd lost ten and fallen back to the middle, the enemy would have lost fifty; seven to one for the middle, ten to one for the inner—by the time the defenders fell back into the house itself, they should have accounted for two hundred and five of the enemy, whose acceptable-loss ratio would be at most one in five, requiring him to muster over a thousand men before he would even consider launching his attack. A thousand men would be visible twenty miles away on the flat plain, giving the family plenty of time to evacuate and go to ground in the horrible rocky wasteland of the Cleir—there were caves up there, any God's amount of them; unless you were very lucky it'd take you a year to flush them out, by which time your men would have mutinied, deserted or starved, provided the defenders hadn't already decimated them with hit-and-run attacks.

Artillery probably wouldn't help a great deal. From the outer wall to the house was three hundred yards as the chamois leaps, and the best trebuchet the Lodge engineers could build from scratch on site had a range of two hundred, pitching incendiaries. If you used your artillery to pulverise the outer wall it wouldn't help you close the range, since the gradient was so steep thereafter that there was nowhere an engine could stand and shoot without toppling over. Besides, by the time your artillery train had rumbled across the dusty plain, everybody worth killing would be long gone.

That would seem to rule out the military option; so what scope was there for the enterprising criminal? The staff had all been in the service of Forza's in-laws for generations. They were exclusively recruited from five villages where everybody knew and was related to everybody else, so there was little hope of a stranger being able to pass herself off as newly hired staff, with or without cooperation from the inside. You might just be able to scramble over the outer wall on a dark night without attracting the attention of a sentry, but the main house had just the one massive door and all the windows were shuttered at night; you could climb the wall at night and hide somewhere until daybreak, but there were sentries on guard all round the house day and night, so shinning up the house wall in broad daylight was pure fantasy. Deliveries? Food and supplies came up from the villages in open carts and were searched three times before they reached the house; all the suppliers were tenants of the family, known by sight and by name. Drainage was a single garderobe on the mountain side, gurgling away down the sheer face of a cliff into a cesspool so noisome that grass wouldn't grow for ten yards all around. The conclusion was, the defences had been designed by someone who kept asking himself, what would Senza Belot do, and knowing the answer.

There was one obvious way in. The aspiring assassin would present herself at the front guard-house and produce valid credentials identifying her as an accredited representative of the Lodge. She would then be escorted directly into the presence, where (if she was very quick and clever) she'd just have enough time to stab Forza Belot before his bodyguards tore her to pieces.

Like many heavy sleepers, Axio was a morning person; once he was awake, he was bouncy and bounding with energy, keen to get on and set about the day's business. He washed in cold water, did his morning exercises, drank a pint of last night's cold tea, dressed and combed his hair with a little silver comb. "Sleep well?" he asked.

"No."

"I'll see about some breakfast."

He went away, giving her time to get out of bed and throw some clothes on. He returned with hot tea, bread rolls, three types of cheese and a selection of fruit on a brass tray.

"It can't be done," she said.

"What? Oh, you mean Forza."

"It's impossible," she said. "The whole place is done up tighter than a drum."

He grinned. "And you want your money back. Relax. There's a way. Actually, it's very simple. If you think about it."

She waited, but he didn't seem inclined to discuss the matter further. Instead, he was packing, throwing things into a bag: shirts, spare pair of boots, comb, a small rosewood box. She stared at it for the brief time it was visible, but he didn't seem to have noticed.

"You wanted artillery," he said.

They'd ridden, on two very fine horses (at a time when anything with four legs that wasn't obviously a pig had been impounded by the cavalry requisitions board) as far as Tin Chirra, once a rather disreputable suburb where rich merchants stabled their mistresses, in timber-frame houses faced with stone cladding. Senza had burned it to the ground during the recent unpleasantness, but a shanty town had since sprung up, cobbled together from commissariat timber and sailcloth rejected by the navy. Tin Chirra was still mostly populated by women and children, but the dresses weren't nearly as colourful.

"Well?"

They'd stopped outside one of the more substantial structures, basically four unserviceable masts and half a dozen galley sails, with a pallet wood door. Someone had painted a sign: *Rightousness Ascendent*. Whoever it was couldn't spell.

"In there."

"Our artillery?"

"In a sense."

You had to lift the door to get it open; its hinges were twisted rope, nailed to the frames. Inside were long trestle tables, government-issue, and benches, likewise. At the far end was a rack of barrels, all burned with the double-eagle brand. Which made sense. Ever such a lot of perfectly good, useful property gets mislaid during a war, either because someone steals it en route to its designated user, or it gets lost in the registers, or its owners have no further use for it, being dead. Half the benches were occupied, mostly by men. Now that was unusual.

They looked up when Axio walked in. He made a sign to one of them, who nodded and got up; the rest followed. "Things are made out of materials and skill," Axio said. "This is the skill."

They formed up outside in groups of ten; there were fifty of them. Most of them carried tools in canvas bags. They didn't speak. Axio handed one of them a leather satchel she hadn't noticed before: wages, in advance.

"How are we going to get these people to the Cleir mountains?" she whispered. "They're going to stick out a mile."

He beamed at her. "No, not really."

And he was quite right. The carts were just like the ones Saevolus had used. The shackles were an inspired touch. A foreman went from cart to cart locking them in, then handed the driver the key. "You've got a signed warrant," she said. "Of course."

"Actually it's forged," Axio admitted. "But very nicely done. Did it myself, as it happens."

No real mystery. Two months ago, these men had been passengers on these very same carts, wearing these very same shackles, until a half-squadron of Lodge cavalry intercepted them on the way to Eousa. Their freedom, just as soon as they'd done a little job for the Lodge. A very good deal, and one they'd been happy to accept. Not that they looked happy. She asked one of the drivers where they were from, originally. Oh, all sorts of places, he replied; Aelia, Scheria, Scona Major, Meroe, the four corners of the earth. No chance of ever going home, it went without saying; but it's better to be free than a slave, isn't it, and once the war was over they'd be able to name their own wages, skilled men like them; they could settle down, build new lives, become pillars of new communities, provided they had the energy to bother.

Axio wanted to ride at the head of the column, so they did. She could tell, the role of master of a slave caravan appealed to him. "Materials?" she asked.

"Don't worry about that. Grows on trees."

At Dui Chirra, fifteen miles further out, they picked up another seven wagons, containing ninety men, similarly chained but different somehow; they were just as quiet, but she could sense a sort of subdued energy that the carpenters so obviously lacked. Also they were younger, and better fed. "Our infantry," Axio explained. "Lodge regulars. The seventh wagon's their kit."

"This is all wrong," she said. "Saevolus' caravans have large cavalry escorts."

"Funny you should mention that."

The horsemen joined them at Boulomai, eight miles down the road; forty no Vei, who suddenly appeared out of a spinney of outgrown fir. "They were the hard part," Axio explained.

"Hard to explain away, when everyone knows they've gone over to us. Mind you, these days, who's in a position to pick a fight with forty horse-boys?"

She did the arithmetic: fifty engineers, ninety infantry, forty cavalry. One hundred and eighty. Even with artillery, the ratios called for a thousand, and that was ignoring the fact that the defence was led by Forza Belot. "This isn't going to work," she said.

"You'll see."

Supplies of food, beer and firewood were waiting for them in barns and derelict sheds at intervals of roughly twenty miles. She was impressed. Quite apart from the level of organisation, which was several orders of magnitude better than the empire had ever managed, there was the simple fact that the Lodge had managed to find food, and beer, and firewood, in deserted, overgrown country. Axio grinned. "There's still a few people left," he said, "in more remote areas. Women and old men mostly. Of course, they'd never have been able to make it if we hadn't taken them under our wing, so to speak."

"In return for a few simple jobs now and again?"

"Exactly." He smiled. "We aren't a charity, you know. Besides, free handouts never did anyone any good. You know the old saying. Teach a man to fish, and all that."

At Mavova they picked up fifteen stonemasons. "You can't just shoot any old lump of rock out of a trebuchet," Axio explained. "The shot has to be rounded and smoothed, which is skilled work. Isn't it wonderful, the way we're encouraging the essential trades? When the war's over—"

"The war will never be over," she said angrily, then wondered why. "I mean, it's gone on so long. I simply can't imagine a world without it."

"Try." The usual grin turned into a solemn gaze. "It'll happen, and sooner than you think. And then we'll have a new world to build, exactly how we want it. Note the word *build*. Things won't just accrue, like silt in a riverbed, by accident or the accumulated whims and mistakes of generations of self-interested halfwits. Things will happen for a *reason*. It's going to be just grand, I promise you."

The villa had been built for easy access to major lines of communication; it's important for important people to be able to run up to town to see to business. The Northern Strategic Road was six miles from the main gate.

A horseman rode up, stopped about two hundred yards away, then rode away again. "Of course they're watching us," Axio said cheerfully. "That's why we've gone to all this trouble to look harmless. They'll only realise we're a threat when we turn off the Northern Strategic and start rumbling up their front drive. By then, of course, it'll be too late."

"Out of interest," she said, "Senza was here recently. It wouldn't have been a problem for him to send a double squadron of cavalry and raze this lot to the ground. Why didn't he?"

Axio shrugged. "Forza wasn't there," he said. "I guess. Or maybe he considered it wouldn't be sporting. If I knew how he plans his campaigns, I'd be a military genius. Instead, I'm just very, very good."

"It's what I'd have done."

"Quite probably. But then, we agreed, you're a criminal, and

your origins are decidedly lower class. Not that there's anything
wrong with that," he conceded generously. "It just means your
mind works in a certain way, which is ideally suited for certain
specific purposes. Other stuff you simply don't understand.
And why should you?"

"I'd have hit this place hard and fast and captured Forza's
wife. He's crazy about her, everybody knows that. He could've
won the war at a stroke."

"In which case, I assume she wasn't there. You see," he added
with a gentle smile, "there's a logical answer to every mystery, if
only you stop and think."

They came to a large stand of ash trees, maybe six or seven acres.
The carts stopped and the carpenters got out. "From now on,"
Axio said, "our intentions will be blindingly obvious, so we
need to be a bit careful. I don't imagine Forza will mount a pre-
emptive strike, he can't afford any losses, but you never know
with military geniuses."

The thought, which hadn't occurred to her, scared her stiff.
So much so that—"Do we really need the artillery?" she said.
"I mean, from what you've been telling me, it won't make a lot
of difference, since the whole idea looks like it's doomed from
the outset."

He laughed. "We need the artillery," he said.

"Look." She gave him her best no-nonsense look. "I know
you love being mysterious and clever, but would it kill you to
let me know what the plan is?"

He gave her a fake scowl. "Security," he replied. "Need to
know. It'll be fine, don't worry about it."

By the time the carts and the horsemen were ready to move on, the carpenters had already dropped a dozen mature ash trees, and were bustling about lopping off the brash. "I told them," Axio said, "the sooner they start, the sooner they'll finish, and then they're free to go. If they really get a move on, maybe they'll be gone before Forza gets here. Nothing like giving people an incentive if you want results."

She shivered. Apart from the ash wood, the surrounding country was open, flat and bare, nowhere to run, nowhere to hide. "If I was Forza, I'd definitely hit us now, before we're ready. I mean, why wait till we've got siege engines?"

His smirk was actually rather reassuring; it said, I know something you don't know, and that something makes all the difference in the world. She devoutly hoped so.

They saw horsemen all the rest of the day: two or three riders, never closer than six hundred yards. "Oh, he's got our number, no doubt about it," Axio said, as though it didn't matter at all.

"Did you leave any soldiers to guard the carpenters?"

He shook his head. "Wish I could've, but we couldn't spare any. They'll be fine."

She lay awake all night, terrified out of her wits, listening for the crack of a twig or the jingle of a stirrup, but all she heard was Axio snoring and the drip of rain on the canvas of the wagon. Dawn came up slow and grudging, soaking the wide sky with red. Forza had neglected to strike them down as they slept, and she couldn't understand why.

Around mid-morning they turned off the road. Shortly after noon, they came over the crest of a long, steep hill and saw below them a shining white house nestling in the gulleys of the lower slopes of a bare-rock mountain. Her first reaction was: how beautiful. Then she remembered what she was here for, and looked for the defensive walls, which weren't hard to spot. All she knew about strategic and tactical theory was what she'd read and failed to understand in technical manuals, so she was hardly qualified to judge, but how he thought he was going to break in there she had absolutely no idea.

"Please tell me," she said, "that your wonderful plan doesn't involve attacking downhill from the side of that mountain. There's no way in hell—"

He grinned. "Actually," he said, "that's the closest you've got so far, though you're still a mile or so wide of the mark." He pointed, apparently at the mountain. "There," he said. "In plain sight. Can you see it?"

"I don't know. What am I looking for?"

"Ah," he said gravely. "That'd be telling."

She didn't want to give him the satisfaction of staring for too long, so she quickly gave up and pretended not to be interested. But the only thing she'd seen that might conceivably be relevant was a thin plume of smoke drifting upwards in the still air from the mountainside. A signal? Maybe, but signifying what? Like I give a damn, she said to herself, fooling nobody.

Everything they did was plainly visible from the house, so there were no more horsemen buzzing them; they had the world to themselves, as far as the eye could see. Axio chivvied the Lodge infantry out of the wagons and drew them up in a long, painfully thin line about five hundred yards from the outer wall, while the horse-archers clustered on the right wing. They didn't seem bothered by what was going on; mostly they talked to each other in low, cheerful voices, and occasionally one of them laughed, as if at a joke or some familiar story. She'd read somewhere that one of the horse-tribes believed that the dead don't go anywhere after they die. They hang around more or less where they've always been, following the wagons and the flocks, raising and folding their tents, drinking milk, eating cheese. The only difference is that we can't see them, or their horses, sheep, goats, wagons, tents. We share the same space; if we happen to coincide with one of them, we walk right through them, or they walk through us, depending on your point of view. Whether they can see us is unknown and mildly disputed among the wise and learned; the consensus view is, they can see us but they really aren't interested. She had no idea if the people who believed this were the no Vei or one of the other nations. The truth was, they all looked pretty much alike to her, though she wouldn't dream of saying so.

Axio was busy seeing to things—she was deeply impressed by his tireless grasp of and attention to detail, though watching him made her feel desperately tired—and so wasn't available for questions and idle chat. She tried to keep from getting under everyone's feet; and there was an interesting point, because hadn't the Triumvirs (one of whom was here with her, doing all the work) given *her* the ghastly job of assassinating Forza Belot? But, as far as she could tell, she was the only one present who didn't have a useful and necessary part to play in the grand scheme; for all the use she'd been so far, she could've stayed on in Rasch for a couple of days, ridden out to join them at a leisurely pace, and still have been here in time to do all this aimless sitting around. She could only assume that her bit came later, and that it was uniquely dangerous and horrible, so much so that nobody else was prepared to do it, direct order or no direct order. That sort of made sense, but it didn't cheer her up an awful lot.

The artillery arrived, trundling along behind the carts. Not trebuchets after all. Instead, the carpenters had built a dozen medium-range onagers—basically an enormous wooden spoon sitting in a wooden frame, with twisted rope for springs. Fair enough; their rate of fire was four times that of the fancy stuff, and they lobbed a seventy-pound stone a hundred and eighty yards—twenty yards further than bowshot, in other words, so they could pound the wall without getting shot at. They were also a better bet for shooting incendiaries, and a crew of three could work one of them all day long. The frame timbers were green wood, with the bark still on, so it wouldn't be long before they shook themselves to pieces, but undoubtedly Axio had factored that into his stupid plan, whatever it was. The stone-masons, it turned out, had been engaged to double as artillery crews, so that was all right.

Axio supervised the lining up of the engines personally, pacing out distances and sticking hazel sticks in the ground to mark where each one had to go. They were surprisingly easy to move, with a few long beams as levers, and wedges under their wheels to stop them shifting out of position when the mighty spoon slammed against the cross-bar. When the last engine had been nudged into place precisely between four sticks, Axio gave a nod of satisfaction and strolled over to where she'd been watching the show. "All done," he said. "With your permission, we might as well get started."

"With my permission."

"Well, yes. This is your circus, after all."

She sighed. "You win," she said. "Whatever the game is, you've won it. Now will you please tell me what the hell is going on?"

He beamed at her. "You haven't figured it out."

"No, I can't say I have."

That seemed to give him enormous satisfaction. He sat down on a folding stool and clasped his hands behind his head. "Well," he said, "it all started about three hundred years ago."

"Oh, come on."

"No, really. Three hundred years ago, when they first built this place—all right, you're the builder. What's going to be one of your main problems on a site like this?"

She tried really hard, then shrugged. "Don't know."

"I'd have thought it was obvious. Water supply."

She shook her head. "No, I read the file. They've got a big underground cistern, which you can only get at through the house, down a long passage cut into the rock. It drips down through the mountain, so it can't be cut off from the outside or poisoned from above. So whatever your plan is, it can't be that."

Axio held up his hand for silence. "They built the cistern, yes. And, being conscientious men, they explored the large underground cavern before building it, to make sure you couldn't get in there any other way apart from the way they'd come. The emperor sent his own corps of surveyors to do the work, as a favour to the family, and they filed a full report. It's in the Imperial archives. Thratta looked it out for me, and I had a copy made."

She nodded. "Fine," she said. "How does that help?"

"Oh, you have to read it quite carefully," Axio went on, "and cross-reference with the expenses sheets and supply requisitions. From which, you'll see that they didn't put in for much in the way of candles, torches, lamp oil or wick. From which we deduce that there was *light* down there, so they didn't need any."

"That can't be right," she said. "Not deep underground."

"That's what I thought," Axio said. "So I sent a man— Musen, I think you know him—and he scrambled up the mountain and poked about—this was some while ago—and he found a crevice in the mountain, far too narrow to get through, but if you dropped a stone down it, after a long while it went *plop!* You see what I'm getting at? It fell into water."

He was waiting for her to say something. "Go on."

"So I had Musen go back up there with a couple of surveyors, and then we cross-referenced their measurements with the plans in the engineers' report. The crevice Musen found is directly above the cistern; just a narrow little crack, but enough to let the daylight in."

She realised she was breathing a little faster. "Go on."

"Well," he said, "at the time it wasn't a major issue; Forza was still very much in post and in favour, so figuring out how to crack this place wasn't a priority. But I went on turning it over in my mind. At first I thought, all we need to do is pour something nasty down through the crack and into the water, but I had someone try it with honey and a lot of it got caught up on the limestone crust. So when Forza got put under house arrest,

I sent a couple of stonemasons up here, and had them quietly ream out the hole, until it was big enough to drop something worthwhile down there. As it happens, half a dozen dead sheep, which would be enough to spoil anyone's day. When they finished, they lit that handy little beacon on the mountain that you were so interested in when we arrived."

She took a deep breath. "You poisoned them."

"I very much doubt it," Axio replied. "For one thing, I don't suppose Forza and his wife and the higher servants drink plain water; I gather his father-in-law had a rather fine cellar, though Forza's more of a tea-drinker, left to himself. But you boil the water when you make tea, so that's not a problem. I imagine the soldiers and the servants drink mostly beer, but water when it's hot and they're working or drilling; just enough to kill one or two and make the rest of them sick as dogs. Forza's a military genius, as we know, but even he's going to have his hands full defending this place against a determined assault with artillery support when three-quarters of his fighting strength is rolling about on the floor with the screaming shits." He smiled proudly. "That's one thing I've learned over the years," he said. "You don't have to do everything all at once with one stroke. Just enough to tip the balance, that's all."

She stared at him. She wanted to laugh. It was ridiculous. And then she remembered wondering why they hadn't seen any riders watching them, or sentries on the wall, or sorties under cover of darkness driving off their horses or burning the supply wagons.

"Even so," Axio went on, "Forza's bound to come up with something utterly brilliant, and with the dozen or so men still on their feet he'll mount a surprise attack, outflank us and slaughter us like sheep. But so what? While he's doing that, you'll have had your chance to slip over the wall and get inside the house; after which," he added pleasantly, "I'm sure you'll know exactly what to do. You're the expert at that side of things and I wouldn't have the impertinence to make suggestions."

The artillery bombardment started mid-afternoon. It wasn't what she'd expected. The stonemasons would chip a lump of rock out of one of the many outcrops that dotted the plain. Then they'd chisel it approximately round—peck, peck, peck, like a patient bird—and then they'd load it into one of the huge wooden spoons and launch it at the outer wall. It left the catapult with a thud that shook her right down to her gums, soared a long way up, stalled and looped down again, slow, graceful and tiny, until it hit the wall; first she saw a puff of white dust (though Axio assured her that what she was actually seeing was steam; the moisture in the shot, or possibly the stone wall, becoming volatile under the furious pressure of impact) and then she heard the thump. Then the pecking once again, as the masons chipped away at the next round. It didn't strike her as a lightning assault by shock troops.

"We're just filling in time," Axio replied, "until the nastiness in the water's had a chance to get busy in their poor little tummies. Also it stops them coming out here and bothering us. I don't suppose you've noticed, but we've blocked that gate up real good."

She couldn't see that sort of detail at that sort of distance, but it seemed inevitable somehow that Axio should have exceptional eyesight. "Do we want to do that?"

He nodded. "Right now, yes. Dead-sheep-in-the-water-disease takes about two days to make you really, really sick. So we want to keep them bottled up for now, and then we'll smash a hole in the wall we can get through. Unless Forza's thought of something clever, in which case it'll happen and there's nothing we'll be able to do about it. But that won't matter, will it? I'm sure you can climb a silly little wall like that, provided everyone's looking the other way."

So she made her preparations: a coil of rope looped over her shoulder and a knife borrowed from one of the stonemasons. When it started getting dark, the masons lit big fires so they could see to work. She took careful note of where they were, so that she could use them as beacons to fix her position.

"Once it's dark we'll start pounding the wall," Axio said. "We'll be hitting a spot about fifty yards to the left of the gate, so stay well clear. Good luck," he added with a grin. "Not that you'll need it. Are you sure you don't want a jemmy?"

"No."

He shrugged. "Please yourself. Personally, I'd take one in case I had to pry open those shutters, but you know best, of course. We may not be here when you come back. If not, I'll see you in Rasch."

"Not if I see you first."

"Funny lady. All right, off you go."

He didn't actually pat her on the top of the head or ruffle her hair.

The walls were no bother, but the house itself was another matter. She crouched under the shadow of the inner wall, blessing and cursing the bright moonlight that allowed her to see the magnitude of the task that faced her, and to be seen by anybody looking out if she stirred from the shadows. It was all very well for Axio to chatter blithely about jemmying windows; a fly might be able to walk up that smooth, sheer wall, but she couldn't. For something to do, she counted the intervals between the thumps of the catapult shot. It could have no possible relevance—

The thumps had stopped. That was odd. Axio had told her they'd keep the barrage up all night, and then move the artillery forward at dawn to start pounding the middle wall. They couldn't have run out of stone, because the ground was littered with the stuff, and they couldn't have breached the outer wall already. In which case—

Forza Belot. He'd made his move, his brilliant tactical stroke, whatever the hell it might be, and the catapults had stopped because their crews were dead or running away. She shivered. Of course she knew that Forza was *supposed* to win, but, even so, the idea that her army, the artillery and the highly trained and dedicated Lodge soldiers, had been swept away and she was on her own, terrified her. All that effort, and here she was, armed with nothing but a rope, a knife and Axio's total confidence in her abilities. And she didn't have a clue what she was going to do next.

Lights; there were lights moving in her direction, coming from more or less where the gate was in the middle wall. She made herself as tiny as she could, and saw a dozen men, walking slowly; tired men who'd just done a very difficult and dangerous job, and succeeded, and were now going home to bed. She guessed one of them was Forza Belot, but there was no way of knowing which. The house gate opened to let them in; not the great double door, but a little sally port twenty-five yards to the right, so cunningly let into the stonework that you wouldn't know it was there.

He might have told me, she thought bitterly; but it was just possible he hadn't known. In which case, she should've figured out its existence from first principles (because, of course, Forza Belot would have a sally port, so he could dart out and attack his attackers in flank). The hell with all this, she thought, and fumbled in her sleeve for her trusty bit of stiff wire, because a sally port would have a lock you could open from the outside, for when you come back after a daring nocturnal raid.

It was a stupid lock, great big wards but no brains. The click as the last ward dropped was so loud she nearly fainted. She froze, waiting for shouts and running feet. Nothing. She was more scared than she could ever remember being. She gave the door a little prod and it swung open.

The light hit her like a punch. Forza Belot kept lanterns burning in his courtyard all night, another thing she hadn't been told. Of course, light's no use if you don't have armed men to see by it; she looked round but there didn't seem to be any. Rolling on the floor with the screaming shits, she prayed fervently, and the few who weren't would be resting after the exertions of Forza's brilliant foray. She took a deep breath and scuttled across the yard like a little mouse. Nobody yelled or shot her dead, and she was at the foot of the main staircase, leading to the family apartments.

Bad place to be. Instead, she ought to be at the foot of the back stair, leading to the servants' quarters, linked to the family's part of the house by connecting passages. That had been the plan; but she thought about it, and decided that going back into that horribly well-lit yard was too great a risk. Instead, why not climb the stair directly above her? If Axio was right, everybody who wasn't groaning and clutching their guts would have been out on the foray, in which case they'd either be in bed or celebrating victory all together in the great hall or the library, though in the circumstances she didn't think that was likely. She tried to think her way into their heads, but she realised she was too scared; like when you're cold and your fingers are too numb for delicate work. She was losing her fine edge, she realised, and there didn't seem to be much she could do about it; which left dumb luck, and a certain gift she had for stabbing innocent people before they had a chance to scream.

Up the bloody stairs, then. She considered throwing away the rope, which she kept treading on or catching in things, but she couldn't quite bring herself to do it; her only possessions in this hostile world were the rope and the knife, and she realised just how much she despised poverty. So she wrapped it round her waist under her coat and addressed the horrible stairs.

On the first-floor landing, she ran into a sentry. She didn't see him until he stepped out of the shadows. He looked at her. She could see his mind working. A stranger, but a woman, unarmed; didn't fit either category, enemy or friend. The time it took for him to think about that was just long enough for her to draw the knife, or would have been if it hadn't caught on the hem of her coat. As it was, she'd run out of time, and the sentry lowered his spear and stabbed her. She grabbed the spear shaft and held it still, controlling his hands, while she cut his throat for him. Wonderful, wonderful rope, she thought, as the light faded in his eyes and he slumped against the wall.

In fact, the encounter cheered her up enormously. Who needs stupid, heavy armour when a coil of rope wrapped round your middle does just as well? And the look on his face had been priceless. Another flight of stairs, and there was the door she'd never expected to reach. She stopped and looked down, for a tell-tale blade of light under it, indicating that someone was in there and awake. No such blade. She tried the door. It wasn't locked. Not so smart after all, General Belot.

Inside it was truly dark, so she forced herself to relax, weight equally on both feet, very small steps, fingers outstretched, so that if her fingertips met anything they'd do so very gently indeed. When they did, she recognised the texture of fabric. She stopped and stroked, as you'd tickle a kitten under the chin. Velvet; unmistakable pile, going only one way. Bed-hangings. Velvet bed-hangings were the absolute must-have about ten years ago, and Forza's in-laws were old-fashioned, conservative in their tastes, just the sort of people to be ten years behind the arbiters of elegance in Rasch.

She walked her fingers across the unseen velvet until she found a seam, then tugged gently. Bed-hangings sliding along a pole. She reached down, and felt a coverlet exactly where a coverlet should be. She edged closer, and her foot touched something that chimed ever so softly. A porcelain chamber pot; she smiled. Then, as carefully as she could, in case there was someone in the bed, she climbed on to it. As the mattress gave under her weight, she heard a gentle moan. Forza's wife.

She stopped and thought as hard as she could. A man who often comes to bed late at night, considerately, so as not to wake his wife. In her sleep, she recognises the sounds he makes, the feel of his weight on the mattress.

The sensible thing, of course, would be to stab her. That way there'd be no risk of her waking up and yelling the place down. The brief hadn't mentioned her either way, and it was therefore quite legitimate to consider her expendable. Strategic value? None, because with Forza dead she'd be worthless. On the other hand—she realised she wanted there to be another hand, which was stupid. But let's suppose Forza, a tactical genius with an infinite capacity for noting detail, enters the room and doesn't hear the customary sound of his wife's breathing. He suspects—

And then all she could think about was her own stupidity, because it made no sense—Forza's wife, who adores him, sleeping peacefully while he's out fighting for their lives. She didn't know what to do. Get out of there, of course, it's a trap, get *out*—

A blaze of light; someone lifting the shutters of a dark lantern. She had no choice but to lift her hand and shield her eyes. Her hand had the knife in it, but that couldn't be helped. Behind her, someone moved; she felt a strong grip on her wrist, and relaxed her fingers. A hand reached past her ear and took the knife from her hand.

"Thanks," said a voice behind the dazzling light. "Careful." She guessed it wasn't talking to her. She felt movement on the mattress as whoever the sleeper was got off the bed, taking her knife away. She heard a faint chink, which proved to be someone lighting a lamp from the lantern. Curious; more light, less dazzle. Now at least she could see who she was dealing with.

Two soldiers, and a third man, who had to be Forza, because he looked so much like his brother, and a thin-faced, grey-haired woman who was holding her knife. "Get that bloody woman out of my bedroom," Forza said, and the soldiers obliged, none too gently.

Came round in a small circular room with no windows; a turret room, presumably, high up, just the sort of place you'd store a dangerous prisoner; someone so very dangerous that you had to knock her out before moving her from room to room. She was tied to a chair with steel chain, the sort you use for restraining a guard dog, which was a compliment if you cared to look at it that way. Judging by the savage cramp in her legs, she'd been there some time; overnight, maybe. Put the monster somewhere safe till the morning and get a good night's sleep.

The last member of the Belot family to ask her searching questions had been Senza, and he'd had her arm broken. It had healed quite well, though she still got twinges in damp weather. She considered what information she held in her head that would be worth prising loose, and realised that there was a depressingly large quantity of it—all the Lodge operatives she'd worked with and for over the years, the names of several Commissioners, of the Triumvirs themselves. And none of it could she give willingly or easily, and all of it would come out eventually, after a world of pain and damage, and—she was no coward, she reckoned she'd proved that over the years, but inflicting pain is one thing, enduring it is another matter entirely, and she'd never been good at the latter, had been unbelievably fortunate, all things considered, to have avoided it to the extent she had; and now it was going to hurt very much for a very long time. She wondered if they'd found the dead guard yet. Almost certainly; and that wasn't going to make her very popular, on top of everything else.

She contemplated these issues for what seemed like hours and hours, and then the door opened, and in came Forza Belot.

He still looked tired, though he'd had a shave and a bath, presumably a night's sleep and something to eat. He brought a small folding chair with him, opened it and shut the door. Then he sat down and looked at her.

"I got this letter," he said. From his sleeve he drew a folded sheet of paper. "Would you like to hear what it says?"

She opened her mouth but couldn't think what to say.

Forza cleared his throat. "Oida to Forza Belot, greetings. You may have heard that I'm dead. To prove this isn't so, show this letter to your wife's brother Mazapa, who can compare the handwriting with the manuscript of one of my songs, which I wrote out for him after a concert in Arossa two years ago and gave him with my own hand." Forza paused and looked up. "Done that," he said. "It's genuine. Surprised?"

She shook her head. Forza nodded and went on: "To prove that I wrote this after my supposed assassination, I can tell you that this morning the price of cinnamon in Rasch market hit a record four angels sixty per ounce." He stopped again. "Haven't bothered checking that, but I'm prepared to take it on trust." He lowered his head and continued reading. "This letter is to warn you that an assassin has been sent to kill you in the name of the Lodge. The officer in question is a woman by the name of Telamon, and she's quite the best in the business. You will therefore need to take every possible precaution. I have no details of how the job is to be done; however, I trust that you of all people will be able to cope, given due notice." He paused, smiled, and went on: "You and I have only met twice, and on both occasions I fear that I made a bad impression, appearing to be vain, shallow and self-centred; which of course I am. It will therefore be difficult for you to trust me. That said, you will also give due weight to the circumstances. In particular, why would I—a confessed Lodge sympathiser—warn you of an attack by the Lodge?"

He paused, looked at her. "Well?"

"I don't know," she said.

"You knew he was still alive?"

"I was supposed to have killed him."

He nodded; right answer. He cleared his throat again. "The truth is that, for the first time in its history, the Lodge is divided against itself, and has split into two factions. The officers who ordered your assassination belong to the rebel or schismatic faction, and their orders do not—underlined," Forza added with a smile "—represent the wishes or the policy of the true leadership of the Lodge." He lowered the paper and looked at her. "Did you know that?"

"No."

"I believe you," he said. "Oh, there's a bit more." He looked back at the paper. "What you do with the assassin is, of course, entirely up to you. If she survives the attempt, the Lodge—I mean the real Lodge—would quite like her back, and would consider her release a valuable favour. Personally, I wouldn't lift a finger to save her."

She stared at him. "Is that it?"

"That's it." He got up, walked over and held the paper in front of her face so she could read it. "Well?"

She thought, for quite some time. Then she said, "Oida couldn't have written that."

He raised both eyebrows. "Really."

"Not in his own handwriting. You see, when I pretended to kill him, I cut off the index finger of his right hand, to show to his brother. There's a scar on it that's unmistakable, and anyone who knows Oida would think he'd never sacrifice that finger, it's the one he plucks strings with. It's also the one he holds a pen with, if you think about it."

Forza stared at her for a moment, then burst out laughing. "So it's a forgery," he said.

"Must be."

"Including, presumably, the appeal to let you go."

She couldn't shrug, because of the chain. "Presumably."

"So someone who wanted to warn me about an attempt on my life pretends to be someone I barely know and who I think is dead, and don't much like, and who I probably wouldn't believe if he told me my name is Forza, and while he's at it he tells me he doesn't give a damn if I execute the woman he's known to have been in love with for years, and, in case that wasn't enough, he gets in that bit about not lifting a finger, which only means something if you're here to tell me about cutting the finger off—which presumably only you and he know about, and which makes it possible for you to declare the letter a forgery." He sighed. "On top of which," he went on, "he says that if I do let you go, the Lodge will owe me a favour, bearing in mind that the Lodge is at war with the empire I've served my entire adult life and I'd do almost anything to see it wiped off the face of the earth. It's a bit too much, if you ask me. And I'm tired, and I've just fought a rather nasty and completely unnecessary battle, and I assume that it was your lot who somehow managed to poison our well, which I have to say I take rather hard. For two pins I'd cut your head off and stick it on a pole."

But he wasn't going to do that. He was angry and confused and sick to death of everything that was happening to him, but he wasn't going to kill her. For the first time since she'd climbed the wall, she felt a tiny spark of hope.

"All right," he said. "Here's the deal. Go back to the bunch of weirdos you work for. Tell them—" he sucked in a deep breath and let it out slowly. "Tell them I have no quarrel with the Lodge. My only concern is serving my emperor on the battle-field. Tell them I'm grateful for the warning, which I take at face value. You might add that, once I've finished off the East, I'll be at liberty to deal with them as they deserve, but that's likely to be at some point in the future, and by then things may have changed; I hope so. I don't actually enjoy slaughtering people, even parasites like your lot." He reached behind her back and gave a little tug on the chain, which fell to the floor with a clatter. "Now, please, get out of my house and never ever come back. Understood?"

As she walked through the breach in the outer wall, she put up a mob of crows. They swarmed and circled, yelling abuse at her, then drifted away in the direction of the mountain.

She didn't make a point of looking, but she recognised some

of the faces, in spite of the mud and the crows. Mostly they were stonemasons, but there were several Lodge soldiers. Further up the road she came across a dozen or so no Vei, all huddled in a heap, like puppies. Whatever Forza and his tiny army had done, it had been very clever and it had worked like a charm. She didn't recognise the siege engines until it occurred to her that the charred stumps sticking up out of the ground couldn't be anything else.

All told, it had been a pretty dismal affair, all to no purpose as far as she could see. Forza had made a point of telling her that seven of his household staff had died from the poisoned water, four of them women, and a dozen more were dangerously ill; two of his soldiers had died, and thirty-one were still sick, but they were veterans, hardened to violent dysentery, and would probably make it. She wondered what on earth had possessed him to let her go. In his shoes, she'd have done no such thing. It must be different if you're a soldier.

Wouldn't lift a finger. He couldn't have written the letter, because he was right-handed, and she'd cut off his finger. Yes, you can write without using your index finger, but your handwriting looks different; the writing in the letter she'd seen had been absolutely typical, characteristic Oida, big letters, flamboyant, a man who'd never had to worry about the ruinous cost of paper or parchment. Anything distinctive and full of character is easy to fake; it's the nondescript that defeats all but the skilled forger. Because it was so right, it could only be wrong, and therefore Oida hadn't written the letter, and someone else had. But nobody else knew about the severed finger, apart from her and—

Axio? Yes, it was entirely possible that he knew his brother's writing well enough to fake it. But he of all people had no motive to sabotage the attack he'd put so much time and energy into organising, and which he himself had ordered.

None of it made any sense, and she was fairly sure that that was why she was still alive. Forza Belot, realising there were things going on which he didn't understand, had wisely decided not to do anything irrevocable, such as cutting a throat, until he knew the relevant facts. She tried to figure out a few of the hypotheses that must have flitted through his mind. For instance: the Lodge arranges an assassination attempt, and then warns him about it, so that he can overcome it and survive. The outcome: he now trusts and is grateful to one faction of the splintered Lodge—though, of course, the Lodge isn't splintered at all, and the whole object of the exercise was to obtain that little handle of gratitude and trust, by which he could be skilfully manipulated on some other occasion for some vastly more valuable purpose. But why choose Oida, or Oida's ghost, as the purported messenger? That part of it still made no sense. And why undermine the whole effort with the obvious mistake of the forged-handwritten letter? She could just about believe in Axio sacrificing a few dozen lives to trick Forza into trusting a useful ghost, but he would never have dragged his brother into it, surely. Also, she was absolutely certain in her own mind that Axio believed Oida was dead. Some things you can't fake, and the overwhelming joy on his face when he'd opened the rosewood box was one of them.

The mystery served the useful purpose of taking her mind off her sore feet, her empty stomach and her parched throat as she trudged down the North Strategic in the general direction of Rasch. She had, of course, no money (no knife, no rope, nothing; and the soles of her boots were parting company from the uppers, and her coat was in tatters, and there was a brisk northerly wind with a nip in it) and Rasch was a long way away— She remembered a derelict farmhouse they'd passed on the way up. There it was; she wasted a significant proportion of her remaining strength and energy breaking down the shutters, but it was completely empty—no furniture, no objects or artefacts of any kind, no food. She wondered if any of the carpenters were still hanging about at the copse where they'd felled the wood for the engines. She found the place. Tree stumps, severed brash, woodshavings, the ruts of cartwheels, a few eggshells and apple cores. This time last year there was constant traffic on the Northern Strategic. Now it was empty in both directions, as far as the eye could see.

The emptiness was getting to her; far more comfortable to think about plots, deceptions and betrayals, because at least they implied that someone was still alive somewhere, and in a fit state to be active. *Wouldn't lift a finger.* Whoever had written that had relied on her seeing it, otherwise it'd be meaningless. Unless it was simply a huge coincidence.

When it started to get dark she got very nervous, which was ridiculous, when you thought about it. The time to be afraid is when there are lots of people around you, not when you know you're completely alone. She stopped and gathered a few dry sticks, but without a tinderbox she couldn't light a fire—you're supposed to be able to rub two sticks together, but it *doesn't work.* There was no ditch to crawl into or hedge to huddle under.

She lay flat on her back and knew for a fact that she wasn't going to sleep, even though she was bone weary.

She'd been lying staring at a cloudy, starless sky for a very long time when she heard something; a rustle, the sort of noise heather makes against the side of a boot. She found she couldn't move. She'd never been so scared in all her life. Another noise, a crunch of withered bracken. It's deer, she told herself, just deer grazing; they'll smell me and go away. All I have to do is keep absolutely still.

She waited a long time, then heard another rustle, but on the other side of her, going away. Just deer, she screamed silently at heaven, got to be, because no human being could track her in the pitch dark. She kept perfectly still for hours and hours, and then the sun rose.

She sat up and looked round, and there was nobody and nothing to be seen. Her legs ached from lying badly, and she'd squashed her left hand under her body. She stood up. Her feet hurt. There was still ever so much road, apparently going nowhere. She started to walk.

Around noon, she stopped and took off her boots. She had a fat, ugly blister on her left heel, and another on her right sole. She tried to tear a strip off her dress to bind them with, but the stuff was too strong, and she burned her hands trying. Then a shadow fell over her, and she froze.

"You got away, then."

She turned her head slowly. "Musen," she said.

He was towering over her, a bow in his left hand. The right side of his face was caked with dried blood. "Did you get him?"

"No. He got me. And then he let me go."

Musen gave her a look of pure disgust, then dropped to his knees beside her and sat down. "You screwed it all up."

"Yes, I suppose I did."

Musen shook his head, then fished about in the cloth satchel he wore round his neck and handed her two oatcakes. "He'll skin you alive," he said.

She nodded. "He made it, then."

From the look on Musen's face, the idea that Axio might not have made it was too bizarre to register. "I guess so," he said. "He legged it the moment the attack started. Me, too, but one of those bastards hit me with something and I fell down. They were running about all over the place yelling, so I thought it'd be clever to stay put and pretend I was dead. When I figured it was safe I got up, and everybody had gone." He shrugged. "And here I am."

She waved the remaining half-biscuit at him. "Thank you," she said with her mouth full.

"There's nine left," he said. "I thought, at least I'll be all right for food, I can shoot a deer or a sheep or something. But there's nothing out here. Like a bloody desert."

She nodded. "Got anything to drink?"

"There's a stream about two hundred yards up the road. It tastes of shit."

She grinned. "Maybe there's a dead sheep in it."

"No sheep up here. No nothing."

He was right, it didn't taste very nice, not if you weren't used to moorland water, which runs through peat. "It's fine," she said. "We used to drink this stuff all the time when I was a kid."

"Picking blueberries."

"That's right. I hate moorland."

"Can't say I'm crazy about it myself."

They had nothing to carry water in, so they swallowed as much of the shitty water as they could stomach. "Rasch?"

"Nowhere else to go," Musen said.

She thought of the sullen, antisocial true believer she'd tried to take in hand at Beloisa. The Lodge had changed him, that was certain, though not necessarily for the better. "Can I ask you something?"

He handed her his knife. "Sure."

She cut two neat strips off her hem and bound them tight around her feet, securing them with triple knots. "Back there," she said. "What the hell was all that about?"

He didn't look like he understood the question. "We were supposed to kill Forza Belot," he said. "Axio had it all planned out, but you made a bog of it."

"That's all?"

"That's all I was told."

She handed the knife back, though she wished she could think of an excuse for hanging on to it. The idea of Musen having the monopoly of armed force all the way back to Rasch didn't sit well with her. "You know Axio pretty well."

"I wouldn't say that."

"Oh come on. You're his hanger-on of choice. His right-hand man."

Musen grinned. "He's left-handed."

"So he is." It hadn't occurred to her, but he was right. "You've worked with him a lot. Does he confide in you? Tell you things?"

"No."

"All right. But reading between the lines. All that stuff with the army and the siege engines. Sledgehammer and nut, don't you think?"

Musen looked at her. "Forza's still alive, isn't he? Anyhow, it was a good plan. It should've worked, only—"

"Yes, I know." How far to Rasch? Seven days? Eight? With Musen for company, the whole way. "Did you notice anywhere inhabited on the way out? Somewhere we could get a horse, maybe."

"No. But it'll be all right. The Lodge will send someone to get us."

Absolute faith. The unsettling thing was, she was afraid he might well be right.

When there was only one oatcake left, Musen got lucky and shot a pig. It was brown with black spots, enormously fat, and came running up the road to meet them. Musen's first shot went over its head; his second hit the top of its head and skidded off, leaving a long red gash. The pig stopped dead, turned round and bolted. Musen hit it again, breaking its back leg. It could still hobble quite fast, but Musen was a good runner; he got in front of it and put an arrow in its neck. It fell over, then got up again. He shot his last arrow just behind the shoulder, and that eventually did the trick.

You need to butcher pigs straight away, or they spoil. To do this you need a frame to hoist them up on, or a tree. No frames, no trees. Musen grabbed the back legs and just managed to hold the carcass up, while she made a horrible job of opening it up and scooping out the warm, slippery guts. You're supposed to drain off the blood, but neither of them knew how. Musen had seen pigs killed, but it always made him feel ill, and he looked away before they got to the blood-draining bit. She cut its throat, but only a few drips came out. You can't be doing it right, Musen said helpfully.

"If there's a pig, maybe there's a farm," she said, as they toasted jagged slivers of pig over a smoky fire of dry heather stalks and bracken.

"Was a farm, maybe. It's probably been living wild for a long time. No people about, no wolves, nothing else big enough to bother it."

She sighed. "I thought you people were great hunters," she said.

"Not me. My job was always walking through the woods making a loud noise."

In its death throes the pig had broken all but two of the arrows. "This lot would last us a long time," she said, "if we had any salt."

"Yes, but we—"

"If there's a farm, there may be salt."

He shook his head. "They'd have taken it with them."

"It seems such a waste, just leaving it."

He shrugged and said nothing. They ate as much as they could force down, and carved off enough for three days, after which the meat would spoil and probably kill them.

It turned out that there was a farm. The people who'd lived there couldn't have seen the raiders coming until it was much too late; the cows were still in the shed, where they'd starved to death, likewise the chickens in their well-built, fox-proof run. The pigs had smashed their way free, but the dog was still there, curled up dead on the end of its chain. The household had mostly died in the yard, though an old woman had hidden under a bed, unsuccessfully, and a white, bloated child floated upright and motionless in the narrow well like some sort of exotic water lily.

"No more than a week ago," Musen said, and she was prepared to accept his expertise on the fine points of human decomposition. "Since we came this way," he clarified. "That's odd."

Odd wasn't the word she'd have chosen, but she applied her mind. "Who do you think it was?"

He thought for a while. "They didn't take any of the livestock," he said, "just the dry food, and the hay barn was cleared out, did you notice?"

Horsemen; wouldn't want to be cluttered up with herds of uncooperative animals, but would have a good use for hay. Not the No Vei or any of the horse-people. So who still had cavalry? "Senza," she said. "Senza's Fifth Lancers."

"Weren't they wiped out at Sabela?"

"What was Sabela?"

Oh dear, she'd missed a major battle. She accepted the reproof stoically. "Senza's always got a strike force of heavy lancers," she said; "they're his signature unit, all his battles involve lancers. And it can't be Forza, because we know where he's been, and, besides, they were his people, Westerners. And you can rule out stragglers and deserters, they'd have taken the stock. Whoever did this was in a hurry."

Musen looked doubtful. "Why would Senza be here?"

Good question. He'd have to know he couldn't storm Rasch, he couldn't have enough men. Then she understood. "He's making a nuisance of himself," she said, "right under the emperor's nose, so they'll have no choice but to give Forza his command back. That's what Senza wants, he wants to finish the fight with his brother. He knows he can't beat the West any more, but that's not the point, as far as he's concerned. He wants to beat Forza in the field and then kill him."

"That's stupid." Musen was poking about in the chicken run, looking for eggs under the straw. "If he wanted Forza, he could've got him at the villa."

"That wouldn't count. I don't think it's about killing each other any more. One of them's got to win."

Musen shrugged, expressing a total lack of interest. "If it was horsemen, we'd have seen hoofprints."

"It's been dry."

"We'd still have seen prints." He found an egg, just the one. No way of knowing how long it had been there. He climbed out of the run and put it in the water butt. It floated. He sighed, fished it out and threw it across the yard. "Look," he said, and the expression on his face suggested that he blamed her for everything. "Do you think the Lodge still needs me? I don't think they do. If I just wandered off somewhere, they'd manage without me, wouldn't they?"

"Sure. Where did you have I mind?"

"This is *stupid*." For a moment she almost believed he was going to hit her. "Everything's ruined, there's nobody left alive, and we're going around killing people. And I don't know what for."

It was in her mind to tell him, about the schism, the split in the Lodge. But he was Axio's—what? Friend? She didn't want him to be put in the position of choosing sides, because he'd undoubtedly choose the wrong one. "I thought you had faith," she said.

"I do. But Axio made me hand over a silver pack so the Lodge could sell it."

"To save Rasch."

"Nothing's going to save Rasch, don't you see?" He sat down on the ground, his absurdly long legs poking out in front of him. "I've got faith," he said. "I'm beginning to think nobody else has."

She knelt down beside him. She thought, a little show of compassion and he's mine, just like he was at Beloisa. "I've got faith," she said. "In the Lodge, and the Great Smith. But maybe it's possible that the people running the Lodge have lost their way. You can't blame them. It's the war."

He looked at her. "You did it with Axio, didn't you?"

Jealous. Should've seen that coming. "No," she said.

"He says you did."

"He doesn't always tell the absolute undiluted truth."

Musen scrambled to his feet. "I thought it was all starting to happen," he said. "On the island, and then when I went to Mere Barton and saw what they'd made of it. I grew up there, did you know that? It was a shithole little village full of stupid people, and then the Lodge came, and they built something so amazing, and I thought, I was right all along, there really is a purpose to it all, it's the Lodge, the Lodge will make everything better."

She nodded slowly. "That was when you met Axio for the first time."

"What's that got to do with it? Yes," he added almost immediately, "that was when he noticed me."

She took a deep breath. "We need to get to Rasch," she said. "I'm a Commissioner now, I can ask people questions. I think you're right. I think the Lodge has lost its way."

"You said that, not me."

"You thought it, though."

Suddenly he grinned. "Don't know if you remember, but I had a friend, from home, Teucer."

"The red-haired man. A good shot."

"That's him." He looked away, undid his bootlace and tied it again, tight. "He was one of the Lodge soldiers. We grew up together. I never liked him much."

"Did he get away?"

Musen shrugged. "I don't know. I think Axio asked for him for this job specially, because he knew it'd upset me. Because I don't like him, and he knew there was a good chance he'd get killed."

"You think he was trying to do you a favour?"

Stone face. "No."

You ought to stick a knife in this fuckup before it's too late, said the voice in her head that always sounded like it knew best. *He's far more dangerous than useful, and I don't suppose you'll be able to give him the slip. Also, you could do with the knife.* One of these days, she'd have to follow the voice's advice, just for the hell of it.

They found horses, three of them, saddled and bridled, although the tack was muddy and the stitching was torn. She guessed the horses had been rolling, to try and get rid of the nuisance. The saddles were Eastern Imperial issue.

"Means nothing," Musen said. "The West buys stuff from Ocnisant, or maybe it was captured."

"Like it matters," she said cheerfully. "I'll take the white one with the brown splodges."

Horses changed everything. True, there was no food in the saddlebags, but even so; three days' fast ride, as against ten days footslogging. And it's so much easier to run out on an unwelcome companion if you're on horseback.

It wasn't till late evening that they found the source of their good fortune. They rode over a narrow humpbacked bridge into a small, deep combe, with woods on their left and a steep, round hill to their right, and as they broke the skyline a black cloud exploded in front of them, causing the horses to shy and backtrack—crows, disturbed and harrassed while about their lawful business. The combe was full of dead men, heaped up on top of each other.

They stood up in their stirrups and looked for a while. Then Musen said, "Ocnisant would've buried this lot."

And then we wouldn't have had to see it; quite. But the dead men hadn't been disturbed, except by the crows and the foxes. They still wore their clothes and armour, which was just beginning to rust—the chestnut-red bloom that starts once the damp has worked its way past the sergeant major's sheeps' grease. "Six days?" she asked, mostly just for something to say.

"Four," Musen said. "You can tell by the swelling and the colour. Mind you, it's been quite mild."

How he'd come by the expertise she didn't want to know.

Perhaps he'd stolen it from a negligently unlocked mind. Anything not nailed down.

"What unit?"

He shrugged. "I ought to know that," he said, "but I don't, offhand. But they're Western. Look at the boots."

Black leather, heavily waxed; the Western quartermasters had recently pulled off a coup, two hundred tons of buffalo hides from somewhere way down south, through Blemyan intermediaries. They'd paid a ludicrous amount of money for them. "Recently issued."

Musen nodded. "And look at their faces." She decided she'd take his word for it. "Old men and boys. I'm guessing they've had the red ropes out in Rasch."

It took her a moment to grasp the allusion, since the press had come in very recently, while she'd been out of town. The recruiting sergeants swept through the backstreets of the city holding each end of a rope dipped in raddle; anybody who got paint stains on their legs was suddenly a soldier. Not the best way to build an army, since it discriminated against the quick, agile and smart.

Musen slid off his horse and started rummaging. Their luck was in: bread (stale, but perfectly good if you scraped off the blue mould), hard biscuit, some marginal looking cheese and half a pound of dried sausage, somebody's leaving present from home. Musen also scraped together half a pocketful of bits and pieces, but it was all garbage, he said; silver-washed copper rings, a folding knife rusted shut, a few base silver lucky charms that palpably hadn't worked. But he found and gave her unasked a perfectly good knife—he must have seen her looking at his and maybe read her mind. It was too long and heavy, but a million times better than nothing.

The next morning she woke up and he'd gone. Instinctively, she ran an inventory. Ah well; he'd left her the horse, the knife and enough stale bread and cheese for four days, and she couldn't remember offhand what else she'd owned at that point. She felt as though a weight had shifted off her shoulders. Presumably he felt the same way.

On horseback, she had a much better idea of where she was, which made a sort of sense; she'd only ever seen the Northern Strategic through a coach window, rattling along at a respectable pace. At walking speed, it looked different; you saw more and the landmarks were further apart. That evening, she passed a burned-out skeleton of posts and rafters that had once been the Divine Mercy, two days' comfortable ride from Rasch, or one day for a well-motivated courier. The Mercy; sixteen years ago she'd played cards for kisses with the under-groom and his friend in the back stables. She stopped and considered the layout of the ruins, but it bore no relation to anything she could remember having seen before. Just an exercise in geometry and some charred beams. She dismounted, knelt down and poked her fingers into the ashes. Still faintly warm. Three days?

Senza Belot and a troop of lancers, heading for Rasch, doing all the spiteful things he could think of to provoke the emperor into sending for Forza. It occurred to her to wonder if the Belot boys mattered any more; Senza was too weak to threaten the city, and he probably had no real interest in harming it, so long as he could get to grips with his brother one more time. Even so; it struck her that she was headed for a city under attack, a few days behind the invading army. Getting into Rasch might not prove as simple as she'd thought. But where else could she go? Besides, she was a Commissioner now, and if anyone was winning it was the Lodge. For some reason, the thought made her want to laugh. She wondered where Oida was, and what he was doing. Somehow, things would be different if he was there; he'd have books, and nice things to eat, and a comfortable coach to ride in and take them somewhere with a roof and clean sheets and a warm fire. Suddenly she saw him as a man in armour, impervious to spears and arrows inside his cap-a-pie of money, charm, success and taste. The whole world could come crashing down, but he'd still have brought her something to read, and figs preserved in honey. It was then that she understood. It was just a matter of semantics, that was all. Like someone who's learning a foreign language, she'd failed to grasp the true meaning of love. All this time, she'd thought it meant something else, to do with fire in the blood and skin tingling at a certain touch, when really it was all about completely different things—food, shelter, comfort, money, a defensible space, something that would still be there in the morning. Stupid, she thought. It takes a valley full of dead bodies and a burned-out inn and her mother's grave and a night with Axio and Senza Belot trashing and torching everything in his path to reveal the true definition of an everyday word. Simpler to have bought a dictionary.

The Northern Strategic runs through a gap in the Eviot hills at Charnac, which is where the naïve traveller from the rustic north gets his first view of Rasch Cuiber. He sees a flat plain, a winding river, a straight line of a road and a great square shape, constrained by the magnificent, inch-perfect walls. From Charnac, on a clear day, you can make out the spire of the Silver Horn, the triple towers of the College and the blazing golden dome of the New Palace, which is, of course, four hundred years older than the Old Palace, most of which was knocked down to build the Painted House, which is where the emperor lives when he's not too scared to set foot in his own capital. He will also notice the columns of black smoke rising from the industrial quarter, usually slanting at an angle like clinched-over nails in the east wind, and the green chequerboard fields where they grow food for all the people, and the shadowy grey forest to the west, preserved untouched for the Imperial hunt.

It was a clear day, and she wasn't in a hurry. So, for the first time, she noticed that the forest had gone, chopped down and roasted into charcoal and long since burned, and the chequer-board was a brown stain with very faint lines where the hedges stood up out of the trash and briars, and there were no smoke nails any more, and the dome—she couldn't see the dome because they'd stripped out and scraped off the gilded tiles to raise a week's pay for a regiment that Senza had wiped out at some point, and Ocnisant had buried them and sold their boots and trinkets and barely broken even.

The sight didn't upset her, because she'd never really liked Rasch anyway, but she felt she had a duty to stop and look at it for a while, as if it was the grave of a close relative you never got on with. Really, she thought, it was time she gave some consid-ered thought to all that side of things, particularly now that she was just beginning to grasp what certain words meant, such as love, and her name. So: what was Rasch to her? She didn't have to think too hard. Rasch was a witness, one of many who'd seen various stages and events in her life, preserved the facts and the narrative independently of her own memories, which were by their very nature fallible and partial. Witnesses are, of course, ambivalent; some of them record what would otherwise be lost and go to waste, while others need to be hunted down and killed before they can tell what they know; and the man who stands on the grave of the last witness owns the truth and is responsible for it, a dangerous trustee. There were places in Rasch that would always remind her of things she'd be very glad to forget—so, if Rasch burned down and vines and creepers overgrew the ruins, she'd never have to remember them again and they would never have happened, just as her mother had never lived and she herself had never been an inconvenient nuisance and a not-very-valuable commodity. If Rasch died, part of her would die with it, but sometimes you have to amputate in order to survive. Still, as the man said just before he died of gangrene, you can't help feeling attached to your leg, even when it's turned against you.

The longer she looked, the more she saw; among other things, flashes of light on the straight road, which proved to be associated with small dark shapes that were in fact moving. That would be Senza, and the blobs were his army.

There's a better view from Sier Top, which is ten miles further down the road. She thought about it for a while and decided to risk it.

Sier Top is close enough to make out human movement, in bulk if not in detail. The dark shapes were definitely an army—cavalry, by the speed they moved at, and thousands rather than hundreds. She watched them for a long time as they inched forward along the dead straight road, slow as a stain sinking into fabric. They were well into the faint remains of the chequerboard now, and she wondered what on earth Senza was thinking of, dashing forward to make some aggressive display in front of the gates he couldn't break down and the walls he couldn't climb. It wasn't like him to make a public exhibition of weakness. If the emperor was at home, possibly he might provoke a fit of pique. But the emperor was far away, barricaded in a massive castle on top of a mountain surrounded by marshland. They said he didn't like Rasch all that much, and had seriously considered moving the capital to another city, or building a new one; or that as soon as his uncle died and the empire was reunited, he'd take possession of Choris Anthropou and rule from there, as though his uncle had won the war and the East had prevailed.

The sun was starting to set, and it was definitely getting colder, but she stayed where she was and watched the grey and brown stain crawling ever closer to the beautiful square. There was definitely a conflict going on down there, between the fixed, regular straight lines and the creeping mass; something wasn't right, and she couldn't think what it was. Any moment now the wave would reach the cliff, break and fall back—but the sea is resigned to failure, men aren't, so why was Senza picking up the pace, as though it mattered when he got there? Because it didn't, it couldn't.

She watched. The brown and grey stain reached the square, and didn't stop, and sank into it; through Florian's Wall as if it wasn't there, through the newly cultivated allotments where the Foregate slums used to be, through the main gate of the inner ring. For a moment she couldn't understand what she was seeing. Then it suddenly made sense. Senza's army had ridden straight into Rasch. The gates had been open.

You don't expect to see things like that. You don't imagine that you'll be watching at the moment when a flaming star falls out of the sky and scoops out a mile-wide crater, or a mountain cracks open and starts spewing out fire, or a wave taller than the spire of the Silver Horn rears up and crashes down on a crowded harbour.

The first thing your mind does is to search for alternative explanations. So; the army she'd been watching hadn't been Senza's Eastern lancers, but some Western reserve hurriedly summoned to reinforce the city. Now that made much more sense. After all, she'd only assumed that what she'd seen had been Senza, because she'd passed evidence that they were nearby, therefore leaped to an understandable but entirely false conclusion. For all she knew, the West had managed to hire some hitherto unknown tribe as mercenaries, and here they were reporting for duty, and when the real Senza showed up they'd sally out and engage him, or man the walls and throw rocks. She felt as though she'd just woken up out of a nastily realistic nightmare, and was only just beginning to realise it wasn't real and everything was still all right—

Smoke was rising from the centre of the beautiful square. Now that made no sense at all.

Not just in one place, but five, six, ten separate plumes of smoke; not in the Arsenal quarter, but somewhere near Sheepfair, Coppergate, the Painted House, the Temple district.

Stupid, dangerous places to light bonfires, because of all the old timber-framed and thatched streets and alleys. The smoke was moving, spreading (like a stain sinking into fabric), the abominable movement that had been outside the square was now inside it, and that couldn't be right, could it? The logical explanation shattered like glass. The enemy were inside Rasch, and had set it on fire.

She stayed where she was. Fairly soon, thousands, tens of thousands of people, would be streaming out of the gates, and the space around the city would quickly be bogged down with them. She didn't want to get trapped in a human quicksand. So she watched, and the smoke swelled and blotted out the crisp, straight lines of the walls, and presumably that was why she couldn't see the crowds of refugees, not until they were clear of the smoke and surging out along the roads. She waited. They were taking their time about it. The sun set, granting her a spectacle that few people could ever have been privileged to witness—two fiery red sunsets, one in the sky, one on the ground, two glaring pools of fire bursting through curtains of black cloud. It would make a fine retrospective prophecy—*on the day of two sunsets, such and such will happen*, and, of course, it would all depend on your vantage point, because if you were lower down or looking at it from the south or the east, the effect would be lost on you. A terrible thought struck her; was she perhaps the only one who could see it as it was supposed to be, if it was to have any meaning, if it was to be capable of interpretation? Was she the only witness; and, if so, was the whole thing solely for her benefit?

She decided she must have missed something. At some point,

surely, the many, many thousands of people who lived in Rasch must have got out, and dispersed. Stupid of her not to have noticed, but it must have happened. When the alternatives are, either the world is completely wrong or you are, it's just common sense to assume the latter.

Just before dawn it rained heavily. The red glow dimmed and faded behind a massive cloud of white fog that slowly filled the valley as the sun rose, until she could barely see ten yards in front of her. When the rain stopped, she got up and picked her way carefully along the road. It was four miles to Rasch.

The further she went, the thicker the fog; as a result, she didn't see him until he stepped out in front of her from behind a smashed cart. He'd drawn his bow as he advanced, and so her view of his face was obscured by the arrowhead, right under her nose.

"Musen, it's me."

For a moment, she thought he was going to loose anyway. But he slowly lowered the bow and let the arrow come forward and off the string. "You're here," he said. "I thought you were inside."

"The city? No, I saw an army headed for it, so I hung back. What's been happening?"

He dropped the bow and sat down heavily on the ground. She dismounted and knelt beside him. "Are you all right?"

He nodded sideways with his head. "It's gone."

"What has?"

"The city." He looked up at her. "All gone. They closed the gates so nobody could get out."

The words ran off her mind, like rain off waxed cloth. "What are you talking about?"

"The soldiers," he said. "Senza Belot's men." He drew a deep breath and looked at her. "I was so lucky, I hadn't quite reached the gate when the outriders came up. I ducked behind some junk and saw the whole thing. Someone opened the gates to let them in."

She nodded. "Yes, I'd guessed as much. Go on."

He looked past her, over her shoulder, into the mist. "They just rode straight on through while I stood there and watched. There were ten squadrons, maybe five hundred each. I think I saw Senza, but I'm not sure, he shot past and there were lancers all round him. And then the gates slammed shut."

He stopped and frowned, as though he'd found a mistake in a ledger. "Go on," she prompted.

"Well, I wasn't going anywhere, so I sat tight and waited to see what'd happen. But it all seemed very quiet, I couldn't hear fighting or anything. So I got up and walked about fifty yards along the wall, and I found this little postern gate, what's the word, sally port, and it was open, an inch or two. So I thought, what the hell, and I opened it and slipped inside. The door clicked shut and wouldn't open when I pushed it, and then I saw the key was in the lock. I don't know," he added with a frown, "I remember taking it out and putting it in my pocket, no idea why, just force of habit. Well, you know what I'm like."

She nodded. "Go on."

"Well, I came out into Marshal's Yard, that little stone coop thing, by the well. I always thought it was a pump house, but obviously not. So I looked round to make sure there was no one about, and the place was deserted, nobody in the streets or the square. I kept going and came out into Foregate, and there were the lancers, sitting on their horses quite still, so I stayed where I was, and a bit after that they all moved off up New Street. And then some of them came back, on foot, and went towards the Gatehouse. I guess they went to lock the gate."

"Why would they do that?"

"So nobody could get out, I guess. I don't know, do I?"

"And then they set fire—"

Musen shook his head. "I think it was an accident," he said. "At any rate, the fire didn't start till long after the gates were shut. I didn't see anything much after that, I stayed put where I was, but then there was shouting and yelling and a big mob of the lancers came charging back into the square headed for the gate, and when they found it was locked they weren't happy, you can bet your life. Then I smelled the smoke, and not long after that the air was thick with it. And more lancers came and tried to bash the gate in with long benches they'd fetched out of one of the buildings, but you know those gates, they're massive. No, I think what happened is that the fire started by accident, and it spread, you know how fires can take hold in Rasch, and there wasn't anybody in charge to deal with it, or if anybody tried they left it too late."

"You made it out."

"Soon as the coast was clear I nipped back through the sally port. I'd got the key, remember? I left it open behind me, but I didn't see anybody come out after I did. Mind you, that whole district went up like a foundry a few minutes after I got out, so maybe they tried and didn't make it."

She thought for a moment. "Whoever locked the main gates," she said calmly, "must've had the keys. Why didn't they open them again when the fire started?"

"I don't know, do I? Maybe they couldn't get there in time. You don't know what it was like, when the lancers were trying to smash in the doors. They were berserk. Like when you've got a bird inside the house, and it flies round and round bashing into the shutters."

She got the impression he didn't want to talk about it any more, which was understandable. "Have you got any food?" she asked.

"Me? No."

"Pity." She stood up. "Me neither."

"What are you drivelling on about food for at a time like this?"

"Because we're going to need to eat, sooner or later."

"Where are you going?"

She nodded towards the mist. "Can't all have been burned up," she said. "It's a huge city, there must be hundreds of miles of cellars, where they keep the siege supplies. It's that or nothing."

"You want to go in there?"

"I don't want to, no. But I do all sorts of things I don't want to, because I have no choice."

He stared at her, as though she was standing on a chair putting a noose round her neck. "About fifty yards from the gate on your right," he said. "It was open when I left it."

She nodded. "I'll bring you back something nice," she said.

The sally port he'd told her about was there all right, and still open; that is, the upper half hung wide at a crazy angle from one hinge. The rest had burned away. She stepped over the lock, which still had the key in it. Her feet crunched on the cinders.

She found herself in a cramped stone gatehouse, its walls black with soot. Through the low arch at the far end she saw an extraordinary sight: open space. In a way she recognised it—Marshal's Yard, a low-rent district where for centuries they'd specialised in cheap wooden tableware, builders' lumber and sheep hurdles. Now it was a wide, flat rectangle, like a parade ground, and the black and grey ground reminded her of moonlight. Hundreds of people, maybe thousands, lived and worked in Marshal's Yard. She felt something under her foot and stooped to pick it out of the ash. It was the blade and ferrule of a chisel, grey with scale. She shuffled around with her toes and turned up a few flat nails, the sort people use to nail wooden shingles to rafters.

Marshal's Yard to Swan Yard to the Shance to Butcher's Row, passing the Sincerity Vindicated and the Golden Legacy—nothing. Six hundred yards away she could see a black, square shape; when she reached it, it turned out to be the Silver Key temple, a sublime masterpiece of middle-period Formalism in shining white marble, with a gilded dome so light and graceful you expected the next breath of wind would float it away over the rooftops. The bronze-faced doors were completely gone, and so was the dome, and the walls were black as charcoal.

From the Silver Key up Westgate to the Flower Market; heaps of rubble where the stone facings of the buildings had fallen in. The lower end of Westgate was mostly high-class clothing and luxury goods, lawyers' chambers, banks, a couple of guild halls.

The big private houses started on the other side of the Flower Market and carried on up the hill to the old Citadel. But apparently the big houses had all been stone cladding over timber frames, because they were all gone. The next thing she came to that was taller than her was the tower of the Salvation—the nave and chantry had vanished, as though they'd been carved from ice, but the bottom half of the tower was still there, with the top half scattered in heaps round its base.

She'd been walking for an hour and seen nobody, no bones sticking up out of the ash. Obviously Musen had got it all wrong. Rasch had seven gates; the other six, therefore, had been opened, and the majority of the population had left through them in an orderly fashion. To prove the point, she went down Moor Street to the Westgate. In Foregate Yard she trod on something and turned her ankle. The something turned out to be a skull, roasted dark brown and black, treacherously nestling in the deep ashes. It wasn't the only one. In fact, she had to give up and turn back, because it was like walking on a beach of rough shingle. But she got close enough to see that the Westgate was shut, because the gate itself (fifty plies of oak, cross-grained) had actually survived, just about; you could see daylight between the cracks where the heat had warped it, but it was still there, resolutely doing its duty, shut tight.

That was all she wanted to see, thank you very much. She stumbled back the way she'd come, remembering at the last minute that there was a military grain store in Hawkers' Yard, just past the Eye theatre, which had vanished without trace. The heavy double doors of the store had burned through, but the fire hadn't been able to breathe in the narrow tunnels where they kept the supplies for the city garrison. There she found a gallery lined with barrels almost as tall as she was, and nothing to open them with. Just when she was about to burst into tears and give up, she found an open barrel. Apples. She decide she liked apples very much, and stuffed her pockets with them until the seams split.

Rasch Cuiber, the biggest city in the world—don't go saying that out loud in Choris if you value your life, but as a matter of cold, impartial geometry the area inside the walls of Rasch is four hundred and seventy-seven square yards bigger. She tried to remember what it had looked like when she was there last, but the fact was she'd had other things on her mind and hadn't really noticed. The streets hadn't been nearly as busy, though that could have been curfews or trading restrictions, or maybe most of the people had no work and no food and had drifted away. Conventionally, the population of Rasch was between ninety and a hundred thousand, though of course it fluctuated, depending on garrison strengths, markets, influx and outflow of seasonal labour, refugees, that sort of thing. And—silly girl, she'd almost forgotten—add in five thousand Eastern Imperial lancers, bashing frantically against the locked gates until the smoke got them.

Five thousand lancers. A significant proportion of all the remaining soldiers in the world.

She stopped dead, up her to her ankles in ash in the middle of what used to be Cutlers' Row. The entire population of Rasch Cuiber and five thousand lancers, *and Senza Belot*, burned to death because the gates that some helpful traitor had opened for them suddenly slammed shut behind them.

Omelettes and eggs, she thought. And who did she know who could possibly think like that?

"I don't like apples," Musen said. "They give me bellyache."

"Tough." She piled them up in a neat pyramid. "That's all there was. Are you hungry or aren't you?"

"I thought you said you found the grain store."

She sighed. "You know where it is. Go yourself."

"Not likely."

She looked at him and came to a decision. "We ought to get a fire lit," she said.

"Why? It's not cold."

"I'm cold. Find some wood."

He shrugged and wandered off. She gathered the apples and put them in a goatskin bag she'd found beside the road. Not that she was desperately fond of apples, but they were significantly better than nothing at all. Then she spent a few minutes carefully selecting the perfect stone; just big enough to close her hand around, smooth, without dangerous jagged edges. No sooner had she found it than Musen came back with his arms full of firewood—broken-up palings, mostly, with some dead twigs for kindling. "Over there," she said, and when he knelt to lay the fire she hit him with the stone, two inches or so above where the neck stops and the head begins. He toppled over without a sound and lay still.

She checked to make sure he was still breathing, then quickly rummaged through his pockets. A few items of interest, things she'd forgotten she had and hadn't missed, also two angels sixty in Western cash money and a small folding knife with a silver handle and a blade that locked when you turned a little collar. She took the last few arrows out of his quiver and broke them, then tugged off his boots and hid them under a smashed-up cart. He wasn't the nastiest man she'd ever met, and it's nice to have company sometimes, but for the time being she'd rather be alone, and the thought of Musen all the way to Iden Astea was rather more than she could cope with, all things considered.

Three days on the Western Military Road; blissfully peaceful, in retrospect, because she didn't see another living soul, not even any farm animals, and she didn't have her gloomy shadow trailing along behind her, and she found a flitch of dusty but perfectly edible bacon in the chimney breast of a burned-out cottage five miles or so outside the ruins of Opopa—three days in her own company, which gave her time to think, then get sick of thinking, then amble aimlessly along with nothing on her mind except where the next fresh water might be. She thought, among other things, about why she was going to Iden Astea, and came to the conclusion that it was as good a place as any. If anyone had managed to get out of Rasch before or during the ... (she couldn't think of a word for what had happened there; disaster didn't chime right, fall wasn't appropriate, recent unpleasantness was rather a mouthful), Iden would be the logical place to head to. The emperor was there, if that counted for anything any more, and where he went the Imperial Guard tended to follow; if there was still a hierarchy, a government, a state, an empire, Iden was the logical place to look for it. And if there wasn't, what the hell. Last she'd heard there were still people there, and that on its own made it a pretty exceptional place these days.

On the fourth day, quite early, she stopped to drink from a rainwater stream that had broken out across the road, dislodging the cobbles and cutting a furrow right down to the gravel. She was lying on her stomach lapping up water like a dog when she heard a noise she'd almost forgotten: horses, plural, and the rattle of iron-tyred wheels on a metalled road.

She jumped up and saw a coach. More of a chaise; a pretty thing, slender and fragile-looking, painted green and yellow, with a fringed canvas hood. Four milk-white horses drew it and there were two seats on the box, one of them empty. She stared at it until it was right up close and slowed down, and then she recognised the driver. An easy man to recognise, because of the scar.

"Director Procopius."

"Small world." He stopped the chaise. "Where the hell have you been?"

"I had a job to do—"

"Did you now?" He frowned, then shrugged. "Don't just stand there," he said. "Hop in."

"My horse—"

"You won't be needing it if you're coming with me."

"Am I?"

He gave her a look. "I think it would be the sensible thing to do. Iden?"

She nodded.

"Me, too. After all, where else is there?"

The back of the chaise was crammed full of trunks and boxes—mahogany rectangular boxes, flat tin boxes, narrow ebony boxes, circular boxes turned out of spalted beech and polished with beeswax until they glowed like the sun. She threw her goatskin bag on top of them and scrambled up on to the chaise. The moment she was settled, Procopius cracked the whip and the horses broke into a swift, long-paced trot.

"Before you ask," he said, "yes, I was in Rasch when the enemy broke in. Rather lucky, really. I'd just finished packing up all my stuff—I'd just got a summons from the emperor to relocate to Iden, effective immediately—and suddenly all hell broke loose. And there's a postern gate down by the main sluice that not many people know about, but I've got a key. Of course, that was before some clown set light to the place."

She looked at him and knew he was lying about something, though what it was she couldn't guess. Also, he didn't seem to care much about whether she believed him or not.

"I wasn't there when it happened," she volunteered.

"Lucky you. I don't know how many of us got out. Not a lot, I don't think." He transferred the reins to his right hand, stretched his left behind him and patted the nearest wooden crate. "All my manuscripts," he said. "Every damn thing I ever wrote: scores, notebooks, works in what I laughingly call progress, the lot. Doesn't bear thinking about."

"Director Procopius—"

"Oh, forget all that stuff," he said cheerfully. "After all, it's not like there's anything left to direct. Or, if there is, I'm through with it. To the best of my knowledge, Imperial Intelligence now consists of you and me. All the rest of them—" He drew the fingertips of his left hand across his mouth, and she knew what that meant; *all dead.* But it was a very localised gesture, specific to just one region.

So she had to ask. "Are you from the Mesoge?"

"No, but I had a nurse who was born in Eyren. Just down the road from your old haunts, isn't it?"

She nodded. "Heneca Cross. Of course, you know that."

That got her a grin. "I expect I read it in your file, but I'm afraid the name didn't stick in my mind. I gather it's a delightful part of the world."

"The Mesoge?"

He smiled. "My nurse thought so. Mind you, she moved away when she was quite young. You were going to ask me something."

She'd forgotten what she was going to say. "What happened at Rasch?"

He pulled a sad face. "Your guess is as good as mine. I was sitting at my desk, trying to sort out a mess I'd made with the string section before I set out for Iden, and a clerk came running in yelling that someone had opened the gates and Senza Belot's lancers were inside the city. I didn't believe him, so he dragged me to the window and I saw for myself. Well, I'm not a brave man. I ran down the back stairs, yoked up the horses to this trap thing and made a dash for the little gate I told you about. Luckily I didn't meet anyone, and I was outside in a matter of minutes. To be honest with you, all I could think about was my music, packed in these trunks. I drove up onto the top of Weal Down, where I could get a good view, and I watched it all happen."

She nodded. "The fire."

"Don't ask me who started it," he said. "Honestly, I think it must've been an accident. There's always fires breaking out in the Osiery, as you know, but under normal circumstances the

Prefect's men are there with a cart and a bowser within minutes. This time, nobody came. I guess the lancers had them all kettled up in the barracks along with the Guards until it was too late. Anyhow, the fire spread from the Osiery to the slums round Waybrook, and then the wind changed and the next thing I saw, all the warehouses downtown were on fire, and it was spreading out in every direction faster than a man could run. But who locked the gates I have no idea. The lancers, presumably, to stop a mass exodus, and then the fire stopped them from getting back to unlock them again. I don't know, I couldn't see very much by that stage because of the smoke." He paused, then went on, "I couldn't see if anyone got out, but once the smoke had lifted I couldn't see anyone on the plain below, and from Weal Top I should've been able to, so I'm guessing—" He closed his eyes for a moment. "I never liked the place much, I'm a country boy at heart. I don't really care for big cities, but even so."

She waited for a moment, then asked; "Does this mean the war is over?"

He shrugged. "That's an interesting question. On balance, I'd say no, it isn't. The emperor's quite snug in Iden, by all accounts, he hasn't got much of an army there but neither has the East, and Rasch didn't actually matter, strategically. In fact, it was more of a hindrance than a help, as witness what happened when Senza laid siege to it a while back. So there's no reason why the emperor should end the war, if it's up to him."

She looked at him. "If?"

"Something like Rasch being destroyed," Procopius said, not looking at her, "it changes things in people's minds. It may not actually be a defeat, but it feels like one. And with Forza out of favour—" He shook his head. "There may well come a point when whoever's in charge of the army figures that enough is enough, and the hell with the emperor. Now, properly speaking, it would be our job to deal with anything like that quickly and efficiently, but of course we aren't there any more, we went up in smoke along with everybody else, so who's to stop the generals from mutiny, if that's what they decide to do? But I don't think it'll come to that. Everything's been Forza Belot for as long as anyone can remember, all the senior staff are a bunch of obedient nonentities, I can't recall half of their names without looking at my notes, which of course I no longer have. If there's anyone with the gumption to stage a coup, I don't know him. So, no, I don't think the war is over. I think it'll carry on until Senza takes Iden. Assuming," he added with a frown, "Senza is still alive, and not a cloud of ash in the ruins of the Haymarket. If he's dead, too, then I have absolutely no idea what'll happen. I'm sorry, that's not terribly helpful, is it? I ought to be full of wise insights, but without my notes I'm as much in the dark as you are."

Travelling with Director Procopius was an odd experience. He'd brought food, in a vast wicker hamper (potted quail, curried hare with saffron, dear little baby beetroot the size of cherries in wine vinegar, pickled pheasant eggs, all packed in glazed red jars sealed with hessian and beeswax) and a crate of elderflower cordial in stone bottles, not forgetting the dainty silver spirit stove and matching teapot. There were cushions to sleep on, mohair throws and rabbit-fur carosses, just as well because he couldn't be persuaded to light a fire, even though it was painfully obvious there wasn't another human being within twenty miles. On the first evening, just as it was getting dark, she plucked up her courage and asked if she might be allowed to look at some of the scores in the solid, coffin-like trunks—

"You can read music?"

She nodded. "I taught myself to when I was in prison once," she said. "That's in my file, too."

"I've never been in prison. What's it like?"

"Depressing."

He thought for quite some time, then nodded. "In the morning," he said, "you can have a rummage in the long brown trunk, that's all published stuff, meaning it's not the only copy. In fact, you can help yourself, if anything takes your fancy." He smiled; she could just make out the glow of his teeth in the dying light. "Don't tell me you're a fan."

"Yes, actually. You won't remember, but—"

"Oida introduced you to me at a concert, the clarinet concerto." He nodded, though of course it wasn't the concerto, it was the overture in D. "Sorry, I've never got the hang of expecting people to like my stuff. It always comes as a bit of a shock."

She took a deep breath. "Why are you going to Iden?"

"I told you, I got orders."

"But by the time we get there, the emperor could be dead, or the Easterners could be camped outside the walls."

She heard him sigh. "The truth is," he said, "I'm going to Iden to resign. Both jobs. If there's still an Intelligence department, I don't want to run it any more, and I'm almost certain there's no longer a Faculty of Music. So I'm packing it all in and getting out. Far away from here as possible. If there's any ships sailing, I rather fancy Blemya. I gather the queen's a fan. I think

Blemya is far and away our best bet, assuming they haven't all been wiped out by a plague while I wasn't paying attention. These days, it's not wise to assume anything."

"Have you been to Blemya?"

"No. You have. What's it like?"

"Hot."

"Pity. I don't do well in the heat. I sweat a lot, and there's nothing I like less than my underclothing sticking to my legs. Cold's all right, you can always do something about it—put on something warmer, throw a log on the fire—but hot just has to be endured, and I'm not the enduring sort. I don't suppose you have that problem."

"I like the heat."

"Women do," he said sagely. "And they whine incessantly if the room drops below the melting point of copper." He turned his head and grinned at her. "One of the two reasons why I never got married."

And the other one—plain as the nose on his face, so to speak. She wondered why he was doing his best to be annoying. A conditioned response, maybe, whenever he had to spend time with a fan, to bypass the gushing and stammering with a stream of drivel of his own. Or maybe this was what he was really like, though she was inclined to doubt it. More plausibly, he was steering the conversation away from hidden rocks on a flood of twaddle. So she asked him a difficult technical question about all-interval tetrachords (she'd researched it a long time ago, to spring on Oida when he wasn't expecting it; she was secretly convinced he knew nothing at all about musical theory, but had never been able to prove it), to which Procopius replied cheerfully, at length and so clearly that for half an hour after he'd finished she could've sworn she'd understood it.

At Sechora, they met some people. They walked into the Tolerance and Hope, or what was left of it, and found three men kneeling on the floor round the hearth, vainly trying to get a fire to light. They jumped up and backed away, then relaxed when they saw her. An old man and a woman travelling together weren't a threat, apparently.

As it turned out they were diplomats, accredited representatives of the Directorate of Scona. They'd come to discuss the terms of a loan their government had reluctantly agreed to make to the Western empire, but when they arrived at Rasch they found it a burned-out ruin, so resolved to press on to Iden Astea instead. She started to explain what had happened but they stopped her; they knew rather more than she did, having encountered a quarter-squadron of Eastern lancers escorting a supply officer who had arrived at Rasch a day late. Yes, there had been a plot to open the gates, though the officer didn't know who was behind it; malcontents, the opposition, the peace party if there was one. The gates would have been shut on Senza's orders, since his intention was to use the population of the city as hostages. There hadn't been any idea of burning the place down, or, if there was, Senza had neglected to mention it at staff meetings. The fire must have started accidentally, or maybe it was the work of death-before-surrender Western loyalists; in any event, the outcome was totally unexpected, and the supply officer protested that he hadn't a clue what he was supposed to do next. He had thirty carts laden with supplies rumbling along the Great West Road but no army to deliver them to, and nobody to take them back to, since Senza's five thousand lancers had been the last army-in-being outside of the Choris garrison. One of the diplomats had jokingly suggested that he keep the stuff for himself and sell it in the next market he came to; to which the officer replied that he'd do that like a shot, except every town and village he'd been through was deserted. One of the diplomats then asked: why now? What had prompted the East to gamble everything on taking Rasch? To which the officer replied that the Eastern emperor was ill and worried that he might not recover, and he was grimly determined to win the war before he died and his nephew the Western emperor inherited his throne. We rather hoped that was meant as a joke, the diplomats added, but the supply officer had previously shown no signs of a sense of humour, so probably it wasn't.

And then one of the diplomats, who'd been staring at Procopius' face, began a sentence with, *Excuse me, but*— And he was a fan, of course, in fact they all were, and they were stunned and deeply honoured to be sharing a derelict ruin with the greatest living composer of serious music; and it would be a privilege and a pleasure if they could ride together to Iden, assuming that would be entirely convenient. A trapped look passed quickly over Procopius' face, and then he said yes, of course, what a good idea. Oh, and this was his assistant; and the diplomats, who'd completely forgotten about her, smiled and bowed and then ignored her for the rest of the journey.

They arrived at the foot of a wall of white-topped mountains. About three hundred years ago, with infinite labour, the roadbuilders had turned a narrow pass, cut by the trickling of melted snow, into a flat, wide road that led to Iden Astea. Because they lived in uncertain times, they'd guarded the mouth of the pass with a wall, fifty feet high and ten feet thick, in the middle of which they set a gate. Four times the gate had been assaulted. The first, second and fourth attacks had been beaten off with heavy losses; the third time, the strongest artillery park ever assembled had pounded the gate for sixty days (to no perceptible effect), while a team of a thousand sappers had burrowed through solid rock to undermine it. The gate collapsed and the invaders poured through, to be wiped out to the last man by the heavy dragoons of Genseric II. Genseric rebuilt the gate, flooded the saps with concrete and supplemented the defences with a moat, crossed by a drawbridge raised and lowered by a hydraulic winch powered by a lock and weir.

She prided herself on not being easy to read; but, as they drew close enough to make out the gatehouse in the distance, Procopius leaned across and whispered in her ear, "I wouldn't get your hopes up."

"What do you mean?"

He didn't reply. They came closer, and she saw that the drawbridge was down and the gates were open. "That's good, isn't it?" she said.

"Arguably."

According to the latest edition of the *Military Survey*, the garrison of the gate and wall was five hundred infantry and three hundred engineers, with around six hundred civilian support staff. They rode closer. The fortress was empty. The horses' hooves clattered appallingly on the iron plating of the drawbridge, echoing off the sheer walls of the cutting, a noise so loud they must have heard it in Iden, but nobody looked out over the walls or called out a challenge.

The supplies in the wicker hamper were starting to diminish; nothing to worry about, but maybe it would be sensible to skip the entrées and the savoury until they found somewhere to resupply. Procopius drank water that night instead of elderflower cordial; there was a spring of the purest water in both empires, which rose in a marble tank decorated with marble bas-reliefs, just inside the gate. They washed out all the empty bottles and refilled them.

"Where is everybody?" asked one of the diplomats, and Procopius hazarded a guess that the garrison had been withdrawn to strengthen the defences of Iden. The diplomat reckoned that was a bit short-sighted; a small force could hold these gates against a mighty army. Yes, Procopius said, and offered no further comment.

Twenty miles from the pass to Iden; some of the richest, most valuable farmland in the empire. Grain yields here were three times the average, and someone had once calculated that you could evacuate the five biggest cities in the West to Iden and feed their populations indefinitely from the cornfields of the Ring without the need for rationing. As they followed the road they put up clouds of rooks and pigeons out of the laid, broken-down fields, where the unharvested grain had been left to rot. One of the diplomats protested that it made no sense; if the emperor had fallen back on Iden, why hadn't the crop been brought in and laid up in the siege granaries? The more he saw of this region, he said, the more he wondered why the emperors had ever bothered with Rasch, which was a liability, hard to defend and impossible to feed in wartime. Anyone with any sense would have cleared the place out and come here, where even a small army could hold out forever against the whole world. Leaving the pass undefended and the farmland derelict—At this point words failed him and he wandered off, muttering to himself, while the other two saw to the horses.

He had a point; and she tried to ask Procopius if he had any idea what was going on, but he waved her away; he was working on a flute sonata, and he needed to concentrate absolutely. So she drove the horses and kept quiet, as the rooks burst reproachfully out of the low-hedged fields and twisted in a black ribbon overhead, and the white blur on the skyline gradually resolved into a great walled city, with spires and towers roofed with blazing copper.

A stone beside the road announced that they were five miles from Iden. It was getting dark, but the diplomats wanted to press on. She agreed that it made sense; the road was straight and level, the sky was clear and the moon was nearly full. They protested that Master Procopius seemed inclined to spend the night where he was, and they'd so wanted to go with him the whole way. She explained that he was in the throes of composition; they understood perfectly, they assured her, and of course it would be criminal to disturb him at such a time. You're so lucky, they said, you'll be able to tell your grandchildren that you were there when a masterpiece was taking shape, note by note, like a stalactite. She smiled vaguely, and the diplomats rode off, talking in low voices so as not to break the spell.

When they were out of sight, Procopius looked up from the

portable writing desk balanced on his knees and said, "Well done. I don't know about you, but they made my teeth ache."

She opened the hamper and chose dinner. "How's it going?"

"What? Oh, the sonata. Finished. Want me to hum it for you?"

She didn't know what to say, so said nothing. Procopius cleared his throat, then mooed like a cow for what seemed like a very long time. "Like it?" he asked.

"Yes," she said. "Very much."

He seemed pleased. "It's a sort of meditation on the fall of Rasch," he told her, "though that's a bit of an oversimplification. I always say that music can't be about anything, it ought to be as close to abstract as it's possible to get in an imperfect world. Otherwise you get stuff like violins trying to sound like rainwater, which is all very well, but rain does it so much better. What's for dinner?"

She told him and he frowned; not quails' eggs in aspic *again*. She handed him a plate, and he scooped quails' eggs into his mouth with his fingers. His idea, his face said unequivocally, of roughing it.

Early start in the morning. The last mile and a half out from Iden is and always has been peach orchards, the very finest peaches anywhere in the world, the only place the wretched things will grow north of Seyanco, because of the uniquely favourable micro-climate. But someone had cut down all the trees and burned the trunks for charcoal. They passed a dozen or more hollowed-out beehive charcoal ovens, the baked clay crumbling into the black embers. The most expensive charcoal the world has ever known.

"Now that's a shame," Procopius said, as they passed the roofless shell of what had once been the Privileges of Integrity. It hadn't been burned down; someone had carefully stripped out the rafters and the floorboards, leaving the roof tiles scattered in heaps. "They used to do a fish curry that made your head spin."

"Someone wanted wood pretty badly."

He shrugged; not interested. "I remember stopping at the Privileges when I was a boy, and my father and I— Hello, who's this?"

Two men had emerged from behind a wall. They had bows in their hands, but no arrows on the string. One of them was a giant, boyish-faced, red-headed Rhus; she thought she knew him from somewhere. The other was short, thickset, grey-haired. "Ride on," she hissed, but Procopius didn't seem to hear her. He drew up, and called out a greeting.

She remembered where she'd seen the red-headed man, but it was too late. He'd already grabbed Procopius by the ankle, while the thickset man jumped up onto the box. She had her knife three parts out of its sheath when he kicked her in the face. She was aware of falling, and then of nothing at all.

When she woke up, she was alone. No chaise, no Procopius, no two Lodge soldiers. She felt the back of her head and her fingers met stiff caked stuff in her hair, so she'd been out long enough for the blood to clot and dry. Her knife was lying on the ground, next to a wheel-rut. Her head hurt and she realised she was seeing double. Not good. Going back to sleep was not recommended under these conditions, she knew, but she did it anyway.

She woke up nauseous, bitterly cold and wet through; there

were pools of water all around her, so she'd slept through heavy rain. The knife was still there, so she put it back in her sheath, then ran the by-now-customary inventory of all her worldly goods. The money was still in her purse, but she had no food and unsatisfactory footwear. Still, she could see the rooftops of Iden from here—assuming some prankster hadn't burned that down too, just to keep her on her toes. She examined her face in a puddle and winced. That's me, she thought. That's what years of dedicated service to my lofty ideals has left me with. Serves me right, presumably.

Nobody to be seen in either direction. She got up; cramp in her back and legs, from lying in a bad position. You want to take more care of yourself. First thing you know, you'll ruin your health.

She knew this road, though not terribly well. It had been a while, and something was horribly different. She figured out that it was the emptiness. This road should be crammed with carts, wagons, coaches, all times of day and night, because they stagger the deliveries of supplies to Iden, to avoid total gridlock on the bridge. She walked on, right up to the gate. It was shut. There was still nobody to be seen. She took a deep breath and, feeling incredibly stupid, balled her fist and knocked on the massive grey oak gate.

Nothing. She took a long step back and looked up. A face was looking down at her from an arrowslit above the arch. She waved. The face looked at her. "Hello," she called out.

The face ducked down out of sight, as though her single word had been an incoming arrow. "Hey!" she yelled, but that didn't work. She had no idea what to do next, though bursting into tears seemed favourite. She stayed where she was, and after a very long time there was a grating noise like a dragon growling, and the left side of the great gate moved back, about a foot, and there in the gap was the face. It looked at her. She stared.

"What?" it said.

She realised she'd been spoken to. "Can I come in?"

"Who the hell are you?"

"Me? Oh, nobody. I just want to come in, that's all."

The porter thought for what seemed like a very long time, then threw his weight against the gate and strained until she thought he was going to burst something, and the gate moved another eighteen inches. Then he stepped aside to let her pass.

She couldn't think of a sensible way to put it, so she said, "Is everything all right?"

The porter looked at her, head a little on one side. "Move along," he said, so she did.

Inside the gate, everything was just as she remembered it, except there were no people. She looked round for the porter, but he'd disappeared, and the gate was shut. For a moment she panicked—shut gates meant trouble, or they had done in Rasch. But that was silly. Standard operating procedure, nothing to be scared of. Welcome to Iden Astea.

She wandered up Foregate, which she had all to herself. The shops were closed and shuttered, which at least suggested an orderly cessation of normal activity, and the nightsoil pots had been emptied and the streets had been swept. She looked up at the first- and second-storey windows, but they were shuttered, too. If Musen had made it this far, she decided, he'd love this place.

Round the corner into the Fishtail, where the two parallel boulevards that led to the palace diverged. The broad pavement was clear of traders' stalls, and someone had cut down the thirty-seven lime trees that shaded the triangle where the military band used to play. She sat down on the paw of the crouching marble lion, loot from the Fire Temple at Solenco back in Gordian's day. People used to come here to feed the pigeons and sparrows, but there were no birds anywhere.

A shadow fell across her, and she twisted round, and her heart stopped.

"There you are. I was worried about you."

It was impossible; but so was the silent, deserted city. She tried to say his name, but for some reason that wasn't possible. She stared at him, and he frowned.

"It's me," he said. "Oida. Don't you recognise me?" And he held up his hand, and there was a finger missing.

"Oida," she repeated, and then; "What happened to your face?"

"I grew a beard. It's a disguise."

And then she burst out laughing.

"Well, it worked, didn't it? You didn't know who I was."

Trust Oida to find, without even looking, the only unbolted and unshuttered wine shop in a desert of barricaded front-ages. True, there was nobody else there. He sat her down on a bench, vanished into a back room and came back with a dusty bottle. "I know you don't," he said, "but right now I think you could do with one." He knocked the top off the bottle. She'd never seen it done before. He made it look easy but she was sure it wasn't. "Sorry, no cups or mugs. Mind you don't cut yourself."

She took three swallows, then choked, then waved him away as he started to fuss. "Of course I recognised you," she said. "I just didn't expect to see you here."

He was disappointed. "In spite of the beard."

"It's awful," she said. "It makes you look like a side of gammon wrapped in an otterskin."

He gave her a filthy look, then grinned. "I'll shave it off when I've got five minutes," he said. "Actually," he went on, as she lifted the bottle, "I'd lay off that stuff if I were you. It's pretty fierce, and you aren't used to it."

"Oida, what's going on? What the hell are you doing here? You're supposed to be dead."

He took the bottle from her and swallowed five gulps without even wincing. "Things have moved on since I saw you last," he said. "You know about Rasch, obviously."

"I was there."

He stared at her. "Inside?"

"Outside. I saw the soldiers go in, and then the fire."

He nodded. "Things have moved on," he repeated. "Let's see, now. First things first. The emperor's dead."

Her head was starting to swim from the firewater. "Dead?"

"Oh yes. Stupid, really. You know he was crazy about his pet dogs? Well, one of them scratched him, and it must've had something nasty in its claws, because the scratch turned bad, and the royal physicians weren't there; he'd sent them away to save money. Three days later, lockjaw. Three days after that—"

And he did the hand-across-the-mouth thing that Procopius

had done, and which she was so very familiar with. "All duly witnessed and attested," he added, "in case you were wondering. The kennel boys saw him get scratched, and he was surrounded by courtiers right up to the end. He wasn't poisoned or got out of the way. It was a stupid accident."

Like the fire at Rasch. He took another deep swill from the bottle, which was nearly empty. Apparently he was immune to it.

"So what now?" she asked.

He did his deep, wide shrug. "God only knows," he said. "It means Glauca's now the sole ruler of both empires, but—" He hesitated. "Things have moved on. Glauca is not a well man. They gave him six weeks, five weeks ago. Of course they could be wrong. I wouldn't believe most doctors if they told me my name."

Her head had stopped spinning, and she thought; so it's true, you can be shocked sober. "So he dies, and—"

"Quite. What then?"

Maybe he was being stupid. "It's obvious, surely. The war's over."

He looked at her, and she remembered what Procopius had said: *don't get your hopes up.* She felt cold down to her bones.

"Maybe," Oida said quietly. "I hope so."

Or maybe it's just beginning. "But for crying out loud," she said. "There's nobody left to fight. There's nobody *left.*"

Wry grin. "It feels a bit like that, doesn't it? Town's deserted because at the end there was nobody here but the Imperial staff, and they all pushed off when he died: nobody to pay their wages, so no reason to hang around. They cleared out the Treasury and everything of value that wasn't mortared into the stonework. Also, all the food, carts and horses. There's a few people left, servants, hewers of wood and drawers of water. But all the men from the State foundry and the armoury have gone."

"What about the soldiers?"

She'd made a joke, apparently. "What soldiers? Oh, hadn't you heard? No, of course you haven't, you've been wandering about the place, out of the loop. They had a nasty little dose of cholera, in the garrison's water supply. They had their own special water, you see, because the CO didn't trust the town stuff, reckoned someone might get at the cisterns and put something horrible in them. Cleared out half the garrison and a third of the general staff, and the rest hopped it so they wouldn't catch it too. I gather they got as far as Moduse, and then they ran into the Aram no Vei. So, officially as of a week ago, there is no Western army. Not one single solitary man, unless you count Forza Belot, and he's been cashiered. Crazy, really, when you think about it." He frowned, as if he'd suddenly remembered something important, which really shouldn't have slipped his mind. "The hell with all that," he said, "what about you? You look absolutely awful."

She wanted to laugh. "I feel how I look," she said. "How about you?"

"What you need," he said, "is something to eat."

"Yes," she said firmly. "But for crying out loud, not quails' eggs. Or guinea fowl in aspic, or sturgeons' roe or sun-dried Aelian ham. I've had nothing else for days and I'm sick to death of them."

He looked at her, but not the way she'd expected. "I've got a jar of pickled cabbage and some rather stale rye bread, or there's Siya Valley cheese."

"Yes, please."

"Coming right up."

He disappeared and came back a minute or so later with a wooden plate heaped with food. She didn't leave him any, and he didn't seem to mind.

"Courtesy of the Western army," he said, while she gnawed the cheese. "The lads I got it from didn't need it, if you get my drift. I loaded four saddlebags, so we won't starve for a day or two."

"You know what," she said with her mouth full, "I think this is the first time you've fed me with ordinary food."

"It's the best I can do."

"I'm not complaining." She swallowed, and said, "Oida, what the hell are you doing here?"

He picked up a cheese rind she'd knocked off the plate and ate it. "I came to meet someone."

"But you got overtaken by events?"

"Actually, no. But all that stuff can wait. We need to find you some new clothes. No offence, but you look like a traffic accident."

He also had a crowbar. She prised open the shutters of the Cortuli Brothers, purveyors of ladies' gowns to the discerning since the reign of Gordian IV. She rummaged around on the racks and chose something flowing in powder blue. It was rather too long, so she tore six inches off the bottom hem. "How do I look?"

He didn't answer that. "Shame the Cortulis didn't do warm outdoor coats," he said. "Come on."

"What are you doing?"

"Leaving the money. Well, they might come back some day and stealing is morally wrong. Don't pull faces, you'll stick like it."

She found a pair of shoes, elegant sea-blue with cork soles and heels, and when he tried to leave money for them as well she snarled at him like a dog. "What?" he complained. "Oh, all right, if it bothers you so much, though I don't see why it should." He closed the violated shutters behind them as best he could, though they no longer met in the middle. "Now I expect you'll want a cutler's. The best was always Fordazi, in New Parade."

He knew her too well. Fordazi's shutters took some opening, but they managed between them in the end. She chose a single-bladed skinning knife with a slight curve to it and a stag's horn handle.

"There," he said. "Feel better now?"

"Much, thank you."

"I worry about you sometimes."

They went back to the wine shop, where Oida had stashed his luggage. There was a rainwater tank out back, and she had a proper wash, for the first time in ages. But the gaunt, thin, middle-aged woman who scowled at her out of the water made her feel horribly depressed. Stupid, really. And this time, Oida hadn't even pretended that he'd come to Iden simply or primarily to rescue her. Not that, well, that sort of thing was going to matter ever again.

"After you left," he was saying, "I holed up in a little country place of mine in the Coen Valley for a bit and grew the beard, and then I took a flying visit to Blemya, and I got back just in time to hear about Rasch. Then I had to scurry about a bit making arrangements, personal stuff, and then I came straight on here. Orders."

She glanced sideways at him. "Personal stuff?"

"Money," he said. "Trouble with being dead is, you can't get at it. Fortunately I've always had a bit of a rainy-day mentality, so I've got bits and pieces squirrelled away all over the shop under names that aren't strictly speaking my own. Of course, all that's been overtaken by events, too, so, cut a long story short, financially I'm a mere shadow of my former self. But since there doesn't appear to be any money left anywhere in the empire, that's actually the least of my problems."

She grinned at him. "You're broke."

"Not exactly. Quite a few of my squirrellings were in Scona, Aelia, Blemya, places like that, so they're all right. But, like I said, I've been cut down to size somewhat since I've been dead. Actually, on paper and in theory, you're considerably richer than me."

That made her stop dead in the middle of the street. "You what?"

He was looking embarrassed. "Fact is," he said, "in a moment of romantic enthusiasm, I made a will. Well, I haven't got any real family, only Axio and the two emperors, and I thought about endowing monasteries to intercede for my immortal soul, but they're supposed to do that anyway without being paid for it. So I left everything to you." He paused, then said, "I hope you don't mind."

All that money—Except that there wasn't any, because the

empires were bankrupt, the banks had failed, it had all gone, evaporated, disintegrated. All that money, a fortune so vast that you'd need a dozen lifetimes to spend a fraction of it. All that money—security, safety, peace, all her troubles over, after a lifetime of worry and fretting and never quite having enough and never knowing where the next stuiver was coming from— had come and gone, blossomed and withered, in the twinkling of an eye.

"Sorry," he said, "are you all right? You look—"

"For God's sake," she snapped, because his voice was getting on her nerves. "You might have told me."

He didn't answer, and what he didn't say was: you were standing there with a knife in your hand and orders to kill me, and I neglected to mention that you were my sole heir. She drove the thought out of her mind, but the stink of it remained.

"Academic now anyhow, like I said. Of course you never know, one day some of it might be worth something again. But I wouldn't get your hopes up."

She noted the choice of words. "Oida," she said, "it may have escaped your notice, but you're still alive."

"Not officially. Not that I can prove in a court of law. Mind you, I don't think there's any of them left either. Look, forget I mentioned it, all right? I only told you because I thought it'd amuse you."

She opened her mouth to tell him what she thought about that, but changed her mind. Yes, once the shattering, numbing shock had worn off, that's what it was, amusing. Like watching *The Orphans' Tragedy* is a form of amusement, or listening to a Procopius symphony—

"Anyhow," he went on, striding ahead so she had to start moving again to keep up with him, "there's absolutely no chance of me coming back to life any time soon, with my delightful brother still on the loose. I meant to ask you. How did he take it?"

"What?"

"The news. The rosewood box."

She stopped again. "He was happy."

Oida's face froze, and then he sighed. "I imagine so, yes."

"Very happy. Like it was the best thing that had ever happened."

He hadn't liked hearing that. "So he believed in it all right. That's the main thing. I'd hate to think all this had been a waste of time."

For some reason, she found that offensive. "Quite," she said. "A bit like the war, in fact. And the end of the world."

He looked at her. "Sorry," he said. "Where did that come from?"

"You do realise what you've done, don't you?" The anger came frothing out—it wasn't what she was really angry about, but it would do to be going on with. "Staging your own death, so you'll be safe and happy in bloody Scona with your squirrelled-away millions. You've seen to it that Axio is going to be the next emperor."

And how did he react? He sighed, very long and deep, then rested his back against a wall and slid down it until he was sitting on the ground. She hadn't expected that, not one bit. "Oida? Are you all right?"

He shook his head. "No, of course not. And don't tower over me like that, it's rude."

She knelt down beside him. "Well?" she said.

"For a start," he said, suddenly brisk, "Axio is my elder brother, so in order for anything to change, he's the one who'd have to die, not me. For another, think just for one moment about this stupid war we've been having. Now ask yourself, if I was still alive, what might very well happen? Axio is proclaimed rightful emperor in, for the sake of argument, the West. Will that go down well in the East? I don't think so. No, next thing I know, someone pops a bag over my head and whisks me off to Choris, where I'm crowned as schismatic emperor of the East, whether I like it or not. And so Axio immediately sends for Forza Belot, and whoever's pulling my strings at that moment sends for Senza, and they conscript all the ten-year-olds and eighty-year-olds, and we have another war. Correction; the same war, phase two." He shook his head violently. "No. Axio's not a wonderful human being, but there are worse things than the absolute monarchy of a psychotic monster. As we've just seen."

It really was the most ridiculous thing, the two of them, crouching on the pavement in a deserted street in an empty city, arguing. Nothing left to argue about, after all. "Fine," she said. "You fuck off out of it and let that lunatic—"

"I was rather hoping you'd come with me."

That's how they hunt the wild boar, or so she'd been told. You stand there in the open, between the boar and its safe haven, while your friends with the dogs goad the stupid creature into red-eyed frothing fury, and it charges you. And at the very last moment, practically when you can smell its disgusting breath, you lower your spear and jam the buttspike into the dirt and let the crazy animal skewer itself, driving the point deep into its own heart, which you'd never have the strength to do. "Say what?"

"Come with me. Share my squirrelled millions. Well, million. Let's get the hell out of this ghastly mess and go somewhere where there's still people and food to eat and things to buy and buildings with the roof still on. God knows, you've earned a bit of peace, even if I haven't." He paused, looking at her desperately to see if there was any sign, any sign at all, that the spear had gone home. "You don't have to marry me or anything, I know you don't like me that way, but we can just be friends. You're the only friend I've ever had, did you know that? The only reason I've stuck it out for so long is—" He stopped. Sometimes the boar just keeps on coming up the spear, neglecting to realise that it's dead, and then it gets you. "You don't fancy the idea. Fair enough. I just thought I'd mention it."

She looked at him, with his big cow eyes and his idiotic beard. "I can't," she said.

"Right, that's fine. Just forget I said anything."

"I can't," she repeated. "I belong to the Lodge. You know that. Body and soul, remember? Unless they let me go, I can't just walk away."

"Dear God." He stared at her, as if he'd just noticed a third arm. "You believe, don't you? You're a goddamned true believer. That's amazing. All these years I've known you and I never realised."

She felt her fists tighten. "Of course I am. The hell with you, Oida, I thought you understood me. But you don't. You don't know me from a hole in the ground."

"Of course." He nodded slowly. "Of course you are, and I've been too stupid to see it. I'm sorry. That's unforgivable."

"And I thought—"

"You thought I'm a true believer, too." He closed his eyes, screwed them tight shut. "Yes, of course I am, I always have been. It's not so long ago that I walked through the gates of Senza Belot's camp with orders to kill him, knowing full well that that would be the end of me. Come to think of it, that was when I made that dumb will. The orders came down, and I hesitated, just for a moment or so, and I lowered my head and did it. Well, obviously I didn't, I got lucky. But I would've. I'd made my mind up to do it, as far as I was concerned I was dead already, and all for the Lodge, no doubts, no questions. So don't you ever tell me I'm not Lodge to the bloody core. It's just—"

"What?"

He lifted his head and looked at her. "The Lodge has no further use for me. They couldn't have made it any clearer. They ordered you to kill me. You know what that means? The Great Smith has decided I'm useless, not fit for anything, not even as scrap. Which means—" He stopped, bit his lip. "That's not strictly true. They figured I could do a job of work by dying. So I died. To all intents and purposes, I died, and that's it. There's absolutely nothing else they want me for. I've done everything I can, and I no longer exist. So—" He spread his arms wide, then let them flop to his sides. It should have been melodrama, but it wasn't. "I tried to find a way of being useful even in death, I saw to it that you'd be all right after I was gone, but even that's been taken away from me. You know what? There's times I wish you'd actually done it, because if I'm no bloody good to Him, what good can I possibly be to myself?"

She tried to find something to say. This was her big chance, to help, to save him, to pay him back, to even the score. But she couldn't think of anything at all.

"And that's not all," he went on, looking away. "You were given an order, and you disobeyed it. The one thing the Lodge can't ever forgive is disloyalty. You're the broken tool, the flawed anvil, the cracked hammer, and there is no health in you. They may not know it at Headquarters, but He does. You really think He wants you after what you've done? Forget it. There's no way back from that. You're finished. Oh, and it's all my fault. Believe it or not, that thought doesn't make me feel a whole lot better."

But she shook her head. "You said," she told him. "You said, there's a schism in the Lodge. Those orders can't have been genuine. I know they couldn't have been. That's why I couldn't obey them."

He didn't seem to be listening. "So anyway," he said. "Here we are, two abominations in the sight of the Almighty. We're no earthly use to anyone except each other. Let's go to Scona and sleep in a room with furniture and eat fresh grapes."

So there it was, out in the open; what she'd decided she wanted most in all the world, or what was left of the world, there for her to accept or reject. It was also a way out, the only one she was likely to get. It was security, money, peace, everything, neatly stowed in a box, and all she had to do was say yes, or, if she didn't feel like speaking, nod her head. But she found she couldn't, because of something he'd said. *Then I had to scurry about a bit making arrangements, personal stuff, and then I came straight on here. Orders.* A fairly typical Oida statement. She'd heard enough of them over the years, and had learned not to encourage them by listening to them too closely. Scurry about a bit; by that he meant lightning-fast journeys in covered chaises, meeting important people, exercising the charm, doing deals, making and using money. It was designed to inspire awe while still preserving the illusion of modesty and self-deprecation, and she was so used to it that she'd taken no notice, until now. I came straight on here, to where you are. Why? Orders. Orders from whom, since he was supposed to be dead—all that spurting, pent-up eloquence, about God forsaking him, not even fit for the scrap-pile, thrown into the darkness outside the flickering light of the forge fire; lies. Because, if he no longer existed as far as the Lodge was concerned, who was giving him orders?

And then she remembered the letter that Forza Belot had read to her, and suddenly she knew that he hadn't written it. When Forza read it to her, having authenticated the handwriting as he'd been instructed to do, she'd told him; he couldn't have written in, in his own hand, because of the missing finger. He hadn't argued with that; he'd accepted the letter as a forgery and refused to try and make sense of it, and once she'd escaped from his house and presence she'd had other things on her mind and hadn't thought about it since. But the letter—

"Oida."

"Yes?"

"Did you write to Forza Belot?"

"Why would I do a thing like that?"

"Did you?"

He took a deep breath. "No," he said. "Of course not. I'm dead, aren't I?"

She hadn't mentioned when the supposed letter had been

written. "You told me," she said, "that there's a split in the Lodge. Is that true?"

He shrugged. "For a while I suspected it. Only way I could make sense of them ordering my death, I guess. But it's none of my business now, is it?" He stood up. "I'm guessing the answer is no," he said. "And, as you're well aware, I never take no for an answer. Well, I do sometimes, but not from you. All right, if you're not coming with me, what do you propose doing next? In case you hadn't noticed, there's not a lot anyone can do around here any more."

"I didn't say no," she replied, quickly and quietly. "If I believed a single word you've just said, I'd come with you like a shot. But I don't believe you. Whether that's enough to stop me coming with you I just don't know."

He gazed at her, as if she was land and he was on a raft, being carried out to sea. "That's fair enough," he said. That was the thing, the whole thing, about Oida. He never ceased to amaze her.

"I'm going to think about it," she said. "On my own, without you buzzing at me."

"All right." He stood up. "You take your time, I won't rush you. Just don't wander off too far, all right? I'll be in the teahouse."

He walked away without looking back.

PART FOUR

PART FOUR

So she went to the Single Teardrop temple, mostly because it was the first building she came to that wasn't locked and shuttered. The name derives from the colossal post-Revisionist fresco that covers the whole of the north wall. The Invincible Sun stands in glory, radiating golden light over all the nations of the earth. His face is serene, totally impassive, and in his left eye glistens a single golden tear. Over the course of a thousand years of passionate debate, opinions have divided sharply over what the tear means, the only consensus being that it must mean something. She looked at it, and decided that the artist had put it in because, without it, the composition was bland and commonplace, and the tear made it rather more interesting.

She tried to concentrate on the points at issue, but instead her mind wandered, breaking out of the confines of the problem to be resolved like goats through a newly laid hedge.

All her life, she realised, she'd had faith, ever since the Lodge bought her from the berry-pickers and told her she had talents which the Great Smith considered useful. She'd believed it instinctively and absolutely, the way a drowning man catches hold of a rope. She had accepted that she belonged to the Lodge, in both senses; she was a member of it—no longer alone, no longer weak—and its property, to be disposed of as the Lodge saw fit, regardless of any wishes of her own. And now, after a long, gruelling campaign of fruitless victories and bloodless defeats, she'd fallen in love with Oida, the man who'd just lied to her, and who she knew she could never trust about anything apart from the fact that he loved her. Faith and love; she didn't really want to think about them right now; it was rather more important to worry out this business of the letter and Oida's slip of the tongue about orders. But she thought about faith and love, and realised that what they had in common was that they can't be acquired by choice. You can't decide to have faith, or be in love. You can't make yourself love or believe. Faith and love steal over you, like sleep. The more you try to go to sleep, the more you lie awake. The priests and the Lodge urge and implore you to have faith, to believe, to trust; how stupid is that? You can desperately want to believe, but the more you try, the less it happens. You can see how much better your life would be if only you could bring yourself to fall in love, but it simply can't be done. By the same token, once you have faith, once you're in love, you can't just snap your fingers and wake up; and once those fingers have snapped and you open your eyes, no power on earth will bring back sleep, faith or love, not even if the emperor were to command it; honour and riches if you comply, a horrible death if you don't. It simply can't be done.

And the Great Smith had ordered her to murder Oida, and she'd done no such thing. Oida had been right about that, even if he was a liar. She'd refused a direct order from the whole of which she was a tiny part. The little finger had refused an order from the brain. That was impossible, because the finger has no will of its own, but nevertheless she hadn't done as she was told, so she no longer belonged. Could that possibly have brought about the end of the world? Unlikely, because she wasn't that important. She only had importance, relevance, meaning as a component part of the whole. But had her dysfunction thrown everything out of joint (the small part that breaks and derails the whole machine)? Highly unlikely. The war had depopulated the empire long before she made her act of rebellion. The likeliest thing was that she'd broken nobody and nothing except herself. There was a degree of comfort in that, but not very much.

But if there was schism in the Lodge, and if the order she'd been given was crooked and unholy—she thought about that, and decided that it made no difference. The brain orders the hand to strike. The little finger refuses, the blow isn't struck, the misguided decision isn't implemented—makes no odds. Thou shalt not second-guess the Lord thy God. If there was schism and treachery in the Lodge, it could only be because the Great Smith had a use for schism and treachery; which was certainly not impossible, given that He has a use for everything, even murder, even Axio and Musen. Everything, that is, apart from her, because she'd been told to do a simple thing and had refused.

She glanced up at the vast image on the wall in front of her. There are no paintings, icons, frescos, mosaics, carvings of the Great Smith. Nobody knows why, there just aren't. She'd always assumed that it was because He didn't like the way He looked, something she could easily relate to. Was there a tear in His eye? She doubted it. Not the contemplative, introspective sort, from what she knew of Him, not an intellectual, very much the man of action. If He saw something that distressed Him, he'd do something about it, instead of snivelling. The Invincible Sun had never appealed to her, even for a moment. What credibility could you find in a god who died every evening, messily and publicly, in a blaze of melodramatic red blood? Priests she'd talked to had been surprised by her attitude. How can you not believe, they told her, when you can see Him, every day of the year, when it isn't cloudy and overcast? To which she was given to answering that she came from the Mesoge, where it was always raining.

She heard a footstep behind her and turned round quickly. She saw a young man, very tall, with red hair. He had a bow in his hand, but no arrow on the string.

"Hello," she said, trying her best to sound casual. "It's Teucer, isn't it?"

"Commissioner."

Who? Oh yes, she'd forgotten. Silly, really, an outcast being a Commissioner of the Lodge. She smiled at him. "What are you doing here?"

"If you wouldn't mind coming with me."

But she did mind, very much. "Why? Where to?"

He was good at looking respectful. Probably he'd learned it at Beal, where there's so very much to respect. It's hard to look respectful while you draw an arrow from your quiver and nock it on the string, all in one fluent movement, without even glancing down. "Is that a threat?"

"Yes, Commissioner."

Over the years, she'd been threatened by the best, and a bow is a pretty poor way of going about it. An archer's only option is to kill or maim you, so he's probably bluffing. "Put that thing down," she said pleasantly, "and tell me who wants to see me. Please."

"I'm sorry. I don't know."

"Fine. Who gave you the order?"

"Captain Musen."

Axio. She'd forgotten about him, too. "Well, now," she said. "He's a captain and I'm a Commissioner. Didn't anyone ever tell you not to point arrows at people?"

Rather to her surprise, he lowered the bow, though the arrow stayed on the string. "I was told not to take orders from you, Commissioner, I'm sorry."

"Really. On whose authority?"

"Triumvir Axio, Commissioner."

She pulled a grin. "You won't be needing the bow, Sergeant," she said, "the Triumvir and I are old friends. All right, lead on. I'm right behind you."

But Axio shouldn't need threats—not unless he'd found out. She did the mental geometry, and wished she'd taken the trouble to learn how to throw a knife. But Sergeant Teucer had learned a thing or two; he kept just enough distance between them to give himself time to draw and loose before she came within distance, and he watched her every step of the way, down Silvergate and across the square to the Mansion House, then down Drovers Yard, which (she remembered now) was where the Lodge had its meeting house in Iden. All properly official, then, though presumably the meeting house had been thoroughly ransacked by Intelligence—sure enough, the doors had been boarded up, and the boards prised off, and two archers were on sentry duty outside. One of them took away her knife, which she guessed was inevitable. Still, it was a shame to let it go, after so brief an acquaintance.

She'd never been in the Warden's office in the Iden house. Turned out she hadn't missed much. It was oak-panelled, but lighter patches showed where various works of art had recently been removed, presumably to fund the war effort. The chair Axio was sitting in was a standard Western issue officers' camp stool, and it was the only one in the room. Musen was standing next to him.

"Thanks, Sergeant," Axio said. "No, don't go, I may need you."

Axio had been in the wars. He had a black eye, and a cut on his forehead, from which he hadn't bothered to sponge off the dried blood. The knuckles of his left hand were skinned, and his clothes were grimy and caked with mud. He looked at her for a moment, then said, "I remembered something. About my brother."

His right hand was resting on the lid of the rosewood box, balanced on his knee. She looked at it, then lifted her eyes quickly.

"He's ambidextrous."

"No he's not."

Axio shook his head. "Yes," he said, "he is. Or at least, he was when he was a kid, and I don't think it's something that goes away as you get older. For some reason, he quit using his left when he was about fifteen, but that was just him being perverse. He can write and play the fiddle just as well with his left as his right."

He opened the lid of the rosewood box, then let it fall to the floor. Salt spilled out everywhere, and something rolled behind the leg of his stool. "I didn't know that," she heard herself say.

"No reason why you should. He's alive, isn't he?"

"No, of course not. I killed him."

"No." Axio glared at her. "He's alive, and you disobeyed orders. He figured the finger would fool me, and it did, for a time. Where is he?"

"He's dead," she said, with as much anger as she could muster. "I stabbed him in the chest—here," she said, pointing to her ribs, "and then in the ear, through into the brain. Then I cut off his finger to show you. It's true. I can take you to where he's buried, if you want."

But he smiled at her. "No you can't," he said, "because I've been there, and the grave's empty. Just a box full of bricks. I don't blame you for that," he added kindly. "You were long gone by the time they played that little charade. I'm guessing he arranged it himself, which is why it was done so badly. No, he's alive all right. Tell me where he is, or I'll kill you."

"I don't know."

Axio nodded, and suddenly she was on the floor, with a strong hand gripping the back of her neck. Then she was dragged to her knees by her hair. "You know about me," Axio said. "Tell me where he is, and I'll let you live."

She opened her mouth, then closed it again. Then Musen kicked her in the face, and all she could think about was the pain.

It wasn't the first time, and she'd been through worse. A part of her that stayed lucid and rational throughout pointed out that

Axio and his men were more enthusiastic than scientific. Too much pain and the subject is swamped by it, and before you know it they die or pass out; which she did, at some point. She came round and saw the ceiling, through one eye. The other wouldn't open, but she could move it under the eyelid, which was reassuring. Her face was wet; they'd brought her round with cold water.

"Tell me where he is," Axio said, though she couldn't see him.

She opened her mouth. Voice not working very well, so probably they'd damaged her throat. "Don't know," she said.

"Is he here? In Iden?"

"Don't know."

She heard Axio sigh. He sounded so very weary, and disappointed, and distressed by all the deceit and wickedness in the world. "Kill her," he said.

"He's in Blemya."

"Hold it," Axio snapped. "Say again?"

"In Blemya. With the queen. She's a fan."

"A what?"

"Fan," she croaked. "She likes his music."

And that was a mistake; it was Procopius she liked, not Oida. She wondered if that was going to cost her her life; but apparently not. "No accounting for taste," Axio said. "All right, take her to the infirmary and get her patched up."

"You're incredibly lucky," the doctor told her. "You came that close to losing the right eye, and how your lung wasn't punctured I just don't know. We might even get that left hand working again, though I wouldn't bank on it."

She asked for a mirror, but he only smiled. "Better not," he said. "I'd count your blessings if I were you. It could've been so much worse."

When she was well enough to have visitors, the chief steward came to see her. He apologised profusely. The food was terrible, the room was dirty, the bedclothes were a disgrace, but with no staff and no supplies other than what the black market could furnish, what could he do? And it was only going to get worse. The traders wouldn't take money any more, they wanted paying in icons, rare manuscripts, ivory triptychs, things they could unload on foreigners, and it was common knowledge, the government had stripped the place bare when the Lodge declared war on the empire. True, a few particularly sacred and indispensible objects had been hidden away, but all of them had gone to keep bread on the table and salt in the jar, and as for hiring servants—

It occurred to her, while the steward was talking, that she must still be a Commissioner of the Lodge and a person of importance. It didn't matter, she assured him. He was doing a fine job in very trying circumstances, and she would make a point of commending him to the Promotions Committee (which she'd just invented, but he didn't know that) at her earliest opportunity. Meanwhile, there was something he could do for her, if it didn't involve breaking confidences or revealing classified information—

Triumvir Axio and his guards had left on the same day that she'd been admitted to the hospital. They hadn't said where they were going, though one of the grooms reckoned he'd heard two of the soldiers saying something about Blemya. Yes, ships were still running between Beloisa and Blemya, that was where the Blemyan traders came to barter looted religious and Imperial artwork for barley flour, so presumably the Triumvir had sailed with one of them, if that's where he'd really gone, though of course you couldn't rely on the word of the working classes, they'd say anything just to draw attention to themselves.

Could he possibly take a letter for her? Of course, no trouble at all. And would he happen to know if Director Procopius, of the Imperial College of Music, was somewhere in the city? He couldn't say, but he could try and find out. There were so few people in town these days that it shouldn't be a problem.

The doctor came twice a day, and he was very pleased with her, as though getting well was something you could decide to do—add that to the list, she told herself, but didn't pursue it any further. In fact, she was doing so well, it might be possible for her to get up and walk once round the courtyard, if she promised to go back to bed for the rest of the day. How long before she was well enough to leave? Let's not push our luck, shall we? It was a miracle she was alive at all.

She asked the steward for something to read. He came back three hours later with a small oilskin bag, containing volumes 8, 9 and 14 of Gannadius' *History of the Aelian Republic*. Lucky to have those, he told her, when she gave him a reproachful look; and she'd better get a move on and read them, because they were promised to a Bessamid trader who'd offered two bushels of wheat for them, sight unseen. She thanked him and said that they were a marvellous improvement on nothing at all, which was actually true.

She woke up out of a deep sleep to find someone standing over her. She blinked. It was someone she knew, and didn't want to see.

"Commissioner," he said.

"General Belot," she replied.

Forza Belot had brought his own chair, which was just as well. He unfolded it and sat down. His face was thinner than it had been the last time she'd seen him, and he looked tired.

"The idiot downstairs," he said, "tells me you're the highest ranking Lodge officer in the city. Is that true?"

"I don't know," she said. "It's possible, certainly. I'm a Commissioner, and that's pretty hot stuff."

He wasn't in the mood. "In that case," he said, "are you authorised to conduct peace negotiations between the empire and the Lodge?"

"I guess so. How about you?"

"Yes."

"Really? Remind me, who's the emperor these days? I'm a bit out of touch."

"I am," Forza said.

She nodded slowly. "Just the West, or is Glauca finally dead? Nobody tells me anything."

"Just the West," Forza said. "I took control yesterday, as a matter of fact."

"Good for you. What are you using for money?"

He gave her a sour look, then converted it to a grin. "Thin

air and optimism," he said. "That's one of the things I wanted
to talk to you about, actually."

"And an army?"

"That was one of the other things."

They talked for a while. She admired his ability to sublimate
the loathing he clearly felt for her into intelligent and construc-
tive diplomacy. He was also disarmingly honest. He had, he
freely admitted, no money and no soldiers, no support from the
few scattered remnants of the old government, nothing in fact
except his name and a total lack of rivals—

"Unless you count that ape Axio," Forza said. "You know
him, of course."

"Slightly."

"My condolences."

"I owe him everything. And of course he's next in line to the
throne. You realise he's Lodge."

Forza nodded. "But he's not here, is he? My people tell me he
left for Blemya. And he'd make a truly awful emperor."

"You're suggesting I make a deal with you behind his back."

They talked a little more. Then she said, "Changing the
subject for a moment, what about your brother? Is he still alive,
or did he die at Rasch?"

"He's dead," Forza said firmly, and she could tell he was
lying. "So, really, there's nothing left to fight about, or at least
nobody left to fight."

She yawned; not deliberately, but she didn't try very hard to
stifle it. "When you say you've got no army, you're exaggerating,
surely. A man like you wouldn't leave the house without a squadron of cavalry. It'd be like going out without your trousers."

She was getting on his nerves. Good. "I've got a hundred and twenty men," he said. "My people, from my wife's estate. You tried to poison them, remember."

"They'll do," she said. "It's a hundred and twenty more than anyone else has got, except for us. Good. I'd like to borrow them, please."

She'd shocked him. "Are you serious?"

"Very. And I need a good officer to lead them. In return, you can be emperor of the West."

He breathed out slowly through his nose. "And the loan?"

"Yes, and the no Vei horse-archers. But not yet. And please bear in mind, any deal we may make is subject to ratification by the head of the Lodge."

That made him grin. "We just discussed that. He's in Blemya."

She shook her head. "Axio's a Triumvir, not the Chief Executive."

"Fine. So who's the real boss?"

Big smile. "I have absolutely no idea."

Folded between the pages of book nine of Gennadius' dismally written and largely inaccurate history, she found a single sheet of parchment. It was very old, and it had been ground blank with sand and brick dust for re-use, probably more than once, so that the ink had soaked into the abused fibres and the letters tended to spread, like coppiced saplings. The handwriting was Reformed Cursive and the language was archaic Mezentine, which it just so happened she could read fluently. It said:

On closer examination, I found evidence of cleaning, probably with some
form of abrasive powder (pumice, millstone wash or corn husks impregnated
with cutlers' grit) in consequence of which the fine raised detail of the relief
had been rounded off and lost; however, I was able to confirm thereby that
the material was solid silver rather than base metal silver-washed. A light
powdery white dust trapped in the crevices also indicated regular cleaning,
and I draw the conclusion that the item was on public display and that
the tarnish was regularly removed by a curator who had little idea of the
significance of the artefact in his charge. Accordingly I felt justified in
detaching a small section from the top left edge, and was able to determine
the purity of the silver, which proved to be .875 fine, which would be
consistent with an item made from melted-down Imperial coinage produced
at one of the North-western mints of that era. I then suffered the sample to
be totally consumed in cinnabar, which revealed slight traces of lead, mercury
and [some word she didn't know]; the first two impurities are common to
all silver, but the third was, in my experience, unique to the silver mines
of Spire Cross, which were in operation for no more than forty years in
the reigns of Simeon II and Antisyrus. This last would seem to me to
be conclusive proof that the item is genuine. I would therefore strongly
recommend that

And that was all. Ain't that the way.

Well, yes, the doctor said, she could get up, if she absolutely insisted, but he wouldn't recommend it, in fact he'd want a disclaimer absolving him of all responsibility, because in his opinion it'd be a very stupid thing to do. So she solemnly absolved him of all blame, forgave him his sins and formally discharged him from her care. On your head be it, he said, and left.

She got out of bed and walked up and down the room for

ten minutes, which made her feel much better. Then she rang the bell. The steward came—you're out of bed, he observed: is that wise?—and she put in an order for clothes and shoes. I'm sorry, we haven't got anything like that here. She told him to go out and steal them. It'll be all right, she said. You can leave the money if it'll make you feel any better. We haven't got any money, the steward told her. In that case, she said, don't leave any.

She walked up and down for an hour, and then the steward came back, looking mildly stunned, as though he'd just had a vision of something disturbing and wonderful. He had with him a sort of grey sack with holes for her arms and head, and stout, good quality ladies' walking boots, brand new, two sizes too big. She tore up a pillow case and stuffed them until they fitted, while the steward stood and gazed at her, reduced to silence by the violent death of bed linen. You wouldn't happen to have, she asked, anything in the way of a weapon? He blinked, as though she'd used a word from a foreign language. You know, a dagger, knife, a small hatchet would do at a pinch. He went away without speaking and came back clutching an Eastern-issue dragoon officer's backsabre, complete with frog, twin belts and fringed tassel. Thank you, she said, that'll do fine. I'm leaving now. It's been an honour, the steward said. Do drop in any time you're in the neighbourhood.

Iden Astea had changed since she saw it last. Most of the shut-tered shops had been broken into, their contents disappeared, the bits of broken shutter thriftily scooped up and spirited away for firewood. There were dead bodies on the pavement, lying like flotsam on a beach. Nobody had come to collect them, but their clothes and boots had gone. She glanced up, looking for a smoking chimney, but the air was clean and sharp with a slight chill. She snapped the backsabre trying to prise open a door that had defeated her fellow looters; she had no reason to believe there was anything worth having inside, but it was the only intact door she'd seen, so her options were limited.

The wine shop where Oida had been staying had been stripped of its doors, window and door frames, threshold and floorboards. She walked in, examined it carefully for signs of life (which took about as long as it takes to sneeze) and left. Of course he wouldn't stay there, once it had sunk in that she'd gone and wasn't coming back. He had more sense. Now, she knew him better than she'd ever known anyone in her entire life, so where would he have gone? She thought long and hard and realised she had no idea. Oida, gone; and with him the food, the transport, the money, the bed for the night, the book to read on the journey, all gone for ever. She prayed to the Great Smith, who never listens to prayers, that he hadn't gone to Blemya, though now she came to think of it he could very well have done. Hadn't thought of that when she put Axio on what she'd fondly believed was the wrong trail; she hadn't anticipated spending three weeks immobilised and incommunicado. She wondered if she should go back to the Lodge house, where they still had some food and a bed to sleep in, but decided she couldn't face the look the steward would give her. The Lodge, so it would seem, was finished, too, just like everything else. She hadn't anticipated that, but maybe she should have. Wherever it was, if it still existed anywhere, it wasn't present and active in the ruins of the Western empire, or it wouldn't have left its house steward in Iden to starve slowly to death. Someone would have been sent, with food and money, or at the very least a large covered wagon, to carry any castaway Craftsmen to safety. She decided that she'd made peace with Forza under false pretences, not that the thought bothered her in the least.

So, she asked herself, where now? Academic question, since there were no carriages, carts, wagons, chaises or traps, and no horses to pull them, and no food to eat along the way, whether she rode or walked. How long would it take the people of a city, devoid of leadership and cut off from all sources of supply, to starve to death? Probably less time than you'd think. It would be a quiet cataclysm, like a fire going out. You could easily miss it if you were out of things for a while, laid up recovering from injuries, say, or otherwise indisposed.

She went to the Single Teardrop, to find the walls bare and the great fresco missing. Someone had chiselled it off the wall in chunks, presumably imagining that they could put it back together again later and finding out too late that fresco doesn't work like that; there were lumps of painted plaster on the floor, in heaps, and she could picture in her mind how it had happened. At first it comes away easily, and they're laying it out carefully on the floor, numbering the segments in chalk. But then they try and move it, and it falls to pieces in their hands. It'll be all right, they tell themselves, and they try and salvage at least some of it, and they carry on trying until they're left with nothing but coloured rubble—it's all still there, nothing's been lost, but no power on earth will ever get it back together again the way it used to be. The truth sinks in eventually, and they give up and go away. Seemed like a good idea at the time, pity it didn't work out.

The hell with it. Overrated, in her opinion, and if it hadn't been chipped off the wall sooner or later the damp would have got into it and achieved the same result. She sat on the floor where the pews had been and stared up into the belly of the dome, too high to reach and strip of its gilded tiles. There were, after all, worse places to end up; and maybe, if she thought long and hard about it, she'd be clever enough to find a way out—if she could be bothered, which she wasn't sure she could be. When the world ends, maybe the sensible thing is to end with it. Later, perhaps. In the meantime, the beating of the heart and the action of the lungs are a useful prevarication, keeping all options open.

To keep herself amused and her mind off food, she asked herself the question, whose fault is this? At first, the answer seemed perfectly simple. The two emperors, East and West, who fell out over something or other—nobody had ever found out what, exactly—and fought each other until everything was gone—a bit like a game of chess which comes down to white king, black king and one other piece, all the others having perished; a perfectly valid way to play the game, if the purpose of playing is to win. But that answer was a bit too simplistic. The emperors were at fault, but they weren't to know that each of them had one of the two greatest generals of all time leading their vast but eventually finite armies, and that these two generals would cancel each other out; two brothers who fell out about something, nobody knew what exactly; two kings left stranded on an empty chessboard, doomed to pace and menace and feint and retreat for all eternity.

The real answer, of course, was staring her in the face. It was the Lodge's fault, for not putting a stop to it. Painfully, shamefully obvious. The Lodge could have murdered, say, Emperor Glauca and Forza Belot. It would all have been over in days, and the world need not have ended. But the Lodge had done no such thing. She wondered about that for a long time, then gave up, for fear of having to face the obvious answer.

She was asleep when they found her. She was dreaming, and in her dream someone called to her: Commissioner, Commissioner Telamon. The dream admitted of no suitable context for that title, so she woke up.

A woman was kneeling over her, someone she recognised. Behind her, a large number of armed men. I must stop coming here, she told herself. "Triumvir Lycao," she said. "What are you doing here?"

Lycao turned her head to look at someone, and she recognised him, too. Last time they'd met, he'd ordered his men to break her arm. No, that couldn't be right. "Excuse me," she said, "are you Senza Belot?"

Nobody seemed able to hear her. Four of the soldiers came over and lifted her up. "It's all right, I can manage perfectly well," she said, and then found that she couldn't. So she let them carry her, out of the temple and into a jet-black carriage, surrounded by a cavalry escort. Lycao got in next to her, and Senza sat opposite, his gilded helmet coddled on his knee, like a baby.

"It's all right," Lycao said to her, which was just plain silly.

*

"You must have been there for days," Lycao told her. "You nearly died. There's practically nothing left of you."

"I don't feel particularly bad."

"Look." Lycao lifted a mirror, and showed her something truly horrible: a skeleton, a loathsome thing with bones sticking through the skin. "We found you just in time. Lucky we knew where to look."

She had no idea where she was, though it was a distinct improvement on Iden. She was lying in a bed in a small, warm room, in comfortable clean bed linen, with a lamp burning. "You knew?"

Lycao nodded. "Well, it was a guess. He said the Single Teardrop was your favourite place in Iden, so we went there first."

He said. Someone who didn't know her very well, because it simply wasn't true—overrated, as previously noted. "Axio?"

Lycao looked at her and frowned. "Oida," she said. "He's worried sick about you. That's why we came."

When she hadn't come back, Oida had gone looking for her. At first he guessed that her answer had been no and she'd slipped away rather than tell him face to face, but then he realised that would be entirely out of character, and, besides, where would she have gone? That gave him pause for thought, so he went to the Lodge house, where discreet enquiries (she couldn't imagine Oida making discreet enquiries) revealed that Triumvir Axio was in town. As to what had happened after that, not a great leap of intuition needed, more of a bunny hop.

So he'd stolen the last remaining horse in Iden and lit out for Headquarters—

"Headquarters?" she had to ask. "Where—?"

She'd asked a bad question. Lycao gave her a nasty look, then continued with the story. At Headquarters, he'd burst in on a private meeting between the two remaining Triumvirs and the head of the Order. There had been a bit of a scene, with Oida making threats, until the Chief had agreed to his demands—

"Which were?"

"To find you and bring you here."

"What threats?"

"You don't need to know that."

"Fine. Where's here?"

"You don't need to know that either." Lycao gave her a look that ought to have chilled her to the bone, but somehow didn't. "I might add, I was against it. Taking action at this stage puts the whole plan at risk, and we could lose everything. To be entirely frank with you, I don't think you're worth it. Luckily for you, though, Oida disagrees." She pursed her lips. "He's in for a shock when he sees you, but that's his problem."

"Why does it matter what Oida thinks? He's not a Commissioner. He's *dead*."

"Something else you don't need to know."

"What's Senza Belot doing here?"

That got her a thin smile. "He's on his honeymoon. As am I. We'd hoped to go somewhere a bit more romantic, but you spoiled all that."

Different doctor, same bedside manner, same quantity and quality of information. She was lucky to be alive, a minor miracle, and somehow it was all her fault, though when she asked what she'd done wrong the doctor just looked at her and changed the subject. It's all right now, he assured her, you're going to be fine.

"Where am I? Where is this place?"

"Plenty of rest," the doctor said, "and no excitement."

An old woman with a lot on her mind looked in on her every half-hour or so and brought her gallons of strong brown broth that smelled and tasted of bones, but which was good for her, apparently. Every time the broth turned up, she pleaded for something to read, but it appeared that that wouldn't be good for her at all, so no dice. Every time the old woman left the room she bolted the door from the outside; read into that what you like. There was a window, but it was shuttered, and the bars were on the other side. She could always kill the old woman and escape. Maybe tomorrow, when she was feeling a bit stronger.

Lying on her back all day, she found it very hard to get to sleep at night, though for all she knew what she assumed was day could just as easily have been night, and vice versa. Needless to say, when at last she had a visitor who wasn't the old woman or the doctor, she'd finally managed to nod off, and the visitor— Triumvir Thratta, no less—woke her up.

"How are you feeling?" he asked.

"Sleepy," she said truthfully. "Where is this?"

"The doctor says you're making good progress," Thratta said, looking at something rather more interesting than she was on the wall behind her head. "Provided you get plenty of rest and don't overexert yourself, in due course you ought to make a full recovery."

"Yes, I know, he told me so himself. Is this Headquarters? I didn't know we had one."

Thratta reached inside his black woollen gown and produced a book. "If I give you this," he said, "you have to promise on your word of honour not to read for more than an hour at a time, with a two-hour interval. Otherwise, the doctor says, it may cause inflammation of the brain."

Which is what all good books do, of course. "Thank you," she said; but he hadn't given it to her yet. He was holding it just outside comfortable grabbing range. "What's going on? Why is everyone going to so much trouble about me? Where's Oida? Is he all right?"

"I've spoken to the doctor," Thratta said, "and he feels that if you continue to make good progress, you may be able to stomach solid food in a day or so. In the meantime, he recommends that you stay on the beef and barley broth. It's particularly rich in the phlegmatic humour, which of course is what you need most at this stage."

"I see," she said. "Thank you. Who's the head of the Lodge? You must know, you were in a meeting with him."

The book wasn't getting any closer, and Thratta was scowling. "Try and sleep," he said. "Sleep is the best medicine for your condition, that's what the doctor says."

"Where's Axio?"

Thratta stood up. He was still holding the book. "I'll be going now," he said. "Don't fret about things that don't concern you. You don't want a relapse, do you?"

Fair enough. She was good as gold for a whole day, and that got her the book. It was Tycho's *Reflections on Infinite Silence*, which she'd been meaning to read for years. Six pages in, she decided it was overrated, all style and precious little substance, but a sovereign remedy for insomnia. Just what the doctor ordered.

Maybe she was getting soft, but she couldn't bring herself to kill the old woman, or even bash her over the head. Maybe it was because she was, for all her many faults, a living and reasonably able-bodied human being, and from what she'd seen lately there were so few of those left that it would be a shame to waste one of them, even a largely unsatisfactory specimen like her. The doctor, on the other hand—the only problem was, how? She had no knife, no belt, no items of crockery or cutlery, and Tycho's *Reflections* was a vellum-bound pocket-size student's edition and no help at all. The chamber pot was a flimsy enamel-tin thing, no heft to it and you couldn't smash it to get a sharp shard. The doctor never brought his medical bag, so no help there. One good thing: there didn't seem to be a guard on the door. So, what would the Great Smith do, He who makes good use of everything, no matter how humble?

Eventually, she decided on the sheet; the bottom one, not the top. Tearing the wretched thing was harder than she'd antici-pated. She had to use her teeth to get it started, but once she'd breached the hem, it came apart quite easily, and she soon had twelve three-foot strips of good-quality linen. Plaiting took a long time, since the old woman interrupted her every half-hour, and it took a while to unmake and remake the bed with the damaged part of the sheet underneath her, out of sight. It helped concentrate her mind to reflect that she only had one chance, since the bedclothes were changed every day. But it was wonderful to be doing something, to have a project, an aim. When at last she'd twisted her rope, she found that it had come up short: three feet down to two and a quarter. She should have allowed for the foreshortening effect of torsion. Silly girl.

In the event it was touch and go; the doctor was stronger than she'd expected, and she was shocked to find how weak she was, in spite of all that strengthening broth—maybe she really was sick after all. She slackened the rope just a bit and asked him about that.

"Of course you're sick," the doctor gasped. "What do you think you're in here for?"

Oh, she thought; still, too late to worry about that now. She tightened the rope. It would be far easier to kill him, but she went the extra mile and throttled him till he went all weak, and then let go. He wore strong leather boots with a good solid heel, just right for knocking a man silly with.

She looked down at him, sleeping peacefully, getting plenty of rest. For her part, she was exhausted; nothing she'd like more than to get back into bed, except that there was a strange man in it. She tied his hands with her beautifully crafted rope and stuffed a sock in his mouth. Time to go.

The flagstones in the corridor outside were freezing cold under her bare feet, and her head was throbbing. Since she hadn't really expected to get this far, she hadn't given any thought to what she intended to do—get out of that horrible room, the limit of her ambitions. Beyond that, her thinking was rather vague. Find out everything, or something along those lines.

Wherever this place was, it had corridors. This one had four doors in it, apart from the one to her room, which she'd remembered to shut after her. At the end of the corridor was a spiral staircase, the sort that always made her feel dizzy. Up or down? She had no coin to toss. She chose down.

Probably a poor choice, since it brought her out into a courtyard, where she'd have been spotted instantly if there had been anyone about. But there wasn't, so that was all right. A substantial place, this, a bit like a college or a monastery. She drew back into the doorway and looked round carefully. There was a long, single-storey building on the opposite side of the courtyard. It had a plainly visible door. That was as good a reason as any. She ran across the yard, wincing at the cobbles, grabbed the latch, lifted it, went through, slammed the door behind her.

The stench hit her like a hammer. The most disgusting smell she'd ever encountered, like a battlefield, but in a confined space. The only light came from a narrow slit of a window high up on the wall opposite, a white-hot glowing bar lying across the floor. It took a moment for her eyes to adjust, and then she saw that she was in a room full of dead dogs.

She didn't actually count them, but she guessed there were well over a hundred. What they'd died of wasn't immediately apparent; probably not starvation, because the bigger dogs would've eaten the smaller ones and there were all shapes and sizes. The only thing they had in common was identical gold collars—

Yes, they'd be gold all right, and none of your low-grade alloy, the stuff they'd been reduced to making coins from. This would be pure, better than ninety-seven parts fine, because only the best was good enough for the late emperor's beloved pets. Which meant she was in the palace, at Iden Astea, about nine hundred yards from the Single Teardrop.

Headquarters.

You spend such a long time yearning for things to make sense, and then you get what you wish for. Serves you right, really.

"What are you doing out of bed?"

Just like her mother. "I wouldn't come any closer if I were you," she said helpfully. "It's not very nice in here."

Triumvir Thratta clearly knew what to expect; he'd stopped at the door, and he had a thick scarf wrapped round his face. "Come out of there," he said. "What are you doing here? Why aren't you in your room?"

"I bashed the doctor's head in," she explained. "Sorry. Touch of cabin fever. I don't like being cooped up for very long." Talking wasn't good. Every time she opened her mouth, she could taste the loathsome smell on her tongue. "I don't think I did him any lasting damage, but I'm no expert. You'll have to ask him, as and when he wakes up."

She could make out at least two soldiers standing behind Thratta, with their regulation scarves over their mouths. Time to come quietly. Besides, she was freezing cold in nothing but a shift.

"We found Doctor Luseric," Thratta said. "You'll be relieved to hear he's all right. Now, I must insist—"

"Yes, of course." She picked her way between a cluster of decomposing dogs. The floor was damp and sticky. "It's all right," she said. "I've answered most of those irritating questions you refused to answer. I'll be a good girl from now on."

One positive result of her tantrum: a new room, with a chair as well as a bed, and an unshuttered window. From it she could look down into the main quadrangle. There wasn't an awful lot to see. From time to time, people came and went, mostly in groups of three or four, well wrapped up in heavy coats and hoods or broad hats, a few soldiers but mostly civilians, about two-thirds more men than women. She kept a careful lookout for tall archers, but there didn't seem to be any of those. The food improved dramatically, and the doctor no longer bothered her. According to the chatty, red-faced woman who brought her meals, he was scared stiff of her and nothing would induce him to go near her, even with an armed escort. No book, and no fire in the grate; but in it she found a finger-long stick of charred elder, and the walls were smooth and whitewashed. She spent a whole day marshalling her thoughts, then started writing on the walls.

"What's all that about, then?" the red-faced woman asked.

"Just a few notes," she told her. "It helps me think."

"That's not proper writing."

"It's Mezentine," she explained. "They use different letters from us."

The red-faced woman wasn't impressed. "It'll have to come off," she said. "Bound to leave a mark. Soot on whitewash always leaves a mark."

"Sorry."

Her apology was neither accepted nor rejected, and, yes, it left a mark, but nothing anyone would ever be able to decipher. Not that it mattered, she knew she wouldn't forget any of it in a hurry. But when the red-faced woman came next, she asked if she was allowed a pack of cards. To her surprise, the answer turned out to be yes. They came in a dark oak box with crudely forged iron hinges and a lock that had been forced, a long time ago. She waited for the red-faced woman to go, then opened the box and took out a rectangular block wrapped in faded red silk. It felt curiously heavy. She unwrapped it. Flat black plates that clattered as they spilt into her lap. A silver pack.

She stared at them, desperately unwilling to touch them. A silver pack, black with tarnish, but traces of white powder clung to the recesses of the embossed shapes. She counted them. There were ninety-two, fourteen more than there should have been. Every pack ever made consists of seventy-eight cards; except for one, the first one ever, the prototype.

Or a clever copy thereof; and she knew nothing about that sort of thing. Only a handful of people did—a handful minus one, if Glauca was dead yet. So she sifted through them, one by one, and found what she'd been expecting, or expected, to find. A thin sliver had been clipped off the top left edge of the Two of Swords. She dropped it as though it was red hot. It landed on the floor and bounced away under the bed.

Not proof, because there's no such thing. You can't be made to believe, you can't make yourself believe, the sheet of parchment had almost certainly been planted in the book for her to find, and if the pack was a fake then so was the sheet of parchment. And she didn't believe in the Invincible Sun, even though He was real enough to blister the skin on the back of her neck when she forgot to cover up in summer, so proof was an irrelevance; proof proves nothing. In another life, she could imagine herself being lectured by her father, excellent reasons why she ought to marry so-and-so, an outstandingly good catch whom she didn't happen to love. Proof and reasons are meaningless. All that matters is faith, and you can't be forced to believe, or fall in love. You can be made to go to sleep (she knew a doctor who could vouch for that one) but only through an act of violence, tantamount to proof or reason, a battering over the head to nullify resistance and induce acceptance and tranquillity. But there was no need for anyone to bash her over the head with a shoe, or to file a corner off the Two of Swords. She looked at the jumble of tarnished silver plates in her lap, and she just *knew*, by the way her skin had crawled when she'd touched them. But so what? She'd already figured it out for herself, when she saw the dead dogs and their golden collars. Confirmation? Maybe. More likely, someone hadn't given her enough credit for being able to make sense of the screamingly obvious.

Be that as it may. Eventually she plucked up enough courage to shift the pack off her lap onto the bed, then fish around on the floor until she found the card she'd dropped. Then she sorted them into suits—*five* suits—and laid them out in order. It took a long time. Then she shuffled them, wrapped them in the faded silk and put them carefully back in the box. When the red-faced woman came in with her breakfast, she handed the box back.

"Thanks," she said. "I'm ready to talk to someone now."

"Right you are," the red-faced woman said. "Now eat your porridge before it gets cold."

Later that day, the red-faced woman escorted her down the stairs and across the main quadrangle, in the middle of which an old man and a tall, skinny boy were driving a stake into the smooth, short grass. "What's that for?" she asked. The red-faced woman said she didn't know.

The old man held the stake straight and steady while the boy swung the big hammer. He was taking great care, and she guessed it was the first time he'd been allowed to do the grown-up's part of the job. Beside the old man on the grass was a large round wicker basket with a neatly fitting lid. The old man said, "That'll do," picked up a small hammer and a long square nail and opened the lid of the basket. He pulled out a man's head by the hair; and then she reached the chapel doorway and she couldn't see any more.

It wasn't *the* chapel, of course, just a private side chapel the Imperial family used for quiet, informal daily worship when there was nobody at court who needed to be impressed. On the cedar-panelled walls hung portraits of all the emperors back to Jovian—guesswork, most of them, needless to say, what they should have looked like but probably didn't, this being an imperfect world. The backgrounds were gold leaf and the frames were silver. On the altar stood a magnificent late Mannerist triptych of the Transfiguration, flanked by free-standing ivory statues of the Fifteen Disciples, middle-period Neo-Decadent school, quite possibly the only complete set to have survived the iconoclast riots of the Insurgency; apart from the set in Rasch, of course, except they were presumably ash now, or buried so deep in rubble that they'd never be found. Someone had placed a chair directly in front of the altar. It was a regulation-issue Western officer's folding camp chair, and the webbing back was torn. A man came out of the shadows under the chancel loft, took off his coat, slung it over the back of the

chair and sat down. He was Senza Belot. He fished a roll of paper
out of his coat pocket and began to read.

"Don't get too comfortable." The acoustics snatched the
woman's voice and bounced it off the walls, but she recognised
Lycao. "She'll be here any minute. Talk of the devil."

Senza looked up and saw her; their eyes met. Senza Belot
stood up, tried to stuff the papers back in his coat pocket, gave
up and let them drop to the floor. He looked straight at her and
smiled. "Commissioner Telamon," he said. "Good to see you
again."

"Can we get on with it, please?" Lycao descended the long
staircase that led to the choir stalls. She was wearing her Beal
tutor's gown, which didn't suit her one bit. Odd choice for a
honeymoon. She crossed the chancel floor and sat down cross-
legged next to Senza's chair. Her feet were bare and the soles
were black from walking on dusty floors.

Thratta pushed her forward. She stumbled, then found her
feet. She'd been trembling when she came in, but now she felt
fine. "Excuse me," she said.

Nobody seemed to have heard her. Thratta sat down on a pew
in the front row. She went to sit next to him but he frowned and
shook his head; no sitting down for her, apparently. Not that it
mattered.

"Excuse me," she repeated.

"Quiet," Lycao said, not looking at her; she was leaning her
head against Senza's knee. Nothing happened for a long time.
She realised that they were waiting for someone.

"Excuse me," she said.

"Oh, for crying out loud," Lycao snapped. "What?"

"Whose head is that? Outside. A man was about to nail it to a pole when I came in."

Senza frowned, clearly puzzled. She couldn't see Thratta's face without turning her head, and she didn't want to break eye contact. "No idea," Lycao said. "Are you sure you didn't imagine it?"

"No," she replied. "And I think it could be one of three people."

"I'm not really interested in your theories," Lycao said.

Senza reached out without looking and put his hand on the top of Lycao's head, as a man might do with a favourite dog. "Don't be mean," he said. "She hasn't done anything wrong."

"Tell that to Doctor Luseric," Lycao said. "He's in his own hospital with a cracked cheekbone."

Senza gave her a weak smile, as if to say, *sorry, one of her moods.* "That was my fault," he said gently. "At least, Luseric's my fault. I know he's got a really bad bedside manner, but he's pulled me through some nasty scrapes and I simply won't have anyone else. I expect he got on your nerves."

She smiled. "A bit. But I wanted to get out of there."

"I know what you mean. I hate being cooped up, too. How's the arm, by the way? No lasting damage?"

"None, thank you."

"That's the spirit. I guess we're even now."

She heard the door open behind her, and footsteps, but she didn't look round. She wanted her guess to be right; and, of course, it was.

"Sorry to keep you all waiting." She recognised Procopius' voice before she saw him. "Fiddling with the coda to the third movement, lost track of time. Ah, there you are, Commissioner. I hope they've been looking after you."

Senza stood up, and sat down on the step next to Lycao. Procopius sat in the chair he'd just left. So I was right, she thought. Then she did her best curtsey, and bowed her head.

She heard someone clapping. "Clever girl," Procopius said. She looked up, and he was smiling at her, a truly horrible sight. "Told you she'd figured it out."

"It wasn't exactly hard," Lycao said. "And so what if she has? We don't owe her an explanation."

"Yes we do," Procopius said firmly. "I have to tell you," he went on, "Lycao didn't vote for you. Neither did Thratta, come to that. But, as I pointed out, the Lodge is not and never has been a democracy. Congratulations, Commissioner. I have great pleasure in appointing you the third Triumvir of the Lodge."

She kept her face completely blank, though it took an effort she didn't know she was capable of. Third Triumvir; therefore, there had been a vacancy, therefore—

"Well," Lycao said. "Say something."

"The head on the stake," she said.

"Oh, that." Senza pulled a face. "She keeps banging on about the stupid head, and Lycao wouldn't let me tell her."

Procopius sighed. "She might as well go and see for herself."

So she went and looked. It gave her no pleasure, much to her surprise. Then she went back in. When she got back, Thratta had moved up to make room for her.

"What about Oida?" she said. "Is he safe?"

"Properly speaking," Procopius said, "we ought to be very annoyed with you." He waited for a reaction, got none and went on: "You concluded a peace agreement with Forza Belot on behalf of the Lodge, with absolutely no authority to do so."

She nodded. "Forza thought I could speak for Axio, and Axio was head of the Lodge," she said. "It was easier to give him what he wanted than tell him the truth."

"Easier," Lycao repeated, glaring at her. Procopius shut her up with a tiny gesture of his hand.

"I knew Axio wasn't in charge," she went on. "But he—well, both of them—were acting like he was. I assumed they were on his side."

"You can't be expected to be right about everything," Procopius said, kindly and just a little bit patronisingly. "You've done very well as it is. Tell me, when we met on the road—"

"Did I know? No."

Procopius nodded. "You just thought us running into each other at that precise moment was a gigantic coincidence."

She smiled. "Actually, yes. Did you write the letter? To Forza?"

Procopius looked at her for a moment before answering. "Oida wrote the letter," he said. "With his left hand. I dictated it, if that's what you meant."

"Is he all right? Is he going to be all right?"

That made Senza grin. Procopius hesitated. "But you figured it out after that. About me, I mean."

She made herself be patient. "Sort of," she said. "I knew Oida had to be right about a schism in the Lodge, though I had my doubts, God knows, right up until I realised he was ambidextrous. So it wasn't hard to work out that Axio was the leader of the breakaway faction, and what he wanted was Oida dead and the throne for himself, in that order. Don't ask me how long all that was going on, because I haven't a clue."

"Longer than any of us realised," Thratta said sadly. "It simply never occurred to us that a Craftsman—"

Procopius frowned at him, and he fell silent. "Go on," he said.

"So Axio arranged for me to be ordered to kill Oida," she said. "Partly because I'd be the only one he trusted enough to get close enough to do it, partly because—"

Lycao, to her surprise, lifted her hand. "Yes, we know. You don't have to say it. I don't think I've ever met anyone with more of a talent for cruelty."

"Axio wanted me to kill Forza," she went on. "That all went wrong."

"Of course it did," Senza put in. "Axio thought he could outsmart my brother. Always a mistake."

"And Forza showed you the letter," Procopius prompted her.

"Yes. And I knew when I saw the bit about not lifting a finger. But I got it right, but for the wrong reason. I thought Oida couldn't have written that because he'd lost his finger and couldn't write."

Procopius smiled. "He wasn't happy about it," he said. "Refused point blank, until I assured him you'd be all right. I told him, Forza's not a naturally cruel man—be quiet, Senza—so he'd spare your life once you'd got his attention and interest. Also, a rapprochement with the Lodge has been on his mind for a while now, and he knew you were something quite high up, or would be; saving you for later, I think you could say. Anyway, eventually Oida agreed to do as he was told. But I thought you ought to know, he didn't do it lightly."

Senza looked straight at her, then shook his head. She filed that away for later reference.

"If you want to know when I knew that you're the head of the Lodge," she went on, "it was when you came in just now and Senza gave you his seat. That's when I *knew*. Before that, it was just a guess."

"Intuition," Procopius said approvingly. "Intuition is the daughter of Faith, as someone or other once said. But that's not what you wanted to talk about, is it?"

She took a deep breath. "No," she said.

"Fair enough." Procopius stood up. "But I don't want to listen to you, so I made you a Triumvir instead. It's always been a rule of mine, in the many positions of authority I've held over the years. If you can't beat them, promote them. Congratulations."

And then he walked out.

Lycao escorted her to her new quarters.

"You'll have to excuse the decor," she said, as she unlocked the door and handed over the key. "Used to belong to the late emperor's second-favourite mistress. You can clear it all out if you want."

It took her a moment to get used to the glare. Everything was gold, or gold leaf, or cloth-of-gold, or gilded mosaic tiles. She sat down on a spindly legged gold chair and kicked her shoes off, and saw that Lycao had followed her in. "Sit down, please," she said, and Lycao perched on the edge of the gold-canopied bed. "You chose this room for me, didn't you?"

"Tart's boudoir? No, actually. There are fourteen habitable

State apartments, and nine of them are already taken. The other five are worse than this."

She shrugged. "Was there something?"

Lycao glared at her, then relaxed. "We don't have to be enemies," she said. "Yes, I resent the fact that you've been made a Triumvir and you haven't done nearly as much as I have to deserve it. But you would have done it, wouldn't you? Killed Oida, I mean. If he hadn't told you the truth, about the schism."

She decided to lie. "Yes."

"I couldn't have done that," Lycao said. "They tried to make me—kill Senza, I mean, or hand him over to his brother, which would have been the same thing. And I wouldn't do it. Which was downright disobeying an order, so properly speaking I shouldn't even be in the Lodge, let alone a Triumvir. So, who am I to throw stones at you?"

"I understand," she said. "How you must have felt."

Lycao thought for a moment. "You know what," she said, "maybe you do. Probably the only one of them who does. Who knows, maybe we'll be friends after all. I doubt it, though, I'm not easy to like." She grinned. "Hard to break the habits of a lifetime."

She waited for a moment or so, in case Lycao wanted to say anything else. Then she said, "You always did love Senza, didn't you?"

"Always." No hesitation. "But he always loved me, and the Lodge realised how useful that made me, the only chink in the combined armour of the otherwise invincible Belot brothers. I wouldn't kill him, but I'd play horrible games with him, that

I was prepared to do, for the Lodge." She shrugged. "You do know the full story, don't you?"

"No."

"Don't you? Damn." Lycao gave her a savage look. "I assumed—Oh, what the hell. I'll make Senza tell you. It'll be good for him."

"Why don't you tell me?"

Lycao smiled at her, then stood up. "Don't push your luck," she said, and left the room.

So she amused herself by exploring for a while. There was plenty to explore. In a cedar clothes press (plated, needless to say, in thin sheets of beaten gold) she found a dozen heartbreakingly beautiful dresses, presumably the property of the room's previous tenant. They could only have been made by the Scocali Brothers of Choris Anthropou, and none of them fitted. She also found jewellery, cosmetics, perfumes and the most beautiful shoes in the whole world (which didn't fit either) but no books. She did find a comb, tortoiseshell decorated with garnets and lapis lazuli, but the knots in her hair were too much for it and it broke.

She was regretting the death of a thing of great beauty when someone knocked on the door. It was Senza Belot. She smiled at him and told him to come in.

"Dear God," he said, looking round. "Is all this stuff real?"

"I think so."

"You could pay six squadrons of cavalry for a year—"

"You could," she corrected him. "Not me, I'm just a burglar. Please sit down."

He opted for the spindly gold chair, which sagged under his weight. She perched on the bed, where Lycao had sat. "She sent me," he said.

"I gathered."

He smiled at her. Most people would say he was the good-looking brother, though if she had to choose she'd have picked Forza. "She said I had to come and tell you the whole story."

"You don't have to if you don't want to."

That made him grin. "She'll know if I don't."

"What are you doing here?"

"I'm on my honeymoon. And then we're off to Blemya, for the wedding."

Blemya. "Who's getting married?"

He looked at her. "The queen. Didn't you know?"

"Who's she getting married to?"

Senza shifted uncomfortably in his chair. "It was Forza who started it," he said.

"You're not going to tell me."

"On the contrary," Senza said solemnly. "I'm going to tell you everything."

We were always close (Senza said). He's a year older than me, but by the time I was thirteen I was much taller and broader than him. We were never apart more than a minute or so all day long. We took our lessons together, hunted together, slept in the same room, did everything together. And we were always competitive, even as kids. I guess we have our father to thank for that. He used to say that strife is creation, and you can't start a fire unless two flints collide.

Anyway, when I was fifteen and Forza was sixteen, our father set us a challenge. I think there were four events, unless I've forgotten one. We had to write a sonnet, cut and stack a cord of firewood, play three games of chess and shoot five ends at a hundred yards. I lost the chess, but I won at everything else. The prize was a falcon, and I really wanted that bird, more than anything in the world. Forza already had one, he'd been given it for his sixteenth birthday, and I wanted to have one, too, better than his and earned, not just given to me as a present.

So, I won the falcon, and a couple of days later I went to the mews first thing in the morning, and there it was, lying on the ground, dead. Someone had crept down in the night and twisted its neck. Forza swore blind it wasn't him, but he kept grinning at me all day, and I'd heard him get up in the night. So I waited a few days, and then I asked him, suddenly, straight out: why? And he looked at me and said: because I can't enjoy anything if you've got it, too. And then he looked me in the eye and said, I'm sorry, I shouldn't have done it, will you forgive me? So of course I said yes. He smiled and thanked me, and we were fine for a long time after that. But I hadn't forgiven him. I guess I developed my tactical instincts quite young.

Anyway, Forza turned eighteen and they all said it was high time he got married, and there was this girl he really liked, our neighbour's daughter, and our father was all for it, because it'd mean sorting out a problem with grazing rights and access to water for the sheep. I think Forza was actually in love with her, or believed he was; also, as soon as he was married, Father would build him a house and give him his share of the land, he'd be a grown-up, independent, and I know he was really looking forward to that. I'd been given some money by our grandmother, and I spent all of it on a wedding present for him. I bought him a pure white falcon. They're very rare, and I knew he'd always wanted one.

So, the night before the wedding, I slipped out of the house and walked over to our neighbour's house. I knew the layout of the place quite well, so I knew which window was hers. I shinned up the wall; luckily it was a warm night so the shutters were open. I'd got some archers' root. It's what poachers use to poison the tips of their arrowheads. You boil the root and then distil it, over a long period of time. I'd been worried sick they'd find my still out in the woods, but I got away with it. I used to take chances then. Anyway, I found a brooch in her jewel box, dipped the pin in the poison and pricked her in the web between her fingers, where nobody would think of looking. The prick woke her up. I remember, she looked at me sort of blearily, and then the light in her eyes went out and she was dead. First time I'd ever seen anyone die, as a matter of fact. That stuff's good, believe me. You probably know about it, of course, in your line of work.

I was back well before dawn and I know nobody saw me, and I'd taken great care not to leave footprints. I'd taken a pair of Forza's old shoes to do the job in, and I pitched them into the furnace on my way back in, snuck up the stairs in my stocking feet. It was a well-planned exercise, though I say it myself. There was absolutely no proof against me, and, needless to say, no proof was needed. There are some things you just know, without needing proof. He knew I'd done it.

We were never friends again after that. I guess it was

inevitable. He completely lost all interest in the estate and joined the Western military, so I went East. We were both horribly precocious; you don't grow up competing with someone every bit as good as you at everything without learning how to win, and beat people. I think we might have forgotten about each other—well, not forgotten, naturally, but got on with our separate lives. Only I made a tragic mistake. I fell in love.

That's something you should never do, because immediately you're giving your enemy a hostage. Trouble is, you can't help it, can you? Anyway, I knew as soon as I set eyes on Lycao that she was the only one for me. She challenged me, just like Forza did, about everything, and I realised I didn't want to win. That's an amazing feeling, for someone like me. Someone you want to lose to. So, obviously, I had to have her. And, obviously, Forza would find out, and I knew exactly what he would do then. My own stupid fault, except I couldn't help it.

Needless to say, I told her all about it, it was only fair, she had a right to know what she was getting into. I told her what I'd done, and she looked at me for a very long time and said, quite probably in my shoes she'd have done the same thing. So we talked it over, and what we decided was, for the time being anyway, she'd make out that she couldn't stand the sight of me— I was weird and I scared her, and she wanted nothing to do with me. So, whenever I could get away from my regiment, the story was that I'd caught up with her and was holding her against her will, and then when it was time for me to go back, she'd manage to escape and go into hiding, supposedly from me, really from Forza. It was damned difficult keeping in touch, because she really did have to make herself very hard to find. But we worked out a set of clues that only we knew about. It was risky, because Forza's no fool; we knew he'd figure them out eventually. But at that stage we were hoping he'd get killed or sent into exile. Kidding ourselves, really, but you've got to have some hope, or what do you do?

Well, Forza figured it out. I sent one of our coded messages, he intercepted it, and got there before I could. He snatched her out of bed in the middle of the night, and handed her straight over to Saevus Andrapodiza; you know, the slave dealer, Saevolus' father. Saevus put her on a fast ship out of Beloisa, and four days later she was in Aelia.

That was where Forza made his one and only mistake. He couldn't resist overdoing it; also, he still believed she couldn't stand me. So he had Saevus tell her that I was responsible for selling her to the slavers—I was going to marry into the Imperial family and I wanted her out of the way—so that even if I did find her again she'd hate me. I reckon that's why he didn't just kill her outright. He had to go one step further than that, I fancy, in order to outdo me, in order to win. But, of course, she knew that wasn't true. And eventually, I did find her. But she had rather a rough time in Aelia—well, I don't need to explain, do I? She's never got over it, and who can blame her? Something like that either kills you or twists you up inside until you can never be right again.

By this time, I was commander-in-chief in the East, and Forza was leading the West. Suddenly we had this chessboard, and everybody wanted us to play. I think both of us under-estimated the other. We both thought we could win. Actually, chess is a good analogy. You know the sort of game where you end up with only four pieces on the board—white king and rook, black king and rook. You don't throw up your hands in horror and concede because you're appalled by the slaughter of innocent pawns. The longer it goes on, the closer you get, the more intense it becomes. And, of course, the degree of skill required increases, and when you're good at something you enjoy doing it for its own sake, and the harder it gets the more pleasure you get out of it. I probably shouldn't say this, but I for one, I've enjoyed every minute of it, and if I had my time over again—well, I wouldn't complain, let's put it that way. They say the only immortality is to be remembered, and nobody's going to forget Forza and me in a hurry, are they?

The question that's bothering me is, did I win? Arguably I did. Got you to thank for that, actually. No, really. You made that crazy peace treaty between Forza and the Lodge. Whether or not he took it at face value I really couldn't say. But when Lycao and her lot—I mean your lot, sorry—found out that under the treaty he was to get an army of Lodge soldiers—Some opportunities are too good to miss, aren't they? So she sent him six hundred Rosinholet horse-archers, knowing that he'd send some of them—a hundred, as it turned out—to protect his home and his wife, who he was genuinely fond of. They burned the house down, slaughtered the in-laws and the servants and stuck her head up on a pole. Probably on balance that puts me ahead in the game, but I don't know.

Anyway, that's why Lycao and I got married. No point keeping up the pretence any more, with Lycao being the only piece left on the board, so to speak. So, we got married, and she's sticking with me closer than a lid on a jar from now on. It's

a risk, but now that you Lodge people are coming out into the
open, and you've got all the money and all the soldiers, I fancy
protecting her will be your job as much as mine. That business
at Beal gave me a real scare, I can tell you, but he won't be in a
position to try anything like that again for a long time. And who
knows? By then he could be dead.

Didn't they tell you? No, the war is now officially over,
now that Glauca's dead. So Forza's signed up with the Vesani
Republic, commander-in-chief of land forces, and I'm to be
the grand marshal of Mezentia. Well, they had no choice, did
they? Obviously the Vesani wanted Forza so they could rub the
Mezentines off the map. I didn't have to offer: they came and
pleaded with me, you're our only hope for survival, all that sort
of thing. So it'll be business as usual, only with a brand new
chess set. I'll be honest with you, I'm looking forward to it. Once
you've got used to practising your trade at the highest level,
anything else would be the most awful anticlimax.

Lycao? Well of course she's coming with me. She says there
are outstanding opportunities for the Lodge in Mezentia. And
in the Vesani Republic. Well, that's what she said. Not sure
what she means by it, but she knows the Lodge business far
better than I do.

"I know exactly what she means," she said. "Now, will you
answer my question?"

"I thought I just did."

"Who's the Queen of Blemya getting married to?"

Senza pulled a sad face. "Well, you'll find out soon enough.
If you must know, it's your pal, the song and dance man. Oida."

She looked at him in total silence, until she realised she was embarrassing him. "Yes," she said, "of course it is. I'm sorry. How silly of me."

She tried to find out how you went about making an appointment to see Director Procopius, but nobody knew. There was no established protocol, because it was something that simply didn't happen. If he wanted to see you, you were told. That was that.

So she started figuring out a plan. The logical person to seize and hold hostage was Lycao, because of her obvious value. Easier said than done, since a dozen very good men went with her everywhere she went, and at night you'd have Senza to reckon with; but she didn't see that she had any choice. It was a good plan, one of her best, and when you're good at something you enjoy doing it for its own sake, as a great man once said; so she was mildly disappointed when Procopius suddenly appeared in the doorway of her room, and the whole thing was suddenly redundant.

She said as much; but Procopius smiled and shook his head. "You really think I didn't know what you were planning? That's why I'm here. So, the plan worked, you got what you wanted, I'm here." He looked round, saw the spindly chair, decided against it and lowered himself slowly onto the floor, tucking his feet under his knees. "What did you want to talk to me about?" he said.

She didn't know whether to stand or sit; either would be mildly ridiculous, as would squatting down next to him on the hearthrug. She gave up and sat on the end of the bed.

"Just confirmation, really. Of course, if you tell me I'm wrong I won't believe you."

He nodded gravely. "Belief," he said, "it's all that matters. Also, I fancy, you want to show off how clever you've been, figuring it all out for yourself. You know, it's a shame we didn't get to know each other years ago. You'd have benefited from a father figure."

She took a deep breath. "How did you do it?"

"Excuse me?"

"How did you start the war?"

"Oh, that." He sounded disappointed, as though he'd been expecting a more challenging question. "To be honest with you, it was luck as much as anything. That's to say, it was sheer dumb luck that Glauca and his nephew were so alike. Stubborn, I mean, and stupid in a clever sort of way. As soon as I realised that, I knew it would be pretty straightforward. I had to control certain variables, of course. The nephew was ideal for my purposes, so I had to get rid of Glauca's wife and his sons, while they were still children. Fortunately, the old fool never showed any interest in marrying again, so that was one less thing to worry about. But, no, mostly it was just making good use of what was offered to me. I stirred up a little bit of fuss in the East, nothing serious but enough to warrant sending the heir apparent out to deal with it, a good chance for him to win his spurs and get a bit of hands-on experience of coping with a situation. Then, while he was there, I cooked up fake evidence that he was conspiring against his uncle. Glauca believed me, of course, I was his chief of security and I was never wrong, he trusted me implicitly, and also I had proof, buckets of it. And, of course, there's nothing so infuriating as being accused of something you really wanted to do but nobly forebore doing; so when Glauca ordered him back home to stand trial for treason, naturally the idiot boy refused and proclaimed himself emperor of the East. I'd made it known to him, you see, that Glauca was terminally ill and couldn't last more than a year or so. A little white lie in a good cause."

He paused and looked at her, waiting for her to respond to her cue. But she didn't, so he smiled and said, "Confirmation?"

"Mostly. But why didn't you just kill them both?"

"You don't know?"

"I want confirmation. A confession."

He shook his head. "That would imply that I've done something wrong."

"Confirmation, then. Humour me. Give me the satisfaction."

That made him grin. "If you insist on finding something to blame, I guess you can have the fact that I was made head of the Lodge at such an early age. Thirty-two, actually, the youngest ever by at least fifteen years, but there, I was the outstanding candidate, there was never really any other possible choice. And it meant I had enough years ahead of me to be able to think long-term. That's a luxury none of my predecessors ever had. I was able to look at the empire and realise that it was basically incompatible with the aims and objectives of the Lodge, and therefore it would have to be disposed of and replaced. I contemplated an invasion by a powerful enemy, but back then the empire was plainly invincible, so it would have to be civil war. The Belot brothers were a gift from heaven, of course. If I was that way inclined, I'd say it was vindication. If the Great Smith didn't want me to succeed, why did he send me Forza and Senza?"

"Hang on, though," she said. "The Belot boys made the war

go on and on, when it could've been wrapped up quickly—"
She stopped. "Sorry, I'm being obtuse. That was the whole
point."

That got her a gentle smile. "You got there in the end," he
said, "that's the main thing. It wasn't the emperors I wanted rid
of, it was the empire. The whole thing: constitution, laws, economy, social and political structures—all too big, too powerful,
too constricting. I think that's the difference between a mortal
Craftsman and the Great Smith. A human will keep on trying to
mend something that's broken, because he knows that making
a new one from scratch is beyond him. Only the Great Smith
has the—well, I guess you'd have to say the self-confidence, to
smash it up, grind down the scrap, put the whole lot in the cruci-
ble, melt it down and pour it into a brand new mould. Sorry," he
added, "I'm not very good at Great Smith imagery. I don't really
believe in Him, not as an individual entity, a person. I think I
may have at one time, but not any more. The further you get in
true faith, the less you need personifications and anthropomor-
phisations. Or don't you agree?"

"I don't matter," she said. "Go on with what you were saying."

"Oh, there's not really much to add, is there?" Procopius
yawned. "Like I said just now, we got there in the end, and
that's what matters. Now we have a huge country, mostly
empty, which we can restock according to our own specifica-
tions; we have the money to buy that good stock, from Saevolus
Andrapodiza in the first instance, and then with refugees from
Mezentia and the Vesani Republic, where they're about to have
a truly ruinous war, and so on; what they call in mathematics
a recursive loop. At Beal we have the resources and facilities to

train the leaders and directors of this perfect society of ours. To keep order, we've got the horse-archer people, and quite soon we'll have Blemya, with a perfectly good army and plenty of money. That'll tide us over until we've bred our first generation of new imperials, and after that it'll all take care of itself. You agree, don't you? It's all worked out rather well."

She chose her next words with a degree of care. "Axio didn't agree, though, did he?"

Procopius shrugged. "He was a great disappointment to me. That's all I want to say about him."

"He knew what you were doing, and he wanted to stop you."

A shake of the head. "That's one interpretation," Procopius said. "I prefer the version that has him down as simply ambitious. He wanted to rule to world. That's never a good thing."

"But that was the whole idea," she persisted. "That was the plan. You recruited him to be your puppet emperor. All he had to do was what he was told. But when he realised that you didn't just want the empire, you wanted vacant possession—"

Procopius held up his hand. "I don't think his motives are particularly relevant, do you? All that matters is that he tried to subvert the Lodge and take it over for himself, thereby defying the ordained chain of command, which is intolerable blasphemy and an abomination in the sight of the Divine. So he had to be dealt with, and it was just as well that I had the foresight to keep a reserve. Who," he added, rather more pleasantly, "will do just as well if not better, so no harm done. And a real stroke of luck for you, so I don't see why you're complaining." He looked at her as if she'd just appeared out of nowhere. "You're not questioning the decision, are you? Where's your faith?"

It was a perfectly valid question. She chose not to answer it. "What happened to him?"

"Axio?" Procopius looked down at his hands. "To be honest with you, I'm not entirely sure. You'd have to ask that Rhus archer, the red-headed boy." He looked up. "Does it matter?"

"Not particularly."

"He had it coming," Procopius said. "There was a warrant out for him." He paused, then added, "I still think he could have been a useful emperor, but we'll never know now, will we?" He yawned again, and slowly got to his feet. "And now I really must be going. I've been awake for forty-eight hours straight, and I need some sleep. We'll be seeing a lot more of each other in the future."

His hand was on the latch. "Director," she said.

He turned to look at her. "Well?"

"Is that it? The end justifies the means, and nothing else matters?"

"Yes," he said. "I thought everybody knew that. Good night."

She sent for the Rhus boy, Teucer, but nobody knew where he was. Nobody had seen him since he brought Axio's head to the front gate, in a bag. The garrison colour sergeant said he wasn't allowed to talk about it.

"I'm allowing you," she said.

Oh well, in that case. It was just rumour, of course, but they were saying that Teucer killed Axio before the warrant actually left the duty officer's desk, and he hadn't known a thing about it. "Came in here expecting to be arrested," the sergeant said, "I'll come quietly or something like that, could've knocked him down with a feather when he heard it was all right and he wasn't a murderer, he was a bloody hero. They reckon he cleared off after that. He'll turn up sooner or later, mind. After all, there's nowhere left to go, is there?"

Indeed. He turned up the next day beside the road, with a bloody head, an empty purse and no boots. She went to see him in the hospital wing as soon as he woke up.

"Yes," he said. "I killed Axio." He frowned, as if he knew he'd forgotten something important. "Am I in trouble?"

"No," she said. "There was a warrant out for him. You did your duty."

"Did I?" The boy tried to smile. "I can't remember any warrant."

"It must have slipped your mind. A bang on the head can do funny things to your memory."

"That wasn't why I killed him. I'm pretty sure of that."

"But you can't remember the real reason. That's an odd thing to forget, don't you think?"

"I suppose it is, really. Are you sure I'm not in any trouble? Surely it's murder, if you don't know the other person's guilty of something."

She gave him a mock scowl. "Well," she said, "I can arrange for you to be hanged if you really want me to, apparently I'm not without influence these days. But it'd be a bit of a nuisance, and I'm really busy right now."

That made him laugh. Easily amused, the Rhus people.

Being not without influence, she found someone to ask about a search party.

The man to ask about everything, it turned out, was an elderly clerk whose face she vaguely remembered from the Intelligence office in Rasch. There he'd been—well, a clerk, someone who copied out copies of copies of letters, for the files. His name was Sutento, and it turned out he was something frightfully grand in the Lodge, though not—now—nearly as grand as she was.

"And all that time," she asked him, "you knew—"

He was one of those craggy old men who don't look like they're capable of smiling, but who look totally different when they do. "Oh yes," he said. "I was Master Procopius' personal clerk."

"In the Department."

He shook his head. "Not in the Department," he said, "in the Lodge. He dictated letters and I wrote them out, I sorted and filed documents for him, all the usual things. You don't imagine he did all that for himself, do you?"

"No, but—" She found she'd run out of words. "But I thought only the Triumvirs knew—"

"That's right. Only the Triumvirs, and me. But a mere clerk doesn't count."

She gave up. "Is that what he's called, then? As head of the Lodge, I mean. Master Procopius."

That was funny, apparently. "Good lord, no. I've always called him that. I was his servant, right from when he was so high. Our family has always been in service with his family, as far back as anyone can remember."

She sighed. "Everyone says you're the man who gets things done around here. I want somebody found. Can you see to that for me?"

"I should think so," Sutento said. "Who did you have in mind?"

She hesitated for a moment, trying to find a way to describe him. "He's an archer, a Rhus, who used to be Axio's right-hand—"

"Oh, him." Sutento nodded. "Musen, the thief. Yes, I imagine he won't be hard to lay hands on. It's so much easier finding people," he added, "now that there are so few people left. They tend to stand out, if you see what I mean."

She got the impression Musen hadn't been cooperative. They'd patched him up with splints and bandages, and his bruises were just starting to come into flower.

"I thought you were my friend," he said.

"Really?"

He gave her a look that bothered her. "I just want to go away," he said. "I've done my share. I've done everything I was told. Why can't you people just leave me alone?"

She smiled at him. "Where is it?"

He was silent for just too long before he answered. "What are you talking about?"

She knelt down beside him. "Axio was going to kill you, wasn't he? But then your friend Teucer showed up, and shot him in the back."

"He's no friend of mine."

"You should have told him that; maybe he wouldn't have bothered."

"He didn't have to kill him."

She sighed. A little of Musen went a very long way. "Tell me what happened," she said.

*

It was in Rasch (he said) before you showed up with that stupid box. Axio said there was a job I had to do for him. It was really important, he said, it was the job he'd brought me into the Lodge to do. I had to break into the old Intelligence offices and steal something, a box, from a big iron chest in one of the tower rooms, and put another one just like it where I'd got it from. He drew me a map, told me exactly where to look. Actually, it wasn't all that difficult. The lock on the chest was about a hundred years old, I had no trouble with it.

The box he wanted was locked, and it was one of those fiddly little locks, you need special tools. I took it to Axio, and he got me to open it. I had to file down a set of keys, it took a long time, and you know he wasn't the most patient man in the world. Soon as I'd tripped the wards, he grabbed me by the hair and threw me out of the room, bolted it behind me. So I ran down into the yard and climbed up the side of the building. He didn't see me looking in through the window.

It was a silver pack, in that box. I watched him counting the cards. That's when I knew what he'd made me steal, the first pack, the one with five suits. That's when I knew what he'd made me do. I wanted to kill myself, for shame, but that wasn't going to put things right. It was bad enough when he gave the other silver pack to the Eastern emperor. It was wrong, he shouldn't have done it. So I knew I had to get it back.

It took me a long time, and I knew if he caught me this time he really would kill me, so I had to be careful. I didn't get my chance till we were on the ship back from Blemya. I picked the lock, took the cards and wrapped them up in my spare shirt, and I put in a load of strips of copper I'd cut from the sheathing on the stern of the ship. Then, when we landed, soon as I could I ran for it.

Just my luck, it was Teucer who caught me. He had every man he could get out looking for me, but it had to be bloody Teucer. I beat the shit out of him before he finally put me down, but by then I'd hidden it where it couldn't be found. Anyway, Teucer took me back to the camp and Axio started smacking me around. Teucer told him to stop but he wasn't listening. I think Axio must've guessed I wasn't going to tell him where I'd put it, I'd rather die first, and he finally lost his rag, he started throttling me and I don't think he could've stopped even if he wanted to. I think he was disappointed in me, most of all. I don't blame him for that. He trusted me, and I promised him, no more thieving. But Teucer didn't have to kill him. When I saw what he'd done, I went for him. I was so mad I wanted to smash his head in, but after what Axio had done to me I just didn't have the strength to finish him off. So I left him lying and crawled off, licked my wounds, so I'd be up to going back to where I'd hidden them. Nearly got there, too, but bloody Teucer found me *again*. One of these days I'll do for him, I promise you. All my life he's been getting on my nerves, and I've had enough of it.

When he'd finished, she stood up. Her back was stiff from crouching, and her ribs ached. "Axio wanted the first pack because he wanted to be head of the Lodge, and the head of the Lodge keeps the first pack. He thought if he got his hands on them, it'd somehow mean he was legitimate. But that's not how it works, he was kidding himself." She smiled. "He wasn't nearly as clever as he thought he was, and look where it got him."

"He was my friend," Musen said. "And Teucer shouldn't have killed him. There was no need for that."

She shook her head. "I really don't give a damn," she said, "not any more. For what it's worth, I think Axio was trying to do the right thing, just like a good Craftsman should, only he would insist on going about it in the worst possible way. Anyway, he's dead now, and the pack needs to come home. I want you to go and get it and bring it to me, and then you can leave. Or stay, if you want to, whatever makes you feel better."

He looked at her for a long time. "They'll be safe?"

"They'll be with the head of the Lodge, where they belong." Suddenly she grinned. "Bless him, he doesn't even know they were ever missing. He's going to have a fit when he finds out."

Musen said there was something he wanted. It wasn't valuable, in fact it was no use to anyone except him, and he reckoned he'd earned it.

So she found a basket and fetched it for him. Axio didn't look quite so handsome now. His skin was chalk-white and the birds had been at his eyes and his lips and the lobes of his ears. "What do you want it for?" she asked.

"I'm going to bury him," Musen replied. "It's the decent thing to do, isn't it?"

Clearly Musen wasn't going to be up to using a pick and a shovel for some time, so she sent down to the kitchens for a big cheese jar, filled with honey. "It won't improve him," she said, "but it'll stop him getting any worse."

"Thanks," Musen said. "You hated him, didn't you?"

She thought about her reply before answering. "It was hard

not to," she said. "But the head of the Lodge reckons he could have been a fairly good emperor, if he'd had the chance."

"What do you think?"

"I agree," she said. "And he was a true Craftsman, after his fashion. He could have been useful, if he hadn't taken a wrong turning."

He looked at her. "He was my friend," Musen said. "And he forgave me, when others wouldn't have. He was worth ten of you. If he'd been in charge of the Lodge, things wouldn't have got in this mess."

When Musen was fit to travel, she let him have a cart and six men with spades and a crowbar. But there was one condition. Musen didn't like it, but she insisted, and he was in no position to argue.

The new word was "reconstruction," though nobody seemed to know what it meant. She attended meetings with Lodge officials from all over the two empires, which would soon be one empire again, who told her about grandiose plans for resettling the deserted areas, reclaiming land that had gone back to scrub and wilderness, reopening mines and quarries, redeveloping shattered communities, renewing vital infrastructure such as roads and bridges; everything they said began with "re-," and it was all terribly exciting and positive, but somehow she couldn't bring herself to believe in it, any more than she could believe that she was an incredibly important person whose approval was needed for all these wonderful projects. She listened politely, trying her best to understand, occasionally asking a question when it became obvious that someone had missed something or misunderstood something that made such and such a Grand

Plan utterly unworkable; and sometimes they tried to talk their way past her, until she had to be firm with them, and sometimes they looked astonished and ashamed, and implored her to tell them how to fix the problem, as if she had the faintest idea. And when she asked where the money was coming from, or all these new settlers, or skilled craftsmen or experienced foresters, stock-breeders, mineworkers, the answer was always the same. Blemya, of course. Because once Blemya rejoined the empire—

Another word beginning with "re-." And then she would nod and let the point go, because she didn't want to hear or talk about Blemya, with its huge surplus population, its vibrant economy, its immeasurable expanses of river-irrigated wheatfields, and its young and easily manipulated queen.

One other common theme emerged from this babble of conversations. Nothing could happen until Blemya was reincorporated into the empire, which would only happen when the emperor married the queen, which could only happen once the emperor had been duly crowned. Eventually she couldn't stand it any more and asked: why hasn't any of this happened yet? To which there was no answer, because nobody knew.

But somebody had to know; and, since she was the second most powerful human being in the empire these days (Thratta seemed to count for less and less these days, she didn't know why and didn't really care) and she didn't know, that really only left Procopius. So she asked to see him, and was told he was busy. He was away; he had a cold; he was finishing a particularly demanding piece of music and couldn't be disturbed on any account. After a while she realised that the people she'd been asking didn't know who Procopius really was, so she sought out

Sutento, who did. He replied that he'd pass on the message and would get back to her shortly. He said this several times a day for a week, and each time she actually believed him. And then she decided to do something about it.

She resolved to start at the bottom. She found out the name of the woman who was in charge of the linen—bedclothes and dirty laundry—and from her she got the name of the house-keeper, who told her which chambermaid looked after the fifth floor of the west wing, where she had an idea Sutento lived. In fact, he was on the sixth floor, but now she was getting some-where. She found the room and a dark corner of the corridor outside with a good view of its door; shortly before the third night watch, she made her way there and settled down to wait. Not long after, the door opened and Sutento came out to start his daily round of duties. It was one of the hardest tailing jobs she'd ever done, since there was precious little cover in the corridors and stairways of the palace, and too many people knew her by sight, so she couldn't get away with pretending to be a servant. She followed him to the kitchens, the wardrobe, the room where the boy cleaned the boots, the stables, the counting house, the cartulary, the housekeeper's room, the pantry, the map room, the linen store. Finally she followed him up a long, winding staircase (which, if her mental picture of the geography of the palace was accurate, simply couldn't exist) with a heavy oak door at the top end. Then and only then she pushed past him and hammered on the door.

"You can't go in there," Sutento said urgently, tugging on her sleeve.

"Go away before I break your arm," she said.

He carried on tugging, and things would have gone badly with him if the door hadn't opened.

"Oh," Procopius said, "it's you. Was there something?"

"I need to talk to you."

He thought for a moment, shrugged and stood aside to let her pass. Shaking Sutento's clawed fingers out of her sleeve, she barged through the door, and the first thing she saw was—

"Hello."

"You."

Oida stood up. He was filthy with caked mud, and his head was crudely bandaged with a length of sailcloth, brown with dry blood. He smiled at her feebly, then sat down again.

"As I was saying." Procopius swept past her as if she wasn't there. "The fifteenth would suit the Aelian ambassador, and if the Mezentines can't get there by then they'll just have to read about it in despatches. Is that all right with you?"

Oida nodded, looking at her.

"Fine," Procopius said, "I'll arrange for formal invitations and let the chamberlain know. He's bound to say it's not enough notice, but screw him, I've had enough of his whining. As far as I'm concerned, the sooner we can get it all over and done with, the sooner we can get on." He waited for Oida to nod, then turned and glared at her. "An unexpected pleasure," he said. "Come in, sit down, I hate being loomed at from doorways."

There was a little three-legged stool, child-sized. She sat on it, her knees under her chin.

"Oida," Procopius went on, "has just come from Blemya. He managed to get himself shipwrecked, which is why we've all been hanging around waiting for him, but he's here now, so no harm done. We've just been deciding the date of the coronation." He paused. "And the wedding."

She turned her head so she couldn't see Oida at all. "Am I invited?"

"You can go if you want," Procopius said, "though I can't see the point in you dragging all the way out there. Thratta will be representing the Lodge, so you won't be needed."

"She can come if she likes," Oida said quietly.

Procopius didn't seem to have heard him. "If I were you I wouldn't bother," he went on. "You'll be far too busy. Once we've got the coronation out of the way, you'll be tied up negotiating the instruments of reunion with the Blemyans. Don't worry, there isn't actually anything to negotiate, but you know how obsessed those people are with doing everything by the book. I think you'll just have to read out the terms of the treaty so they can say 'we agree' at the end of each section."

"I think I'll go," she said.

Procopius shrugged. "Suit yourself," he said. "So long as the work gets done, it's up to you how you do it. Right." He turned his back on her. "You'd better go and get yourself seen to, and then you'll need to see the tailor. Your blasted cousin was completely the wrong size, so none of his robes and regalia are going to fit you, and they reckon it'd be easier to make new ones from scratch than try and let out the old ones. He had an unusually small head, apparently, so we can't even reuse the crown."

Oida stood up, and she saw that his right foot was bare and grimy with sand and silt. He limped past her and the door closed behind him.

"Now, then," Procopius said. "What do you want?"

She couldn't remember, and he told her to go away. She ran down the stairs, nearly tripping and breaking her neck, but by the time she reached the corridor it was empty.

Fine, she told herself, he's safe and well, and he's going to be crowned emperor. On balance, she wished him well. He'd saved her life once or twice, tried to save her life a few times but turned up too late, only putting in an appearance when she'd saved her own life perfectly efficiently, but it's the thought that counts; he'd been there when she needed him more often than she could remember, and he'd helped bury her mother. He was the best, the only friend she'd ever had. He'd lied to her and used her, got her into desperate trouble, made her do appalling things, and whether he actually cared a damn for her she really didn't know. It made no odds. He was going to marry the beautiful young Queen of Blemya and breed heirs for the reconstituted empire, his duty to the Lodge, the world, the future. And he wrote quite jolly tunes, but he was no Procopius— And he'd left her his vast, ridiculously easily earned fortune, out of sheer altruism and love, and then neglected to die, and lost most of it through politics and war. None of which mattered. Instead, she was a Triumvir of the Lodge, with responsibility for building the Kingdom of Heaven on Earth, and that ought to be enough for any serious-minded person, surely.

So, all that being the case, she stayed in her room for the next three days, holding meetings there, having all her meals and official papers sent up, so he'd be sure to be able to find her, if by any chance he were to come looking, though why he should feel the need she couldn't say.

Meanwhile, she met with the leaders of the Aram Chantat and the Rosinholet, who said they were perfectly happy to act as the Lodge's army, or the empire's if that was what they wanted to call it, just so long as they were earning more than they could get anywhere else. She met the dean and chapter of Beal, who reluctantly agreed to second a number of members of faculty to the Imperial court, to train and supervise local governors, parish headmen, teachers for village schools. She met high-ranking Lodge officials from places she'd never heard of, listened to their reports, took an intelligent interest, realised that they knew far more about the people and problems of their regions than she could assimilate in a lifetime, and gave them permission to carry on doing whatever it was they did. She met confessors and experts on doctrine, architects and town planners and mining engineers and experts on supply and demand, Treasury officers and revenue officers and logistical planners and men who knew about drains, disease and malnutrition. She met Saevolus Andrapodiza, who promised her a quarter of a million farmers at three angels a head for ten years, farm implements and live-stock not included. It was all quite ludicrous. In her little room she was building the Great Society, taking careful thought for all the real difficulties and dangers that no king or politician could ever hope to tackle, but which she could deal with easily because she was starting with a clean slate; the land would belong to the farmers, not carls or abbots or conglomerates of investors; taxes would be enough to cover essential services but nothing more, no vanity wars or monstrous sinecures or jobs for someone's son-in-law; everything would be planned and thought out in advance, learning from the mistakes of history, doing the right thing, balancing the needs and abilities of the people—here, in her little room, on paper or in earnest dialogue with intelligent, motivated men of goodwill. It was probably all a game, or an aptitude test, and all the people she met were probably actors. And it didn't really matter; outside the magical walls of the palace, if ever she left them, she would find empty roads, burned-out towns, fields choked with brambles and thorn saplings, and if she got down on her hands and knees and scrabbled about, sooner or later the skulls and bones of dead soldiers, dead farmers' wives, dead men's dead children, dead because of Procopius, dead so that she could have her clean slate. And, in another reality, in a few days' time she would stand in the palace chapel and see the new High Priest of the Invincible Sun (appointed by her; he was an idiot, but biddable) crown Oida as supreme ruler of the world, which he wouldn't be, just another loyal Craftsman obeying orders. And then Blemya, for the wedding. Fair enough. She'd never had the least bit of luck in bloody Blemya, but this time, presumably, she wouldn't have to murder anyone unless she wanted to.

Procopius came to see her (had the nerve to show his face, was how she saw it). He sat down unasked in the comfortable chair and helped himself to sugared almonds from the jar.

"It had to be you, of course," he said—they'd been discussing road-mending schedules. "Nobody else could do it."

She smiled at him. "Bullshit."

He waved away the affront, like a father parrying a child's punch. "You were born in poverty and raised a slave. As a field agent, you've seen more of the empire than anyone I know—"

"Except Oida."

"More than him, even. And you read: philosophy and history and ethical theory, for pleasure. And your judgement is mature and your instincts are good, but when you have to, you do something unexpected and shocking, but which makes sense when you come to analyse it."

"Like killing a political officer."

"No great loss," Procopius said, and for a moment she hated him. "And, most of all, you didn't want the job. You didn't think you were capable of it, you have absolutely no ambition, and your faith is unshakable. I'd like to take credit for all that and say I had my eye on you from the day you were born, I trained you, carefully chose all your miseries and experiences to shape you into the perfect instrument for the great work ahead." He clicked his tongue. "Actually, you grew like a weed in a crack in the wall, and I wouldn't have noticed you if it hadn't been for Oida. But he kept talking about you—" He stopped, frowned. "You wouldn't be here now, doing this job, if Oida hadn't insisted."

"I don't understand. Insisted on what?"

Procopius looked away, deliberately turning the good side of his face toward her. "He refused point blank to marry the queen unless I made you a Triumvir. I pleaded with him, yelled at him, gave him a direct order, but he can be as stubborn as a mule sometimes. And now look: you're so perfectly suited for the job, and I had nothing to do with it."

She gave him a long, cold stare. "Silly me," she said. "I was under the impression I got promoted on merit."

He stood up. "Don't push your luck," he said, and left before she could say anything she'd live to regret.

*

One thing she'd promised herself. No power on earth was going to keep her from being at Oida's coronation. The look on his face when they put the golden hoop round his silly head would, she felt sure, make up for a great deal—

So, of course, she missed it. On Coronation Day morning she was up bright and early, to get through the day's paperwork. In with a load of other stuff for her to sign—requisitions for supplies and materials, travel permits, counter-signatures to show she'd read stuff she hadn't read but should have—was a death warrant. She fished it out and glanced at it, feeling she owed the poor bastard that, whoever he was. She saw that one Musen had been condemned to death for desertion, dereliction of duty and stealing two horses, saddles, harness, clothing and sixty-five angels cash from Lodge resources. Execution was scheduled for noon that day. It had already been signed, by some functionary whose name she didn't recognise. This copy was for information only.

For crying out loud, she thought; but she jumped up, dragged on the first coat that came to hand, and scuttled down six flights of stairs into the stable yard. No grooms around—off early to find somewhere to watch the coronation from—so she wasted an insufferably long time finding a harness and forcing it on a singularly unhelpful horse; then an hour's gallop, the stirrups galling her slippered feet, to the guard outpost where Musen had been caught. By the time she got there, the sun was dangerously close to its zenith. It occurred to her as she jumped off the horse and wrapped its reins round a broken rail that she had no way of proving her identity and authority to the perfect strangers who were in charge here, which might mean— Of course, she'd come out without her knife. Probably just as well.

Ridiculous, she thought. I'm *not* going to murder half a dozen loyal, innocent Lodge soldiers just to rescue that worthless son-of-a—But, by pure fluke, the outpost commander had just been transferred from guard duty at the palace, and she'd had occasion to be very rude and unpleasant to him about a week ago, so he remembered her just fine.

Even so. Yes, he conceded, she was entirely within her rights to countermand the warrant and order the prisoner's release, but there should be a form; to be precise, a writ of countermand. If she wasn't familiar with the precise form of words, he had the book of precedents in his office, if she'd care to consult it. So she spent a ludicrous half-hour reading the form out to him while he wrote it down in painful, scrupulous longhand; then he copied it out twice; then she signed all three copies and he handed her one copy back, for her records.

There were no cells at the outpost, only a root cellar. They lifted the trapdoor and she lowered herself in, hung by her fingers and dropped six inches to the floor. Something moved in the darkness. They handed her down a lamp.

"You," Musen said. "What are you doing here?"

It occurred to her that nobody had bothered to tell him the good news. "Rescuing you, idiot," she said. "We're friends, remember?"

He shrugged. "If you say so. Am I—?"

She nodded. "And as far as I'm concerned, you're welcome to piss off and not come back. You realise I'm missing the coronation because of you."

She listened to what she'd just said, and noted that Musen had the sense not to answer.

"Come on," she said. "Let's get out of here, before I change my mind."

The horses, saddles, saddlebags and money were in the guardhouse (evidence). She had to sign receipts for them. "Where will you go?" she asked.

Another shrug. "I thought the Lodge was my home," he said. "Apparently not."

"Don't be stupid," she said. "I'll find you a job somewhere."

"No thanks."

"You can go to Beal and teach thieving."

She could see he was tempted. But he shook his head.

"I don't want anything more to do with the Lodge," he said.

His face was a picture of sullen misery. She understood. He hadn't lost his faith, but the thing he believed in had. "Axio," she said.

"Yes, as a matter of fact," he spat back. "He understood. He knew what the Lodge ought to be about. He saw what they've been doing, and he was going to put a stop to it."

The terrible thing was, she couldn't argue with that. "He left it a bit late," was the best she could do.

"Yeah, sure. But at least he knew that what you've been doing is wrong. That's something. That's honesty."

She took a deep breath, then let it go. "Sixty angels won't get you very far," she said. "I'll make it five hundred."

"I don't want your money, thank you."

Everybody else's, just not hers. That was her told.

"He'd have won," he said. "I don't think you realise that. He was that close. The horse-boys would've followed him, and he'd have killed your lot and taken over the Lodge, if that arsehole Teucer hadn't shot him."

That shocked her. "Balls," she said; he didn't reply, because he knew he was right and she was wrong. She shuddered. That close? She'd have to ask someone about that. "And anyway, if he hadn't, you'd be dead."

"Maybe," Musen replied. "Or maybe he'd just have beaten me up a bit, like he did before. Wouldn't have made any odds."

She could feel her temper fraying. He had that effect on her. So did the truth. "You shouldn't have stolen the bloody thing, then, should you?"

He looked at her. "No," he said. "No, I guess I shouldn't have."

There was only so much of that sort of thing she could take. "Good luck," she said. "Next time, I won't be there to save your useless neck, so try a bit harder not to get caught. Go somewhere, a long way away, and don't even think about coming back."

He didn't dignify that with a reply, and she walked away.

"You missed a good party," Thratta told her. "It's been a while since anyone's had a chance to let their hair down. Did them all a power of good, I reckon. Where were you, by the way?"

Saving the man who saved us all, she wanted to say. "Something came up."

He shrugged. "I can see why you wouldn't want to be there," he said. "Painful for you. Still, it's for the best."

"I'm going to the wedding," she said.

He looked surprised. "You sure? There's no need, you know."

"Yes there bloody well is," she said, and left him staring at her back.

"I'm sorry," Procopius said. "You can't go."

She gave him an icy look. "Really? Why not?"

He sat down next to her. It was warm in the back quadrangle, the benches there were comfortable and he looked tired. "Because I'm dying," he said.

She suddenly couldn't think of anything to say.

"The doctor told me what to look out for," he said. "When certain things start to happen, it means I haven't got long left, days rather than weeks, and that's if I'm lucky. It's fine," he added, "I've known it was coming for some time, but it was gracious enough to wait for me to finish my work. My ninth symphony," he added. "The only thing I've ever done that's any good. And I know I can never top it, so, really, what's the point in hanging on?"

It was possible, more than remotely possible, that he was lying; that, as soon as the ship sailed for Blemya, he'd make a spectacular recovery. But she couldn't risk it.

"I'm sorry," she said. "Truly I am. But why does that mean I can't go?"

He gave her a reproachful look. "Three Triumvirs," he said, "one of whom must succeed me. Lycao's going to have her hands full with Senza Belot, and, besides, I sounded her out and she refused, point blank. Thratta feels he's not up to the job, and I agree with him. And in any case, I think I'd have chosen you, even if Lycao had been prepared to do it. She has brains and a compelling personality, but she's needed where she's going, and, besides, you get things done. And you have absolute, perfect faith. Surprisingly, that's the most important thing."

She felt as though the sky had just fallen on her. "Me," she said. "You're joking."

"I have a lively sense of humour, but no, I'm not. So, obviously, you can't go, you'll be needed here. There's a great deal I have to tell you, things I have to pass on to my successor by word of mouth because they can't be put down on paper, and only a short amount of time. I'm very sorry, but there it is."

"I can't," she said, and she felt more wretched than she'd ever done in her whole life. "The head of the Lodge is— It's the most important thing in the whole world. It's out of the question. You'd have to make decisions, and they'd have to be right. No, I'm sorry. I can't do it, I don't have the brains, or the strength."

He didn't seem to have heard her. "There's no formal investiture, obviously. What happens is, I stop breathing, you start work. You ought to know by now, promotion in the Lodge isn't something you're happy about, it's not something you *want*. It's an insufferable, crushing weight that squeezes the life out of you. It starts when you wake up in the morning and it never ever stops. That's what Axio never understood. He wanted it. Which, of course, is why he couldn't possibly be allowed to have it. Trust me, it's the worst burden anybody could ever inflict on anybody else. And you have absolutely no choice."

She turned her head and looked at him. She looked at the scar, which his father's knife had left, and which he'd worn all his life, like a badge of office. "Ah well," she said. "If you put it like that, how can I possibly refuse?"

He stood up. "Good girl," he said. "That's the ticket."

He was right. There was a lot to learn. She had to know the names of agents and representatives in every town in the reunited empire, their life histories, abilities, defects, their dark and poisonous secrets that nobody else could ever be told. She had to assimilate and properly understand a vast body of doctrine, abstruse and esoteric, which would form the basis for every decision she'd ever take. She had to learn the art of identifying the lesser of two evils, or six, or twenty. She had to commit to memory the mind-bending scope of the Lodge's assets and possessions, the stupefying wealth it had squirrelled away, the arcane, twisted structures by which it secretly owned money, resources, means of production—and the more she learned, the more she came to realise that the utopian schemes, the aptitude tests she'd been doing for the last few months were actually true and for real, because the Lodge truly did have the money, and the power, and the influence, and the authority to do all those impractical, impossible things. That horrified her: decisions, choices she'd made on the basis that it was all strictly make-believe now turned out to be very real and about to happen. She desperately wanted to go back and do them all again, but Procopius wouldn't let her; it's too late now, the decision's been made, the orders have been given, your word is law and your actions are irrevocable. Also, he added casually, you got it right the first time.

"Is it a sort of inspiration?" she asked. "When I decide

something, is it actually the Great Smith talking through my mouth and putting the thoughts into my head?"

That made him smile. "You don't still believe in the Great Smith, do you? That's so sweet. Nothing wrong with it," he hastened to assure her, "if you find it's helpful, it's an entirely valid perspective, though personally I've always regarded Him as a sort of extended metaphor. But the country people like someone solid to believe in. A figurehead, if you like. A bit like the emperor."

"Not inspiration, then."

"I wouldn't say that. It's entirely possible that you work things out in the back of your mind and then hear them as the voice of the Great Smith, and that gives you the confidence to believe in your own decisions. Not a bad way of going about it, not bad at all. Confidence is nine-tenths of the battle, in my opinion."

She looked at him. He'd gone downhill a lot since the ships sailed for Blemya. His skin was grey, his voice was little more than a whisper and he closed his eyes when he talked, as though making a great effort. "You said you chose me because I have faith. And now you tell me the thing I have faith in doesn't exist."

He laughed. "That's like saying that if you hate the hat I'm wearing, you hate me too. The difference between us is, you worship an old man in a leather apron and I worship an extended metaphor. Different hats, that's all. Can we get on now, please? We've still an awful lot to get through."

There was still an awful lot to get through when his voice grew so quiet that she couldn't make out the words, and when she tried to tell him that, he couldn't hear her. So he went on painfully revealing the crucial, quintessential truth, which she couldn't hear, until at last he fell into a deep, slow-breathing sleep. Twenty hours later, he woke up for the last time, and she asked him, "How do I let everyone know I'm the new leader?"

He told her, but she couldn't hear. And then he died.

She sat beside the bed looking at him, his white face, a skull bound in parchment like a book, his empty, useless body. I stop breathing, he'd told her, you start work. She had absolutely no idea what she was suppose to do next.

The door opened and Sutento came in. He looked at the thing in the bed and nodded. "All done, then."

An odd way of putting it, but she wasn't going to quarrel with it. "Yes."

"You'll be wanting to see the day-book."

"Will I?"

"Yes."

"What the hell is the day-book?"

"I'll fetch it down directly."

The day-book was old, fat, covered in dark brown leather and written in a code she couldn't read. She stared at it for a while, then closed it and let her mind wander. A little later, Sutento came back and took it away, and she never saw it again.

Since she had no idea what work she was supposed to be doing, she carried on with what she'd been doing before she'd started her sessions with Procopius. It was the same work, but she found it a hundred times harder, because she knew there was nobody to review it, check it, stop her, point out her ridiculous mistakes and make her do it again. She was so busy that she couldn't spare the time to attend Procopius' funeral, to which was annexed the premier of his last work, the ninth symphony. Sutento told her there was almost nobody there for the service or the concert. Fair enough; the death of a musician, even one as eminent as Procopius, was something and nothing in the ruins of a great empire. The Mezentines sent a cultural attaché, but his carriage broke an axle on the atrocious roads and he arrived two days after the event.

She never left Procopius' old tower room these days. Outside, they told her, things were already starting to happen. Fifty thousand Aram no Vei horsemen had arrived to garrison the city and the northern frontier—she vaguely remembered signing something to do with that, but it was a long time ago and she'd had so much else to think about since then—but she didn't see or hear them; all she could do was take the reports on trust; believe in them, have faith. The first fleet of grain ships from Simmeria docked at Beloisa and unloaded its cargo on to a thousand newly built carts, for onward transmission to relief depots all over the empire, to feed the starving survivors in the famine districts. The Resettlement Commission made its first set of recommendations, which she couldn't find time to read. Five thousand miners (from Saevolus Andrapodiza at practically cost, prisoners from some war Senza Belot was fighting in a faraway country of which she knew little) arrived at the Weal Teuchisma and set about reopening the collapsed shafts. She knew she'd ordered or authorised all that, having sifted the relevant data and reached an informed decision, but there was so much of it all that she couldn't keep track, let alone take more than a passing interest. She opened the hidden lock gates and oceans of money flowed out through them. She felt more hopelessly alone than she'd ever done starving and footsore on an empty road in the wilderness. Most days, the only other human being she saw to speak to was Sutento, who brought her letters and the books she'd asked for and her meals on a tray. Gradually she came to understand why Procopius couldn't believe in the Great Smith; for the same reason that the Great Smith doesn't believe in the Great Smith. And Axio had wanted this job. The sad, deluded fool.

One morning, no different from all the other mornings, Sutento said to her, "Oida would like to see you."

That didn't make sense. "He's in Blemya."

"No, he's here. Can you spare him five minutes?"

She wanted to scream. "He's in Blemya. What's wrong with you?"

He was staring at her. No way for the leader of the Lodge to behave. "Of course," Sutento said. "So I'll tell him you don't want to see him."

She looked round the room. She'd hardly left it since Procopius died. Still his books, his furniture, his writing slope on the small desk by the window, where he sat to write music. It was enough to make you believe in reincarnation. "Tell him I can spare him ten minutes."

It wasn't fair, she protested to herself. It shouldn't be allowed; the emperor, making an unscheduled call. What was the Lord Chamberlain thinking of? The emperor should ride into Iden in a chariot drawn by milk-white horses, or on the back of an elephant, while awe-struck crowds gazed in stunned silence from behind the shields of a wall of impassive, arm-linked soldiers.

And a servant shouldn't announce him as simply Oida, because the man she used to know by that name was dead. She should know. Obedient as ever to the commands of her superiors, she'd killed him.

He'd shaved the stupid beard. He was dressed in a simple monk's habit—a well-cut monk's habit, of course, with neatly hemmed sleeves, made from the best Aelian bleached wool, and was that a lining poking out from the back of the collar? He'd caught the sun, the ferocious Blemyan sun. It suited him.

"Oh, it's you," she said. "I've got something for you."

He opened his mouth to speak. She turned her back, went to Procopius' desk, opened the secret drawer she'd discovered quite by chance, and took out a plain rosewood box. "Wedding present," she said.

He opened it, shuddered and closed it quickly. "Is that—?"

She nodded. "The rest of him's buried somewhere, I have no idea where. Musen—you remember him?—he insisted, I had to bargain like mad just to get that much. But I thought you might like something to remember him by."

Oida grinned weakly. "They do say, an eye for an eye. But I'm not sure it's meant to be taken literally." He put the box in the pocket of the robe. "Congratulations," he said.

"Likewise."

For the first time, she found she couldn't talk to him. Always it had been so easy; talking to him came as fluently and naturally as thinking, or breathing. Now, she had no idea what to say, and neither, it seemed, did he. Oida, lost for words? It really did have to be the end of the world.

"What are you doing here?" she said, and it came out all wrong. "Shouldn't you be in Blemya?"

He sighed. "Properly speaking, yes."

"Properly speaking? What does that mean?"

She hadn't told him he could sit down, and he was still standing. "The chamberlain tells me that the official honeymoon for a king or queen of Blemya is precisely six weeks, followed by a series of receptions to allow the nobles and senior government officials a chance to offer their formal good wishes, followed by an extended tour of the provinces. But she'd got to the stage where she couldn't stand the sight of me, and I was itching to get away and not making a very good job of hiding it. She said, go, for crying out loud. So I went."

"Really. That doesn't augur well."

Oida laughed. "Actually, we were both amazed we stuck it out for as long as we did. She was desperate to get back together again with Daxen—you remember him—and I—" He shrugged awkwardly. "Well, I wanted to be here, obviously."

"Obviously? What's obvious about it?"

He gave her his puzzled look. "Maybe you don't know the situation with her and me."

"Clearly not. Is there one?"

"But didn't Procopius tell you? He must've done."

"He didn't say anything about it." Not strictly true. He'd told her that she'd got her promotion to Triumvir because Oida had insisted, thereby spoiling the whole thing. "What didn't he tell me?"

"The deal," Oida said. "Between him and me. And the Blemyans, of course. Oh, come on, he must've told you. Otherwise—"

"Told me what, for crying out loud?"

Oida looked round, identified a chair, dragged it across the floor and sat on it. And why not? He was, after all, the emperor. "This marriage," he said. "Strictly and totally political."

"To get Blemya back into the empire. Yes, I'd figured that for myself."

"Political, and that's all." He laid a lot of stress on the last word. "She's madly in love with Daxen, I'm—well, you know about me. Strictly political. We haven't—well, if that's what you were thinking."

She frowned. "What about an heir? Your first duty to the empire, surely."

That got her a scowl. "Let's say Daxen's standing in for me on that one. We both insisted; actually, it was bloody comical. Both of us, in the same room, saying not under any circumstances, not if the fate of the known world depended on it. No, the next emperor won't have a drop of the true Imperial blood in his veins. Which is a damn good thing, if you believe in heredity."

She looked at him. He'd turned scarlet, and she wanted to laugh. "Why not, for pity's sake? I didn't get a close look at her, but I got the impression she's not exactly hideous."

"Oh, come on," he said angrily. "You know perfectly well."

She took a deep breath, then let it go. "You're assuming rather a lot, aren't you?"

"Am I?"

So here we are, she thought; the point at which only a simple yes or no will do. Like faith; do you believe or don't you? A question you answer either in a split second or not at all. "What the hell," she said irritably, "do you see in me? I've always wondered, and for the life of me I can't guess. Is it just that I'm the only one you could never have? Is that it? The born collector's desperate frustration at missing out on the complete set?"

He just looked at her. I deserved that, she thought. Very well. Here goes nothing.

"I could forgive you," she said, "for lying to me all those times. I could handle that, it's what I'd come to expect, and I always knew it was for the Lodge. I'd probably have done the same, in your shoes. But what I can't forgive is you twisting Procopius' arm to get me promoted. Do you realise what you've done? You made everything I ever managed to achieve worthless. That wasn't just thoughtless. It shows what you really think of me."

He nodded slowly. "I realise that now," he said. "That's why I wanted you to chuck it all and go to Aelia with me." He hesitated, watching her like a fencer. "That offer still stands, by the way. God knows if we'd be able to get away with it, but I'm game if you are."

That was more than flesh and blood could stand. It was a lie, of course, a bluff, a brilliant counter-move, worthy of the Belot boys at their very best. She gave in, and burst out laughing.

"You clown," she said.

He shrugged. "I don't know what's so funny," he said.

At which point, something clicked into place; the brake, bringing the mighty, racing machine of her train of thought grinding to a sudden, catastrophic halt. He'd meant it, for God's sake. He'd actually meant it. No bluff. What a general he could have made, she thought. How could you beat someone who's prepared to throw away everything, just to win?

"You're serious."

"Of course I am. We'd have to change our names, obviously, and make ourselves very, very hard to find. But it could be done, if that's what you want."

"What about you? Is that what you want?"

"You know perfectly well what I want."

And for a split second the thought did cross her mind; to escape, to be free, just the two of them. Hadn't they earned it, for God's sake? But she let it go, and the tiny moment when it might have been possible was over and gone for ever.

"Don't be stupid," she said. "Emperors don't just sneak out the bathroom window and disappear. Besides, what makes you think I'd want to? Give up everything, just to be with you? Nothing to do all day but sit around the house or go for a picnic in the woods? I'd die of boredom in a fortnight."

"Well?"

"Well what?"

"Well?"

Faith, hope and love; no rational debate, no careful weighing of the evidence, balancing the merits, persuasion, not even a supreme effort of will. No options, no choice. They catch you unaware, like sleep, and won't let you go till they're ready. "You do realise it's hopelessly impractical? You'll be off presiding at ceremonies all day, and I have all this bloody work to do. We'll be lucky if we get five minutes a week."

He closed his eyes, and opened them again. "Five minutes will be fine," he said.

She looked for it everywhere, in every enclosed space in every room in the palace. Eventually, when she'd given up all hope, there it suddenly was, the familiar box with the forced lock, hidden under a pile of Procopius' shirts in a linen press. She took it and opened it, unwrapped the faded silk, laid the tarnished plates out one by one on the writing slope under the window. Five suits. She'd made enquiries. All the scholars who could tell if it was genuine were dead now. There was no way of knowing for sure.

All through our lives, there are witnesses—parents, family, friends, people we work with, people we love and who love us, people who hate us and we hate. One by one they die, until the world seems empty, and eventually there are no independent witnesses to testify to our crimes and our achievements. Only we remember them, there's nobody to contradict our version. If we want it to be, it can be the truth.

She picked the cards up one by one, and put them back again, in neat rows, like soldiers. No witnesses needed, no evidence, no facts. It was the first pack, because she knew it was.

She closed her eyes and chose one at random. Two of Swords. There is no Two of Swords in an honest pack.

He'd been away for a week, dedicating some bridge in the Mesoge. Come to think of it, she'd ordered it to be built. It would cut two weeks off a carter's round trip; wool and butter going down the mountain, grain and manufactured goods going up. It would bring life, like a drop of water falling on dust. And he'd be home today. She wondered what present he'd bring her this time.

extras

orbit

meet the author

K. J. PARKER is the pseudonym of Tom Holt, a full-time writer living in the south-west of England. When not writing, Holt is a barely competent stockman, carpenter and metalworker, a two-left-footed fencer, an accomplished textile worker and a crack shot. He is married to a professional cake decorator and has one daughter.

Find out more about K. J. Parker and other Orbit authors by registering for the free newsletter at www.orbitbooks.net.

if you enjoyed
THE TWO OF SWORDS: VOLUME THREE

look out for

DEVICES AND DESIRES

by

K. J. Parker

When an engineer is sentenced to death for a petty transgression of guild law, he flees the city, leaving behind his wife and daughter. Forced into exile, he seeks a terrible vengeance—one that will leave a trail of death and destruction in its wake. But he will not be able to achieve this by himself. He must draw up his plans using the blood of others...

In a compelling tale of intrigue and injustice, K. J. Parker's embittered hero takes up arms against his enemies, using the only weapons he has left to him: his ingenuity and his passion—his devices and desires.

1

"The quickest way to a man's heart," said the instructor, "is proverbially through his stomach. But if you want to get into his brain, I recommend the eye-socket."

Like a whip cracking, he uncurled his languid slouch into the taut, straight lines of the lunge. His forearm launched from the elbow like an arrow as his front leg plunged forward, and the point of the long, slim sword darted, neat as a component in a machine, through the exact center of the finger-ring that dangled from a cord tied to the beam.

It was typical of Valens' father that he insisted on his son learning the new fencing; the stock, the tuck, the small-sword and the rapier. It was elegant, refined, difficult, endlessly time-consuming and, of course, useless. A brigandine or even a thick winter coat would turn one of those exquisite points; if you wanted to have any chance of doing useful work, you had to aim for the holes in the face, targets no bigger than an eight-mark coin. Against a farm worker with a hedging tool, you stood no chance whatsoever. But, for ten years, Valens had flounced and stretched up and down a chalk line in a drafty shed that hadn't been cleaned out since it was still a stable. When he could hit the apple, the instructor had hung up a plum, and then a damson. Now he could get the damson nine times out of ten, and so the ring had taken its place. Once he'd mastered that, he wondered what he'd be faced with next. The eye of a darning-needle, probably.

"Better," the instructor said, as the point of Valens' sword nicked the ring's edge, making it tinkle like a cow-bell. "Again."

It was typical of Valens that he suffered through his weekly lesson, face frozen and murder in his heart, always striving to do better even though he knew the whole thing was an exercise in fatuity. Fencing was last lesson but one on a Monday; on Wednesday evening, when he actually had an hour free, he paid one of the guardsmen four marks an hour to teach him basic sword and shield, and another two marks to keep the secret from his father. He was actually quite good at proper fencing, or so the guardsman said; but the tuck had no cutting edge, only a point, so he couldn't slice the grin off the instructor's face with a smart backhand wrap, as he longed to do. Instead, he was tethered to this stupid chalk line, like a grazing goat.

"That'll do," the instructor said, two dozen lunges later. "For next week, I want you to practice the hanging guard and the volte."

Valens dipped his head in a perfunctory nod; the instructor scooped up his armful of swords, unhooked his ring and left the room. It was still raining outside, and he had a quarter of an hour before he had to present himself in the west tower for lute and rebec. Awkwardly—it was too small for him at the best of times, and now his fingers were hot and swollen—he eased the ring off his right index finger and cast around for a bit of string.

Usually, he did much better when the instructor wasn't there, when he was on his own. That was fatuous too, since the whole idea of a sword-fight is that there's someone to fight with. Today, though, he was worse solo than he'd been during the lesson. He lunged again, missed, hit the string, which wrapped itself insultingly round the sword-point. Maybe it was simply too difficult for him.

That thought didn't sit comfortably, so he came at the problem from a different angle. Obviously, he told himself, the reason I can't do it is because it's not difficult *enough*.

Having freed his sword, he stepped back to a length; then he leaned forward just a little and tapped the ring on its edge, setting it swinging. Then he lunged again.

Six times out of six; enough to prove his point. When the ring swung backward and forward, he didn't just have a hole to aim at, he had a line. If he judged the forward allowance right, it was just a simple matter of pointing with the sword as though it was a finger. He steadied the ring until it stopped swinging, stepped back, lunged again and missed. Maybe I should have been a cat, he thought. Cats only lash out at moving objects; if it's still, they can't see it.

He cut the ring off the cord with his small knife and jammed it back on his finger, trapping a little fold of skin. Rebec next; time to stop being a warrior and become an artist. When he was Duke, of course, the finest musicians in the world would bribe his chamberlains for a chance to play while he chatted to his guests or read the day's intelligence reports, ignoring them completely. The son of a powerful, uneducated man has a hard time of it, shouldering the burden of all the advantages his father managed so well without.

An hour of the rebec left his fingertips numb and raw; and then it was time for dinner. That brought back into sharp focus the question he'd been dodging and parrying all day; would she still be there, or had his father sent her back home? If she'd left already—if, while he'd been scanning hexameters and hendecasyllables, stabbing at dangling jewelry and picking at wire, she'd packed up her bags and walked out of his life, possibly forever—at least he wouldn't have to sit all night at the wrong end of the table, straining to catch a word or two of what she said to someone else.

If she was still here....He cast up his mental accounts, trying to figure out if he was owed a miracle. On balance, he decided, probably not. According to the holy friars, it took three hundred hours of prayer or five hundred of good works to buy a miracle, and he was at least sixty short on either count. All he could afford out of his accrued merit was a revelatory vision of the Divinity, and he wasn't too bothered about that.

If she was still here.

On the off chance, he went back to his room, pulled off his sweaty, dusty shirt and winnowed through his clothes-chest for a replacement. The black, with silver threads and two gold buttons at the neck, made him look like a jackdaw, so he went for the red, with last year's sleeves (but, duke's son or not, he lived in the mountains; if it came in from outside, it came slowly, on a mule), simply because it was relatively clean and free of holes. Shoes; his father chose his shoes for him, and the fashion was still for poulaines, with their ridiculously long pointy toes. He promised himself that she wouldn't be able to see his feet under the table (besides, she wouldn't still be here), and pulled out his good mantle from the bottom of the chest. It was only civet, but it helped mask the disgraceful length of his neck. A glance in the mirror made him wince, but it was the best he could do.

Sixty hours, he told himself; sixty rotten hours I could've made up easily, if only I'd known.

Protocol demanded that he sit on his father's left at dinner. Tonight, the important guest was someone he didn't know, although the man's brown skin and high cheekbones made it easy enough to guess where he was from. An ambassador from Mezentia; no wonder his father was preoccupied, waving his hands and smiling (two generations of courtiers had come to harm trying to point out to the Duke that his smile was infinitely more terrifying than his frown), while the little bald brown man nodded politely and picked at his dinner like a starling. One quick look gave Valens all the information he needed about what was going on there. On his own left, the Chancellor was discussing climbing roses with the controller of the mines. So that was all right; he was free to look round without having to talk to anybody.

She was still here. There was a tiny prickle of guilt mixed in with his relief. She was, after all, a hostage. If she hadn't been sent home, it meant that there'd been some last-minute hitch in the treaty negotiations, and the war between the two dukedoms, two centuries old, was still clinging on to life by a thread. Sooner or later, though, the treaty would be signed: peace would end the fighting and the desperate waste of lives and money, heal the country's wounds and bring the conscript farmers and miners back home; peace would take her away from him before he'd even had a chance to talk to her alone. For now, though, the war was still here and so was she.

(A small diplomatic incident, maybe; if he could contrive it that their ambassador bumped into him on the stairs and knocked him down a flight or two. Would an act of clumsiness toward the heir apparent be enough to disrupt the negotiations for a week or ten days? On the other hand, if he fell awkwardly and broke his neck, might that not constitute an act of war, leading to summary execution of the hostages? And he'd be dead too, of course, for what that was worth.)

Something massive stirred on his right; his father was standing up to say something, and everybody had stopped talking. There was a chance it might be important (Father loved to annoy his advisers by making vital announcements out of the blue at dinner), so Valens tucked in his elbows, looked straight ahead and listened.

But it wasn't anything. The little bald man from Mezentia turned out to be someone terribly important, grand secretary of the Foundrymen's and Machinists' Guild (in Father's court, secretaries were fast-moving, worried-looking men who could write; but apparently they ruled Mezentia, and therefore, by implication, the world), and he was here as an observer to the treaty negotiations, and this was extremely good. Furthermore, as a token of the Republic's respect and esteem, he'd brought an example of cutting-edge Mezentine technology, which they would all have the privilege of seeing demonstrated after dinner.

Distracted as he was by the distant view of the top of her head, Valens couldn't help being slightly curious about that. Everyday Mezentine technology was so all-pervasive you could scarcely turn round in the castle without knocking some of it over. Every last cup and dish, from the best service reserved for state occasions down to the pewter they ate off when nobody was looking, had come from the Republic's rolling mills; every candle stood in a Mezentine brass candlestick, its light doubled by a Mezentine mirror hanging from a Mezentine nail. But extra-special cutting-edge didn't make it up the mountain passes very often, which meant they had to make do with rumors; the awestruck whispers of traders and commercial travelers, the panicky reports of military intelligence, and the occasional gross slander from a competitor, far from home and desperate. If the little bald man had brought a miracle with him (the ten-thousand-mark kind, rather than the three-hundred-hour variety), Valens reckoned he could spare a little attention for it, though his heart might be broken beyond repair by even the masters of the Solderers' and Braziers' Guild.

The miracle came in a plain wooden crate. It was no more than six feet long by three wide, but it took a man at each corner to move it—a heavy miracle, then. Two Mezentines with grave faces and crowbars prised the crate open; out came a lot of straw, and some curly cedar shavings, and then something which Valens assumed was a suit of armor. It was man-high, man-shaped and shiny, and the four attendants lifted it up and set it down on some kind of stand. Fine, Valens thought. Father'll be happy, he likes armor. But then the attendants did something odd. One of them reached into the bottom of the crate and fished out a steel tube with a ring through one end; a key, but much larger than anything of the kind Valens had seen before. It fitted into a slot in the back of the armor; some kind of specially secure, sword-proof fastening? Apparently not; one of the attendants began turning it over and over again, and each turn produced a clicking sound, like the skittering of mice's feet on a thin ceiling. Meanwhile, two more crates had come in. One of them held nothing more than an ordinary blacksmith's anvil—polished, true, like a silver chalice, but otherwise no big deal. The other was full of tools; hammers, tongs, cold chisels, swages, boring stuff. The anvil came to rest at the suit of armor's feet, and one of the Mezentines prised open the suit's steel fingers and closed them around the stem of a three-pound hammer.

"The operation of the machine..." Valens looked round to see who was talking. It was the short, bald man, the grand secretary. He had a low, rich voice with a fairly mild accent. "The operation of the machine is quite straightforward. A powerful spiral spring, similar to those used in clockwork, is put under tension by winding with a key. Once released, it bears on a flywheel, causing it to spin. A gear train and a series of cams and connecting rods transmits this motion to the machine's main spindle, from which belt-driven takeoffs power the arms. Further cams and trips effect the reciprocating movement, simulating the work of the human arm."

Whatever that was supposed to mean. It didn't look like anybody else understood it either, to judge from the rows of perfectly blank faces around the tables. But then the key-turner stopped turning, pulled out his key and pushed something; and the suit of armor's arm lifted to head height, stopped and fell, and the hammer in its hand rang on the anvil like a silver bell.

Not armor after all; Valens could feel his father's disappointment through the boards of the table. Of course Valens knew what it was, though he'd never seen anything like it. He'd read about it in some book; the citizens of the Perpetual Republic had a childish love of mechanical toys, metal gadgets that did things almost but not quite as well as people could. It was a typically Mezentine touch to send a mechanical blacksmith. Here is a machine, they were saying, that could make another machine just like itself, the way you ordinary humans breed children. Well; it was their proud boast that they had a machine for everything. Mechanizing reproduction, though, was surely cutting off their noses to spite their collective face.

The hammer rang twelve times, then stopped. Figures, Valens thought. You get a dozen hits at a bit of hot metal before it cools down and needs to go back in the fire. While you're waiting for it to heat up again, you've got time to wind up your mechanical slave. Query whether turning the key is harder work than swinging the hammer yourself would be. In any event, it's just a trip-hammer thinly disguised as a man. Now then; a man convincingly disguised as a trip-hammer, that'd be worth walking a mile to see.

Stunned silence for a moment or so, followed by loud, nervous applause. The little grand secretary stood up, smiled vaguely and sat down again; that concluded the demonstration.

Ten minutes after he got up from the table, Valens couldn't remember what he'd just eaten, or the name of the trade attaché he'd just been introduced to, or the date; as for the explanation of how the heavy miracle worked, it had vanished from his mind completely. That was unfortunate.

"I was wondering," she repeated. "Did you understand what that man said, about how the metal blacksmith worked? I'm afraid I didn't catch any of it, and my father's sure to ask me when I get home."

So she was going home, then. The irony; at last he was talking to her, and tomorrow she was going away. Further irony; it had been his father himself who'd brought them together; *Valens, come over here and talk to the Countess Sirupati.* Father had been towering over her, the way the castle loomed over the village below, all turrets and battlements, and he'd been smiling, which accounted for the look of terror in her eyes. Valens had wanted to reassure her; it's all right, he hasn't actually eaten anybody for weeks. Instead, he'd stood and gawped, and then he'd looked down at his shoes (poulaines, with the ridiculous pointy toes). And then she'd asked him about the mechanical blacksmith.

He pulled himself together, like a boy trying to draw his father's bow. "I'm not really the right person to ask," he said. "I don't know a lot about machines and stuff."

Her expression didn't change, except that it glazed slightly. Of course she didn't give a damn about how the stupid machine worked; she was making conversation. "I think," he went on, "that there's a sort of wheel thing in its chest going round and round, and it's linked to cogs and gears and what have you. Oh, and there's cams, to turn the round and round into up and down."

She blinked at him. "What's a cam?" she asked.

"Ah." What indeed? "Well, it's sort of..." Three hours a week with a specially imported Doctor of Rhetoric, from whom he was supposed to learn how to express himself with clarity, precision and grace. "It's sort of like this," he went on, miming with his hands. "The wheel goes round, you see, and on the edge of the wheel there's like a bit sticking out. Each time it goes round, it kind of bashes on a sort of lever arrangement, like a see-saw; and the lever thing pivots, like it goes down at the bashed end and up at the other end—that's how the arm lifts—and when it's done that, it drops down again under its own weight, nicely in time for the sticky-out bit on the wheel to bash it again. And so on."

"I see," she said. "Yes, I think I understand it now."

"Really?"

"No," she said. "But thank you for trying."

He frowned. "Well, it was probably the worst explanation of anything I've ever heard in my life."

She nodded. "Maybe," she said. "But at least you didn't say, oh, you're only a girl, you wouldn't understand."

He wasn't quite sure what to make of that. Tactically (four hours a week on the Art of War, with General Bozannes) he felt he probably had a slight advantage, a weak point in the line he could probably turn, if he could get his cavalry there in time. Somehow, though, he felt that the usages of the wars didn't apply here, or if they did they shouldn't. Odd; because even before he'd started having formal lessons, he'd run his life like a military campaign, and the usages of war applied to *everything*.

"Well," he said, "I'm a boy and I haven't got a clue. I suppose it's different in Mezentia."

"Oh, it is," she said. "I've been there, actually."

"Really? I mean, what's it like?"

She withdrew into a shell of thought, shutting out him and all the world. "Strange," she said. "Not like anywhere else, really. Oh, it's very grand and big and the buildings are huge and all closely packed together, but that's not what I meant. I can't describe it, really." She paused, and Valens realized he was holding his breath. "We all went there for some diplomatic thing, my father and my sisters and me; it was shortly before my eldest sister's wedding, and I think it was something to do with the negotiations. I was thirteen then, no, twelve. Anyway, I remember there was this enormous banquet in one of the Guild halls. Enormous place, full of statues and tapestries, and there was this amazing painting on the ceiling, a sea-battle or something like that; and all these people were in their fanciest robes, with gold chains round their necks and silks and all kinds of stuff like that. But the food came on these crummy old wooden dishes, and there weren't any knives or forks, just a plain wooden spoon."

Fork? he wondered; what's a farm tool got to do with eating? "Very odd," he agreed. "What was the food like?"

"Horrible. It was very fancy and sort of fussy, the way it was put on the plate, with all sorts of leaves and frills and things to make it look pretty; but really it was just bits of meat and dumplings in slimy sauce."

To the best of his recollection, Valens had never wanted anything in his entire life. Things had come his way, a lot of them; like the loathsome pointy-toed poulaines, the white thoroughbred mare that hated him and tried to bite his feet, the kestrel that wouldn't come back when it was called, the itchy damask pillows, the ivory-handled rapier, all the valuable junk his father kept giving him. He'd been brought up to take care of his possessions, so he treated them with respect until they wore out, broke or died; but he had no love for them, no pride in owning them. He knew that stuff like that mattered to most people; it was a fact about humanity that he accepted without understanding. Other boys his age had wanted a friend; but Valens had always known that the Duke's son didn't make friends; and besides, he preferred thinking to talking, just as he liked to walk on his own. He'd never wanted to be Duke, because that would only happen when his father died. Now, for the first time, he felt what it was like to want something—but, he stopped to consider, is it actually possible to want a person? How? As a pet; to keep in a mews or a stable, to feed twice a day when not in use. It would be possible, of course. You could keep a person, a girl for instance, in a stable or a bower; you could walk her and feed her, dress her and go to bed with her, but.... He didn't want *ownership*. He was the Duke's son, as such he owned everything and nothing. There was a logical paradox here—Doctor Galeazza would be proud of him—but it was so vague and unfamiliar that he didn't know how to begin formulating an equation to solve it. All he could do was be aware of the feeling, which was disturbingly intense.

Not that it mattered. She was going home tomorrow.

"Slimy sauce," he repeated. "Yetch. You had to eat it, I suppose, or risk starting a war."

She smiled, and he looked away, but the smile followed him. "Not all of it," she said. "You've got to leave some if you're a girl, it's ladylike. Not that I minded terribly much."

Valens nodded. "When I was a kid I had to finish everything on my plate, or it'd be served up cold for breakfast and lunch until I ate it. Which was fine," he went on, "I knew where I stood. But when I was nine, we had to go to a reception at the Lorican embassy—"

She giggled. She was way ahead of him. "And they think that if you eat everything on your plate it's a criticism, that they haven't given you enough."

She'd interrupted him and stolen his joke, but he didn't mind. She'd shared his thought. That didn't happen very often.

"Of course," he went on, "nobody bothered telling me, I was just a kid; so I was grimly munching my way through my dinner—"

"Rice," she said. "Plain boiled white rice, with noodles and stuff."

He nodded. "And as soon as I got to the end, someone'd snatch my plate away and dump another heap of the muck on it and hand it back; I thought I'd done something bad and I was being punished. I was so full I could hardly breathe. But Father was busy talking business, and nobody down my end of the table was going to say anything; I'd probably be there still, only—"

He stopped dead.

"Only?"

"I threw up," he confessed; it wasn't a good memory. "All over the tablecloth, and their Lord Chamberlain."

She laughed. He expected to feel hurt, angry. Instead, he laughed too. He had no idea why he should think it was funny, but it was.

"And was there a war?" she asked.

"Nearly," he replied. "God, that rice. I can still taste it if I shut my eyes."

Now she was nodding. "I was there for a whole year," she said. "Lorica, I mean. The rice is what sticks in my mind too. No pun intended."

He thought about that. "You sound like you've been to a lot of places," he said.

"Oh yes." She didn't sound happy about it, which struck him as odd. He'd never been outside the dukedom in his life. "In fact, I've spent more time away than at home."

Well, he had to ask. "Why?"

The question appeared to surprise her. "It's what I'm for," she said. "I guess you could say it's my job."

"Job?"

She nodded again. "Professional hostage. Comes of being the fifth of seven daughters. You see," she went on, "we've got

389

to get married in age order, it's protocol or something, and there's still two of them older than me left; I can't get married till they are. So, the only thing I'm useful for while I'm waiting my turn is being a hostage. Which means, when they're doing a treaty or a settlement or something, off I go on my travels until it's all sorted out."

"That's..." That's barbaric, he was about to say, but he knew better than that. He knew the theory perfectly well (statecraft, two hours a week with Chancellor Vetuarius), but he'd never given it any thought before; like people getting killed in the wars, something that happened but was best not dwelt on. "It must be interesting," he heard himself say. "I've never been abroad."

She paused, considering her reply. "Actually, it's quite dull, mostly. It's not like I get to go out and see things, and one guest wing's pretty like another."

(And, she didn't say, there's always the thought of what might happen if things go wrong.)

"I guess so," he said. "Well, I hope it hasn't been too boring here."

"Boring?" She looked at him. "I wouldn't say that. Going hunting with your father was—"

"Quite." Valens managed not to wince. "I didn't know he'd dragged you out with him. Was it very horrible?"

She shook her head. "I've been before, so the blood and stuff doesn't bother me. It was the standing about waiting for something to happen that got to me."

Valens nodded. "Was it raining?"

"Yes."

"It always rains." He pulled a face. "Whenever I hear about the terrible droughts in the south, and they're asking is it because God's angry with them or something, I know it's just because Dad doesn't go hunting in the south. He could earn a good living as a rainmaker."

She smiled, but he knew his joke hadn't really bitten home. That disconcerted him; usually it had them laughing like drains. Or perhaps they only laughed because he was the Duke's son. "Well," she said, "that was pretty boring. But the rest of it was…" She shrugged. "It was fine."

The shrug hurt. "Any rate," he said briskly, "you'll be home for harvest festival."

"It's not a big thing where I come from," she replied; and then, like an eclipse of the sun that stops the battle while the issue's still in the balance, the chamberlain came out to drive them all into the Great Hall for singing and a recital by the greatest living exponent of the psaltery.

Valens watched her being bustled away with the other women, until an equerry whisked him off to take his place in the front row.

Ironically, the singer sang nothing but love-songs; aubades about young lovers parted by the dawn, razos between the pining youth and the cynical go-between, the bitter complaints of the girl torn from her darling to marry a rich, elderly stranger. All through the endless performance he didn't dare turn round, but the thought that she was somewhere in the rows behind was like an unbearable itch. The greatest living psalterist seemed to linger spitefully over each note, as if he *knew*. The candles were guttering by the time he finally ground to a halt. There would be no more socializing that evening, and in the morning (early, to catch the coolest part of the day) she'd be going home.

(I could start a war, he thought, as he trudged up the stairs to bed. I could conspire with a disaffected faction or send the keys of a frontier post to the enemy; then we'd be at war again, and she could come back as a hostage. Or maybe we could lose, and I could go there; all the same to me, so long as...)

He lay in bed with the lamp flickering, just enough light to see dim shapes by. On the opposite wall, the same boarhounds that had given him nightmares when he was six carried on their endless duel with the boar at bay, trapped in the fibers of the tapestry. He could see them just as well when his eyes were shut; two of them, all neck and almost no head, had their teeth in the boar's front leg, while a third had him by the ear and hung twisting in mid-air, while the enemy's tusks ripped open a fourth from shoulder to tail. Night after night he'd wondered as he lay there which he was, the dogs or the pig, the hunters or the quarry. It was one of the few questions in his life to which he had yet to resolve an answer. It was possible that he was both, a synthesis of the two, made possible by the shared act of ripping and tearing. His father had had the tapestry put there in the hope that it'd inspire him with a love of the chase; but it wasn't a chase, it was a single still moment (perhaps he couldn't see it because it didn't move, like the ring hanging from the rafter); and therefore it represented nothing. Tonight, it made him think of her, standing in the rain while the lymers snuffled up and down false trails, his father bitching at the harborers and the masters of the hounds, the courtiers silent and wet waiting for the violence to begin.

if you enjoyed
THE TWO OF SWORDS: VOLUME THREE

look out for

THE COURT OF BROKEN KNIVES

Empires of Dust

by

Anna Smith Spark

In this dark and gripping debut fantasy that Miles Cameron calls "gritty and glorious!" the exiled son of the king must fight to reclaim his throne no matter the cost.

It is the richest empire the world has ever known, and it is also doomed. Governed by an imposturous emperor, decadence has

393

blinded its inhabitants to their vulnerability. The Yellow Empire is on the verge of invasion—and only one man can see it.

Haunted by prophetic dreams, Orhan has hired a company of soldiers to cross the desert to reach the capital city. Once they enter the palace, they have one mission: kill the emperor, then all those who remain. Only from the ashes can a new empire be built.

The company is a group of good, ordinary soldiers for whom this is a mission like any other. But the strange boy Marith who walks among them is no ordinary soldier. Though he is young, ambitious, and impossibly charming, something dark hides in Marith's past—and in his blood.

Dark and brilliant, this new fantasy series is for readers looking for epic battle scenes, gritty heroes, and blood-soaked revenge.

Chapter One

Knives.

Knives everywhere. Coming down like rain.

Down to close work like that, men wrestling in the mud, jabbing at each other, too tired to care any more. Just die and get it over with. Half of them fighting with their guts hanging out of their stomachs, stinking of shit, oozing pink and red and white. Half-dead men lying in the filth. Screaming. A whole lot of things screaming.

Impossible to tell who's who any more. Mud and blood and shadows and that's it. Kill them! Kill them all! Keep killing until we're all dead. The knife jabs and twists and the man he's fighting falls sideways, all the breath going out of him with a sigh of relief. Another there behind. Gods, his arms ache. His head aches. Blood in his eyes. He twists the knife again and thrusts with a broken-off sword and that man too dies. Fire explodes somewhere over to the left. White as maggots. Silent as maggots. Then shrieks as men burn.

He swings the stub of the sword and catches a man on the leg, not hard but hard enough so the man stumbles and he's on him quick with the knife. A good lot of blood and the man's down and dead, still flapping about like a fish but you can see in his eyes that he's finished, his legs just haven't quite caught up yet.

The sun is setting, casting long shadows. Oh beautiful evening! Stars rising in a sky the color of rotting wounds. The

Dragon's Mouth. The White Lady. The Dog. A good star, the Dog. Brings plagues and fevers and inflames desire. Its rising marks the coming of summer. So maybe no more campaigning in the sodding rain. Wet leather stinks. Mud stinks. Shit stinks, when the latrine trench overflows.

Another burst of white fire. He hates the way it's silent. Unnatural. Unnerving. Screams again. Screams so bad your ears ring for days. The sky weeps and howls and it's difficult to know what's screaming. You, or the enemy, or the other things.

Men are fighting in great clotted knots like milk curds. He sprints a little to where two men are struggling together. Leaps at one from behind, pulls him down, skewers him. Hard crack of bone, soft lovely yield of fat and innards. Suety. The other yells hoarsely and swings a punch at him. Lost his knife, even. Bare knuckles. He ducks and kicks out hard, overbalances and almost falls. The man kicks back, tries to get him in a wrestling grip. Up close together, two pairs of teeth gritted at each other. A hand smashes his face, gets his nose, digs in. He bites at it. Dirty. Calloused. Iron taste of blood bright in his mouth. But the hand won't let up, crushing his face into his skull. He swallows and almost chokes on the blood pouring from the wound he's made. Blood and snot and shreds of cracked dry human skin. Manages to get his knife in and stabs hard into the back of the man's thigh. Not enough to kill, but the hand jerks out from his face. Lashes out and gets his opponent in the soft part of the throat, pulls his knife out and gazes around the battlefield at the figures hacking at each other while the earth rots beneath them. All eternity, they've been fighting. All the edges blunted. Sword edges and knife edges and the edges in the mind. Keep killing. Keep killing. Keep killing till we're all dead.

And then he's dead. A blade gets him in the side, in the weak point under the shoulder where his armor has to give to let the joint move. Far in, twisting. Aiming down. Killing wound. He hears his body rip. Oh gods. Oh gods and demons. Oh gods and demons and fuck. He swings round, strikes at the man who's stabbed him. The figure facing him is a wraith, scarlet with blood, head open oozing out brain stuff. You're dying, he thinks. You're dying and you've killed me. Not fair.

Shadows twist round them. We're all dying, he thinks, one way or another. Just some of us quicker than others. You fight and you die. And always another twenty men queuing up behind you.

Why we march and why we die,
And what life means... it's all a lie.
Death! Death! Death!

Understands that better than he's ever understood anything, even his own name.

But suddenly, for a moment, he's not sure he wants to die.

The battlefield falls silent. He blinks and sees light.

A figure in silver armor. White, shining, blazing with light like the sun. A red cloak billowing in the wind. Moves through the ranks of the dead and the dying and the light beats onto them, pure and clean.

"Amrath! Amrath!" Voices whispering like the wind blowing across salt marsh. Voices calling like birds. Here, walking among us, bright as summer dew.

"Amrath! Amrath!" The shadows fall away as the figure passes. Everything is light.

"Amrath! Amrath!" The men cheer with one voice. No longer one side or the other, just men gazing and cheering as the figure passes. He cheers until his throat aches. Feels restored, seeing it. No longer tired and wounded and dying. Healed. Strong.

"Amrath! Amrath!"

The figure halts. Gazes around. Searching. Finds. A dark-clad man leaps forward, swaying into the light. Poised across from the shining figure, yearning toward it. Draws a sword burning with blue flame.

"Amrath! Amrath!" Harsh voice like crows, challenging. "Amrath!"

He watches joyfully. So beautiful! Watches and nothing in the world matters, except to behold the radiance of his god.

The bright figure draws a sword that shines like all the stars and the moon and the sun. A single dark ruby in its hilt. The dark figure rushes onwards, screeching something. Meets the bright figure with a clash. White light and blue fire. Blue fire and white light. His eyes hurt almost as he watches. But he cannot bear to look away. The two struggle together. Like a candle flame flickering. Like the dawn sun on the sea. The silver sword comes up, throws the dark figure back. Blue fire blazes, engulfing everything, the shining silver armor running with flame. Crash of metal, sparks like a blacksmith's anvil. The shining figure takes a step back defensively, parries, strikes out. The other blocks it. Roars. Howls. Laughs. The mage blade swings again, slicing, trailing blue fire. Blue arcs in the evening gloom. Shapes and words, written on the air. Death words. Pain words. Words of hope and fear and despair. The shining figure parries again, the silver sword rippling beneath the impact of the other's blade. So brilliant with light that rainbows dance on the ground around it. Like a woman's hair throwing out drops of water, tossing back her head in summer rain. Like snow falling. Like colored stars. The two fighters shifting, stepping in each other's footprints. Stepping in each other's shadows. Circling like birds.

The silver sword flashes out and up and downwards and the other falls back, bleeding from the throat. Great spreading gush of red. The blue flame dies.

He cheers and his heart is almost aching, it's so full of joy.

The shining figure turns. Looks at the men watching. Looks at him. Screams. Things shriek back that make the world tremble. The silver sword rises and falls. Five men. Ten. Twenty. A pile of corpses. He stares mesmerized at the dying. The beauty of it. The most beautiful thing in the world. Killing and killing and such perfect joy. His heart overflowing. His heart singing. This, oh indeed, oh, for this, all men are born. He screams in answer, dying, throws himself against his god's enemies with knife and sword and nails and teeth.

Why we march and why we die,
And what life means . . . it's all a lie.
Death! Death! Death!

Chapter Two

"The Yellow Empire...I can kind of see that. Yeah. Makes sense."

Dun and yellow desert, scattered with crumbling yellow-gray rocks and scrubby yellow-brown thorns. Bruise-yellow sky, low yellow clouds. Even the men's skin and clothes turning yellow, stained with sweat and sand. So bloody hot Tobias's vision seemed yellow. Dry and dusty and yellow as bile and old bones. The Yellow Empire. The famous golden road. The famous golden light.

"If I spent the rest of my life knee-deep in black mud, I think I'd die happy, right about now," said Gulius, and spat into the yellow sand.

Rate sniggered. "And you can really see how they made all that money, too. Valuable thing, dust. Though I'm still kind of clinging to it being a refreshing change from cow manure."

"Yeah, I've been thinking about that myself, too. If this is the heart of the richest empire the world has ever known, I'm one of Rate's dad's cows."

"An empire built on sand...Poetic, like."

"'Cause there's so much bloody money in poetry."

"They're not my dad's cows. They're my cousin's cows. My dad just looks after them."

"Magic, I reckon," said Alxine. "Strange arcane powers. They wave their hands and the dust turns into gold."

"Met a bloke in Alborn once, could do that. Turned iron pennies into gold marks."

Rate's eyes widened. "Yeah?"

"Oh, yeah. Couldn't shop at the same place two days running, mind, and had to change his name a lot…"

They reached a small stream bed, stopped to drink, refill their water-skins. Warm and dirty with a distinct aroma of goat shit. After five hours of dry marching, the feel of it against the skin almost as sweet as the taste of it in the mouth.

Running water, some small rocks to sit on, two big rocks providing a bit of shade. What more could a man want in life? Tobias went to consult with Skie.

"We'll stop here a while, lads. Have some lunch. Rest up a bit. Sit out the worst of the heat." If it got any hotter, their swords would start to melt. The men cheered. Cook pots were filled and scrub gathered; Gulius set to preparing a soupy porridge. New boy Marith was sent off to dig the hole for the latrine. Tobias himself sat down and stretched out his legs. Closed his eyes. Cool dark shadows and the smell of water. Bliss.

"So how much further do you think we've got till we get there?" Emit asked.

Punch someone, if they asked him that one more time. Tobias opened his eyes again with a sigh. "I have no idea. Ask Skie. Couple of days? A week?"

Rate grinned at Emit. "Don't tell me you're getting bored of sand?"

"I'll die of boredom, if I don't see something soon that isn't sand and your face."

"I saw a goat a couple of hours back. What more do you want? And it was definitely a female goat, before you answer that."

They had been marching now for almost a month. Forty men, lightly armed and with little armor. No horses, no archers, no mage or whatnot. No doctor, though Tobias considered himself something of a dab hand at field surgery and dosing the clap. Just forty men in the desert, walking west into the setting sun. Nearly there now. Gods only knew what they would find. The richest empire the world had ever known. Yellow sand.

"Not bad, this," Alxine said as he scraped the last of his porridge. "The lumps of mud make it taste quite different from the stuff we had at breakfast."

"I'm not entirely sure it's mud..."

"I'm not entirely sure I care."

They bore the highly imaginative title The Free Company of the Sword. An old name, if not a famous one. Well enough known in certain select political circles. Tobias had suggested several times they change it.

"The sand gives it an interesting texture, too. The way it crunches between your teeth."

"You said that yesterday."

"And I'll probably say it again tomorrow. And the day after that. I'll be an old man and still be picking bloody desert out of my gums."

"And other places."

"That, my friend, is not something I ever want to have to think about."

Everything reduced to incidentals by the hot yellow earth and the hot yellow air. Water. Food. Water. Rest. Water. Shade. Tobias sat back against a rock listening to his men droning on just as they had yesterday and the day before that and the day before that. Almost rhythmic, like. Musical. A nice predictable pattern to it. Backward and forwards, backward and forwards, backward and forwards. The same thinking. The same words. Warp and weft of a man's life.

Rate was on form today. "When we get there, the first thing I'm going to do is eat a plate of really good steak. Marbled with fat, the bones all cracked to let the marrow out, maybe some hot bread and a few mushrooms to go with it, mop up the juice."

Emit snorted. "The richest empire the world has ever known, and you're dreaming about steak?"

"Death or a good dinner, that's my motto."

"Oh, I'm not disputing that. I'm just saying as there should be better things to eat when we get there than steak."

"Better than steak? Nothing's better than steak."

"As the whore said to the holy man."

"I'd have thought you'd be sick of steak, Rate, lad."

"You'd have thought wrong, then. You know how it feels, looking after the bloody things day in, day out, never getting to actually sodding eat them?"

"As the holy man said to the whore."

Tiredness was setting in now. Boredom. Fear. They marched and grumbled and it was hot and at night it was cold, and they were desperate to get there, and the thought of getting there was terrifying, and they were fed up to buggery with yellow dust and yellow heat and yellow air. Good lads, really, though, Tobias thought. Good lads. Annoying the hell out of him and about two bad nights short of beating the crap out of each other, but basically good lads. He should be kind of proud.

"The Yellow Empire."

"The Golden Empire."

"The Sunny Empire."

"Sunny's nice and cheerful. Golden's a hope. And Yellow'd be good when we get there. In their soldiers, anyway. Nice and cowardly, yeah?"

Gulius banged the ladle. "More porridge, anyone? Get it while it's not yet fully congealed."

"I swear I sneezed something recently that looked like that last spoonful."

"A steak...Quick cooked, fat still spitting, charred on the bone...Mushrooms...Gravy...A cup of Immish gold..."

"I'll have another bowl if it's going begging."

"Past begging, man, this porridge. This porridge is lying unconscious in the gutter waiting to be kicked hard in the head."

A crow flew down near them cawing. Alxine tried to catch it. Failed. It flew up again and crapped on one of the kit bags.

"Bugger. Good eating on one of them."

"Scrawny-looking fucker though. Even for a crow."

"Cooked up with a few herbs, you wouldn't be complaining. Delicacy, in Allene, slow-roasted crow's guts. Better than steak."

"That was my sodding bag!"

"Lucky, in Allene, a crow crapping on you."

"Quiet!" Tobias scrambled to his feet. "Something moved over to the right."

"Probably a goat," said Rate. "If we're really lucky, it'll be that female goa—"

The dragon was on them before they'd even had a chance to draw their swords.

Big as a cart horse. Deep fetid marsh rot snot shit filth green. Traced out in scar tissue like embroidered cloth. Wings black and white and silver, heavy and vicious as blades. The stink of it came choking. Fire and ash. Hot metal. Fear. Joy. Pain. There are dragons in the desert, said the old maps of old empire, and they had laughed and said no, no, not that close to great cities, if there ever were dragons there they are gone like the memory of a dream. Its teeth closed ripping on Gulius's arm, huge, jagged; its eyes were like knives as it twisted away with the arm hanging bloody in its mouth. It spat blood and slime and roared out flame again, reared up beating its wings. Men fell back screaming, armor scorched and molten, melted into burned melted flesh. The smell of roasting meat surrounded them. Better than steak.

Gulius was lying somehow still alive, staring at the hole where his right arm had been. The dragon's front legs came down smash onto his body. Plume of blood. Gulius disappeared. Little smudge of red on the green. A grating shriek as its claws scrabbled over hot stones. Screaming. Screaming. Beating wings. The stream rose up boiling. Two men were in the stream trying to douse burning flesh and the boiling water was in their faces and they were screaming too. Everything hot and boiling and burning, dry wind and dry earth and dry fire and dry hot scales, the whole great lizard body scorching like a furnace, roaring hot burning killing demon death thing.

We're going to die, thought Tobias. We're all going to fucking die.

Found himself next to pretty new boy Marith, who was staring at it mesmerized with a face as white as pus. Yeah, well, okay, I'll give it to you, bit of a thing to come back to when you've been off digging a hole for your superiors to shit in. Looked pretty startled even for him. Though wouldn't look either pretty or startled in about ten heartbeats, after the dragon flame grilled and decapitated him.

If he'd at least try to raise his sword a bit.

Or even just duck.

"Oh gods and demons and piss." Tobias, veteran of ten years' standing with very little left that could unsettle him, pulled up his sword and plunged it two-handed into the dragon's right eye.

The dragon roared like a city dying. Threw itself sideways. The sword still wedged in its eye. Tobias half fell, half leaped away from it, dragging Marith with him.

"Sword!" he screamed. "Draw your bloody sword!"

The dragon's front claws were bucking and rearing inches from his face. It turned in a circle, clawing at itself, tail and wings lashing out. Spouted flame madly, shrieking, arching its back. Almost burned its own body, stupid fucking thing. Two men went up like candles, bodies alight; a third was struck by the tail and went down with a crack of bone. Tobias rolled and pulled himself upright, dancing back away. His helmet was askew, he could see little except directly in front of him. Big writhing mass of green dragon legs. He went into a crouch again, trying to brace himself against the impact of green scales. Not really much point trying to brace himself against the flames.

A man came in low, driving his sword into the dragon's side, ripping down, glancing off the scales but then meeting the softer underbelly as the thing twisted up. Drove it in and along, tearing flesh. Black blood spurted out, followed by shimmering white and red unraveling entrails. Pretty as a fountain. Men howled, clawed at their own faces as the blood hit. And now it had two swords sticking out of it, as well as its own intestines, and it was redoubling its shrieking, twisting, bucking in circles, bleeding, while men leaped and fell out of its way.

"Pull back!" Tobias screamed at them. "Get back, give it space. Get back!" His voice was lost in the maelstrom of noise. It must be dying, he thought desperately. It might be a bloody dragon, but half its guts are hanging out and it's got a sword sunk a foot into its head. A burst of flame exploded in his direction. He dived back onto his face. Found himself next to new boy Marith again.

"Distract it!" Marith shouted in his ear.

Um...?

Marith scrambled to his feet and leaped.

Suddenly, absurdly, the boy was balanced on the thing's back. Clung on frantically. Almost falling. Looked so bloody stupidly bloody small. Then pulled out his sword and stabbed downwards. Blood bursting up. Marith shouted. Twisted backward. Fell off. The dragon screamed louder than ever. Loud as the end of the world. Its body arched, a gout of flame spouted. Collapsed with a shriek. Its tail twitched and coiled for a few long moments. Last rattling tremors, almost kind of pitiful and obscene. Groaning sighing weeping noise. Finally it lay dead.